AMANDLA

AMANDLA

ALIX JANS

COPYRIGHT © 2020 ALIX JANS
All rights reserved.
AMANDLA
ISBN   978-1-7349368-1-0   *Paperback*
        978-1-7349368-0-3   *Ebook*
        978-1-7349368-2-7   *Audiobook*
Cover and interior layout design: John van der Woude, JVDW Designs
Cover image: Modified from "Nelson Mandela Capture Site", photo by Darren Glanville, Flickr.com. Licensed under the *Creative Commons Attribution-Share Alike 2.0 Generic* license.

For Rochelle and Kathryn—a legacy.

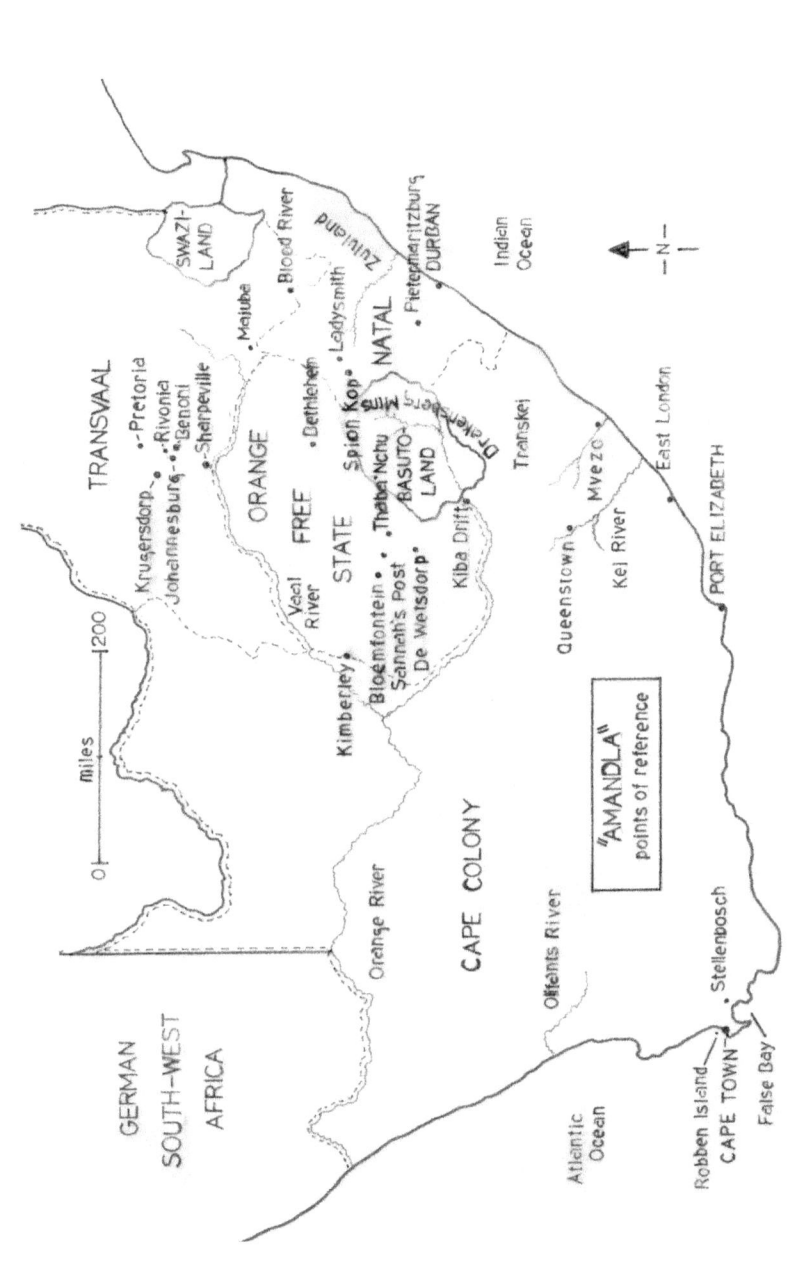

"Amandla": Nguni, literally: power

Power tends to corrupt, and absolute power corrupts absolutely.

—Lord Acton

The tree of liberty must be refreshed from time to time with the blood of patriots and tyrants. It is its natural manure.

—Thomas Jefferson

PROLOGUE

2010

"It's time, Madiba—time to wake, time to die."

Nelson blinked, trying to adjust to being so rudely woken and to what he thought he had just heard. He struggled upright and stared in disbelief at the man sitting on a chair near the foot of his bed...with a gun in his hand. He didn't recognize the man, but there was something about the gun that evoked long-forgotten memories.

I must be dreaming, he thought, closing his eyes, willing it to be so.

He had gone to bed at peace with his retirement from public life, revered as father to his people, survivor of twenty-seven years in prison, winner of the Nobel Peace Prize, and the first in a succession of black presidents of South Africa. But even though the landscape of his life was littered with the debris of a violent struggle against the brutal machinery of apartheid, he had never imagined facing death in the comfort of the Groote Schuur mansion in the heart of Cape Town. Yet, out of nowhere, an assassin had invaded his privacy to kill him—in bed—on a Sunday morning.

He pinched the bridge of his nose and massaged his tired eyes, but when he opened them the stranger was still there, the rich blue-black finish of the gun stark against the pale skin of the man's hand.

It was no dream.

The man looked formidable in the low light, his face smeared in dark colors, a black sweater tight over a khaki shirt, his long pants discolored by dirt stains, his boots scuffed and muddy. He was built like a heavyweight and exuded the aura of a boxer on fight night—breathing hard, sweating lightly—as though he had just finished his pre-fight routine and was ready for the opening bell, except this man wasn't wearing gloves and showed no intention of abiding by the Queensbury Rules.

"Do you recognize the gun?" asked the man, twisting his hand to show him a side view of the weapon.

Nelson looked at the pistol's angular profile, so familiar yet so alien. It was like scanning a code that unlocked a vault to his memory. A tremor ran down his spine as he recalled his sense of pride and purpose training at the military camp outside Addis Ababa to prepare for the war against the apartheid regime—learning the fundamentals of guerrilla warfare and how to handle various weapons, before the sudden recall to South Africa to lead the armed struggle—and his pleasure when the Ethiopian colonel had given him the pistol as a parting gift, together with two hundred rounds of ammunition.

"It's a Makarov semiautomatic pistol," he said dismissively.

The man looked at him, a hint of amusement in his eyes. "Yes, but not just any Makarov—*your* Makarov. And it still works perfectly well," he added, resuming his aim, "although your ammunition needed to be replaced."

Nelson glanced at the pistol's chrome-lined barrel, the dull glint like an ominous shroud for the 9 mm cartridge lying in the chamber ready to explode in a deadly flash of light. He wondered if he would see the bullet emerge before it tore into the threadbare fabric of his ninety-two-year-old body.

A smile flickered across the man's mouth. "Fifty paces from the kitchen at Liliesleaf, near an oak tree. That's where you said you buried it—the first gun of the revolution. Many tried to find it. No one ever did."

"So how did *you* find it?" asked Nelson, his mouth dry, his palms damp.

"I was there the night you buried it," said the man with grim satisfaction. "I watched you do it."

Nelson's thoughts swirled, caught in a vortex of disbelief as he recalled that dark night at his secret hideout nearly fifty years ago. Had he already been under surveillance, his movements tracked, his hideout discovered, even before he was betrayed and captured? But he was also intrigued. The man was here to kill him yet had addressed him by his clan name and showed no sense of urgency.

And he apparently wanted to talk.

"Indulge an old man," began Nelson, breaking the ominous silence that seemed to fog the bedroom. "I've been a troublemaker all my life, shaken many trees over the years, faced death many times. If I am to die today, at least tell me why."

The man stared dispassionately at him for several moments.

"'Proclaim it from the rooftops—free at last! Free at last!' That's what you declared, Madiba, quoting Martin Luther King. But the ANC shows contempt for the principles of democracy—power is all that matters—and the only thing I hear proclaimed by your people is 'Bring me my machine gun' and 'Shoot the Boer' and 'One settler, one bullet.'" The man was flushed, breathing hard. "The ignorant barbarity of it all is almost apocalyptic, like a death star collapsing and extinguishing the light of freedom in a black hole of demagoguery."

"I reject that," retorted Nelson indignantly. "But even if true of some, I recall your Afrikaner Broederbond cared nothing for democracy. They put the *Volk* ahead of all else, and power was the only thing that mattered to them."

"We had no choice," hissed the man. "We faced extinction. But your people had a choice. You were supposed to be the golden key to unlock a future of reconciliation and justice. You promised a rainbow nation would emerge from the storm of apartheid, that together we would rebuild our country and hand the baton to the next generation.

"Well, the next generation has taken the baton, Madiba, but it's running the race in reverse—back across the rainbow bridge—back into the anguish and oppression of our past, but this time caused by your people, not mine."

The man paused, grinding his jaw as though chewing on indigestible gristle, before continuing. "Instead of regenerating itself with leaders from your stock, the lifeblood of the ANC has been poisoned by the cancer of corruption and tyranny, a desecration of the ideals you were prepared to die for and convinced our people to believe in."

The man let out a sigh that seemed to tear itself from the core of his being and stretch across the space between them.

Then he raised the pistol.

"And so our beloved country needs a blood transfusion," the man added, his tone tinged with regret. "It needs yet another generation to give its full measure of devotion to refresh the tree of our liberty with its blood—the blood of patriots—starting with yours."

The downward movement of the man's thumb on the left side of the Makarov was unmistakable, as was the metallic click.

The pistol's safety was disengaged.

"Don't do this," implored Nelson. "I don't care if I live or die—I prepared for death many times. But for our country's sake—for our peoples' sake—don't do this thing."

The man shrugged. "You were prepared to do the same thing all those years ago—to plunge our country into civil war with acts of terror to bring about your revolution." He shook his head. "I wonder if the Academy in Oslo knew they were awarding the Peace Prize to one trained in weapons of terror, commander of a terrorist organization that killed innocent women and children."

Nelson stared defiantly at the man, only too aware of his role in planning acts of sabotage and revolution, first commander of Umkhonto we Sizwe, the "Spear of the Nation." But that was the means—it was the end that mattered.

He took a deep breath. "It was never our intent to kill the innocent, but without our armed struggle, without the violence, there would have been no negotiation. And without negotiation there would have been no peace. Your people would have clung to power, and the streets would have run with blood—the same color blood, yours and mine."

"You were a damned terrorist," sneered the man. "You and Umkhonto were to us what Osama bin Laden and al-Qaeda were to the Americans."

Nelson bristled. "I care nothing for labels," he replied. "I fought the fight that was forced on me. I met violence with violence after peaceful methods failed. Your people did the same against the British. And you called yourselves freedom fighters! But you know what they say, 'one man's terrorist is another man's freedom fighter.'"

"You were not just *one* man's terrorist," countered the man. "Even the Americans and British—Reagan and Thatcher—branded you a terrorist. And despite your early distrust of communists," continued the man, "you got into bed with them and prostituted your ideals for thirty pieces of Soviet silver."

Nelson was stung by the indictment, but before he could respond the man spoke again.

"No comment, Madiba? Can't say I'm surprised. Your people warped the concept of freedom to cloak the abomination of communism."

"And your people warped the concept of Christianity to cloak the abomination of apartheid," he shot back, ignoring the gun pointed at his chest. "At least we are free of that!"

A fateful silence descended on the room, disturbed only by a peal of church bells drifting through the window. On any other Sunday, the bells resonated with an uplifting, spiritual quality, but on this day they sounded discordant, as though unsure for whom they tolled.

"It is a long walk to freedom," said Nelson, breaking the silence. "Your own people know how long and hard it is—you fought two wars for your freedom against the British. But when you finally came to power, you protected your freedom with apartheid. My people still struggle, every day, with its legacy. But now we have the power. We control our own destiny."

He glared at the man, then added in a softer tone, "We have only just begun the journey... for all the people of our country. We are not there yet."

PART ONE

1838—1902

The Cape of Good Hope is amongst the stormiest capes of them all. It is also midway by sea from Europe to the East Indies. The Dutch established a fortified refreshment station at the Cape in the 17th century to support their trade with the Indies. The station eventually became a colony, and Dutch, German, and French Huguenot settlers spread into territories inhabited for millennia by progeny of Africa's cradle of mankind.

In the early 1800s, as part of the European resolution of the Napoleonic Wars, the Dutch colony at the Cape became a British colony, and waves of British settlers arrived, especially during the 1820s. In the 1830s, Britain abolished slavery at home and initiated the gradual abolition of slavery in all her colonies. Many of the original Dutch settlers found British ways intolerable, including the new attitudes towards slavery and racial equality, and chose to pack their wagons and trek into the interior. One of their leaders, Piet Retief, declared the hope that the British government "would allow us to govern ourselves without its interference in the future."

Early reconnaissance efforts had identified two fertile regions believed to be largely unpopulated—one in the interior on the Highveld beyond the Orange River, the other on the Indian Ocean side of the Great Escarpment and bordering the Zulu Kingdom. Some of the trekker parties headed deep into the Highveld, while others, including Retief's party, headed down the escarpment towards the ocean, with its port access and better rainfall.

Retief's party of trekkers attempted to negotiate a grant of land from the Zulu king, Dingane.

1

THE WIZARDS

1838

Ten-year-old Gadla Mandela was startled when Dingane leapt to his feet with his arms held high and shouted the command over the heads of his dancing warriors.

"*Babulaleni abathakathi,*" the king bellowed. "Kill the wizards!"

The king's warriors immediately swarmed over the white men, who fought back desperately with bare hands and bush knives.

Gadla held his breath, transfixed, the frenetic blur of fighting partially obscured by a cloud of rising dust. Even from where he stood just inside the main entrance to Dingane's great kraal, there could be no doubt about the outcome. Then, out of the dust came the warriors, hauling their struggling captives across the arena to shouts of wild celebration, past where he stood, all the way to the outer hedge of the kraal. Once outside, the warriors tied the men's hands and legs and dragged them down the hill across the stream to the rocky hill on the far side, a place feared by all—*kwaMatiwane*—the place of execution.

The rumor among elders was that Dingane had granted land to the whites as a reward for recapturing stolen cattle from one of his rivals and had invited the white leaders to a farewell celebration at his Great Place. But the white men had been told they could not enter the king's presence with their guns. Gadla's task with some other boys had been to stack the guns outside the entrance to the king's kraal. It was a vast oval camp bordered by a thorn hedge, known to all as the Great Place Surrounded by Elephants, enclosing nearly two thousand huts, four royal cattle kraals—each with herds of distinct colors—and special huts for food and war shields. The king's own hut stood on the far side, opposite the main entrance.

Gadla had seen the reluctance in the eyes of the white men as they handed over their weapons. Once inside the kraal, the king had entertained the visitors with beer and warrior dancing—even the king had danced as the beer was served. But as the men sat cross-legged near the king in the center of the oval arena, the dancing of the warriors rushing back and forth became more and more frenetic, until they had closed in on the men on all sides.

That was when the king had sprung his trap. And now all sixty or seventy of them were on their knees at the king's place of execution.

Gadla hated to watch as the warriors clubbed and skewered the men to death but could not turn away, especially when the young one, son of the white leader, was killed in front of his father before the father too was clubbed to death. Gadla winced as a warrior sliced open the father's chest and cut out his heart, even though he knew that body parts of powerful enemies were a source of strength for the warriors.

The sun had hardly moved by the time it was all over, as though the wizards had to be killed quickly before they could conjure up magic in their defense.

Gadla turned away and walked back to his father's hut. He had mixed feelings about the Zulu kings, especially Shaka, celebrated for his military prowess but notorious for his cruelty. And now there was Dingane, the unpredictable half brother who had murdered Shaka to become king. But Gadla was very careful to keep his feelings to himself, not least because he was a Thembu, not a Zulu, from a group of Thembus who had been caught up in Shaka's campaign of conquests and absorbed into the Zulu empire. His father had become one of the king's advisors, and his uncle was a veteran in the king's army.

Gadla didn't really understand Dingane's fear of the whites, even though his father had spoken of it many times. But he knew the prophecy—everyone did—that white traders would come first, then missionaries would follow, and then the soldiers in red would come to take their cattle and conquer their kingdom. The traders and missionaries had come, and the soldiers in red were already making war against the Xhosa in the south and heading north towards the Zulu kingdom. But now these other whites had crossed the mountains—the barrier of upturned spears—and were poised to enter the kingdom, waiting in the foothills for the king to give them land. And these whites, with their horses and guns, had already defeated rival warriors as feared as Shaka himself.

But it was the haunting that seemed to have forced the king's hand. The white leader and his men had camped nearby and, during the night, their horses had been heard moving around the king's kraal. Word had quickly spread through the regiments that these whites were wizards who had haunted the king's kraal and would attack in the morning—this very day—and that the prophecy of conquest was about to be fulfilled.

Whatever the explanation, it seemed the king believed he was threatened from all sides by whites, who encroached on his land, preached at him, killed his elephants, stole his cattle and offered little in return, not even guns that worked properly. Perhaps the king had been right to strike the first blow.

Later the same day, when the sun was at its highest, he watched as several of the king's regiments assembled in the arena. In a loud voice full of urgency, the king ordered the warriors to kill the rest of the whites camped between the river and the mountains—to take them by surprise and kill them all. There was no time for the usual rituals and preparations for battle.

Within minutes the warriors rushed from the arena.

Over the next several days, the stillness that blanketed the king's Great Place was broken only by the screeching of the big birds squabbling over the scraps at *kwaMatiwane*, while many more soared overhead, waiting their turn.

Eight-year-old Johan de Beer woke to such dreadful sounds of shouting and screaming and barking that he thought it must be a nightmare. He sat up on his blanket, confused, until he saw the river a few feet away and remembered.

"Come, Johan, we must go," urged the family friend who had taken him fishing and was already on his feet, rifle in hand, holding the reins of their horses.

The screams were real. So were the dogs. But by the time they reached the main camp less than a mile away, the only sounds were of anguish, like those of mortally wounded animals, and the shouting had stopped.

Johan reined in and stared. It looked like the devil had swept across the campsite, destroyed everything in his path, then fled to avoid the rising sun. A veil of smoke swirled as though possessed by angry spirits, blowing this way and that over dead cattle, goats and dogs. Torn pages and pillow feathers leapt among the charred wagons as though trying to elude the spirits. And scattered about like rag dolls lay mothers, daughters and babies, sprawled at grotesque angles, disfigured and bloody, his playmates among them—lifeless—as though frozen in gory motion.

The smoke burned his eyes, seared his nostrils, and reached deep into the bowels of his being, churning and twisting, until it became the stench of death.

The scavengers had already gathered. Hyenas laughed brazenly behind glowing eyes. A pack of wild hunting dogs barked in delight. Vultures circled overhead, floating silently on the smoke-tainted breeze, their ugly heads angled downward, contemplating the meal to come.

He leapt from his pony as dread replaced disbelief, hoping his mother and baby sister had somehow been spared, determined to save them from the scavengers if they had not. He joined others, searching... calling... slipping on the blood-soaked grass as they stumbled through the desecration.

The father who had taken him fishing found his daughter. For a moment he seemed rooted in horror at the naked violence of the girl's death before dropping to his knees and covering her with his jacket. Then he covered his face with his hands and bowed his head, his shuddering grief testament to the pain that saturated the horrific scene.

Johan shut his eyes and mumbled a prayer. After several minutes he mustered the courage to speak. "Please, uncle, please help me with my mother and sister." He used the usual term of respect, even though there was no family connection.

At first the father seemed not to have heard, then nodded, wiped his daughter's hair from her unseeing eyes, kissed her forehead, and rose to his feet.

When they reached the remains of the De Beer family wagon, Johan recognized the gentle face of his mother lying face up with his baby sister clutched to her chest. But his sister seemed attached by a stick that went through her back and pegged both mother and child to the ground. He stood transfixed, staring in disbelief at the incomprehensible sight. When his numbed senses finally succumbed to understanding, he dropped to his hands and knees and heaved violently, the taste of last night's roast pigeon and homemade candy bitter in his mouth.

"Dear Jesus...dear Jesus," he sobbed as he hunkered on all fours like an animal, swaying and groaning, just a few feet from where their family Bible lay open, its singed pages rustling in the breeze.

The father knelt beside him with a hand on his shoulder. "I will take care of it, son."

Johan nodded, grasped the Bible and, his eyes closed, intoned the Lord's Prayer. At the "amen," thinking the man must be done, he opened his eyes just as the man tore the spear out of both bodies in one upward jerk, his boot braced against the small of his baby sister's back. Johan pitched forward again in a series of dry heaves as the image scoured his gut and scorched his heart.

"Goddamned devils," swore the man as he flung the spear aside. Then, still breathing hard, he said, "Son, you take the little one. I will carry your mother."

Johan managed to stand but could barely see through the tears as he lifted his baby sister into his arms. He held her as he had done so many times to burp her. There would be no burp this time.

The small group collected their loved ones, wrapped them in salvaged fabric of various sorts and loaded them into the back of a usable wagon to be buried in a field nearby. Johan tried not to look at the limp bodies stacked irreverently on top of each other like carcasses after a slaughter.

He stumbled through the macabre scene, struggling to grasp the difference a day had made. Yesterday he had waited for his father to return with their leader, Piet Retief, and about seventy others, bringing a land treaty signed by the Zulu king. But in the night the king's warriors had come, bringing instead a decree of death. Yesterday the families camped with them in the foothills of the Drakensberg—the Bothas, Prinsloos, Van der Merwes, Liebenbergs, and De Beers—had been full of joy, anticipating land to call their own. Today their joy congealed in dark splotches amid the broken bodies of loved ones. Yesterday his mother had fretted about him being away from the camp in an area teeming with all sorts of wild animals, big and small, even though he was with an adult. Today she died with her baby in her arms, while he had been spared as he slept under the stars beside a trout stream.

He didn't understand why everyone was dead, or why he was still alive, or why his father had not protected his mother and sister. Even the miracles made no sense—like how his twelve-year-old friend, Johanna van der Merwe, had survived more than twenty stab wounds. He mumbled a passage from the psalms about how God's rod and staff would comfort him as he walked through the valley of the shadow of death. But he was not comforted. And he still didn't know what had become of his father.

All he could think to do was to stay close to the man who had helped him, a high school teacher from the Cape whose wife and daughter had both died in what his people were calling the "Great Murder," and who now treated him as a son.

Spring came and brought hope of a savior.

It had been a terrible time for the remnants of the trekkers. Their leader was dead, along with more than a hundred fighting men, fifty women, a hundred and eighty children and two hundred servants. To compound their wretchedness, their meager provisions were almost exhausted, disease was rampant and most of their cattle were in Zulu hands. For many, the dream that had inspired their great exodus from the Cape had been trampled in the terror of Dingane's deceit. Some spoke of giving up and making the long trek back to the Cape, back to British domination.

By the time Andries Pretorius arrived in the spring with sixty-eight wagons and a commando of horsemen, he was already a hero. And he had a plan—to advance deep into Zulu territory and to lure Dingane into battle against a fortified laager of wagons.

True to his word, in early December, Pretorius led nearly five hundred horsemen and sixty-four wagons into the heart of the Zulu empire, together with about three hundred black and colored scouts, wagon drivers and horse attendants. And Johan went with them, having convinced his guardian to take him to help with the horses and cattle, perhaps even to help load the rifles during battle.

Every night their preacher climbed on top of one of the cannons to speak to the men. Nobody minded Johan worming his way up to the cannon to hear the stories from the Old Testament that celebrated God helping the outnumbered Israelites fight for their freedom and a homeland.

The message was clear. Just as God had rescued the Israelites from slavery in Egypt and given them victory over their enemies in the promised land, so too had God rescued the Boers from British oppression in the Cape. And surely God would also give them victory against their enemies in their promised land.

As they drove deeper into the heart of Zululand, the preacher added an extra element—a solemn covenant that if God did give them victory against the Zulus they would commemorate the day every year as a day of thanks. And their children and their children's children would do the same, forever giving God the glory of the victory.

In mid-December, just as they were crossing a flooded river, scouts reported thousands of Zulu warriors heading towards them on the run. A murmur of consternation arose among the men. The burly, potbellied Pretorius stood tall in his stirrups to survey the terrain. Then he wheeled his horse and ordered everyone back across the river. Once across, he instructed the men to form the wagons into a rough circle between the prongs of the "V" created by the river and a long stormwater ditch.

The logic of the site was clear to all—to force the Zulus to attack through the narrow, open ground between the two prongs, or risk forging the swollen river or scaling the deep ditch.

The men worked feverishly through the afternoon to lash the wagons together with chains. The scouts and wagon drivers helped too, and Johan found himself working side by side with black and colored strangers. Together they filled the gaps between wagons with fighting gates—wooden screens with gaps between the slats to use as firing ports—and covered the wagon wheels with strips of rawhide. By the time they were finished, the protective wall of wagons around their camp looked as though it was rooted to the ground, immovable and impregnable.

That night Johan joined in the singing of hymns by the light of lanterns. There was little doubt the warriors were moving into position in the dark, just beyond the wagons. After the singing he tried to sleep, but he could no sooner close his eyes to the brilliance of the night sky than ignore the fear of what lay in the darkness beyond the wagons.

By the time the men took up their fighting positions just before dawn, the knot in his stomach was so tight he could hardly breathe.

The cold season passed and the rains and heat came back.

So did the wizards.

The king's messengers were dispatched into the kingdom to muster the regiments to deal with the threat. The valleys echoed with commands shouted from hilltops in every direction. The warriors responded quickly, knowing any delay would enrage the king, and assembled in the Great Place as soon as the entire army had arrived.

Then it was time for the doctoring ceremony—to purify, fortify and bind the warriors together for the battle to come.

Gadla watched in awe as the mass of warriors went through the rituals. First, the men were taken to the stream, where they had to swallow medicine made by the king's war doctors before vomiting into special holes in the ground. Then a black bull was killed, the first of many, its flesh roasted in strips and smeared with special powders, before the strips were thrown into the air among the warriors, who took bites, chewed and spat out the pieces. Next, the army gathered around pots of foul-smelling medicine boiling over large fires. As the warriors filed past the pots, the war doctors used oxtails dipped into the medicine to sprinkle their shoulders with the protective potion.

After the sprinkling, the warriors gathered again before Dingane, who raged against the wizards, insisting they were coming back to avenge the death of their leader and the others, and to take the king's cattle and land and ivory. They had to be stopped, their wagons destroyed, their cattle taken and their people killed so they would never again march against the Zulu kingdom. He would not lead them into battle himself but assured the warriors they were ready, protected by the war doctors from whatever dark forces the wizards could invoke in battle.

Then it was time. The king, who had been ritually cleansed by his war doctors in the privacy of the royal hut, gave the order and the army began to march, led by the most senior regiment.

Its commander was a fearsome sight, cloaked in leopard skin beneath a feathered headdress, a single assegai and knobbed stick in one hand, a white cowhide shield with black spots in the other, with monkey skins around his waist and oxtails hanging from his arms and legs. A thousand warriors followed in a wave of shields, assegais, feathers, pelts and oxtails. Next came a similar-looking regiment, but wielding red-spotted shields. Then another with gray shields, then one with black shields, and on and on, regiment after regiment, until all had passed from the arena.

Gadla was so excited by what he had seen that he persuaded his father to let him be a baggage boy—one of many boys needed to carry the warriors' sleeping mats, headrests and tobacco—who trailed behind the army driving the cattle it needed for food. He was proud to carry his uncle's things, and that his uncle was part of the loin of the army, together with thirty Thembu veterans. The loin would be held in reserve until needed, but all the men thirsted for a chance to prove their bravery against the wizards.

The march to the battle site was brutal, the pace hard, the ground wet and the rivers in flood. His feet were not hardened like the warriors' feet into soles like the hooves of cows, impervious to thorns and rocks and pain. Although they had started in single file, as was the custom, the army soon split into two main groups, with rival regiments desperate to be the first to drink the dew of battle.

Gadla was exhausted and could barely see his hand in front of him by the time he reached the battle site. The sun had set behind him and he could only just make out the circle of wagons ahead, dimly lit by lanterns, and was surprised to hear the sound of singing drifting through the dark towards him.

As tired as he was, he knew there was no rest for the army forming under cover of darkness, the chest of the army to attack the wagons from the front, the two horns—like encircling arms—to surround the wagons left and right, and the loins to remain in reserve. He found his uncle to give him his mat and headrest and tobacco, then rejoined the baggage boys in the deep shadows of the night.

But sleep was impossible—his heart beat so loudly he was afraid he would betray the warriors' position to the enemy.

2

RIVER OF BLOOD

1838

Johan squinted through the gloom as the early-morning sun dispersed the layers of night from the low-lying hills beyond the wagons. He was sure he could see a dark mass moving down the open area between the hills, as though the night was making one last advance towards the wagons even as it retreated elsewhere.

It was suddenly hard to breathe, hard to swallow, as the air turned heavy with dread, saturated by sounds that seemed to rise from the bowels of the earth—horrible groaning and hissing noises as if the darkness was in pain as it moved.

Then it stopped and the hideous sounds quieted.

For a few moments a terrible silence enveloped the wagons. Then, without warning, the air split apart—as though cleaved by the devil to make way for his minions—and a thunderous rumble swept over the wagons like a herald of impending doom.

Panic tightened its chokehold on Johan's senses as the dark mass grew bigger and louder and seemed to dance like a multi-faceted phantom across the murky horizon above the laager. Just as he felt his legs begin to buckle the mass gained definition in the early light and he realized the warriors were beating their spears against shields that appeared to float like ghosts across the high ground.

As though on cue, the warriors stopped beating their shields as the dawn illuminated the front ranks of the fearsome sight. An unnatural stillness descended upon the landscape. All of creation seemed to pause for a moment of silent reflection before the impending conflagration.

Then, as one, the warriors rose and raced down the open ground, screeching and yelling, their shields and spears held low at their sides, a ferocious tidal wave of uninhibited violence that would surely crash over the wagons and destroy everything in its path.

Johan looked frantically at the men around him—everyone seemed frozen by the sound and fury of the attacking warriors, struck dumb by the onslaught. Even the three cannons placed in small openings in the wall of wagons were inexplicably mute. Then, just when it seemed the warriors were about to leap into the wagons, a deafening fusillade erupted from the cannons and rifles.

His ears rang, his eyes watered, and a choking cloud of gunsmoke filled his throat. A moment later his eyes cleared. He could hardly believe what he saw. It looked like the unstoppable force had crashed against an immovable but invisible object—perhaps the hand of God—but the warriors had stopped short of the wagons. Some were reeling, others falling, while those still on their feet were scrambling back towards safety.

The respite did not last long. The warriors rushed the wagons again and again, seemingly impervious to the cannons and rifles, the screams of the wounded and death throes of the dying. Some tried to launch their throwing spears, but most needed to get close enough to use their stabbing spears. The ebb and flow of the attack was broken only by brief lulls as the warriors regrouped before charging again. Despite the piles of bodies and deadly firepower from behind the wagons, the warriors kept up the attack in wave after determined wave.

The men all had more than one rifle, firing the first while someone loaded the second. And they fired in rotations of several men to each firing position. Only seconds elapsed between each shot from every position.

From his station next to a wagon wheel, Johan loaded rifles as fast as he could, knowing his life depended on it. He was sweating, breathing hard, his eyes filled with grit and smoke. He could pour powder and load lead shots as fast as most adults, but there were times the barrels got so hot he thought the powder might explode. And sometimes he barely had enough time to fling a handful of powder into the pan and drop a shot down the barrel before the rifle was needed, before he even had a chance to ram the shot all the way down onto the powder charge.

At the height of the frenzied assault, fresh warriors suddenly attacked across the river and through the ditch. The men were now fighting on all fronts, the battle so fierce that he had to leave his reloading station to help control the frantic horses and oxen. And just when it seemed they were at the limit of what could be endured, shouts of alarm went up all around the perimeter—the men were almost out of ammunition. They had to end the battle quickly or the warriors would finish it with their stabbing spears.

Amid the alarm, Pretorius gathered his best horsemen. Their only hope was to force a Zulu retreat with the last of their ammunition—they would charge the attacking warriors.

Johan helped the men mount the skittish horses.

Gadla rose at the horns of the morning, when it was just light enough to see cattle horns against the sky, a perfect time to attack an unwary enemy. He climbed a tree for a view of the king's magnificent army in action.

But as he climbed, an unnerving sound rose from the murky darkness. As he peered through the low light, it seemed the dark earth beneath him was alive and on the move, groaning and hissing, advancing slowly down towards the circle of wagons. Then the noise stopped and the entire mass seemed to sink even lower in deference to the rising sun ahead.

In the silence his mind went blank, but only for a moment before a deafening clamor burst around him and thundered across the battle site, as though all of Africa's ancestors had risen up in rage against the intruders with a roar like a thousand lions. He took off like a scalded monkey, climbing higher, as fast as he could, trying to escape, trying to discern what was happening.

Then he saw and understood, the dawn revealing what the darkness had concealed.

The earth beneath him was carpeted with a mass of warriors, all beating their shields with their spears. Dread turned to thrill as the sound enveloped him. He looked down the shallow slope to the puny circle of wagons, half expecting the whites to flee in terror. He wondered if they knew the left and right horns of the army had encircled them in the night and that the fearsome chest of the army was about to sweep down and crush them like insects beneath Dingane's heel.

The beating suddenly stopped, the thunderous clamor instantly replaced by a terrible silence. But a moment later an awful howling erupted, as though the warriors' shields were shrieking from having been beaten. Then, out of the half-light, Gadla saw the first wave of chest warriors stream down the open ground towards the wagons in a blur of oxtails, skins and feathers, their shields and stabbing spears held low, shredding the predawn silence with their war cries as they raced towards the circle of wagons.

Victory was inevitable. There could be no doubt the wave of warriors would crash over the white wizards with devastating effect. And the silence from the wagons surely meant the whites had been turned to stone, paralyzed by fear, knowing they were about to die. But just as the warriors reached the wagons, a terrifying blast drowned their war cries and cut them down like an unseen machete slicing through rows of mielies.

Gadla watched in disbelief as those who had been chosen to be the first to taste the dew were the first to die, and those who were still on their feet milled about in bloodied confusion before they turned and fled.

From his vantage point, it became clear the attack was uncoordinated. The river and donga must have stopped the left and right horns of the army from forming overnight to surround the wagons. Only the chest of the army had mounted a proper attack, but it had attacked along the narrow neck between the river and donga, straight into the guns of the wizards.

Gadla watched with mounting despair as wave after wave of warriors rushed the wagons, trying to get close enough to batter the enemy with their war shields and stab them with their spears. But the guns kept them away. Some used their throwing spears from a distance but with little effect against the wall of wagons. Then, to avoid the narrow neck of death, some in the left and right horns tried to cross the river or to scale the donga. But the river was swollen and the donga was steep. Those who climbed the donga still couldn't get close enough to use their stabbing spears, while those in the river had no footing and were too crowded to throw their spears effectively.

Gadla looked for his uncle among the Thembu warriors in the loin of the army, held in reserve behind the chest. As he searched, he saw some in the loin become so agitated at the failed efforts of the younger men that they tried to fight their way through the ranks to get a chance to attack, to blood their spears against the wizards.

As confusion gave way to chaos, he saw his uncle, his war shield a luminous white with a distinctive pattern of black markings, being pushed towards the river by the retreating warriors.

Then, just when it seemed the warriors had survived the worst of the gunfire, the wizards burst from the wagons on their horses, shooting at the warriors, forcing them to break ranks and flee.

As he watched, his uncle stopped at the riverbank with a small group of his fellow Thembu warriors. Crouched behind their shields, they faced the horsemen while all around them warriors were jumping into the deep hippopotamus pool, only to be shot as they hid in the reeds or tried to swim across the pool.

Gadla could see it would not end well and felt his panic rise as the horror of defeat unfolded. He saw his uncle become isolated as warriors to his right and left fell. Then his uncle's white shield spun away from him, his shield arm hanging useless at his side. But still he held his stabbing spear and prepared to fight a potbellied wizard riding straight at him, aiming his long gun. But the man's horse suddenly veered sideways, throwing the wizard to the ground right in front of his uncle.

Gadla watched wide-eyed as the man scrambled to his feet, desperately parrying his uncle's stabbing spear with his hands. Then, just when he thought his uncle would surely deliver the killing blow and thrust his spear up into the man's abdomen, his uncle staggered as though punched in the chest by an unseen fist and tumbled slowly off the embankment into the river, still clutching his spear.

Gadla stared dumbly at the river, now a murky reddish brown, its surface uneven, broken everywhere by floating bodies. He shook his head to dispel the images of death. He barely noticed the potbellied man being helped to his horse by another horseman, his long gun still smoking, or heard the cheers from the wagons as the man remounted and galloped off to lead the attack.

It was all so crushing, so unexpected, as though the order of his world had been thrown down and trampled underfoot by a strange and terrible breed.

Perhaps they really were wizards.

By midday the battle was over. The Zulu army was in full retreat, harried by a relentless mounted pursuit.

Johan wandered through the battle site in a daze. He couldn't believe they had survived, let alone won. Everywhere he looked, black bodies lay in tangled heaps, some right up against the wagons. Gone were their expressions of pride and bravado, replaced now by masks of death, some of shock, some of pain, others just blank stares as though death had come too quickly for any emotion to register.

But the most vivid image of the battle was the color of the river—it ran red with the blood of the warriors.

Although they had not captured Dingane or destroyed his army, nobody could deny their victory, especially at the cost of only three wounded, including Pretorius, who had a deep cut in his hand from defending himself against a warrior's spear after being thrown from his horse. The men counted about three thousand warriors dead, with many more wounded.

It was some consolation for the Great Murder that had taken so many innocent lives.

Gadla felt the weight of death pressing on his spirit as he carried his uncle's belongings back to the king's kraal.

It was a long march amid a disorganized mass of somber and fearful warriors, thankful to have escaped the guns and the horsemen but afraid of what was in store for them at Dingane's Great Place. He understood as soon as he reached his father's hut. The king was in a rage, threatening to execute everyone responsible for the defeat, especially those who had no blood on their stabbing spears.

It was time, said his father, to slip away amid the terror and confusion. The king's kraal had become a dangerous place, even more than before. They would go back to their own Thembu people living peacefully among the Xhosa, to their village of Mvezo, on the banks of the Mbashe River.

Sitting around a campfire that Christmas Eve, one of Pretorius's men recounted riding into Dingane's Great Place after the battle. The Zulu king had set fire to his compound within days of the battle and had fled with his herds into the heart of Zululand.

The man also spoke of the horror of Dingane's place of execution—the mass of rotting corpses and whitened bones. And among the bodies were Retief's men, their arms and legs broken, their skulls crushed, many impaled on wooden spikes, the land grant signed by Dingane still in Retief's pouch. They had buried their comrades near the place of execution—it was the only thing they could do.

Nobody noticed Johan in the shadows of the campfire—or saw his tears.

Not long afterwards, while exploring the foothills of the

Drakensberg with his guardian, Johan found a respectful resting place for his family in the valley of a cold mountain stream that tumbled precipitously from a peak shaped like a cathedral. If there could be no funeral from a church, then at least they could be memorialized within sight of a cathedral.

The only disquieting feature of the terrain was the rock formation directly overhead. It was shaped like a huge baboon's skull that seemed to leer malevolently at him through cavernous eye sockets carved into the rocky outcrop by the elements.

He chose a plateau about half way to the top of the rock formation and found a boulder to serve as a memorial to his family. Then, with his guardian's help, he rolled the boulder into a spot overlooking the tranquil mountain stream. When they were done, he read a few verses of Psalm 23 from the charred family Bible he had salvaged after the Great Murder. He still found no comfort in the Lord's "rod and staff," whatever that meant, but understood only too well how it felt to walk through the valley of the shadow of death. He vowed to return someday to somehow sanctify the sacrifice his family had made in their quest for land to call their own.

As he turned to leave, he looked up into the rocky depths of the baboon's skull. In a searing flash, the cavernous eye sockets came alive, broiling with such awful scenes of violent and bloody death that he staggered back and fell as though struck down by the force of the baboon's malice.

He covered his eyes and sobbed so fiercely he thought he might choke on the flood of memories that threatened to rupture his soul. He was still heaving with emotion when his guardian helped him into the saddle of his pony for the ride back to camp.

He hoped to leave the terrible images behind him but knew they would follow him to his grave.

3

PROPHECY AND PROMISE

1848-68

The story of the Thembu elders, how well they fought and how well they died at the river of blood, became part of the oral tradition Gadla passed on to his family, retold many times in the comfort of his home on the banks of the Mbashe. He was especially proud that his uncle had stabbed one of the settler horsemen before he died.

But the serenity and comfort of the village did not last long after news came of the war against the Xhosa. Gadla's people lived among the Xhosa, and soldiers and settlers from the land of a queen called Victoria were taking their lands, and their cattle had no defenses against the diseases that came from across the seas.

As desperation reached into every village, a prophet influenced by missionaries told the people he had been to heaven and spoken to God, who said he was unhappy with the whites for killing his son and would help the Xhosa by making them invulnerable to the white man's bullets. But after two more years of war, the warriors' vulnerability to British bullets was all too obvious.

Then a sixteen-year-old captured the people's imagination with her prophecy that if they slaughtered all their cattle and destroyed all their grain, the ancestors of all Xhosas would rise from the dead at the new moon in February 1857, and together the renewed Xhosa nation would drive the white people into the sea.

The people believed her. As the date approached, more than four hundred thousand cattle were slaughtered and mountains of grain destroyed. The new moon came and went, but no ancestors rose to drive the whites into the sea. Without cattle and food, thousands of their people died, and many more left their homes to find work in the Cape Colony.

Gadla's family survived only because his father refused to be taken in by the prophecy. His father knew they could not survive without plowing their fields and nurturing their cattle, but all around them neighbors were without food. The family shared what they could, but they had so little and the suffering was so great.

Finally, with his father's blessing, Gadla left Mvezo for Queenstown in the Cape Colony, where he found work as a blacksmith's helper and stable hand. He saved as much money as he could and returned to Mvezo whenever possible to take money home to his family.

Then he heard the stories of the stones.

Everybody was talking about a place where great riches could be dug out of the earth with nothing but a strong back and a pickax. He did not understand why white people would pay money for stones—it sounded like nonsense—but if the stories were true, he was only in his early forties, bigger than most men and as strong as an ox. He was confident no man could dig deeper or wider or work harder than he could.

Afraid the stones might all be found before he got there, Gadla used some of his savings to buy a mule, bade farewell to his family, and set out to find the place of the stones.

It was some comfort to Johan that his people did not forget their vow—that the day of their victory over the Zulus at Blood River would forever be celebrated as a holy day, the Day of the Covenant. But as for land to call their own, what his people had achieved by the spilling of blood the British achieved by the stroke of a pen when Great Britain simply annexed Natal, the territory they thought they had won from the Zulus.

For most of the families, the prospect of living under the heel of the British Empire was intolerable. They had come too far, suffered too much trying to escape its interfering laws and voracious appetite, but it had followed and found them. Now, once again the hated symbol of the Empire flew over their heads. Many loaded their wagons and headed back over the Drakensberg into the interior, where they settled among their own in two adjacent Boer republics—the South African Republic north of the Vaal River and, on its southern border, the Orange River Colony.

Johan's guardian had married a fiercely independent widow who had once brazenly told the British high commissioner that the Afrikaner people would rather climb barefoot back over the Drakensberg to death or independence than submit to British rule. True to her word, she packed up her family and they headed west, over the mountains, to Bloemfontein—the fountain of flowers—capital of the Orange River Colony.

Success came early to Johan when he was appointed an advisor to the first president of the colony—now recognized by the British as the independent Orange Free State—despite being only twenty-four and homeschooled by his guardian. It helped that he was tall and broad-shouldered and had been recommended by his pastor at the Twin Spire Church in the heart of Bloemfontein.

One of his first tasks was to draft a constitution. Undaunted, he drew from a wide range of sources, including the American Constitution, Bill of Rights and Supreme Court decisions. In one section he incorporated guarantees of equality and individual freedoms as well as freedom of speech and of the press. In another he incorporated the opinion of the American chief justice in the Dred Scott case that blacks were "an inferior order, altogether unfit to associate with the white race, either in social or political relations, and so far inferior that they had no rights which the white man was bound to respect." Although he was troubled by the dissenting opinion in the case—that it was "more a matter of taste than of law" to say that the black man, Scott, was not a citizen—the chief justice seemed to speak directly to their frontier predicament. For despite the freedoms promoted by their constitution, they were surrounded and vastly outnumbered by the natives.

But if they weren't bound to respect the rights of the natives, they could more easily protect their own.

Johan's prominence did not go unnoticed. Deemed eligible and handsome, he soon formed an attachment with Susannah, a vivacious young soprano who sang in their church choir. After a brief romance, he married her in the spring when the roses were in full bloom, even as rumors of a civil war in America challenged the ideals he had borrowed so confidently and written into the constitution of the young republic.

As time passed, he became increasingly troubled by reports of the American Civil War. So many battles, so many dead, so much blood—year after year—with no end in sight, tearing families apart. The tipping point came when he read about the battle at Gettysburg and Lincoln's speech afterwards—that America was dedicated to the proposition that all men are created equal. Something in the core of his being seemed to shake loose. All he could think to do was to make a change and start again, far from

Bloemfontein and the constitution he had written. Besides, his early years had been so filled with pioneering drama that city life just didn't sit well.

His chance came when diamonds were discovered just west of Bloemfontein. He knew he was being impulsive, but he couldn't resist the opportunity for a new adventure. Susannah resisted—she was still attached to her mother's apron strings and enjoyed her status in the community—but she finally relented, assured of being taken only about a hundred miles from her parents' home.

His plan was simple—to support his family by living off a small farm and, with a little luck, to make his fortune by finding some of the diamonds everybody was so excited about.

The mining town of New Rush was like a carnival, complete with a merry-go-round, fortune-tellers, saloons and hotels. And there were people from all over the world, some from places he had never heard of before. It was clear that anyone who could afford the price could buy a claim.

Johan loved the gritty, uninhibited exuberance of the town, and his efforts to find diamonds yielded modest results. But to his surprise, he found himself working his claims alongside owners who were not white like him but yellow, brown, and even black, some of whom spoke languages he had never heard before. And the fever spread when an even richer outcrop of diamonds was discovered nearby. Diggers descended on the new mine like flies to an open wound, gouging such an enormous hole in the ground that people started calling it the Big Hole.

New Rush was a hotbed of rumor and half-truths—it was all part of the allure. There were stories of men buying up multiple claims, like Barney Barnato, son of a London pub owner, and Cecil

Rhodes, son of an English country pastor, and Alfred Beit, son of a Hamburg merchant. And day and night, in every store and saloon, every barber chair and brothel bed, men and women talked like chattering monkeys about who struck it rich that day, how many carats the stones weighed, and how much dealers were paying per carat.

There were also rumors of a different kind, rumors that made white diggers lower their voices and black diggers nervous, the latest of which was that the rules of ownership were going to change. Everyone knew the problem. The patchwork of surface claims had disappeared as the diggers dug deeper and deeper and the mine came to resemble a huge sinkhole more than a thousand feet wide and hundreds of feet deep. And as claims collapsed into each other, the boundaries between neighboring claims became increasingly difficult to identify. Tensions between diggers were rampant and, as alliances formed to protect common interests, there was no more compelling alliance than the color of a digger's skin.

A "diggers' committee" had sounded innocuous enough. Johan had long thought there had to be some organization to control the multiple claims in such a confined area. And he had been a unanimous choice for the committee after serving in a republican government with expertise in the law. But the committee's new rules transformed the free-for-all spirit of the mines. Nonwhite diggers were no longer allowed to own claims or possess diamonds without satisfactory explanation—they could only be laborers, were no longer able to move freely around the mining camps, and would be flogged for violating the rules.

Aside from his committee duties, Johan continued to enjoy the frenetic energy and optimism of the mining experience—until the day a digger found a high-quality diamond in a rented claim on the De Beer farm. Overnight Johan was offered a king's ransom for his farm. He didn't want to sell, but his long-suffering wife insisted—she said their ship had finally come in and there was no longer any need for him to work so hard shoulder to shoulder with all the strange and godless people of New Rush. His compromise was to keep four claims for himself and to send her back to Bloemfontein to be with her parents.

He enjoyed the change. It gave him more time to spend in town and at the mine that had consumed his farm, now owned by the Englishman, Cecil Rhodes.

Gadla's journey from Queenstown took longer than expected after his mule was swept away trying to cross the Orange River.

When he finally arrived at the mining camp of New Rush, he quickly realized many others had also heard the stories of the stones. There seemed to be thousands of people of all colors, some speaking languages he had never heard, and from places he could not even imagine, all hoping to work a claim in one of the mines.

His first challenge was to buy a claim. The Big Hole mine was the richest, but the claims were too expensive. The De Beers mine was not quite as rich, but the claims were more affordable. After he bought his thirty-by-thirty-foot claim and the shovels, sieves, and pans he needed, he had only a few pounds and shillings left. He knew it was a risk, but he was confident he would soon find enough stones to survive and, hopefully, to recover his expenses and turn a profit.

He kept to himself, lived frugally and worked diligently. The relentless digging, carrying, washing and sifting of heavy soil, mud and gravel was not hard to master, just exhausting to sustain. The riskiest part was trying to get a fair price for his stones. He learned the hard way which of the buyers to trust. But then he began to worry about how to keep his money safe, for there were many in the camps, black and white, looking for an easier way to make money than digging for stones.

The solution came to him one night as he sat in his tent on the outskirts of town—he would hide his money inside his walking stick. It had a thick stem and a knob on one end to hold as he walked, and he could deliver a vicious blow with the knobbed end if he needed to use the stick a weapon. But there was enough bulk in the stem to carve out a hiding place.

Over the course of several nights, working by candlelight, he carefully cut out a foot-long section about half the thickness of the stick, starting just below the knob. The piece separated neatly from the rest of the stick. Then he carefully hollowed out the two exposed sections of wood. When he was done, the separated piece slotted neatly back into place, creating a hollow tube-like space inside the stick. To hold the separated piece in place, he wrapped that section of the stick in strips of decorative cloth to conceal the cut marks, then wound wire tightly over the cloth.

He was pleased with his handiwork. He could hide tight rolls of banknotes inside the hollow space and still use the stick for walking. But he knew it was now almost useless as a fighting stick.

He found ten stones during the first year. Although some diggers had found more, many had lost everything through gambling and drinking and women, while others had found much less and were reduced to penury. And when a dealer paid over one thousand pounds in crisp banknotes for his best stone, it made up for the many long days when his backbreaking efforts had yielded nothing. He soon amassed a small fortune in tightly rolled banknotes almost too bulky for the cavity in his walking stick.

Many spoke of having safe-deposit boxes in the bank. He had a safe-deposit chamber in his stick, and he always carried it with him.

4

CAT-O'-NINE-TAILS

1870

Gadla should not have worked that day. The mine seemed determined to repel intruders with icy fingers of wintry air that raked its surface and then plunged into the mine with such fury that it seemed the maze of ropes, pulleys, ladders and wooden platforms was possessed by frigid spirits incensed by his intrusion.

But the situation aboveground had forced his hand. The volatile mining existence was now even more perilous after a change in rules by the diggers' committee.

He had heard about the Servants' Registry Office when it opened but didn't bother to register because he was an owner with papers to prove it. But the diggers' committee had become aggressive and decreed that blacks could have no status other than laborer and that all claims owned by black diggers were forfeited.

He had to take the chance to work in conditions that kept prying eyes away. If he could stay in the shadows for just a little while longer, he was sure he could find a few more good stones before he went home. Besides, it was hard to tell who was an owner and who was a laborer at the digs, where people of all colors worked the claims. And there were always buyers willing to make a deal regardless of the seller's color.

Still, he should not have worked that day.

The bitter wind swirled through the cavernous landscape, slinging gravel and mine dust into his eyes and mouth. And although the digging should have warmed him, the sweat under his thin shirt quickly turned cold against his skin. By noon, his hands were so numb he nearly missed what the rockface tried so hard to conceal. But, after digging a little more to free the stone, he wiped away the grit and immediately knew he had found a good one, maybe the last one he needed. And he was definitely done for the day.

He cleaned the stone as best he could, then put it in his mouth—he didn't want to risk losing it through the holes in his pant pockets. He quickly made the sixty-foot climb to the rim, despite the lack of feeling in his hands. But, as he clambered over the edge, his foot struck an iron stake used to secure a mining rope. He tripped and fell, landing hard on his chest, driving the breath from his lungs and the stone from his mouth.

He knew he was in trouble when a boot crashed down on his hand just as his grasping fingers closed around the diamond.

Johan had thought to dig that day, but after walking the perimeter of the mine to the point closest to his claims, he already felt stiff with cold despite his heavy jacket. He decided to take the day off—a decision evidently shared by many other diggers—and began the walk back to camp, deep in thought about being separated from Susannah.

He noticed a black man climbing out of the mine just yards ahead of him and was startled when the man suddenly tripped and fell face-first at his feet. To compound his surprise, an object flew from the man's mouth and landed a few inches from his boot. And when the man lunged for the object, he instinctively stepped on the man's wrist.

"Open your hand," he demanded as the man twisted on the ground, trying to free himself. "Let me see."

Diggers materialized, as though from nowhere. The prospect of entertainment, perhaps even a whipping, was in the air.

"What have you got there, kaffir?" shouted one. "A diamond?"

Still on his stomach, the writhing man rasped, "It's my stone… from my claim."

"Hah! Lying bastard," yelled another. "You stole it."

The black man shook his head. "No, I found it. It's my stone."

"Show us your pass, kaffir," barked someone in the gathering crowd.

The man twisted and pulled in an effort to free his hand. Johan resisted, putting more weight on the man's wrist. But, with a crowd already surrounding them, there was no way the man could escape. He lifted his boot.

The man scrambled to his feet, raised his clenched fist to the crowd, and called out, "This is my stone… from my claim. I do not need a pass. I am an owner."

Johan was surprised the man did not appear intimidated. "But you're not allowed to be an owner," he stated matter-of-factly. "You have no pass and you have a diamond in your hand." His summary was succinct, the evidence damning.

An aggressive murmur rippled through the crowd. Then one digger yelled, "Give me the diamond," and lunged for the stone.

Johan saw the black miner jerk back his balled fist holding the diamond and, with a short jab, punch the lunging digger on the side of his head. Perhaps it was the stone in his fist that made the difference, but the digger crumpled to the ground and didn't move.

There was a moment of stunned silence before the crowd roared its outrage and leapt at the man. The next few moments were a blur. In the melee that followed, amid flailing arms and fists and legs, Johan saw a black arm appear just long enough to fling the stone directly at him. Despite his surprise, he scooped up the stone, turned his back on the one-sided brawl and headed back into town.

Within an hour the diggers' committee assembled on the porch of Graybittel's canteen. A crowd also gathered. It was a novel situation—a black owner charged with possession of a diamond to which he had been entitled before the rules were changed.

"So, De Beer, you were there," began one of the committee members. "The kaffir has no pass, he was caught with a diamond, and he attacked a digger." The crowd howled. "This is what you lawyers like to call an open-and-shut case, hey." The man chortled. "So, what's it to be? I say the maximum—fifty lashes!"

Johan paused. A sequence of questions was forming in his mind as he stood on the porch, fingering the man's diamond in his pant pocket, appraising the black digger who stood below him in front of the canteen's raised porch. He was a big man with a round, bulldog-like head. One of his eyes was swollen and he was bleeding from a split lip. Despite the rules change, the man had said he owned the claim. If that was true, then he should have a digger's license and a deed to the claim.

"What is your name?" he asked in a loud voice.

Drawing himself erect, the man replied, "I am Gadla Mandela, related by blood to the great Ngubengcuka, king of the Thembu."

Johan did not recognize any of the names or attribute any significance to what the man had said, but he did recognize the pride in the man's bearing and voice.

"Show me your deed."

The man reached into his pant pocket, drew out a grimy document that had been folded several times, and held it up for all to see. Johan took the document, unfolded it and read it.

"He's an owner," declared Johan. "The deed is genuine." Then he passed it to the committee member who was demanding fifty lashes.

The man immediately tore the deed into pieces.

"Like hell he is," the member scoffed, stomping on the shreds as they fell. The crowd cheered. "We know the rules—we made them. Only whites can be owners." More cheers as the member glared at him. "Come on, De Beer, don't waste our time. How many lashes? I say the full count." The crowd cheered again.

Johan stared at the man, then at the crowd, thinking of the constitution he had drafted for the republic, carefully crafting a contract for the people they could live by and depend upon for their rights. And although this was a black man—who, according to the American chief justice, was so far inferior to whites that he had no rights the white man was bound to respect—he had a written contract that was being ignored by a mob that would just as soon see the man lynched as flogged. Was it more a matter of taste than of the law to say this man was not an owner? Besides, had not Dingane signed the treaty only to disregard it and slaughter so many in the Great Murder? It seemed hypocritical to condemn Dingane's deceit yet inflict the same betrayal on this poor wretch.

The chanting of the enraged crowd interrupted his thoughts. "Fifty...fifty...fifty...fifty."

He waved his hands, trying to quiet the crowd's rage, but there was no stopping it, no explanation that could contain it. The crowd surged as though to attack the man unless he intervened.

But he knew fifty lashes could kill a man, even one as strong as this Mandela.

"Twenty-five lashes!" he shouted as loudly as he could. "Twenty-five!" The chants turned to jeers but the surge slowed. "And fetch the German," he added in a carrying voice. "Do it now!"

He could almost see the mob's thinking pivot to the spectacle that was to come. The German was notorious. If anyone could make twenty-five lashes feel like fifty, it was the German sailor whose savage flogging skills had transferred easily from ship to shore.

Johan shook his head in dismay, his distaste for the travesty as unexpected as it was bitter.

By the time the German arrived, Mandela had already been stripped to the waist, his arms tied to the horizontal railing of the raised canteen porch, his head facing the committee members sitting on the porch.

Behind Mandela, the sailor's footsteps crunched in the gravel as the big man strode back and forth, caressing the knotted leather strands of his cat-o'-nine-tails, enjoying his notoriety, acknowledging the roars of the crowd with obvious relish.

Johan sat with the committee, overlooking the scene. Mandela was looking straight at him. He noticed the man's high cheekbones, the coal-black eyes, the tuft of white hair above the man's forehead.

The crack of the first lash took them both by surprise. Mandela's eyes bulged and blinked but then cleared and his gaze held steady, even after the next lash tore at his back. He stood tall and stared, as though his tormentor was not the sailor behind him but the miner directly in front of him who had stepped on his wrist.

The German was renowned for his ability to keep a steady pace.

He alternated between overhead forehands and backhands in an unbroken rhythm of bloody lashes as the crowd counted, chanting the number of every lash.

Johan watched in silence. He had seen it all before—how the flesh tore from the victim's back and hung in strips until cut by the next diagonal lash, how the blood ran down the victim's legs into pools at his feet. He could not imagine the pain but he could see Mandela's face, and the coal-black eyes that glared unflinchingly at him.

Lash after lash he saw Mandela's face and body contort—his eyes bulge, his jaws grind, his muscles convulse and the blood splatter. At some point after fifteen lashes Johan could no longer hear the count, and every lash of the whip felt like the slash of a knife into his conscience.

He abruptly pushed himself out of his chair. He had seen enough. He would sell his claims the next day. He was done with the diggers' committee and the Big Hole. It was time to go home to his wife.

He turned and headed for the door of the canteen.

Gadla grasped for an image of courage to give him strength. After the shock of the first lash, he saw in his mind's eye the Thembu elders on the banks of the river, his uncle facing the big man who was thrown from his horse, then lunging at him with his stabbing spear.

His eyes narrowed, his jaws clenched. He would face this miner called De Beer just as his uncle had faced the big horseman in his moment of greatest peril.

With each lash his spirit grew more resolute even as his flesh succumbed to the knots of the whip. And like muffled background noise, the relentless count, the exultant crowd, and the grunting

German became little more than a distraction to his determination to endure. But when, through the blur of sweat and pain, he saw De Beer get up, he seized the moment just as his uncle had with his stabbing spear. He filled his lungs with air and his mouth with bloody mucus and spat as hard as he could.

The splat of gob hitting De Beer's boot—the same boot that had crushed his wrist—was the last thing Gadla heard before another lash tore into him and ripped consciousness from his being.

When the darkness lifted, Gadla didn't need to move to know he was lying on his stomach on the floor of his tent.

He did not know who had brought him to the tent or who had rubbed ointment into his wounds that smelled like crushed leaves. He was thankful but painfully aware his circumstances had inescapably changed. He had lost his claim and was branded a thief. Even if he could get work as a laborer, he could never accept such a position.

He had no choice—he had to leave the mine. At least he had a good amount of money safely hidden in his walking stick.

After darkness fell, a digger he knew materialized in his tent.

"Gadla," the man whispered urgently in Xhosa, "you must go quickly... You must leave this place."

He blinked hard and looked at the man in confusion. "What? Why must I leave?"

"The digger you struck—he is coming for you. Others, too, with guns!"

"Ugh," he groaned, shaking his head at this latest twist of the knife. "Tomorrow. I will go tomorrow. Tonight I must rest."

"Listen to me, Gadla," the man insisted. "The diggers are coming now. Tomorrow will be too late. Come, I will help you. Get up."

He grumbled and struggled to his knees. "But my things. What of my things?"

"Leave them. The diggers are nearly here."

He rose slowly. "I will come. But fetch my stick... I must have my walking stick... and my blanket."

The man lit one of Gadla's candles and looked around the small tent until he found the stick and blanket. Then he stuck the candle into the ground near the cooking pots, draped Gadla's free arm over his shoulder and helped him shuffle awkwardly through the tent flap.

A dreary day had given way to a dismal night.

Gadla turned and looked forlornly at his tent. It seemed even his spirit was reluctant to leave as the glow of the candle next to the pots created an odd silhouette against the tent wall, as though he were still inside, hunched over the fire, sitting on the floor of the tent.

He sighed, then turned and shuffled away.

The two had no sooner rounded a mound of mining dirt than a shout was heard behind them. "That's his tent... There he sits!" someone shouted. "Shoot him. Kill the kaffir dead!"

A volley of gunshots rang out.

"Burn the bastard, burn him!" yelled another.

Spurred on by the violence behind them, the two men lurched forward as fast as they could down a little-used path towards the main road. Once on the road, his helper bade him farewell.

"Stay safe, Gadla. Go well," said the man before he disappeared into the night.

The only direction Gadla could think to head was east, back to Thembuland and the comfort of his family. Perhaps he would come across a medicine man to help him if he stayed on the main road. But many people used the road, and he knew he was in danger because of what had happened at the mine. Then again, if he left the road, he would probably die of hunger, thirst or his wounds.

With that unhappy prospect, he began the long walk home.

5

THE GORDIAN KNOT

1871

Johan's ox wagon moved slowly away from what once had been his farm. The landscape was unrecognizable, as though some huge creature was squatting over it, scraping and clawing the earth to create a giant hole for its eggs—eggs that were constantly hatching, sending thousands of multicolored progeny scurrying about like tiny insects on an endless and desperate quest for sustenance.

He turned away. The road to Bloemfontein was slow going, with wagons and mules and people of every color heading towards the diamond fields. Hardly anyone was heading east, away from New Rush. But, at about midday, he came across another heading away from the diamonds, a blanket over his shoulders, his unsteady gait steadied by a walking stick.

As he drew near, he saw the back of the man's head and lost interest—black men going this way or that were of little consequence. But, as he passed the man, he happened to glance down and found himself looking into the same coal-black eyes he had last seen at Graybittel's canteen.

The black man stopped, his unwavering glare fixed.

Johan stared over his shoulder as his wagon trundled past the man. Then, without thinking, he stopped his wagon. The solitary black figure remained motionless on the road about thirty feet behind him.

With a shake of his head, Johan stepped down from the wagon and reached back into his belongings. His hands moved across the barrel of his rifle until he found what he was looking for. Then he turned and walked slowly back towards the man, who raised his stick and adopted a fighting stance.

He stopped about ten feet away from the man he knew as Mandela.

Gadla immediately recognized the miner on the wagon. And the instant their eyes met, he knew the miner recognized him.

He was not surprised the wagon kept moving. But then it stopped. He felt his muscles tighten. Even if he could run, it would be pointless—the whites always had guns and, like his uncle, he would rather be shot in the chest than in the back.

He stood his ground and waited.

His stomach began to knot when the miner called De Beer climbed down and reached back into the wagon. But it was not a gun the man pulled from the wagon, although he could not see what it was. And when the miner started to walk towards him, he could only think he meant to beat him for having spat at him at the canteen.

Gadla braced himself and lifted his precious money stick above his head, holding it at the opposite end to the knob. Like his uncle against the potbellied settler, he hoped to get in at least one good blow before the end came. But then the miner stopped, just out of reach of the stick. Gadla tensed, his wounded back forgotten.

But the white man just stood, saying nothing. Then he stepped forward, his hands extended.

Gadla flinched and was about to attack when he recognized the objects in the man's hands. Sheer relief washed over him, dousing the instinct to fight. He lowered his stick, sank slowly to one knee, then the other, and settled back on his haunches. He did not understand, but he was too tired and in too much pain to argue.

He laid his stick aside and reached out with both hands.

The man unscrewed the cap of the canteen before handing it to him. He raised it slowly to his lips and drank sparingly. The water was warm, but it tasted so good it almost brought tears to his eyes. Keeping his eyes on the man, he drank again. Then he took the strip of dried meat. His jaw hurt with the effort to chew, but the salty meat reminded him of home. He drank more water and then held the canteen up to the man.

The man shook his head and gave him the canteen cap. Then he reached into his pocket. "This belongs to you," said the man, handing him a stone. Then he turned and walked back to his wagon.

Gadla fingered the rough diamond in disbelief as he watched the miner climb aboard his wagon and crack his whip. He was relieved the man was leaving. But when the wagon moved, it moved in reverse. He tensed again as the wagon came towards him. He had no idea what to expect next.

The wagon stopped a few feet away.

"You are walking east," said the miner, pointing down the road in the direction they had both been heading.

Gadla looked at the man in silence for several moments, then nodded.

"I can take you as far as Bloemfontein," said the man, looking around as though concerned someone might overhear the invitation.

Gadla thought for a moment, then nodded again.

"Keep the canteen," said the man as he turned to face forward.

Gadla gasped as he pulled himself into the bed of the wagon—the effort quickly reminded him of his wounded back—but he was grateful to be riding instead of walking.

He flinched as he heard the whip crack, anticipating the lash on his back. But there was no lash and no pain this time. Instead, the wagon jerked into motion.

The sight of an ox-drawn wagon with a white man driving and a black man sitting in the back was not unusual. But Johan was thankful nobody could see the tangle of his thoughts. He had acted without thinking—offered the injured man food and water, then a ride in his wagon—all before the Bible story occurred to him.

Now he had to decide what to do next.

He had been raised on the teachings of Scripture, and since the terror of the Great Murder and the victory against Dingane, his worldview had been further molded by a sense of divine purpose. And now, with this injured stranger in the back of his wagon, the story of the Good Samaritan was inescapable, the moral imperative unyielding. The story was simple enough. Three travelers separately came across an injured man beaten and clinging to life beside a road. The first two ignored the man and left him to die. The third stopped to help him, then took him to the next town, where he cared for the injured man at his own expense.

Johan could no sooner deny his role in the beating and whipping at Graybittel's canteen than deny the fact that he had come across the injured man beside the road, and that the man now sat in the back of his wagon. Perhaps God had brought them together on the road as a test of his faith. But he only had to think of what the Samaritan had done, or to ask himself what Jesus would do, to know what he had to do next.

The decision gave him little comfort when he finally reined in outside the home of his wife's parents. After a few minutes of reflection to prepare himself for the inevitable confrontation, he climbed down from the wagon.

"Wait here," he said to Mandela, who sat mute and unmoving in the back of the wagon. He climbed the steps to the front door, knocked loudly and entered. His formidable mother-in-law met him almost immediately in the hallway. After a perfunctory greeting he gave a brief account of the man in the wagon, hoping for a sympathetic hearing. His hope was short-lived.

"Johannes Nicolas de Beer, have you taken leave of your senses?" she cried, her eyebrows arched, her outrage visceral. "You're away nearly a year and then you come home out of the blue with a kaffir thief and expect me to take care of him in my own home!"

Johan knew the tone—he had heard it many times from his wife. "Please, Ma. Just a few days until I can find another place for him."

Susannah appeared behind her mother and gave him an awkward hug. She was even more lovely than he remembered, the soft curls of her brown hair draped around her shoulders, the shape of her body beneath the long, off-white dress as alluring as ever. He wished they had a minute alone—she would never kiss him properly in front of her mother.

"I heard, Ma," she said. "The cellar is cool. He can come in the back."

At that, her mother threw up her hands as if to say, *Do whatever you want*, then turned and strode down the hall into the parlor.

Johan drove the wagon to the back of the house and, with help from the family's black housemaid, led Mandela to the cellar. The maid spread the blanket on the floor in a corner, then helped him lie down on his stomach. Susannah hovered in the background, but when she saw his back—the stark contrast between the lacerated black skin and pink flesh—her hand flew to her mouth.

"Dear Jesus, Johan. He needs a doctor. I've never seen anything like it."

He nodded. "I know, but who will treat him?"

"I know someone," said the housekeeper. "I know a medicine man."

"Fetch him," said Johan. "But bring him through the back straight to the cellar. I will pay him."

"And give this one some food and water," added Susannah.

"I will buy another farm," announced Johan after dinner that night.

He and his father-in-law had retired to the living room and were talking over a glass of Madeira in front of the fire. The meal had been his favorite—leg of lamb with roast potatoes, green peas and carrots, followed by a milk tart dessert—and the fortified wine a perfect compliment to the flavors he relished.

"I miss the quiet life," he continued, "the gifts of God from the fields to my table. If I can make some money, that would be an added blessing. But I made enough at the mines, especially after I sold the farm. I don't need a lot to be content."

"What about Susannah?" asked his father-in-law. "You know she wants to be near her mother. And she wants to start a family."

"Ja, well, I will give her children, but it will be on a farm. City life is not for me. Perhaps I can buy a place close to town so she can visit."

The old man thought for a moment. Then his wizened features broke into a grin. "How about somewhere near Sannah's Post? It's only twenty miles east—good farmland, plenty of water—and you can call your farm Su-Sannah's Post," he said with a chuckle. "She will like the sound of that."

Within a few days he had found a farm and Susannah was satisfied. The new De Beer farmstead was modest but comfortable, with two bedrooms, an outhouse and a barn. While Susannah busied herself cleaning up the second bedroom that would be the nursery, Johan settled Mandela in a corner of the barn with help from a maid Susannah had borrowed from her mother. Then he instructed his new foreman, Solomon, to take care of applying the medicine man's ointment. Solomon was head of the black family living on the farm that would be his farmworkers. He was young and strong and eager to learn the basics of farm management.

The third morning at the farm, Johan rose early as was his custom. Just after sunrise, while eating his oatmeal, the maid informed him that Gadla wanted to speak. He was surprised but picked up his bowl and went outside.

He sat in one of the two chairs and gestured for Gadla to sit on the wooden bench that also served as tea table. For a long while the two men sat in silence. The porch was similar to the one at Graybittel's, just smaller. It was impossible to avoid recalling what had so recently transpired in so similar a setting.

"I don't understand," began Gadla. "First you accuse me, then you punish me, then you help me."

Johan stopped eating and stared off into the distance. "I don't understand either," he said after a while. "I'm not proud of the diggers' committee or the flogging, and I'm not sure helping you made it any better." He did not want to talk about Bible stories and divine intervention, but there was an alternate explanation, the potential truth of which he found equally disturbing. "Perhaps I only helped you to help myself, to help me feel better about what happened at the mine."

Gadla shook his head. "I do not believe that. I am also a man. I have done bad things that I am not proud of, and I have done good things to make the bad things better." His eyes narrowed. "But sometimes we do good just because it's the right thing to do. That is the way of men. Beasts cannot think like this, only men."

Then he was silent for a few moments as though rehearsing what he wanted to say next.

"The flogging was wrong," he began, his tone heavy. "Each of the twenty-five lashes was wrong. The claim and the diamond were mine. You knew all this. But I knew the rules had changed. And I knew the punishment. If you had left me on the road, the vultures would have found me. Because of the thing you did, I will see my home again and I will be able to take care of my family. It is a strange story that makes my heart heavy. But there is some good in the story, and I will take the good with me to my grave."

Johan had stopped eating. He stared at Gadla, ignoring a fly that buzzed around his porridge.

Gadla clicked his tongue and shook his head. "But this thing between our people is not good." He stared into the bowl of his unlit pipe. "I have seen our people fight each other, a sight that stays with me always. So many bodies, so much blood. Even the river was red."

"You were at Blood River?" asked Johan, astonished. "At our battle against the Zulus?"

Gadla nodded. "I watched from a tree. Some of my Thembu people were there. They fought well."

"I was there also, inside the wagons, loading guns."

The two men looked at each other. Neither spoke for several moments.

"Too much blood has been spilled," added Gadla as he got to his feet. "We must throw away the spears and the guns. We must do the right thing for our people and for our children." Then he turned and walked away, clicking his tongue.

Gadla left a few days later. He had waited outside the house until Johan and Susannah emerged on their way to church. The parting was brief—a nod of thanks for the kindness and for the horse. Then he was gone.

They sat on the porch after church drinking their Sunday morning tea. And, as was his habit, Johan read the newspaper, including reports from the diamond fields. He was surprised to learn that New Rush had been renamed "Kimberley" after some British lord and politician.

He wished the magic that had wiped away the old name of the mining town could also wipe away his memory of the flogging at Graybittel's. He knew it was an infantile idea. Names on signs could change, but there was no magic that could erase that day from his soul.

He knew it would stay with him all the days of his life. And, as Gadla had said a few days before, it made his heart heavy.

6

THE LION'S TAIL

1899

The war started slowly.

The Boer siege of the British-held towns of Ladysmith, Mafeking, and Kimberley seemed endless, and the effort stalled the Boers' early momentum. Despite the impasse, Johan was convinced it was the real thing—that the mightiest empire in the world would not be so easily defeated as it had been in his people's First War of Freedom.

He had thought to join then and wished he had fought in their great victory at Majuba nearly twenty years before. This time he was determined. It seemed no matter how far his people moved, the British were never far behind, constantly frustrating their efforts to escape the shadow of the Union Jack. And now, since the discovery of diamonds and gold in their two new republics, the far-flung territories that once seemed beyond the Empire's setting sun suddenly shimmered like a treasure trove and, like rapacious pirates, the British wanted it all.

In a matter of days, the war took a dramatic turn as news of the Black Week suffered by British troops spread like wildfire through the Boer communities. Table talk that Sunday when Johan visited

Susannah's parents after church was all about the spectacular series of Boer victories.

"My God, man," enthused his father-in-law, "I still can't believe it! They were so many and we were so few. That Louis Botha is a magician, a real general's general. He outfoxed that pompous old fool Redvers Buller as though he was playing hide-and-seek with a child. Hah! I only wish I had been there to see it."

The old man tapped out the burned tobacco from his pipe before refilling it from a pouch he kept in his waistcoat pocket. Then he held a lighted match above the bowl and sucked hard until the tobacco glowed.

"But now all the talk is about the new British commander, Field Marshal Roberts, whose son was killed at Colenso fighting under Buller," he continued. "And of Roberts's Chief of Staff, General Kitchener, who apparently believes in victory at any price."

He paused to take several deep draws on his pipe to reignite the burn. Then he shook his head and smiled. "Anyway, I thought Kruger was mad to give the British an ultimatum to withdraw—as foolish as pulling on a lion's tail. Truth is, we'd be in real trouble now if we didn't have the field guns and rifles and smokeless bullets we got from the Germans."

He sat back contentedly, like an old dog settling down in front of a log fire, and blew a cloud of pipe smoke into the air. "And now we've got the great British lion running with its tail between its legs. Hah!"

Johan gazed around the table at his family, sharing their pride in the resilience of their people, enjoying the delight in the eyes of his seventeen-year-old son, William, and his fifteen-year-old daughter, Esmé. Caught up in the moment, he heard himself translate unspoken thoughts into words.

"Ja, Oupa, I know what you mean. And I'll be there...at Botha's next battle...to do my part."

The family's reverie about faraway victories was shattered in an instant. Although everyone knew the Boers relied on volunteers, nobody around their family table had imagined Johan would be so foolish as to throw his aged hat into the ring. His wife, daughter, and mother-in-law all erupted in a cacophony of protest, while his son just stared open-mouthed.

"Susannah, please," he implored in a firm voice, "we'll talk about this at home."

"Oh no, we won't," his wife insisted. "We will talk about this right here and right now," she cried, glaring at him. "For heaven's sake, Johan, you're nearly seventy—old enough to be Botha's father and far too old to run off and fight a war on the other side of the Drakensberg. How can you even think about leaving us alone on the farm?"

She turned to her father. "Talk to him, Pa. Tell him."

The old man's pipe seemed suspended in air, his face shrouded in smoke that curled delicately towards the ceiling.

"This is not just about fighting with Botha, is it, Johan?" said the old man matter-of-factly. "Why don't you tell us the real reason for wanting to fight hundreds of miles away when there is a perfectly good war to fight right here on our doorstep against the very same enemy?"

Johan had not anticipated having to explain to his ever-perceptive father-in-law. For a moment he had the sense of being suspended in the web of his people's pilgrimage, able to reach backwards into their sacred past or forwards towards their promised future, but unsure which threads would provide the best support for his current position.

He looked around the table. "Did you read Kruger's speech last Sunday on the Day of the Covenant?" he asked quietly. "The day after Botha's victory at Colenso against Buller?" The speech in

Pretoria had been widely publicized. Kruger had spoken of God's bounty, that just as He had delivered them at Blood River and then at Majuba, so too had He now delivered them at Colenso. And He would continue to bless and lead His people to victory in this war and in the quest for their promised land provided they remained faithful to their covenant with Him.

Johan looked from one uncomprehending expression to the next—the bewildered resentment of Susannah, the stoic fortitude of William, the innocent fear of Esmé, and his mother and father-in-law, the one so fearsomely self-righteous, the other so tempered by the vicissitudes of frontier life. He could sense the question hanging in the air above the table, as though each were asking, *So what has all that got to do with you running off to fight with Botha in Natal?*

"It was there," he began, lowering his voice, "where Dingane battered and clubbed my father to death with Retief's men and then butchered my mother and sister in the Great Murder." He paused, his voice trembling. He could taste the bitterness in his mouth, the indelible taste of roast pigeon and homemade candy from that terrible night forever imprinted on his brain. "It was there where we stood before God and prayed for victory against Dingane." A tear slipped from his eye and came to rest in the stubble of his beard. "And it was there where we defeated Dingane at Blood River."

He closed his eyes for a moment as the images flashed across his mind's eye, grotesquely framed by the skeletal eye-socket of a baboon's skull. He shuddered then looked around at his family through eyes blurred by the recollection.

"I said goodbye to my mother and father and tiny sister under that monstrous rock with nothing but a boulder to mark their passing." He swallowed hard, blinking until his eyes cleared. "And after all that the damned British just march in and declare that Natal belongs to them. And now they want to do the same in the Transvaal and the Free State just because the Queen of bloody England thinks that wherever the sun shines it all belongs to the British Empire." He paused, gathering himself. "Well, I say they can stick their damned sunshine right up the Queen's imperial arse!" He glared at his stunned family, as though daring any to contradict him or to criticize his vulgarity.

"I made a vow to God and to my dead family," he declared. "I must go back to where they died, to fight there for the sacrifice they made."

Susannah turned to her father, the unspoken plea evident to all. The old man slowly shook his head. At that, her shoulders sagged, and a look of immense sadness enveloped her.

"May God help you... and us," she said with quiet resignation. "But you will not go until after Christmas. And Willie will go with you," she added, her voice trembling, "not to fight—you must promise me that. Just to look after you and to bring you home."

A strained Christmas passed.

Early in the new century came news that Boer forces were to attack the British at Ladysmith. General Buller was moving to reinforce the defense of the town. Boer leaders expected a massive confrontation and were calling for every able-bodied man to join General Botha in Natal.

The news was not lost on Johan. The next day he took William with him to the quartermaster general in Bloemfontein to collect their new rifles. He was reluctant to discard his favorite rifle until the quartermaster explained the advantages of the German Mauser's rapid-fire capability, its five-round clip, and that it had smokeless bullets that would not betray his firing position with telltale puffs of smoke.

There was no hiding their excursion from Susannah when they returned to the farm. He still struggled to come to terms with taking William anywhere near a battlefield. But he was proud of his son. The boy was already as big and tall as he was, handled the farm animals with a sixth sense for their well-being, was firm but fair with the farm workers, treated the soil with a deep respect for the nourishment it provided, rode horses with the easy familiarity of one born to the saddle, and was a crack shot with a rifle. Despite the promise to keep him from the front lines, he knew William would be very helpful on commando. But he worried about leaving Susannah and Esmé alone on the farm. He felt torn between the vow made to his dead family and the duty he owed to his living family.

"The time has come, Susannah," he announced later that afternoon as they sat at the kitchen table, softly lit by a setting sun streaming through the small window above the washbasin. She was darning a pair of his socks, while he sat fidgeting with an unlit pipe. William was out in the stable tending to their horses, while Esmé sat on the porch, staring out over the fields.

"When?" she asked curtly, without looking up.

"At first light," he said, laying his pipe aside. "Botha needs us now."

"You must do what you have to do," she replied, laying the needlework aside. Then, in a more conciliatory tone, she said, "We'll be fine, and the headman—"

"Solomon."

"Yes. And Solomon will tend to the animals and the milking and the crops."

"But—"

"And if trouble comes close, we'll go to Bloemfontein and stay with my parents."

There was no further discussion. It helped that her father was supportive, although her mother had not made it easy, her silent hostility a thunderous rebuke. But everything that had to be said had been said, and there wasn't much packing to do. Aside from a fresh shirt and a bedroll, they would carry their water canteens, rifles, ammunition and some strips of dried meat—whatever could fit in their saddlebags.

Susannah prepared his favorite lamb dish for dinner, followed by milk tart. They held hands as he said grace and prayed for safe passage through the war and protection for loved ones left behind.

"I promise to write or send word whenever I can," he offered.

Susannah kept eating until, at last, she looked up. "Don't make promises you can't keep, my dear husband. There's only one thing I want from you—to come back to me. And one promise you must keep—to protect our son from the fighting. Promise me."

He recognized the tone—part warning, part ultimatum. "Ja, ja, Susannah. I promise, I promise."

"You too, Willie," she said. "Promise me. No fighting." Without giving him a chance to respond, she added, "And take care of your father. I need a live husband, not a dead hero."

The morning was crisp and quiet, the silence broken only by the soft clip of hooves as Solomon led their horses to the porch. Johan held Susannah close, trying to comfort her, reminding her of things that needed to be done on the farm, while William stood with his arm around his sister, saying nothing.

Johan looked at Solomon. "Listen to the madam, Solomon. You must help her with the farm until I come back. Understand?"

"Ja, my master," said Solomon. "Go carefully with the young master," he added diffidently, "and stay safe."

After an awkward family hug, the two men mounted and rode slowly out of the farmyard. Johan turned once and waved his felt hat towards the dark figures of his wife and daughter on the porch and of Solomon on the ground below them, their images no more than shadows in the pre-dawn twilight. Then he turned towards the dark horizon outlined by layers of light from the rising sun and urged his horse into a canter.

As the crow flies, it was a little over two hundred miles to Ladysmith from the farm, but they could no sooner fly than wish away the British Empire. Instead, their route took them around the edge of the Drakensberg mountain range, its great peaks and spires rising like armed sentinels watching over all.

By the time they reached the Boer positions three days later, all the talk was of Buller's forces advancing and of Botha pulling back into the hills near Ladysmith, hills dominated by one peak—Spion Kop. The British were crossing the Tugela River and massing to the south of the Kop, the Boers regrouping in the hills to the north. All agreed it was key to their siege of Ladysmith—whoever controlled the Kop controlled the road to Ladysmith.

They sought out William's two cousins, John and Isaac Malherbe, with the Pretoria commando, and found them digging a trench in the Rangeworthy Hills about a mile from Spion Kop. Isaac was already a corporal and the commander was only too happy to have them join. The flexibility of the commando system suited Johan perfectly—fighting units of friends, relatives and neighbors, drawn from the major towns or districts where they lived, and every man free to come and go as he pleased. But, orders were still orders and, apparently taking Johan's age into account, the commander instructed them to help with the supply wagons, a duty that would keep them both a good distance behind the front lines.

Johan shrugged off the disappointment. At least he was there, close enough to feel the tension, smell the gunpowder and hear the cannons, but far enough away that William was safe. And the company around the campfire that first night was good, including a young man, Deneys Reitz, who struck up a friendship with William. But even as Johan reconciled himself to their assignment, he knew battlefields were like wildfires in a hot wind—their situation could change in an instant.

7

AN ACRE OF DEATH

1900

The sound of gunfire split the night air.

Johan sat up in the dark, groping for his rifle, trying to make sense of what was going on. The shooting sounded close, but night sounds were deceptive. Then it stopped just as abruptly as it had begun.

Muted voices in the dark from the small supply group camped with him agreed there was nothing to be done until the morning. At least the Tommies weren't shooting at them. But he slept fitfully—his thoughts filled with images of being attacked by lion-headed Tommies, their fur coats bright red, their huge canines like bayonets.

At first light as they sat drinking coffee, a messenger galloped into their camp with a message from Isaac that the Tommies had taken Spion Kop—they had climbed the steep southern slope in the dark and were now entrenched on top.

"What are our orders?" asked Johan.

"To take it back," replied the rider. "Botha's calling for volunteers," he yelled over his shoulder as he wheeled his horse. "The Pretoria commando is already there and the Carolina commando is on its way!" Then he galloped away.

The commander looked ashen as he addressed the men. "I've seen the Kop," he said bleakly. "If the Tommies are on top, it will cost us dearly to move them. But if any man wants to volunteer, follow me."

"Come, Willie. Let's go see what's happening," said Johan as he reached for his saddle.

There was surely no harm in watching the action, he thought, as they galloped off with Reitz and the others to where Botha waited at the northern foot of the Kop, surrounded by hundreds of riderless horses. The empty saddles signaled the obvious—the men from the Carolina and Pretoria commandos were already scrambling up the Kop.

Johan could see Boer fighters being cut down by unrelenting rifle fire from the crest line of the Kop. The Tommies had evidently learned from their defeat at Majuba to aim low when firing downhill. The crash of battle rapidly escalated when explosive cannon fire added to the rattle of rifle fire.

He closed his eyes to say a silent prayer for Willie's two cousins, somewhere on the deadly slopes. But when he opened his eyes, William was sprinting across the short distance to the slopes of the Kop.

"No, Willie, stop... In heaven's name, stop!" he yelled as he dismounted. But if William heard, he showed no sign of it. Sacred covenants and imperial arrogance were instantly forgotten. He had to stop his son before it was too late.

He climbed as fast as he could, keeping low to avoid the unseen scythe of death cutting through the air above his head, trying to shut out the sights and sounds of battle that enveloped him in a terrifying fusion of dust and death. Even the grit that caked his mouth tasted of death, and all around him men were screaming and shouting, some writhing in pain while others lay still. And every now and then he glimpsed William's head bobbing and weaving through the obstacles as he climbed straight into the murderous Tommy rifle-fire from the crest of the hill.

Unexpectedly, the deadly gunfire lifted on his side of the hill even though there was no letup in the sounds of battle. He looked up in time to see a melee of hand to hand fighting on the crest before William disappeared over the edge with other Boer fighters. All around him men were on their feet, climbing frantically. Somehow they must have pushed the Tommies back from the crest line.

Johan scrambled up the hill, but when he topped the crest he saw that what he had thought was the crest of the Kop itself was just a lower plateau. The Boers were behind a fringe of rocks a few feet from the edge, firing at the Tommies behind a second line of rocks only about twenty yards away. Inexplicably, the Tommies were not on the high ground but had dug in on a lower part of the Kop and were terribly exposed. Boer fighters were not only in front of them but also on both their flanks, firing into the length of the Tommy trench from nearby hills and knolls with deadly rifle-fire and devastating salvos from heavy field-guns.

To make matters worse, the hailstorm of bullets that filled the space between the two lines of fighters at almost point-blank range added an element of apocalyptic horror from which there was no escape. Rocks shattered all around, sending a vicious mixture of rock shards and ricocheting bullets tearing into the men from every angle. The lucky died instantly from clean shots, the unlucky from gruesome wounds.

As he huddled behind bodies beneath a choking blanket of smoke and dust, it seemed as though hellfire and damnation had descended upon the Kop, a jarring reminder that his son was in mortal danger and his promise to Susannah already broken. He also realized he had not yet fired a shot.

"Where's the Pretoria commando?" he called to a big man with red hair who seemed to be in charge.

The man looked at him in surprise before pointing towards their left flank and the aloe-covered knoll beyond. "That way," he yelled.

Johan crawled on his stomach, holding his rifle in both hands ahead of him, keeping as low as possible. But he soon reached the end of the scanty protection afforded by the rocks. Ahead was a gap in the fringe of rocks, an open area that provided no protection from the Tommy guns—the body lying half way across the gap was proof of that. He shook his head in despair. But in the next instant a crash of cannon fire exploded in the Tommy trench.

Without more than a half-formed thought that the explosions were a sufficient diversion, Johan rose and began to run, his entire being focused on reaching the rocks ahead of him.

An eerie silence enveloped him as he ran, the sound of battle oddly muted and somewhere behind him. But then, as though his ears suddenly unplugged, the sound of battle burst over his head, and he heard again the scythe of bullets cutting through the air around him.

Oh God...have mercy, he thought as desperation fueled his tired and aged limbs.

It felt as though someone had jabbed him in his right rib cage with a sharp object, nothing more. He didn't understand why his legs were slowing, why his breathing was suddenly so hard, why he was falling.

The impact knocked the air from his lungs and filled his mouth with a spurt of warm fluid that tasted familiar. He gasped and lay dazed, trying to catch his breath. Then he began to crawl towards the rocks ahead of him, just a few yards away, but the pain in his chest was so sharp he had to stop. To relieve the discomfort, he rolled slowly, awkwardly, onto his back.

He blinked as he gazed through the swirling smoke at the bright midmorning sun, the cloudless sky a deep, distant blue. Warm fluid began to fill his mouth. As he fought for breath, he had the strange sensation of rising to meet the sky, or perhaps the sky was descending to greet him, cloaking him in its azure embrace. He could no longer hear the sounds of battle—he assumed it must be over.

Images began to float across his vision—feathers drifting in smoke over the bodies of his mother and sister impaled by a spear...a grotesque baboon leering at him through sunken eyes...a circle of wagons and bodies like swollen pumpkins floating in a river of blood...a black man glaring at him with coal-black eyes as a whip cracked over his head...his wife and daughter alone on the farm...his son disappearing over a crest of death—before they slowly dissolved in the brightness. Or had they faded into darkness?

Then, after a moment of exquisite lightness, it made no difference.

William was thirsty and dog-tired.

He had made it across the gap but hadn't found his cousins. And now he was trapped with other fighters, unable to move, hunkered behind whatever rocky cover they could find. Volleys of gunfire rolled back and forth across the open ground between the Boer and Tommy lines. Some even took refuge behind the bodies of friends, a gruesome shield against the deadly rifle fire and lethal shrapnel.

As bad as it was for the Boer fighters on the Kop, he could see the Tommies were taking a terrible beating as Boer rifles and field-guns fired round after round into the shallow Tommy trench. And every now and then, in efforts that seemed foolhardy but were surely born of desperation, the Tommies tried to rush the Boer lines. And every time they did, they were forced to retreat.

William had seen large numbers of fighters gathered at the foot of the Kop, but none had climbed to help in the fight. He assumed his father was with them, minding their horses.

Sometime past noon, when the sun was at its hottest and sweat blurred his eyes, a group of about two hundred Tommies suddenly emerged from behind their rocky trench with their hands in the air. He thought he must be hallucinating, that the heat was playing tricks on him, until a handful of Boers rose and advanced with their rifles pointed at the Tommies.

The firing between the lines sputtered and stopped as the two groups approached each other. But just when the surrender seemed certain, a Tommy officer suddenly materialized between the two groups.

"I'm in charge here," bellowed the officer. "Take your men back to hell!" he yelled at the startled Boers. "I allow no surrenders."

William watched in disbelief as the Boers obeyed. His comrades scampered behind their rocky cover, while the Tommies scrambled back into their trench. Moments later every rifle on the hill seemed to fire simultaneously. He could never have imagined such a scene, but he had seen it with his own eyes.

As the afternoon wore on, he noticed Boer fighters slipping over the edge and down the hill. By the time the flame-orange sun had set through the haze of battle dust, it seemed there were just a handful of Boers left on the Kop. And after the gunfire finally petered out, the stillness that descended on the Kop was unnerving, broken only by the groans of the wounded and the murmurs of survivors.

Despite his best efforts to stay alert, he felt himself slip into exhausted sleep. When he woke with a start a short time later, shivering from the cold, he was completely alone. Even the few comrades he had seen earlier in the afternoon were gone, and the Kop was shrouded in a tomblike silence. The only thing he could think to do was get back to where he first crested the hill.

He moved in a low crouch, carefully navigating the vague contours of the hill still visible under the moonless sky. He paused when he reached the gap between two lines of rocks he recalled crossing under fire that morning, but the danger had passed. Still, he moved as quickly as possible across the gap, nearly tripping over a body that lay in his path. And after he crossed, he very nearly gasped out loud when a huge shape suddenly rose up like a phantasm before him.

"Who goes there?" demanded the apparition in a familiar accent.

"De... De Beer," he stammered, before dropping into a shallow depression behind the line of rocks among about twelve other men.

"My God, De Beer, I nearly pulled the trigger," growled Commander Opperman, a bull of a man with a shock of red hair, known as Big Red.

"Where are the rest of our men?" asked William breathlessly as he turned on his stomach to face the Tommy positions, thankful the big man had not shot him by mistake.

"Gone," said a familiar voice. It was Deneys. "The cowards pissed themselves in the dark. We're the only ones left on the Kop unless Isaac's men are still here somewhere. I tried to follow them across the gap but the Tommy fire was too hot."

"Ja, I know," said William. "I made it across but I never found Isaac." He looked around at the grim faces. "So what do we do now?"

"We watch and wait," growled Big Red. "And we keep our bloody heads down."

After a short silence he spoke again. "The Tommies fucked up last night when they entrenched in the wrong place—they must have thought they had the high ground. We should've kicked the shit out of them when we had the chance. Now the Kop is lost. Goddamn!"

As the darkness deepened, William began to imagine dying on the Kop as sounds from the Tommy trench suggested reinforcements moving into position to resume battle in the morning. He even thought of Solomon trying to find his body after Deneys told the story of a kaffir servant who had climbed the Kop looking for his master, only to be shot in the head as he peered over the rocks.

"Ag, fuck it," swore Big Red a few hours later. "Time to get the hell off this damned Kop. We'll be no match for the Tommies in the morning."

William was too tired to feel relieved as he stumbled down the Kop. Several times he kicked or tripped over something soft and was dimly aware of trampling on the bodies of his comrades. When they reached the bottom, only a few horses were still there, including his own and his father's. But his father was nowhere to be seen.

As the dejected men rode away from the Kop in the dark, William asked if anyone had seen his father. To his surprise, Big Red recognized his description.

"Ja, De Beer," he said in a weary voice. "I remember the old man. It was early, after Malherbe and the Pretoria commando had gone around to the left flank. He asked where they were. I told him. That's the last I saw of him."

William stared at the big man as comprehension dawned. His father must have climbed up the Kop into the teeth of the battle to go after him but had not come down, his empty saddle mute proof of that awful fact.

"I must go back," he cried, wheeling his horse, just as General Botha appeared and exhorted the men to return to the Kop. The men reluctantly agreed but refused to climb it in the dark.

William couldn't wait for daylight. For the second time that day he sprinted to the hill of death and began to climb, this time joined by another from the supply wagon he knew only as Jacob, a slightly-built fellow trying to find his older brother, one of Isaac's men. Together they climbed and together they searched, disentangling lifeless limbs, looking into sightless eyes, trying to find their loved ones.

It was nearly midnight by the time they reached the rocks he recognized as the start of the gap he had sprinted across to reach his cousins that morning. They could hear the Tommies moving and decided to wait until the enemy fell quiet and hopefully asleep.

He lay back, thinking about the day, his eyes heavy.

William came slowly awake under the first rays of the sun. He turned to face the Tommy trench as the fog of sleep cleared. Something was not right. It was impossibly quiet, as still as a graveyard.

He shook Jacob awake and gestured for him to stay quiet. Then he hung his hat on the barrel of his rifle and hoisted it tentatively into plain view, expecting it to be instantly shredded by multiple Tommy bullets. But the hat hung undisturbed—not a single shot rang out from the Tommy trench. Jacob tried the same ruse with his own hat from a different position. Again, no shot, the morning stillness suffused with nothing but the breath of God drifting over the recently departed.

He looked inquiringly at Jacob, who nodded. Together they stood and tentatively climbed over the perimeter rocks, ready to duck again. But the quiet held—no shots, no sound, no movement, nothing to interrupt the awful stillness that blanketed the Kop as they slowly approached the Tommy trench.

As his gaze swept the area for any sign of danger, something in the corner of his eye caught his attention. He felt his chest constrict as he turned and stared at one of the bodies lying in the gap in the fringe of rocks. There was no doubt. The green jacket, the shaggy gray-brown hair and beard, the unmistakable profile lying face up as though basking in the early morning sun.

Jacob's shout broke the quiet.

"William, it's unbelievable! Come see, come see."

He ignored Jacob's call and walked slowly towards the prone figure, hoping against hope he was wrong, recalling the body he had nearly tripped over the night before when he crossed the gap. As he drew near, he saw the terrible exit wound under the armpit on the left side. He knelt and looked into his father's glazed eyes. Where he expected to see an expression contorted in the anguish of death, he saw instead an expression smoothed by the tranquility of rest.

He said a silent prayer, then closed his father's eyelids.

"Ag, Jesus. Your pa?" asked Jacob behind him.

William nodded.

"Too bad," said Jacob. "Shot through the lungs—must've drowned in his own blood," he added matter-of-factly. "Ag, sorry man, but you must come see the Tommy trench. It's unbelievable."

William stayed where he was for several more moments, then rose slowly, wiped his eyes on his sleeve and joined Jacob at the trench.

Big Red had been right. The Tommies must have thought they had reached the high ground and tried to entrench. But they had only reached a lower plateau, too rocky for a good trench, and had tried instead to build a wall of rocks around the shallow trench. It had become their grave. Hundreds of contorted bodies were piled on top of each other, some lying three deep. It was hard to believe so much death could be concentrated in so small a place, perhaps no more than an acre.

"Jesus," said William. "They're all dead, and those who aren't are long gone."

He stared at the jumbled mass of bodies, into the vacant eyes of men whose families would never see them again and would never know the horror of how they died. It reminded him of stories his father had told of Blood River, of the tangled mass of Zulu bodies after the battle. He shook his head. Aside from himself and Jacob, only the dead occupied the Kop.

He walked back towards the edge of the crest, where his father lay, and was surprised to see hundreds of Boer fighters gathered at the foot of the Kop. He raised his rifle with one hand and his hat with the other and waved. Jacob did the same. A cheer went up from below as the men rushed back up the hill to occupy what had seemed lost only hours before. He lost sight of Jacob during the celebration and never heard if he found his brother. But he was relieved when Isaac and Deneys joined him on the crest, although Isaac was not celebrating. Deneys had seen Isaac's brother while climbing the Kop during the battle—he had been shot between the eyes.

General Botha gathered the men together on the crest to give thanks. God had clearly intervened, the miracle evident to all— they had snatched an improbable victory from the jaws of defeat. They said prayers and sang psalms for their dead and wounded, and also for the Tommies. Then the general offered his condolences to the Tommy medical officers and William and others helped the Red Cross doctors and the stretcher-bearers with their macabre tasks.

The Tommy dead were buried in the trench where they had fallen and their wounded carried off the Kop.

William sat on the rocky ledge of Spion Kop in a solitary wake with his father's body. He was trying to decide what to do and hoping for inspiration as he gazed out over the Tugela River valley at the retreating Tommies. He knew his father had wanted to visit the memorial to his own father, mother and baby sister. Maybe he should bury his father at the same place. But his mother would want him buried at home on the farm.

As the sun reached its zenith, he made his decision. Isaac had already carried his brother's body off the Kop and now helped him carry his father down. A fighter in the Bethlehem commando recognized his description of a rock formation that looked like a baboon's skull near a mountain shaped like a cathedral and agreed to show him the way.

It was less than a day's ride from the Kop. He found the memorial boulder easily enough on a plateau about half way to the top of the rock formation. But the wild baboons that looked down on him from the shadows of the belligerent-looking rock that bore their likeness unsettled him. Their hooded eyes, set close together above doglike muzzles, added a sense of menace that sent a spasm of dread down his spine.

He dug in silence with the help of his companion before laying his father in a shallow grave that reminded him of the burial trench on the Kop where so many Tommies had fallen. Then he stood for a moment, his father's charred Bible open in his hands, thinking he might read a passage. But nothing came to mind before his eyes blurred. He closed the book and offered a short prayer instead.

The baboons watched in silence as he mounted and rode down towards the cold mountain stream.

He had thought to go straight home but realized he was not yet ready to face his mother. He knew in his heart that his father had died trying to save him from his impulse to join the battle. Now, as the consequence of his folly settled into the marrow of his soul, he could not imagine how he would tell his mother the awful truth. He knew he was just delaying the inevitable, but he decided to stay with his companion and join the Bethlehem commando until he was ready to return to Sannah's Post.

Besides, even though she might never forgive him, there was still a war to fight. And now, with his father dead, his promise to avoid the fighting after the carnage at Spion Kop seemed like a promise made in a different age by a different person.

8

A HOLY WAR

1900

The father of their struggle stood on a butcher's block in the rain. The huge man looked as though he had descended out of the storm to promise them salvation, except that angels did not wear baggy black suits and black stovepipe hats, or scraggy gray beards with round eyeglasses perched on bulbous noses.

And there was nothing angelic about the seventy-year-old Paul Kruger's voice or the way he spat into the dirt for emphasis as he spoke:

"We are the chosen people of God," declared Kruger, his voice rolling over the people like thunder off the highest peaks of the Drakensberg, "a people in covenant with God. If we keep the faith, God will keep his promises. Our God is the only true God, and we are His instruments in the world. He delivered our people from Dingane and gave us a great victory at Blood River. And He will do so again in this war against the Beast."

William sensed the morale of those around him revive with the reassurance from President Kruger himself that God was on their side. This was a Holy War. But even as Kruger's words made his spirits soar on that St. Patrick's Day in 1900 in the small town of Kroonstad that was their temporary wartime capital after the fall of Bloemfontein, he could not dispel the image of his people being devoured by the Beast that was the British lion. It was one thing to proclaim faith in God as their source of hope for victory, but how were a few thousand farmers supposed to win a war they were already losing against the most powerful empire on earth? The Tommies had over two hundred thousand troops already in the field with more on their way.

The fact the Tommies were using kaffirs to help their war effort just added insult to injury.

Kruger made sure they were under no illusion. Aside from the guns they had received from Germany, they should expect no more than moral support from family and friends in France, Holland, Germany and Russia, and the few who had gone to America. But he insisted that God was not fickle. He had chosen them and given them victory over their enemies before. He would do so again if they kept the faith.

But how? That was a question with no obvious answer.

Then, as though inspired by God, General Christiaan de Wet proposed a change in their tactics. No more wagon trains, heavy baggage or set-piece battles. The key was speed and stealth—flying columns behind enemy lines to hit the Tommies then disappear into the shadows like leopards into the night. If the Tommies thought they were winning the war by capturing cities and relieving sieges, then the Boers would simply change the definition of the war.

William was thrilled. The plan was bold, the imagery vivid—a hunting cat, all muscle and bone, striking when least expected, then vanishing before being caught. Best of all, the general's first target would be the waterworks at Sannah's Post that supplied Bloemfontein with all its drinking water. The few hundred

Tommies guarding the pumping station would be no match for two thousand of De Wet's boys.

He desperately wanted to join De Wet in time to fight the next battle in his own backyard. But before he could be God's instrument against the Beast, he had to go home. His mother still did not know what had happened at Spion Kop. And he still did not know how to tell her.

Susannah convulsed at the news, as though on a rack of grief being tortured by the devil himself. But there was no anger directed at William, just all-consuming sorrow at the loss of Johan. For days she wandered around the house, trying to find some purchase in reality, some tangible focus for her sorrow.

"What about a memorial?" suggested Esmé, interrupting the heavy silence as they sat together one night in the small living room.

"What did you say?" asked Susannah, looking up from her knitting.

"A memorial, Ma, like a grave but with nobody in it," explained William. "Like Pa did for his family under that rock shaped like a baboon."

The fire in the hearth sizzled and popped as it spread through the slightly moist wood, its flames sporadically piercing the gloom before retreating, as though dueling with the darkness.

"Where?"

"I don't know, Ma," said Esmé. "Maybe down by the river near the willow tree, where Pa and Willie used to fish. Or even under the tree."

Susannah looked from Esmé to William.

"It would give you a place to go, Ma, a place to think and be with Pa," he said.

Susannah nodded and swallowed hard. "It's hard to know what to do without Johan, especially now that Lord Roberts and the Tommies are in Bloemfontein. They're so close to the farm!" She sniffed and blew her nose. "What will we do?"

"We start with the memorial, Ma," he said. "Then we'll worry about Roberts and the Tommies."

The next morning he found a large oblong river stone with one flat side and called his mother to approve. With a nod she asked him to write *Johan de Beer, Loving Husband and Father*, on the stone.

"What about Pa's middle name?"

"Ag, leave it off for now, Willie—there is not enough room on the stone. Besides, I only called him Nicolas when I was angry with him, and I'm past being angry. We can add it when we get a proper headstone."

It took him several hours to carve the inscription into the flat side of the rock with one of his father's mining tools. Next he dug a depression under the canopy of the willow tree and stood the stone upright with the flat side facing the farmhouse. Then he called his mother and sister to the tree.

The family knelt beside the stone for several minutes, holding hands in silence, before Susannah led them in the Lord's Prayer. Around them, the shroud of the willow's melancholy limbs hung low like a curtain, shifting in the gentle breeze, sweeping the ground as though in penance for the folly of men.

"I will not go to Bloemfontein," said his mother that night during dinner. "My place is here, on the farm, with you and Esmé... and Johan." After a pause, she added, "Let little Lord Roberts do as he pleases. If he thinks our men are fighters, he has not yet met our women. God is with us."

William shook his head. "Ag, Ma, you know it's safer for you in Bloemfontein with your parents. Even President Kruger wants families to evacuate the farms. It's just not safe to stay. If the Tommies think you're helping our men continue the fight, they will bring the fight to you, Ma. And I've heard terrible stories of the things they do to our women."

She shook her head. "General Botha says we should stay on the farms—that the time has come to sacrifice everything for our independence. That's good enough for me. So I'm staying—and that's the end of it."

He sighed. "Ja, Ma, okay. But if you stay, how can I go?"

"What do you mean?" she asked, her forehead instantly creased. "Go where?"

"I have to do my part, Ma. I can't just sit on the farm while others fight our war. I must do something."

She was quiet for several moments. "You already did something, Willie. You went with Pa to fight the Tommies at Spion Kop. Our family has already done its part... and paid a heavy price."

"Ja, Ma, we did pay a heavy price. But now the war has come to us, and I can't dishonor the sacrifice Pa made. You know how he always spoke of Blood River, how our people vowed the generations who followed would keep the covenant." He paused to make sure he had her attention. "I am the next generation, Ma. And now the enemy is the British. They want to take away our freedom and our independence, everything Pa and his family died for fighting against the Zulus."

She sighed and shook her head. "Ag, Willie. I'm sick to death of all the talk about covenants and vows and sacred victories that so consume our people. What kind of God would conceive such a plan? The God I worship doesn't want our covenants and sacrifices. He wants us to act justly... to love mercy... and to walk humbly before Him." She shook her head. "I wish our people had stayed in the Cape and made their peace with the British."

He stared at his mother, shaken by the heresy. Even Esmé appeared stunned by what she had just heard.

"Well, anyway, Ma," he pressed on, "I'm nearly eighteen. People will say I'm a coward if I stay on the farm milking cows instead of fighting. Pa would turn in his grave. He would want me to fight, Ma, just like he fought."

"And died," she said. "All I have left of him are memories and a cold stone stuck in the ground." She wiped her eyes, her bottom lip trembling as she sniffed.

"You will stay until it's time to go, Willie. We'll both know when that time comes."

9

THE WAR SCOUT

1900

Henry Mandela was born five years after his father returned from the mines. He grew up as a member of the Thembu royal house and, soon after his initiation ceremony, traveled to Queenstown with his father to visit the English blacksmith's shop where his father had worked nearly twenty years before.

The settler family still lived in the same place—the blacksmith's sons were now in the trade—and they remembered Gadla. The family agreed to teach Henry the trade in exchange for his help in their stables. He was a quick learner and soon became accustomed to English ways and prejudices, especially about the Boers.

He went home as often as he could to spend time with his father, to sit with him and to hear again about the old days. His father was only too happy to have an audience for his stories—the great battle at the river of blood, digging for diamonds at the Big Hole, being flogged by a German sailor, and the strange ways of a Boer named De Beer and his farm near Sannah's Post.

Although Henry had never been to the faraway places his father described, he absorbed the stories of his father's life until they were part of his lifeblood. He even had a token of those times—the rough stone that had triggered the flogging—which his father had prized for as long as Henry could remember and then given to him.

Henry instinctively favored the British when the war came between them and the Boers. He had no ax to grind with them, whereas the Boers had killed the Thembu elders at the river of blood. Besides, the family in Queenstown had treated him and his father well and happily shared news of the war with him, especially reports of British victories.

His father was proud to have lived to see in the new century and that it coincided with such momentous events. But there were signs his time was drawing to a close—he said he could feel it in his bones. Word went out to gather the Madiba clan, and they all came together on a cool evening at the family home in the foothills outside Mvezo. The feast was full of familial warmth in honor of their patriarch. And Gadla had a few special words for Henry at the end of the meal.

"You are young and strong, Henry, the pride of our family. And the great Qamata, god of the Xhosa, is proud that a grandchild of Ngubengcuka has grown into such a fine young man. Use your strength wisely for the good of our people."

The words of his father still echoed in his head the day his father died. But despite his intentions to honor his father's wishes, he was torn between two emotions—saddened by the loss yet frustrated by the timing. He knew he should assume his role as head of the family after a period of mourning, but he desperately wanted to see the great British army flex its imperial muscle before it was too late. With all the news of British victories, he was convinced he had to go quickly if he was ever to see this glorious sight the English family in Queenstown described so enthusiastically.

He decided to share his heart with his mother one night as they sat on mats in her cooking hut with a single candle burning between them. The smoky aroma of the evening meal still hung in the air.

In a hushed tone full of despair, his mother said, "Tell me again why you wish to do this thing"

"My mother," he began hesitantly, "the Boers killed some of our people at the river of blood. They should pay with their blood but I cannot fight the Boers by myself." He took a breath. "But if I can help the soldiers in their fight against the Boers, then perhaps I can avenge the deaths of our people."

His mother gazed at the embers in the fire pit. "You say this, my son, but you are just one man. What can you do to help the soldiers?"

He grasped the opening. "The blacksmith says the British use our people to help drive their wagons, care for their horses and scout the land. I can do these things." He looked intently at his mother. "But I must go now, Mother. Otherwise, the war will be over before I can do anything to strike a blow against the Boers."

His mother closed her eyes and seemed to retreat into herself like a wise old turtle. He watched, afraid to breathe. After what seemed like an impossibly long time, she began to exhale with a low moan that sounded to him like the collective despair of generations of his people.

Without opening her eyes, in a barely audible voice, she said, "Then go, my son. I will say I sent you away to find work."

"Thank you, my mother," he said respectfully, trying hard to keep the excitement from his voice.

"But remember your father's words, Henry. You must come home to your people when you have done this thing and finished with the Boers."

He nodded. "I will not forget, Mother," he said as he backed out of the hut.

Henry set off while the village still slept, before even the roosters were awake.

At a small town south of Basutoland, a herder told him that British troops were in the area of the town called Thaba 'Nchu, just beyond the northern border of Basutoland, and that the most direct route lay through the mountains of Basutoland. He would need a horse for such a journey and, after working for the blacksmith, knew enough about horses to buy a sturdy animal.

He was excited to know where he was going but not at all sure what reception he would get when he found the soldiers. It proved easier than expected. The first soldiers he came across were handing out pamphlets on Boer farms urging the Boers to turn in their weapons in exchange for being left in peace. The addition of an African scout who could speak English and rode his own horse was welcomed.

But distributing pamphlets was quickly abandoned when word came that a large force of six to seven thousand Boers had moved into the area.

Henry was astonished by the turn of events—so readily accepted as a scout, so quickly close to conflict, and so suddenly forced to retreat. He expected to have to scout ahead, but the only order he heard was to get to the waterworks at Sannah's Post as quickly as possible. He joined the leading group of soldiers in a headlong rush to safety and reached the waterworks just after the sun had set.

As more soldiers arrived, the exhausted men just dropped to the ground wherever they found space between wagons and field guns. A group of black drivers and scouts kept to themselves beyond the wagons.

Henry wanted to do the right thing, but nobody told him what to do. Thinking he might stand guard, he led his horse carefully through the sleeping men to the perimeter. But a sentry told him not to worry and to get some sleep, that the Boers had been left far behind and there was no danger.

As he lay in the dark with his head on his saddle, staring at the night sky and thinking about the day's events, it struck him there was something familiar about the name of this place—Sannah's Post. It was his last thought before his eyes closed.

He came awake to the sound of dawn patrols leaving the camp. He offered to join but was assured it was routine, nothing to worry about. He watched the patrols return just after first light—bored, unhurried, unconcerned. The men looked like they had paid little attention to the terrain, but that even if they had, they would have looked without seeing.

The thought had no sooner crossed his mind than he heard distant booms like rolling thunder, followed moments later by ear-splitting explosions right in the middle of the waterworks. He scrambled to his feet and only just managed to control his horse as panicked troops scattered in every direction to avoid the bombardment.

The only orders heard above the commotion were to get out of the waterworks and to head for Bloemfontein.

William's hands froze on the cow's teats. The stream of milk abruptly stopped and the cow bellowed, either from annoyance or fright at the thunderous sound that seemed to explode directly overhead.

He scrambled out of the milking shed and rushed towards the house. His wide-eyed mother was coming out the front door, still in her nightgown.

"They're here, Ma," he yelled as he ran to meet her. "It must be De Wet shelling the garrison at the waterworks!" He flinched as another salvo exploded overhead. "Please, Ma," he said, breathing hard, staring into her eyes, his hands on her slender shoulders. "The time has come."

She blinked, shaking her head. But then she nodded. "So be it, Willie. And may God be with you," she added as the rage of battle lit up the early morning sky, shaking the ground beneath their feet.

He cupped her face in his hands and kissed her on the forehead. Then he ran to the house to fetch his rifle and saddlebag, and back to the barn to saddle his horse. When he emerged, his mother and sister were waiting on the porch. He checked his fervor while his mother said a short prayer. Then he gave them each a brief hug, mounted his skittish horse and galloped down to the stream.

He angled into the shallows just upstream of the willow tree but couldn't decide which way to go—the sound of battle was all around him. As if in answer to his quandary, he heard shouting—"Hands up, hands up!"—and urged his horse towards the sounds. As he rounded the next bend in the river, he was astonished to see Tommy soldiers standing in the stream, their hands in the air, staring up at Boer fighters on the riverbank waving their rifles in triumph.

"Come on, man, the party's already started," yelled the Boer closest to him. "Damn Tommies with their fancy uniforms don't look too fancy now, do they?" he said, laughing to a chorus of guffaws.

"Who are you? What commando?" called William.

"The best, man, only the best. De Wet's boys."

"Where's the fight? Which way?"

"That way, man. Around the next bend," shouted the man, pointing.

William urged his horse past the Tommies towards the sound of battle.

Henry found himself in the midst of a crush of wagons, horse artillery, troops and civilians, all heading down the muddy road towards the safety of Bloemfontein. But the disorganized procession had no sooner settled into some semblance of order than it came to an abrupt halt.

From his vantage point standing in the stirrups, he saw a group of mounted soldiers with horse-drawn cannons stopped at a river crossing ahead. The crossing appeared to be blocked by a large group of armed men not in uniform. Amid the confusion, he saw a panic-stricken soldier run back from the crossing and past him to the commander of a second group of mounted men and cannons following behind.

"Major! Major! The Boers are there," the soldier yelled, pointing towards the river crossing. "They were waiting for us and have got in among the convoy and the guns."

The major immediately gave the order to turn his six guns around. As they left the road and wheeled a wide left turn, a volley of rifle fire cut down three horses, several gunners, and caused one of the gun carriages to crash over onto its side.

With hardly a thought except that his help might be needed, Henry yanked the reins of his horse towards the gun carriages and kicked his horse into a gallop. The artillery unit raced back along the side of the road, adding to the confusion and scattering stragglers in its path. The major reined in about a thousand yards from the crossing, wheeled his horse to survey the scene at the river, then ordered his men to get the guns into position and ready to fire.

No questions were asked when Henry dismounted and helped carry shells from the munitions wagon to the guns.

The gunners aimed for the bank of the river crossing, where the Boers appeared to have dug themselves into trenches. But it quickly became clear the Boers were deadly with their rifles, even at such a great distance. Although the gunners managed to fire several rounds, they were being shot down one after the other, and when a bullet tore through the sleeve of Henry's shirt and burned the skin of his arm, he threw himself to the ground next to the wheel of one of the gun carriages.

The guns soon fell silent. There were only a handful of gunners left alive, and all were taking cover to avoid the Boers' rifles. Henry was close enough to the major to hear a messenger relay an order from the general to save the guns at all costs. But there were not enough able-bodied men left to move them, especially under constant fire from the Boers.

In the next moment the major broke cover and ran towards a group of railway buildings not far from the guns. Henry instinctively followed, ignoring the bullets cutting through the air around him as he sprinted after the major. He reached the buildings just in time to hear the major berating a group of men cowering behind the buildings.

"Cowards!" yelled the major. "I will shoot the man who doesn't go out and fight. Either fight or help me with the guns. Choose now or I begin shooting."

The terrified men elected to help rather than fight. Together with the remaining gunners, they managed to move four of the guns out of range of the Boer rifles. After a few more desperate minutes trying to harness the gun carriages to the horses, the major led the artillery unit at a gallop towards an alternate crossing higher upstream.

Henry stayed with the major as they crossed the river.

William leapt off his horse when he heard Mausers firing from the riverbank above him and tied the reins to an exposed tree root. Then he clambered up the riverbank and almost fell headlong into a shallow depression alongside a handful of commandos.

He quickly learned De Wet had ambushed a battery of Tommy field guns and taken five of them. But a second battery was now firing at them from hundreds of yards away. He settled into a firing position with his rifle resting on the ridge of the depression and squinted over his sights at the distant figures manning the guns.

Despite their size, one of the Tommies stood out from the rest by the color of his skin. *Bastards*, thought William, *using our kaffirs to fight their war.* He squeezed off two quick shots at the dark figure and kept shooting until his five-shot clip was empty. It was impossible to tell if he hit anyone, but it felt good to be in the firing line.

He was amazed how accurate De Wet's boys were with their Mausers. In less than ten minutes, the field guns were silenced, and only about a dozen Tommies were still on their feet out of the original fifty or so manning the battery. But the survivors managed to drag four of the guns out of sight of the Boer Mausers. Soon after, horsemen galloped into view pulling the field guns away from the ambush at the main crossing.

He glimpsed the black man among the Tommy riders and snorted in disgust.

The celebration that night around the Boer campfires was almost riotous. They had hoped De Wet's new tactics would bag the small garrison at the waterworks, but a much larger Tommy force had dropped into their laps. And they had taken the waterworks at a cost of only three dead and five wounded. The Tommies had been routed, sent packing with their tails between their legs, leaving behind six or seven field guns, about a hundred wagons full of supplies, and over a hundred and fifty soldiers dead or wounded.

William had his own reason for celebrating. He had been part of the action, part of a Boer commando, and not just any commando. He knew his father would have been proud.

10

THE WARNING

1900

Henry rode into Bloemfontein with the remnants of the artillery unit. The blood-spattered major became an instant hero for having saved four of the field guns, while Henry fell into the familiar routine of doing chores around English stables with the other black scouts.

But the mood was somber—the defeat had been costly and a chance lost to trap the elusive De Wet commando.

Two weeks later, on a mid-April morning, Henry overheard a burly sergeant address a section of men on the parade ground in front of the stables.

"Sannah's Post," the sergeant said bluntly. "We're going back. Today!"

The eight men exchanged glances. "Why?" stammered the corporal after clearing his throat.

"To teach the Boers a lesson," said the sergeant, his tone belligerent. "Someone helped that bastard De Wet get into position to ambush us. Our job is to find them, flush them out, then burn their damn farms to the ground—every farm within ten miles of the waterworks."

"What about women and children?" asked the corporal.

The sergeant smirked. "Well, boys," he began, "all I've been told is to turn them loose after we're done."

"What about a scout?" asked the corporal. "We don't want to go anywhere near that damn place without a scout in case De Wet's still in the area."

"Good thinking," said the sergeant. "Go find that scout who helped the major with the guns. Take him to the quartermaster for some kit. Then tell him to report to me on the double."

"You mean the black one?" asked the corporal.

"I mean the one who didn't run and hide when Boer bullets were flying. That's the one I mean, Corporal. I don't give a shit what color his skin happens to be."

Within the hour Henry found himself heading out of the city behind the sergeant and his men. Once they were in open veld, the sergeant signaled him to move forward and take up position south of the road and about half a mile ahead.

He was uncomfortable in the clothes of the soldiers. The quartermaster had given him extra large in everything, yet the clothes were tight in all the wrong places.

But he was more than uncomfortable—he was troubled. He had recalled why Sannah's Post sounded familiar. The Boer named De Beer had taken his father there after the flogging, to a nearby farm. And now he was on his way with the soldiers to burn all the Boer farms around Sannah's Post and to deliver the women and children into the hands of the Tommy soldiers.

He knew what he had to do, what his father would expect him to do—the right thing. It sounded simple enough, but how? He began by slowly increasing the distance between him and the soldiers. He had to be able to move freely, unseen, and to find the De Beer farm before the soldiers.

He drew a deep breath when he reached the stream—the recent crossing under fire from the Boers still made his heart race. He rode down into the riverbed and realized he could not see the soldiers, which meant they could not see him. He turned south, away from the road, and quickened his pace.

Just as he splashed past a willow tree on the bank of the stream, a family of startled warthogs ran out from under the tree, including three little ones, their short curly tails pointing straight up, their tiny legs a blur of movement. He reined in to control his horse and noticed that something appeared out of place as he peered through the low-hanging limbs of the willow. He had grown up sensitive to natural features and could not help seeing the oddly placed large stone under the willow's canopy.

After a moment's indecision, he dismounted and ducked under the branches. He was surprised to see writing carved into the flat side of the stone. Although he couldn't read, he knew from tavern signs in Queenstown what the English name for "beer" looked and sounded like. He recognized the shape of the same word carved into the stone, part of the name his father had spoken about.

It had to be the right place—the coincidence was too strong. He peered through the willow's branches and saw a farmhouse about a hundred yards away, partially obscured from the road by a ridge that ran parallel to the road. Although the ridge provided some cover, he knew he would not be able to get to the house without being seen from the road. He looked right and left and noticed a drainage ditch running from the stream towards a barn and outhouse close to the farmhouse.

He tied his horse's reins to a branch of the willow tree, waded through the stream to the ditch and was relieved to find the ditch was a good depth, about four feet. He checked for any sign of the soldiers then ran the length of the ditch at a crouch, painfully aware of the ill-fitting army boots, hoping he would not be seen from the road. When he reached the far side of the barn, he realized he couldn't reach the house without crossing open ground. He was sure he would be seen if he tried.

He was trying to plot his next move when he heard activity in the barn. Before he could decide what to do, a tall girl emerged and crossed to the outhouse close to the ditch. She was singing and skipping, her skirts sweeping the ground, her braids swinging around her slim shoulders and slapping against her young breasts. He heard the door close and moved quickly to get as close as he could to the outhouse.

He knew the situation would be awkward but it might work if he could convince the girl to stay and listen. Her age was hard to judge—she was young but already showed signs of womanhood—perhaps fifteen years old. He hoped she would understand what he needed to say. He crept forward and knocked on the back of the outhouse.

"Please, young madam," he whispered, "don't be frightened. Is your father home?"

He heard the sharp intake of breath and rustle of clothes, but the girl said nothing.

"Madam?"

"Go away," came the response, the girl's voice tight and fierce. "How dare you sneak up on me like that? Go away at once!"

"Please, young madam, I mean no harm. It is very important that I speak to your father."

"My father is dead," she said tersely, "and my brother is on commando. Now go away."

He was momentarily taken aback. "Then I must speak to your mother." His shirt was damp with sweat, and he was acutely aware of how little time he had before the sergeant noticed his absence.

He heard the girl give an annoyed snort. "My mother has nothing to say to you. Now go away before I fetch a gun."

He threw his head back in exasperation. "Please, young madam. My father knew your father at the mine where they found the diamonds. He asked me to give something of great value to your family," he continued, improvising. "But some robbers are chasing me. I have to hide or they will catch me. Please fetch your mother quickly so I can give this thing to her."

He held his breath to sounds of shuffling and more rustling of clothes, hoping the girl would take the bait.

"Wait here," came the abrupt response before the girl burst out of the outhouse and raced towards the house, yelling, "Ma, come quickly, come quickly!"

He cringed, hoping the soldiers' attention was focused elsewhere. Moments later, an older woman appeared at the farmhouse door. He watched the girl lead the woman towards the outhouse, talking excitedly as she walked. Keeping the outhouse between him and the road, he stood and removed his hat as the women approached. The older woman looked severe in a long black dress with her brown hair pulled into a single braid behind her head. She stood taller than her daughter and looked strong, as one accustomed to hard work.

"What is this? Who are you?" demanded the woman when she saw him. Her scrutiny was fierce, her displeasure evident.

"He has diamonds for us, Ma," said the girl, her eyes bright. "From Kimberley."

"No, madam, no diamonds," said Henry quickly. "The only diamond I have is the one that brought me to this place. And I will never give it away."

"What are you going on about? Talk sense or leave!"

"Madam, do you remember the man from the mine who was whipped, who stayed here on the farm to get well?"

The woman looked stunned. "What of it?"

"He was my father, madam. I am Henry Mandela, son of Gadla."

The woman looked at him closely. "You have the same manner, the same slanting eyes and tuft of white hair above your forehead." She paused. "I remember. My husband helped your father. But what do you want?" she asked in a kinder tone.

"I have come to warn you, madam. The soldiers are coming to burn your farm and to chase you off the land."

The woman's eyes went wide with fright.

"Ag, what nonsense," interjected the young one.

"I speak the truth, madam. Lord Roberts told them to burn all the farms near the waterworks because of the battle that happened there. You and the young madam must go quickly from this place before the soldiers find you."

The woman stared intently at him, as though trying to pierce his heart with the steel of her gaze. "Why are you wearing the khakis of the Tommies?"

"They made me a scout, madam. That is how I know these things. And the soldiers are already near the crossing. They will be here very soon."

The woman nodded slowly, as though considering the information and its source. Then, without taking her eyes off him, she said, "Esmé, go quickly and pack a small bag, only as much as you can carry. Change into some of Willie's clothes—make yourself look like a boy—and get dried meat and bread from the pantry."

The girl looked at her mother with wide eyes. "Ma? You believe this kaffir, this nonsense story?" she cried.

"Yes, Esmé, I do. Now go, do as I say. Quickly."

The girl turned on her heel and stomped off towards the house.

"Where should we go?" asked the woman after a moment.

"I'm not sure, madam. Nowhere is safe. And the soldiers are so close." He looked around at the farm's landscape. Then he had an idea. "Madam, go to the stone by the tree. Hide under the branches until the soldiers have passed. After that I do not know. Perhaps you can find your fighters or go to Bloemfontein."

The woman nodded. "What about you?"

"I will try to lead the soldiers away from this place. Now I must go, madam."

The woman held up her hand as though to wave, hesitated, then stretched it out towards him. He had never touched a white person before. He tentatively took her hand, first in one hand, then in both.

"Thank you," said the woman.

"Thank you, madam, for helping my father. Go well and stay safe with the young madam." Then he turned, ducked into the ditch and ran back to the stream, keeping as low as possible, before remounting his horse and heading for the far side of the crossing.

The horse kicked up so much spray as he rode that he nearly missed seeing a second group of soldiers approaching the crossing from the waterworks. He reined in behind a large overhanging tree and watched. When they disappeared into a depression just short of the crossing, he ducked low, urged his horse through the crossing and rode for another fifty yards before emerging from the riverbed.

He saw the sergeant wave at the approaching waterworks soldiers, then turn and signal to him to come closer. He rejoined as the two groups met but kept his distance while the soldiers exchanged stories about the battle two weeks before.

"So where are the nearest Boer farms?" asked the sergeant, interrupting the flow of war stories.

The corporal in charge of the patrol scratched his head and looked around. "Well, there are three farms north of the road and one south of the road, just beyond that ridge over there," he said, pointing. "Just follow the trail along the riverbank and it will take you almost all the way."

"Good. Thank you, Corporal. Our orders are to burn all the farms within ten miles of the waterworks, so don't raise the alarm when you see the smoke."

The sergeant looked across the stream, surveying the landscape north and south of the road, before he turned to Henry.

"South," he ordered. "Get moving, scout. And don't miss the trail."

11

THE KNOT TIGHTENS

1900

William reined in just below the crest of a hill south of the farm. It had always been a pleasant ritual to stop and enjoy the view after being away. Now it was a necessary precaution. He would stay only a few days to make sure all was well before rejoining the commando at De Wet's hideout.

He reached into his saddlebag for the telescope that had been his father's. He worried that a reflection off the lens might reveal his presence to Tommies in the area but decided to risk it. He dismounted, left his horse on trailing reins and crawled up to the crest to observe.

As he swept the landscape through the telescope, he noticed a group of mounted soldiers moving along the road from Bloemfontein towards a second group moving up the road from Sannah's Post. It seemed the Tommies had reoccupied the waterworks after De Wet's commando left. He switched his focus to the farm and caught his breath. A figure in khaki—a black soldier—was sneaking along the ditch from the outhouse towards the stream.

His stomach tightened. His first instinct was to get to his mother and sister as quickly as possible, but logic told him to wait and watch. Besides, a gallop down the hill would only attract the attention of the mounted Tommies.

The furtive soldier reached the river and emerged into view moments later on a horse, riding fast through the shallow water. But then he pulled up hard at the river crossing, waited for several moments, then ducked and accelerated just as the soldiers from Sannah's Post entered a depression that obscured the rider from their view.

What the devil is he up to? thought William. The man seemed to be trying to avoid being seen by anyone, including the soldiers on the road. But the thought no sooner crossed his mind than the rider rode out of the water and up onto the riverbank in full view of the soldiers.

Within minutes, the two groups of soldiers met at the river crossing and were joined by the black one. As he watched, the men engaged in an animated conversation before one of the soldiers from Sannah's Post pointed in the direction of the De Beer farmhouse. The next moment, the soldiers from Bloemfontein swung their horses off the road and headed down the riverbank towards the farmhouse.

The black rider led the way.

"Goddammit!" swore William out loud. But before he could decide what to do, movement at the farmhouse caught his eye. He swung the telescope just in time to see his mother and sister running from the farmhouse with bags in their hands towards the river.

"Ag, dear Jesus, what now?" He could barely breathe, let alone move, as he watched them disappear under the canopy of the willow tree.

William knew with crushing certainty that the black rider, obviously a scout, was leading the soldiers directly towards the willow tree and the farm, and he knew with equal certainty that he could not reach the tree before the soldiers did. And although he did not know whether the soldiers intended any harm to his mother and sister, his instinct and the stories he had heard left little doubt they were in danger.

He needed a diversion. Only one thing came to mind. He leapt onto his horse and launched a furious gallop down the hill, on a diagonal away from the river past the back of the farmhouse towards a rocky outcrop on the far side of the farmhouse. And to make sure he had the soldiers' attention, he let go of the reins and fired two snap shots in their general direction. To his surprise one of the horses stumbled, spilling its rider to the ground.

The chase was on.

He rode as hard as the horse would carry him, disappointed to see only three riders giving chase, but gratified to see the black rider leading the gallop to try to cut him off before he reached the gap in the rocky outcrop he was racing towards. He could tell he was cutting it very close as the soldiers narrowed the angle towards him, but if he could get to the gap he might have a chance—he knew the nooks and crannies of the outcrop like the back of his hand. He twisted in the saddle and fired another snap shot. No one fell, but the black rider pulled up fractionally, forcing the other two to veer around him, slowing them all down just enough to make a difference.

He raced through the gap, wrenched the reins hard left and galloped into the shelter of a familiar grove of trees amid large boulders, where he pulled up on the horse's reins with all his strength. He leapt off the heaving animal as it shuddered to a stop, slapped its rump with the stock of his rifle, then scrambled up the back of a large, flat-topped boulder as the startled horse took off like a jackrabbit. He had no sooner dropped into a firing position when the Tommies thundered into view no more than twenty yards away and galloped straight towards him, two in front, one behind.

William rammed the butt of the Mauser into his shoulder, used the bolt action to chamber a round, forced himself to take a deep breath and slowly exhale. Just as his lungs emptied, he brought the open sights into alignment with the chest of the rider on the right, squeezed off a shot, chambered the next round, adjusted aim and fired at the chest of the second rider.

He looked up just in time to see both riders tumbling from their horses in a tangle of arms and legs. The third rider, the black one, was so close behind that his horse swerved to avoid the falling riders, launching him headfirst off his horse. The three horses slowed as they passed the boulder where William lay, as though offering proof they were now riderless.

He was astonished his ruse had worked. But he still had a score to settle with the black soldier. He jumped off the rock and cautiously approached the men on the ground. The first was bleeding from his stomach, the second from his chest, both in their last throes of life. He knew the look of the mortally wounded—he had seen it before on the acre of death that was Spion Kop. He stepped between the two soldiers to where the black man hunkered on his hands and knees, apparently dazed from the fall.

"Bastard," he swore as he worked the bolt to chamber the next round. Then he raised the Mauser to his shoulder, aiming at the man's glistening forehead, right between his coal-black eyes.

For the third time in as many minutes, William squeezed the trigger. But this time there was no shot. Nothing. Just a dull click as the firing pin failed to detonate a cartridge. The black man blinked but did not flinch.

William lowered the rifle and stared at the mute Mauser. Then it came to him—three shots from horseback, two from the boulder—the five-round clip was empty.

Before he could think what to do next, the man leapt at him and grabbed the rifle, his hands like black clamps, his breath hot and sour as they stood face to face, glaring at each other, wrestling for the rifle.

Henry was surprised to be alive.

He thought he had been shot off his horse, yet aside from being winded by the fall, he felt no pain. But the reprieve was short-lived when he looked up and saw the Boer standing over him, aiming a rifle at his head. He hoped he would feel no pain, but when the Boer's rifle failed, he didn't second-guess his good fortune. He leapt at the man, grabbed the rifle and came within inches of a white face turned red with rage.

The image distracted him. He never saw the knee that crashed into his groin. He staggered backwards, doubled over in agony, then tripped over one of the soldiers. As he sprawled to the ground, his outstretched right hand hit something hard and his fingers closed over a soldier's rifle. Through eyes blurred by dust and pain, he glimpsed the Boer looming over him, lifting his rifle high above his head, both hands on the barrel.

He managed to swing the soldier's rifle in front of him—one hand on the barrel, the other on the stock—just as the Boer swung his rifle down, its stock splintering as it crashed against the trigger guard of the rifle he held inches from his face.

"Bastard," screamed the Boer as he drew his rifle back for another swing. "Spied on my mother and sister...led the Tommies to them...you black devil!"

Henry scrambled to his feet, holding his rifle ready. There was something in the Boer's words, something about his mother and sister and the farm. Could this be the brother the girl had spoken of—the son of the Boer who had helped his father?

As he blocked the next blow, he shouted, "Stop...I was trying to help them." But his words only seemed to inflame the Boer.

"Lying bastard. I saw you," the man yelled as he swung the rifle again, this time in a vicious roundhouse swing.

Henry realized there would be no reasoning with this Boer as he held the rifle in front of him, right hand over left, its stock pointed to the sky and prepared to block the next blow. He also realized that fighting with useless rifles was just like stick fighting, which he had learned as a child and learned well.

The moment the rifles smashed together, he thrust his upper hand forward, rotating his rifle's stock over the Boer's rifle. Then, with a sharp upward jerk of his right hand and push with his left hand, he hit the Boer with the stock of his rifle, a jarring blow under the man's jaw.

The Boer's eyes went wide with shock before they rolled to white and he crumpled to the ground.

Henry stood for a moment, breathing hard, surprised by the sudden end to the fight. Then he tossed the mangled rifle aside, scooped up the second soldier's rifle, and made sure there was a round in the chamber—he didn't want to make the same mistake as the Boer. Next he checked the soldiers for signs of life—there were none—but the Boer began to groan and slowly sat up.

Henry sank to his haunches near the Boer and tried again. Perhaps the blow to the man's jaw had cleared his head. "Listen to me," he began. "I am Henry Mandela. Your father helped my father after he was hurt at the mine and cared for him at your farm." The Boer squinted, brow creased, his eyes glazed in dull confusion. "I tried to repay the kindness...to warn your mother—"

The sound of a galloping horse interrupted his explanation. He looked up and was surprised to see the sergeant rounding the edge of the rocky outcrop.

Henry made a snap decision and hit the Boer with the butt of his rifle. Blood spurted from the man's nose as he fell back and lay deathly still. Then he aimed the Lee-Enfield two inches to the side of the Boer's head—the side the sergeant couldn't see—and fired a shot into the ground.

"What the devil happened here?" demanded the sergeant as he reined in about ten yards away.

"The Boer ambushed us, Sergeant. Shot these two," he said, gesturing towards the two lifeless forms. "Then his rifle jammed. We fought. I won."

The sergeant looked to where the soldiers and the Boer lay. "Damnation! Not exactly an even trade," he said, shaking his head with obvious distaste. "But quite the cold-blooded coup de grâce you delivered, Mandela. I didn't think you had it in you. And reassuring to see Boers bleed just like the rest of us."

The sergeant looked around. "Drag these two miserable sods out of the sun and under those trees," he said, pointing at the grove. "We'll bury them later after we finish at the farm. But leave the Boer in the sun for the vultures." Then he turned and galloped back towards the farmhouse.

Henry was relieved to see the sergeant disappear from view. But now he had a problem—the Boer would soon wake up. Then what? The Boer would either try to resume the fight or try to rescue his mother and sister. Even if he just disappeared, the soldiers would notice a missing dead Boer when they returned to bury their comrades.

Whichever way he looked at it, it seemed his execution ploy would soon be exposed. The only thing he could think to do was create some distance between the Boer and the soldiers, then hope for the best.

He dragged the Boer into the shade of the trees and tethered the man's horse to a nearby limb. Then he walked the soldiers' horses to where their riders lay, hooked each of the soldiers by a boot into a horse's stirrup and mounted his own horse. Then he rode slowly around the outcrop towards the farmhouse leading the two horses with the dead soldiers dragging behind.

He unhooked the lifeless limbs near a solitary tree not far from the farmhouse, left the bodies in the meager shade and rode to the farmhouse with the soldiers' horses.

"Sergeant," yelled one of the men as fire and smoke billowed out the doors and windows of the old farmhouse, "farm burning is thirsty work."

The sergeant nodded, loosening the buttons of his tunic as he turned away from the burning house.

"What took you so long, Mandela?" he demanded when he saw Henry approach.

"I brought the bodies of the soldiers closer," he said, "to save the trouble of going far to fetch them."

The sergeant grunted. "Collect the canteens. Fill them at the river. And don't take all day about it." Then he turned and yelled at his men to give their canteens to the scout.

Henry collected the canteens and set off towards the river. He had walked only a few steps when he remembered the willow tree—it was in a direct line from the house to the river. He had no idea if the Boer women had taken his advice, but he hoped fervently they were long gone, anywhere but under that tree, especially if they had seen the chase and thought like the son that he had led the soldiers to the farm.

He angled away from the tree and headed down the embankment to the water's edge. But he had no sooner unscrewed the cap of the first canteen than he was startled by a sudden eruption of hysteria behind him. He turned but was slow to rise, partly out of astonishment at the sight of the Boer girl jumping down the embankment in a bustle of skirts—not dressed like a boy as her mother had instructed—and rushing at him, screaming.

She was on his back in an instant, clawing and scratching like an enraged feline, throwing him off-balance, sending them both crashing headfirst into the shallow water. It took an effort to lift himself out of the water on his hands and knees with the girl still on his back.

"Black devil," she screamed as she flailed at him, spitting and slapping his head from behind. "You lied...now Willie's dead and Pa's dead...and our house is burning...and I hate you, I hate you, I hate you!"

He was thankful for the embankment and the roar of the farmhouse fire. He didn't think the soldiers could see or hear what was happening at the river, but he knew he had to get control of the situation before thirsty men came looking for water.

He timed the move perfectly. Just after she had slapped him again on both sides of his head and would be lifting her arms for another assault, he collapsed his arms and straightened his legs in one powerful movement. The girl catapulted off his back into the water in a spread-eagled belly flop that would have raised a good laugh under any other circumstances.

Then he heard the mother jump into the water behind him. He turned just as she slapped his ear.

"You gave your word," she yelled, "then betrayed us." She slapped his other ear. "And what of my son? We saw you chase him. What have you done to my son?"

"I kept my word, madam, and your son is alive," he said, grabbing the woman's forearm as she tried to slap him again. "It's the truth, madam," he said, pushing her firmly away. She stumbled backwards and fell on her bottom into the river, her eyes wide with fright as he stood over her. "I tried to lead the soldiers away. But they were told by others where to find your farm. And then your son started shooting."

The words were no sooner out of his mouth when the girl threw herself at him from behind. He turned to defend himself. "Stop it," he shouted in her face. "Your brother is alive...I saved him...and I tried to save your farm."

"Liar, liar, liar," screamed the girl, her cotton blouse clinging to her wet chest, her braided hair whipping around her face and shoulders like cords of righteous indignation as she slapped at him with both hands. "We saw you...black devil!"

He brushed the girl aside in frustration. She was just like her brother—trying to reason with her would be impossible. He turned and took a step towards the mother, still on her bottom in the river.

"You must listen...I tried to save your farm," he said as the mother scuttled backwards through the shallow water like a frightened crab.

That was when he saw the soldier standing on the embankment, rifle in hand, staring at him with a look of disbelief written large on his sunburned features.

Before either man could speak, the mother marched out of the river straight at the soldier. She stopped a few feet away and glared up at him, hands on hips, her skirts dripping wet.

"Coward!" she yelled. "The great British Empire can't beat our men on the battlefield, so it makes war on our women and children. And to make matters worse, you use kaffirs as your dogs to sniff us out and burn our farms."

The soldier stood his ground, looking bewildered. Into the lull came the girl, who ignored the soldier and flew at Henry, screaming and slapping at him from behind. The girl's efforts seemed to encourage her mother, who resumed her harangue, first at the soldier, then at Henry, who had his hands full trying to shield himself from the enraged despair of the two Boer women.

A head-jarring explosion brought an abrupt silence to the scene.

"Shut up, all of you, not another word," commanded the soldier, his smoking rifle pointed at the sky. "You, Mandela, hands behind your head. One false move and I will put a bullet through your double-crossing black heart. And you two"—he gestured with the rifle at the women—"fill up those water canteens and come with me."

"You can go to the devil," replied Susannah, "and take your canteens with you."

The soldier shook his head. "Bloody-minded to the last, you Boers," he said, his bewilderment replaced by bemused resignation. "Mandela!" he barked, regaining his composure, "you fill the damned canteens." Then he pointed the rifle at the women. "And no more nonsense from you two."

Henry did as instructed. The two sodden women stood with their arms folded in sullen resentment until he returned with the filled canteens.

"Come, Mandela," said the soldier as the women stomped up the embankment past him, "you have an appointment with destiny."

William sat up slowly. It felt as though he had been kicked in the head by a mule. He opened his eyes. Nothing came into focus as he tried to shake off the blanket of fog covering the membrane of his mind and picked at the dried blood encrusting his nose.

Then it came back to him—the farm, the chase, two Tommies shot dead, then the fight with the black one. And he recalled the man speaking. Something about his father and the farm...and something else...his name. Mandela!

He stood up a little too quickly. Waves of nausea immediately crashed over him, forcing him to put his head between his knees until it passed. When he stood again, he was surprised to find himself in the grove of trees with his horse tethered to a nearby branch. He looked to where the soldiers had fallen but saw nobody. All he could see was a broken Lee-Enfield and a shattered Mauser—the dead Tommies had vanished.

It made no sense, but there had to be an explanation, perhaps on the farm side of the ridge.

He drank from his canteen, stuffed the telescope into his belt and climbed the rocky outcrop. He expected to see fields bathed in the orange glow of a late afternoon sunset. Instead, the sun's glow was suffused with shades of crimson and ochre as its dying rays fought to pierce a curtain of smoke from multiple fires, the conflagration magnified by his telescopic gaze.

Their farmhouse was engulfed in flames, its thatched roof completely consumed, its white walls charred. The outhouse appeared unscathed, but the barn was burning and cattle lay everywhere, immobile on a landscape in the throes of a fiery death.

Movement caught his eye. A group of Tommies were standing around a campfire on the far side of the stream, not far from the willow tree. It looked like they were roasting a small animal on a spit, perhaps a lamb, but they seemed more interested in a second group about thirty feet away. He focused the telescope on the smaller group—the light was still good enough to make out some detail.

He caught his breath when he recognized his mother sitting cross-legged on the ground. Then he saw his sister. She was kneeling in front of one of the Tommies. Her waist-length hair only partially covered her nakedness.

As he watched, the man pulled his sister's head towards him.

Her face and the man's groin came together. "Oh my God," he cried aloud, not sure what he was seeing except that it looked vulgar and wrong. But he was too far away to do anything—he didn't have a rifle and couldn't get there in time to stop whatever was going on.

All he could do was watch.

When the Tommy was done, he stood back and a second Tommy pushed Esmé to the ground, turned her on her back, and spread her legs apart. The man's pale buttocks were illuminated by the firelight as he lowered himself over her, thrusting forcefully, again and again, before collapsing across her slender body.

Rage and nausea welled up in William. This time he knew what he was seeing—he had seen farm animals do the same thing.

"Oh my God...no...no..."

Unable to watch, he focused on his mother. For some inexplicable reason she just sat there, her hands behind her back, doing nothing except swaying as though in a trance. Then he saw the man behind his mother, a black man—Mandela. He too just stood there, hands behind his back, as though witnessing nothing more consequential than the plucking of a chicken.

He looked back at Esmé and, just as it seemed the men were done, one of them reached down between her thighs. She squirmed but couldn't get away. The men appeared to laugh. Then they strolled back to the campfire to a round of backslapping from the other men.

William's last impression of his sister as the light faded was the sight of her naked body curled in a fetal position.

He wept.

12

A PROMISE MADE

1900

"So, Mandela, was it worth the price of admission?" asked the corporal. He was silhouetted against the glow from the campfire as he stood staring at the girl, having finally responded to the mother's pleas.

"I should have shot you on the spot. But it doesn't really matter. Sergeant says you'll be executed by firing squad in Bloemfontein tomorrow, a lesson to all about the cost of betraying the Queen." He shrugged. "So be it, but I don't understand what goes on in that black heart of yours, to be brave for us one day and betray us the next."

Henry met the corporal's gaze but said nothing. He knew he would not be reprieved even if he could explain his actions. And there was nothing he could do with his feet tied at the ankles and his hands tied behind his back.

The corporal looked down at the mother, then drew a knife from a sheath around his waist. "What is your name?"

"De Beer, Susannah de Beer," she stammered, transfixed by the sight of the long blade.

"Well, Mrs. De Beer," he said, stepping behind her, "we'll turn you and the girl loose in the morning. But the only place for you to go is wherever your men are hiding. We'll see how long they survive with women and children to worry about, without farms to feed and support them." Then he cut the rawhide that bound her wrists.

The mother flung herself down beside her daughter, covering as much of her body with her own as she could, kissing her face and smoothing her hair, whispering words of comfort.

"Not you, Mandela," said the corporal as he resheathed his knife. "You'll stay tied until we reach Bloemfontein. Actually, you'll stay tied until the rawhide rots off your dead body. And if you need to take a piss between now and then, go ahead...piss in your pants...and get used to it. It'll be the last thing you do before you die unless you shit yourself instead." Then he turned and rejoined his men at the campfire.

Henry stared morosely at the soldiers. He had done the right thing, but at what cost? Once they were in the saddle to Bloemfontein there would be no escaping the firing squad. He had to get away before sunrise.

He looked at the two guards standing nearby, their backs turned, listening to war stories being exchanged between the men around the campfire. The guards were the same two who had acted like dogs with the girl.

Feeling helpless amid the soldiers' frivolity and the mother's anguish, he did the only thing he thought might bring some comfort to the mother. Using his heels, he dragged himself inch by inch to where the girl's clothes lay in a heap, then rolled onto his back on top of the small pile, grabbed the fabric with his bound hands, and dragged himself to within a few feet of the mother.

"Madam, here are the young madam's clothes behind my back,"

he whispered. The mother seemed to ignore him. He tried several times before she finally snatched them from his hands.

"Now get away from us," she hissed. "Go on, get away."

"Madam, please listen to me," he implored. "I must escape. You heard the soldier. They're going to shoot me in the morning."

"Good riddance," she said. "I'd shoot you myself if I had a gun."

He glanced over his shoulder, about to respond, when he noticed her struggling to dress the girl. He looked away and waited until she was finished, until he thought he had her attention.

"Madam, please, you don't understand. You need my help...but I can't help you if I'm dead."

"Hah!" she scoffed. "There's nothing I need from you. But even if there was, I wouldn't trust you farther than I can spit."

He winced—this was not going to be easy.

"Madam, I did not do this thing to you and the young madam." Before she could respond, he pressed on. "I tried to lead the soldiers away from your farm. And I saved your son's life after I chased him. These things I know to be true. I also know I cannot prove them to you, but we can't quarrel now. You heard the soldier. They will just leave you on the veld tomorrow. All the farms are burned and your people are gone. You have no home, no food, and your child is hurt."

He paused to check the soldiers could not hear them. "And madam, after what happened tonight, who knows what the morning will bring, what the soldiers may do before they leave you?" He knew he was evoking the mother's worst fears, but it could not be helped. He heard her gasp, but she did not interrupt. "If you help me, if you untie me, I will carry the young madam away from this place and I will take you to your people."

He held his breath as he waited for a response.

She broke the silence with a contemptuous hiss. "You think I'm a fool, Mandela? I trusted you once. Why should I trust you again? As soon as I untie your knots, you'll run away and leave us."

He was encouraged—she was thinking despite her fears.

"Madam, I have heard your General de Wet hides near the town named after his father. It is far, but I am strong. We will take the soldiers' horses and we can get food and water from the Sotho people." He paused. "And I will give you a soldier's gun so you can shoot me if I try to run away."

He waited in the darkness, afraid to breathe, his life's thread twisting in the storm he knew was raging through the mother's heart. He heard her exhale, as though expelling the tempest that tortured her.

"All right," she said at last, "but if you leave us, Henry Mandela, I swear before almighty God that I will hunt you down and cut out your lying tongue before I shoot you dead, even if it's the last thing I do on this earth."

"I understand, madam," he said, admiring her bravado, relieved by the prospect of escape. "But we have to be ready as soon as the guards fall asleep. Now we must pretend to sleep."

He rolled onto his side, facing their guards and the group around the campfire. He hoped the guards would soon succumb to the combined effects of a hot day's work, roasted red meat and their exertions with the girl.

The last flames flickered and died. The glowing embers cast a crimson hue over the khaki-clad soldiers around the campfire. Their stories exhausted, a quiet settled over the group, until one by one the five men lay back, spread out like spokes radiating from a burning hub. The last to succumb was the sergeant. He looked over at his prisoners and the guards before laying his head on his blanket roll.

Not long afterwards the heads of the two guards came together in a whispered exchange. They glanced at their sleeping comrades and at their prisoners. Then they lay back and stretched out for the night, apparently intent on guarding nothing more than the insides of their eyelids.

Henry forced himself to be patient as he waited in the dark. Aside from a tiny glow from the embers of the campfire, the only light on the landscape came from a pale moon. It was also unnaturally quiet, until a dog barked somewhere in the night. He flinched—it sounded so loud, so close, but none of the soldiers reacted.

Satisfied, he looked to where the women lay. "Madam, are you ready?" he whispered. "We must go quickly." Hearing no response, he scooted closer. "Madam?"

"I'm ready," she said, her tone abrupt.

"First, untie my feet," he said, hoping to strike the right tone to persuade her to follow his instructions.

"Move closer," she said. "But I'll be watching," she warned as he rolled over and extended his feet towards her. "And I'll do what I said if you betray us again. Don't think I won't!" He was tempted to defend his honor but held his tongue as she worked the knots around his ankles until they came loose. "Now turn around," she said. He felt her struggle with the knots around his wrists until the rawhide fell away.

The dog barked again. He stiffened and heard the mother's sharp intake of breath behind him. He stared at the guards and the group around the campfire. One soldier raised his head for a moment, then sank down again.

"Madam," he whispered. "Stay here. I will find a canteen—with water, not whiskey—and a rifle."

It proved easier than expected. It seemed nothing but a Boer cannon would wake the soldiers, although their snoring was loud enough to wake the dead. Within minutes he returned carrying two canteens, a rifle and a bandolier, all of which he handed to the mother.

"To the horses, madam," he whispered as he lifted the girl into his arms and backed away from the soldiers into the darkness.

The horses were in a nearby grove, some standing, some lying, all still saddled. The mother supported the girl while he selected the best horses for them and found his own.

"Madam, you must get up. I will give the young madam to you. I will take her when we're ready," he said as the mother slung the bandolier over her shoulder, strapped the rifle across her back and mounted the horse he held for her. Then he lifted the limp girl into her mother's arms, relieved the girl did not weigh much more than a calf at birth. "Now I must get the other horses," he said as he moved away.

Working quickly, he tied the reins of each horse to the pommel of the next horse until all six were tied together in a loose line before tying the reins of the lead horse to the pommel of his saddle. Then he mounted, took the girl from her mother, and sat her in the saddle in front of him, his arm around her waist. He tried to ignore the menace in the mother's glare as she unstrapped the rifle and aimed it at his chest. He had no doubt she was more than capable of using the rifle against him or the soldiers.

He took a moment to orientate himself. The dark landscape loomed as an unfriendly wilderness beneath the majesty of the night sky. He knew Dewetsdorp lay south of Sannah's Post, and for the moment it was all he needed to know as he searched the heavens for the group of stars that hung like a cross, its long axis pointing due south.

"That way, madam," he said, pointing towards the constellation that would be their guide as he nudged his horse forward. He held the girl close against his chest to prevent her head flopping back and forth. He imagined an ugly scene if she woke to find herself in his arms.

He shook his head in silent dismay. His life was threatened by British soldiers who planned to execute him as a traitor, by Boer fighters who would shoot him for serving as a scout and, if that were not danger enough, by a distraught mother looking for any reason to exact revenge.

As the predawn light eroded the gloom, he saw what he was looking for—a distant thread of willow trees that meandered across the veld. He brightened when they came across a well-worn trail that led directly towards the trees and a river crossing obscured by the drape of willow trees. The crossing turned out to be a good size when they reached it, about thirty feet across, and the trail resumed on the far bank of the river.

The mother immediately dismounted and headed to the water's edge, where she laid the rifle aside, washed her face and neck, and drank from cupped hands. He sat and waited until she was done.

"Madam, there are more soldiers at Sannah's Post who have horses. They may look for us. We must hide our tracks." She scooped up the rifle but said nothing. "We must drive the soldiers' horses across the river, then chase them away on the far side. But we will stay in the river and walk our horses as far as we can. Anyone looking for us will follow the tracks of the soldiers' horses. They will not see we went a different way."

The mother looked across the river and then along its course in both directions. She nodded. "It is a good plan. But first we must rest and wash my child. Get off the horse, Mandela, but remember I am watching and my finger is on the trigger."

"I hear you, madam," he said as he lowered the girl into her arms before dismounting. "But before we do that, I must go behind those bushes," he said, pointing. "I will stand where you can see my back. And then I must take off these boots that hurt my feet."

When he returned, relieved and barefoot, he saw the mother had laid the girl on the riverbank and was kneeling next to her, trying to wipe the girl's face with her scarf. She shook her head as he approached, apparently dissatisfied with her efforts.

"I must bathe her to wash away the Tommy filth," she said. "Turn around, Mandela. We must do this now before she wakes."

He turned his back and heard her talking to the girl, reassuring her as she removed her clothes. He felt something brush against his hands from behind.

"Here, take her wrists, Mandela... Don't turn around... I will take her ankles."

Fortunately, the water was not too deep, nor too cold, as the mother lowered the girl's legs and buttocks gently into the water. He held the girl's wrists and arms while the mother washed the girl with her scarf. After a while, he felt her lift the girl's legs.

"That will have to do," said the mother. Then they walked back up the riverbank where they laid the girl on her skirt.

He went back to the river. The taste and gentle current reminded him of home, of mountain streams and rolling hills, of family and friends, of familiar things. For a moment he was lost in place and time. Then the girl cried out behind him. Assuming the cold water had revived her, he prepared for the scene that was sure to follow. But she merely stared at him with dull incomprehension when he approached.

"She is not herself," said the mother. "I don't think she remembers."

"Do you think she can ride her horse, madam?"

The mother looked unsure. "She might be able to stay in the saddle if we don't go too fast."

He nodded. "I will check the river," he said, then mounted and rode cautiously into the middle of the crossing. His feet got wet, but the current remained gentle. Satisfied, he broke a sturdy switch off a willow tree before rejoining the women.

"Madam, tell the girl to stay here. Then you take that side," he instructed, pointing upstream. "I will drive the horses across between us." The mother nodded and spoke to the girl before mounting and moving into position in the river.

He flicked the willow switch at the rump of the horse nearest him before quickly rounding on the others. They responded with little hesitation—they had obviously forded rivers before. As the horses emerged on the far side, he lashed at as many rumps as he could reach with the switch. The startled animals shot forward and stampeded the rest into a furious gallop up the far bank onto the trail and away from the river.

He watched until the horses disappeared from sight, then sat quietly as the mother helped the girl into the saddle and then led her horse by its halter into the river. The girl swayed precariously, despite holding the pommel of her saddle with both hands. It did not bode well for their journey.

Henry led the way, walking the horses carefully through the water. The river made several wide turns along the course of a shallow valley surrounded by rocky hills. He judged they had ridden a good distance when they came across a rock formation that rose like steps from the water onto dry land.

"Madam," he called over his shoulder, "this is where we leave the river."

The plains were hot and devoid of life, the nights cold and full of menace. Even on the high ground, the stench of death was layered into every breeze that drifted across the landscape. And at every turn, especially after darkness fell, the threat of capture by Boer or Brit hung over his head.

Henry chose their routes and resting places as best he could to avoid being ambushed by day or discovered by night. Towards the end of the third day, he decided to walk his exhausted horse as they threaded in single file along a narrow rocky path into a shallow valley surrounded by low-lying hills. He knew they had to stop soon for the night and was heading for the shelter of a stand of trees in the valley ahead. Behind him, the mother had also dismounted, although the girl remained slumped in her saddle, her hands draped loosely over the pommel.

He turned to tell the mother of his plan and saw the girl swaying as though she was falling asleep. The fact that she was about to fall from her horse occurred to him an instant later. He leapt forward like a jackrabbit past the startled mother as the girl toppled in a lazy arc headfirst towards the rocky path below. At the last moment he dove at the disappearing gap between the girl's head and the ground, twisting his torso to land on his back underneath the girl, hoping to cushion her fall.

But the sudden activity caused the girl's horse to lash out with its hooves. He saw her head snap sideways just before she crumpled in a tangled heap on top of him.

The mother screamed and moments later landed on her knees beside them. As he lay winded, she dragged the girl off him and cradled her head, exposing a ragged gash near her temple, already vivid with blood streaming down her cheek and onto her neck and shoulders.

"Dear Jesus! Esmé, talk to me, talk to me...please God!" implored the mother, rocking back and forth, smoothing her child's hair, kissing her cheeks.

"I'm sorry, madam," said Henry, spitting out a muddy gob. "It happened too fast," he added, glaring at the girl's horse grazing nearby as though nothing out of the ordinary had just happened.

The mother seemed to nod and shake her head at the same time as she stared at her stricken child. Then she blinked several times to clear her eyes, took a closer look at the wound and tied her scarf around the girl's head, covering as much of the wound as possible.

"I will carry the young madam to the trees over there," said Henry, pointing at the stand of trees he had seen earlier. "It's not safe to stay in the open." He got to his knees and lifted the girl into his arms. "You must bring the horses, madam."

Henry was nervous. The trees provided some shelter, but he felt exposed and vulnerable in a landscape so recently devastated, as though by some great beast that roamed the earth with a cataclysmic appetite for all living things.

The only thing Henry knew for certain as he watched the mother clean the girl's wound with water from her canteen was that he could no longer get the two women to De Wet's commando as promised. It was too far, the terrain too hard, the girl too weak. They had to find refuge and help. He had seen such an injury when a horse kicked a childhood friend at his village—it had not ended well.

He was startled when, ignoring his presence, the mother unbuttoned the top of her dress, exposing her breast and then offered it to the girl. He had grown up with mothers nursing their young, but he didn't know white women did the same thing. Besides, he didn't think there could be any milk, and yet, as tears forced channels through the dust on her cheeks, the mother was pushing her nipple into the girl's limp mouth.

He turned away and busied himself with the horses.

"Madam, I'm going to the top of that kopje," he said without looking at her, pointing towards a nearby hill. "I must see what lies ahead. I'll be back before the sun is gone." He thought she might protest, remind him of her threat if he deserted them, but she said nothing. With that he led his horse out from under the trees and rode off at a slow canter up the gentle slope.

The rolling landscape was already mottled with shadows by the time he reached the top of the hill. He looked for signs of life but saw only signs of death. A pall of black smoke hung over the hills. But between him and the smoke, vultures circled over dark forms sprawled on the ground. A herd of dead cattle, he guessed—easy pickings for winged scavengers.

He saw movement a little distance from the cattle and squinted, trying to pierce the encroaching gloom. A solitary figure was walking slowly away from the cattle. He nudged his horse into a trot, confident he could handle a single person on foot, especially one that looked so small. He rode a slow, wide circle around the cattle, keeping upwind of the stench, not wanting to alarm his horse with the smell or the stranger with an aggressive gallop.

As he rode closer, he recognized the familiar figure of a boy in loincloth, a village herder, doing as he too had done in his youth. He was about a stone's throw away when the boy turned, stared for a moment, then took off like a gangly wildebeest, moments after birth, trying to escape a predator.

Henry kicked his horse into a gallop. And although the boy darted every which way, he judged his jump perfectly, grabbing the boy's shoulders as they crashed to the ground in a tangle of limbs. As they wrestled, he spoke into the boy's ear, trying to reassure him that he meant no harm. He had no idea if the boy could understand him, but he hoped the clicking of his Xhosa tongue would assuage the boy's fear. After a few more minutes of frantic effort, the boy gave up the struggle.

He kept hold of the boy's wrist as he sat up and adjusted to face him. He smiled broadly in response to the wide-eyed fright in the boy's chocolate-brown eyes set within bulging orbs of the purest white. He guessed the boy's native tongue was Sotho, a language he knew just well enough to be understood.

"*Dumela*, young one," he said. "My name is Henry Mandela, from the Transkei. What is your name?"

"Jonas," said the boy tentatively.

"Ahh," he said with a smile. "A good name. And where is your village, Jonas?"

The boy glanced at Henry's clothes and shook his head.

"These?" said Henry, tugging on his khaki shirt. "Not mine, Jonas. I am not a soldier," he said, shaking his head. "Not a soldier. Understand?"

The boy frowned but nodded.

"So tell me, Jonas, where is your village?"

The boy pointed towards the southeast.

"How far?"

The boy shrugged.

"Will you take me there...to your village?" he asked, confident the village could not be far away and that the boy would not decline. He did not. Henry led the boy by the hand to his horse and hoisted him into the saddle before mounting behind him.

It was a short ride back to the stand of trees. The mother was in the same position as before but was no longer trying to nurse the girl. If the boy was surprised to see white women, he did not show it.

Henry dismounted and knelt at the mother's side. "Madam, the boy will take us to his village." Her expression was vacant.

"Madam," he urged, "we must go to the boy's village. There will be food and shelter. But we must go now, before the darkness comes."

She blinked and nodded as comprehension filled her eyes.

"Come, madam. I will take the young madam. You must ride with the boy," he said as he helped her climb awkwardly into the saddle behind Jonas and handed her the rifle. Then he draped the girl over the saddle of her own horse, mounted behind her and lifted her into a seated position in front of him. Holding her firmly with his free hand, he rounded up the third horse and led the way up the hill.

At the crest, he urged the mother to follow him in a loping canter down into the valley past the carrion that was all that remained of the boy's cattle.

13

THE HORROR

1900

The night shroud lifted slowly from the rocky outcrop where William lay, but the rising sun did little to lift his spirits. As he gazed in solitary vigil over the scorched landscape, it felt as though he were a sole survivor of his people's quest for freedom, adrift on a sea of suffering with nothing to slake his despair.

He lifted his head and gazed bleary-eyed through the telescope at the soldiers' campsite, expecting to see nothing but indolent inactivity. Instead, as he brought the scene into focus, he registered signs of great agitation among the Tommies—a lot of pointing and running this way and that—and no sign of his mother and sister, or the Tommy horses, or the black man. He came fully awake in an instant. Had his mother and sister been released, or had they escaped in the night riding Tommy horses? Perhaps Mandela had been sent to scout for their trail or to look for the missing horses.

His heart raced as he tried to think where they might have gone. Bloemfontein was the obvious choice, but that would mean risking the cordon of Tommy soldiers. The more he thought about it, the more likely it seemed his mother would try to reach him and the commando at their hideout near Dewetsdorp. With a bit of luck, he might be able to pick up their trail and track them down.

Staying as low as possible, he scrambled off the outcrop, leapt onto his horse and set off at a gallop.

It was almost noon before he came across a fresh trail, although the number of tracks puzzled him—more than what he expected from two horses, but fresh and heading in the right direction. He followed the tracks to the banks of a river crossing and picked them up on the far bank, but again his sixth sense nagged at him. Now there seemed to be fewer tracks than before, although the horses had broken into a gallop that muddled the imprints on the trail. He pressed ahead but eventually lost the tracks over rocky terrain. Cursing, he backtracked and picked up the tracks where they had left the trail.

It was nearly dusk when he found the horses grazing contentedly near a stand of trees. He couldn't see anyone, yet the horses were saddled. He approached cautiously, his rifle at the ready, scanning the area for any signs of the riders. There were none.

"Goddammit," he swore at the unresponsive landscape and unsympathetic horses. A wasted effort—his mother and sister nowhere to be found.

It was too dark now to track anything more than the stars in the sky. He watered his horse and set off for Dewetsdorp, the Southern Cross pointing the way just as surely as if it were the finger of God.

It was noon when he reached the town and rejoined the general's commando at their hideout. There was no news of his mother and sister. A week later when the commando moved out, there was still no sign or news of them. He decided to wait, convinced that Dewetsdorp was the most likely place to hear news of their whereabouts.

Two weeks later he was still waiting. The only news of any

kind was of a commando led by General Jan Smuts moving south towards the Cape Colony with about 250 men. Perhaps his mother had found Smuts's commando instead.

It took several days of hard riding before he caught up with Smuts near the canyon where the Orange River tumbled out of the mountains of Basutoland. But his relief was short-lived—nobody had seen his mother and sister, and all the talk was of the Tommies tightening their grip on the republics. He decided to stay with Smuts—at least he was among friends, including Deneys Reitz, his friend from Spion Kop. The search for his family would have to wait.

"Uncle Jannie," as everyone called the general, was only twenty-eight years old. He was tall and thin with a girl's complexion, wore a short pointed beard in the French style, and had a law degree from a famous university in England. But there was nothing soft or girlish about Smuts's gray-blue eyes or his military prowess. Before Pretoria fell, he had spirited away almost £500,000 in gold and cash from under Lord Roberts's nose and taken all the Boers' reserve ammunition. He now planned to open a third front in the Cape Colony, where he hoped to inspire settled Afrikaners to join the fight against the Tommies.

The day after William joined the commando, as he waited to pay his respects outside the general's tent, he overheard Smuts talking. "The horror is beyond description," the general was saying. "The veld is covered with slaughtered cattle and horses, sheep and goats, and the dams are full of rotting animals. Surely such outrages on man and nature will lead to certain doom."

He edged closer to the tent, hoping to hear more news, when, without warning, the tent flap was suddenly swept aside and the general stepped through the opening, almost crashing into him.

"Who the devil are you?" Smuts's eyes burned with indignation.

William thrust out his hand. "De Beer, General," he said in a rush to cover his embarrassment. "I was at Spion Kop and with General de Wet at Sannah's Post. Now I want to join you, General, to continue the fight." He stood stiffly, his hand hovering in the space between them.

Smuts's frown turned friendly. "Ahh, yes. Good to have you, De Beer." The general's handshake was firm but brief. "Better still if you know a route across the Orange River into the Cape. The canyon is deep, the cliffs are steep, and the Tommies control the usual crossing points."

He shook his head. "Sorry, General, I've never been this way before."

"Too bad," said Smuts. "So, you fought with De Wet at Sannah's Post—a brilliant victory. Good, good, we need good men. We—"

The general was interrupted by a group of commandos galloping into the camp shouting news of Tommy troops closing in on their position. The commando hastily struck camp and, in the dead of night, followed a local farmer down a precipitous trail that cut through the canyon to the crossing at Kiba Drift that, unknown to Smuts, the Tommies had inexplicably abandoned the day before.

The next day, as the sun's rays washed over the depths of the canyon, William splashed across the Orange River into the Cape Colony with his new commando.

William was mesmerized. The ocean was impossibly big, a shimmering canvas of aquamarine with specks of roiling white as far as the eye could see. Even his horse seemed intimidated as its hooves sank into the soft sand.

Then one of the men shouted "The sea!" and galloped down the dune towards the water, setting off a stampede as sixty or seventy men vied to be first to the water. Within minutes the men had stripped off their clothes, thrown off their saddles and were riding bareback through the surf.

The exuberance was intoxicating after so many months of tension, privation and discomfort. The Tommy pursuit had been relentless. But Smuts had proved himself equal to the task and had led the commando from one side of the country to the other, through multiple skirmishes and narrow escapes, before finally calling a halt a few miles from the Atlantic coast. And, on a bright and sunny day, the general let it be known that those who had never seen the ocean could report for an outing near the mouth of the Olifants River. In some measure it helped ease the disappointment of failing to inspire an Afrikaner uprising in the Cape Colony.

William emerged from the sea after several minutes, led his horse to a makeshift corral on the beach, then lay down on the sand with his head resting on his saddlebags. As he did so, he heard a scrunching inside the bag and recalled the newspaper he had salvaged from a train weeks before after a treacherous night spent evading a Tommy trap by sliding off a muddy mountain in the dark.

He smiled. He had not had a chance to read the news, but now seemed a perfect time to do it while basking naked in the sun beside the seashore in the middle of a war. A glorious feeling of contentment coursed through his body as he retrieved the newspaper and settled back to catch up on some news.

The news was not good, outdated though it was. Kitchener had supplemented Roberts's scorched-earth policy with a network of eight thousand fortified blockhouses, guarded by more than fifty thousand troops and sixteen thousand African scouts, patrolled by flying columns of mounted troops. The blockhouses were all within rifle range of each other and connected by barbed wire, covering thirty-seven hundred square miles, a grid of steel and bullets designed to trap the Boer commandos like rats in a cage.

To add insult to injury, Smuts's commando was described as riffraff and Kitchener had called on all Boers under arms to surrender.

William snorted and was about to toss the paper aside when another article caught his attention. He read it several times before its full import penetrated his sun-drenched contentment.

A woman from England, Emily Hobhouse, had caused a scandal with claims that thousands of Boer women and children were dying in special Tommy camps. And it reported seventy thousand women and children already in the camps with a death rate of over three hundred for every thousand prisoners, and that more women and children were being forced off their farms every day and taken to the camps. The article quoted a British politician saying the war was being conducted by "methods of barbarism," while another described "a barrier of dead children's bodies" rising up between the British and the Boer races in South Africa.

William stared at the article, his numbed senses defaulting to denial, until the next paragraph brought the horror home. Hobhouse had been to a camp outside Bloemfontein, where she discovered "a death rate such as had never been known except in the times of the Great Plagues" and where "the whole talk was of death—who died yesterday, who lay dying today, who would be dead tomorrow."

The rest of the article blurred under a veil of emotion, but he had read enough. Had his mother and sister been caught in Kitchener's net and thrown into the Bloemfontein camp? The more he thought of their escape from the farm and their failure to reach Dewetsdorp, the more fearful he became.

The ocean seemed suddenly threatening, the salt air corrosive, the beach like quicksand, the sunshine like the devil's embrace. He had to speak to the general immediately. He pulled on his trousers, saddled his horse and galloped back to camp.

His route to camp intersected the road from the south, where he came upon an astonishing sight—a cart with two British officers carrying a white flag being escorted by his friend Deneys Reitz and two other commandos. Deneys was tight-lipped. The Tommy officers carried a message for Smuts and had to be taken directly to the general.

William waited impatiently in the shade of a tree until Smuts came out of his tent and bade farewell to the British officers. Most of the men were sure the British had offered to surrender and to restore the Boer republics. But instead of calling the men together to deliver the good news, the general said nothing and retired for the night.

With Smuts inaccessible, William did the next best thing and looked for Deneys. He found him sitting on a campstool near the perimeter of the camp, smoking his pipe, gazing into a smoldering fire pit.

"Bit dangerous sitting in the firelight smoking," said William as he approached and sat on the ground near Reitz. "This is not Spion Kop. Damn Tommies could be anywhere."

"Ag, no, my friend. That danger has passed," replied his friend with surprising equanimity.

"What do you mean? What's going on, Deneys? The men are really confused."

"Ja, man, I know. It's a confusing time." He paused to draw on his pipe. "Smuts showed me the message from Kitchener. The Tommies want our leaders to go to a meeting to discuss peace."

"About bloody time," said William. "The sooner the damn Tommies give up and go home, the better." His bitterness mixed awkwardly with relief, as though oil and water were being compressed through the same narrow channel into his soul. Despite himself—for just a moment—the thought of peace transported him to another time and place.

"Ja, I agree," said Reitz. "But it's not that simple."

"Huh? What are you talking about? They surrender and go back to bloody England, and we get to go back to our farms and live in peace in our republics. Seems pretty simple to me."

"It doesn't look good for us, William," Ritz said, lowering his voice. "Smuts is not optimistic."

"But... but we won, didn't we?" he stammered as his stomach muscles tightened.

Reitz took a long pull on his pipe and slowly shook his head. Then he lifted his head and gazed into the night sky as though seeking an explanation from a silent and distant God.

"Jesus, Deneys, what are you saying? It can't be true." He could feel his earlier relief congealing in the pit of his stomach.

"It's true, William. Unless we surrender, they will kill us all," he said with unexpected bluntness.

It felt like his heart had been ripped from his chest—like Retief must have felt at Dingane's place of execution. As time stood still, images flooded his mind's eye—the bloody battles, the murders and deaths, the burnt farms and scorched earth, and now the camps where women and children were dying like flies, perhaps even his own mother and sister. Was it all for naught?

He forced his thoughts back to the present. "When is the meeting?"

"Smuts and two aides leave tomorrow. I'm going with him. A British ship will take us to Cape Town. From there we'll go north by train."

"To where?"

"Vereeniging. We meet on the banks of the Vaal."

"Any chance I can go with?" he asked, his hopes rising. Vereeniging was not far from Bloemfontein and perhaps from his mother and sister.

"Ag, sorry, man. Smuts is lucky to be allowed even two aides. And the other is his brother-in-law."

William looked off into the darkness, his options as bleak as the inky horizon. Despite what Reitz had told him about the war, he didn't trust the Tommies. But there was no way to get through Kitchener's barbed wire and blockhouses alive if he tried to go it alone on horseback.

"When will you be back?" he asked.

"As soon as the meeting is over. We'll come back to deliver the news."

William was silent for a few minutes. "Deneys, you must do something for me."

"What?"

"Help me find my mother and sister."

"How so? Aren't they on the farm?"

"Read this," he said, handing Reitz the newspaper and pointing to the article about the camps.

Reitz read intently, his brow increasingly furrowed. When he was done, he looked across the firelight at William. "My God, William. I heard rumors, but if even half of this is true it's more terrible than I ever imagined."

"Does the general know of these things?"

"I'm not sure. I don't think so. He has spoken of camps for our people, but we thought the camps were for their safety." Reitz shook his head. "So what do you want me to do?"

"Make sure Smuts reads this. Then find out what you can at the meeting. Ask if there are lists of names showing who is in the camps. Start with the Bloemfontein camp. If my mother and sister are not listed there, then try nearby camps." He swallowed hard and paused to check his emotions. "But Smuts must be told, Deneys. He must stop the dying. How can we make peace with people who do such things to our women and children?" he insisted as fear and anger churned through his gut in equal measure.

"I will do my best, William, but I can't promise anything."

"Ja, I understand." He wiped his nose on the back of his hand and got to his feet.

"Before you go, William, there's something you should know."

"Ja. What now?"

"Look at this," said Reitz with a grim smile as held up another page of the newspaper. "Kitchener says any Boer caught wearing a British uniform will be executed on the spot as a spy."

"Ha! That means you and me both," scoffed William as he brushed the lapel of his friend's British tunic. Both wore clothes taken from the Tommies after Smuts's victory at the Battle at Elands River over the death-or-glory boys of the 17th Lancers, renowned for their heroics in the Charge of the Light Brigade against Russian guns in the Crimea. The chance to replace their rags with sturdy clothes had been irresistible, even if they were British uniforms. "So, my good man," he added in a mock English accent, "we are all spies...and guerrillas...and riffraff."

The two men laughed and shook hands, a brief flash of levity before the reality of their situation and news of the camps overwhelmed the moment. With a somber nod to his friend, William turned and walked away into the night.

14

ANOTHER THREAD IN THE KNOT

1900

Susannah could not believe what was happening—that it must surely be a terrible dream to be dispelled as soon as she woke. But there was nothing dreamlike about the jarring gallop of the horse beneath her or the awkward press of the black boy against her chest as they entered the small village, already deep in shadow from the setting sun.

The village appeared deserted except for the telltale signs of smoke leaking through the roofs and doorways of several of the round, thatched-roof huts set in a ragged circle around an open central area. The boy led them into the heart of the village, then leapt to the ground and raced into one of the huts.

Susannah looked inquiringly at Henry, who nodded reassuringly.

Several villagers appeared before the boy emerged from the hut with a sturdy middle-aged woman, who kept a protective hand on his shoulder. She wore an off-white wrap from her chest to below her knees and an ochre-colored blanket draped over her shoulders. An intricately beaded necklace lay across her chest, its white beads like night stars against her complexion.

Henry addressed the woman. "*Dumela*, mother," he said with

great deference. "I am Henry Mandela from the Transkei. Forgive me for intruding, mother, and that I stay on my horse, and that I do not speak your Sotho very well."

The woman smiled. "And I do not speak your Xhosa very well, Henry Mandela from the Transkei—my tongue does not click so easily as yours. I don't know why the gods gave us so many languages—perhaps they too speak many languages—but they all seem to agree on English. That's what the missionary told me," she added with a laugh, "so let us speak that language." Then her features clouded. "But I see you travel with two white women, and that you are dressed as a soldier. That is very strange...in any language."

Henry nodded. "It is a difficult story, mother. But I beg you, this young one is very sick—she has been kicked by a horse and treated badly by the soldiers. And that one," he said, pointing, "is her mother."

The woman stepped closer to look up at Esmé, draped like a half-empty sack over Henry's arm. After a moment's hesitation, she said, "Very well, my Xhosa friend, take her into my cooking hut. Jonas will show you."

Then the woman turned to her. "You are a Boer?"

Susannah was caught off guard by the question—it sounded like an accusation. She nodded tentatively. "We had a farm at Sannah's Post."

"Ahh. I was told of a battle at that place between the soldiers and the Boers. I heard it did not go well for the Boers living there after the battle."

Susannah choked back a cry and covered her mouth. The woman's features softened as she reached up, inviting her to dismount. She felt her chest constrict. For a moment the woman's arms and hands distorted into black vines reaching up to drag her off her horse into the abyss. She held her breath as their hands touched. The woman's firm grip was disconcerting, especially when she did not let go as they came face-to-face.

"You will be safe here," said the woman, the smile in her eyes as warm as the tone of her voice.

It was all too much. Susannah's reserve ruptured and a flood of emotion wracked her body. The woman responded with a deep sigh that seemed to fill the void between them before she folded her into her arms. Susannah stiffened at the unexpected intimacy but slowly relaxed as the woman rocked her from side to side. In some inexplicable way, the embrace seemed to represent a truth as comforting as it was unsettling.

The villagers watched in silence before drifting back to their huts.

"Come inside," said the woman after a while. "It is getting cold."

Susannah was relieved by the prospect of spending at least one night under shelter, but her brow creased in distaste as soon as she entered the hut. The smell and gloom of the cramped interior were like an alien and impenetrable fog through which her sensibilities all but refused to pass.

In the center of the floor stood a cooking pot on an iron grate over a depression in the floor containing the embers of a fire. There was just enough light from the embers for her to make out where Esmé had been laid under a plaid blanket. She knelt to smooth her child's hair, vaguely aware of Henry and the boy off to one side.

"Show me," said the woman.

Susannah carefully unwrapped the scarf from Esmé's head. The wound was a mess of tangled hair and dried blood. The woman knelt beside her and gently fingered the area of the wound. Esmé whimpered.

"Jonas, light the candle and bring it to me," the woman said.

"Then put some water in the pot over the fire and bring me the sharp knife."

Susannah gasped. The woman looked up, her eyebrows arched inquiringly. "I am afraid for her life," whispered Susannah, swallowing hard. "And afraid of the knife."

The woman nodded. "What is your name?"

"Susannah... My child is Esmé."

"I am called Miriam, a name the English missionary gave me."

"It is a good name," said Susannah as Jonas approached with a knife. "Please be careful," she added, her voice trembling. "She is all I have left."

"I must use the knife and I must clean it before I can clean the wound," said Miriam, dipping the knife blade into the boiling water and wiping it dry. "The missionary taught me—he said 'Cleanliness is next to godliness.'"

Then she turned towards Esmé. With Jonas holding the lighted candle, she carefully cut away the patch of hair surrounding the gash before washing the wound with warm water. After rewrapping it with one of her own scarfs, she turned to Susannah.

"In the morning I will mix some medicine—it is too dark now to find what I need. Give her some water and let her sleep. I will sleep here with you tonight where it is warm. My sleeping hut is too cold for the child."

Susannah nodded as she lifted Esmé's head to dribble water into her flaccid mouth. Then she lay down with one arm under her child's head. As an afterthought, she turned to Miriam. "If I need to go outside in the night, where do I go?"

"Behind the hut about thirty steps. It is clear ground and the moon will be high. Wake me if you need help. Tomorrow I will show you a better place."

"Thank you, Miriam. You are very kind." With that, she closed her eyes, as much out of weariness as wanting to shield herself from the reality of her surroundings. Her skin crawled with visions of what might be sharing the dirt floor with her—so many of God's creatures were tolerable only so long as they kept their distance and knew their place.

She could hear Esmé's labored breathing, the hiss and crackle of the fire, and Miriam and Henry whispering to each other. She was uncomfortable in so many ways, and now she also felt like an eavesdropper.

"Jonas will show you where to sleep," Miriam was saying. "He told me about the cattle—that is very bad for the village. But I am glad you found my boy."

"Thank you, mother," he said. "Have the soldiers troubled you?"

"We have seen them, but they have not been here."

"And the Boer fighters?"

"Ow," said Miriam. "They have come many times. They take our food and leave us with nothing."

Susannah went rigid. This was the first she had heard of such a thing. And here she was at the villagers' mercy, asking for their help.

After a silence Miriam asked, "Do you know who killed the cattle? Jonas said they were dead, but he did not say how."

"It was the soldiers, mother," said Henry. "They are killing everything and burning all the food and the farms."

"I don't understand. Why do they do such things?"

"Because of the Boer fighters, mother. The soldiers cannot find them and they cannot beat them, so they kill all the animals, destroy the crops and burn the farms."

"But what about the women and children—like these two?"

"I don't know, mother. Some are just left after the farms are burnt, some are chased off the farms and told to find their men, and some are sent to camps."

"Camps?"

"The soldiers have made many camps for the people, camps with tents and food and hospitals. Some are near the big towns. That is all I know."

"How do you know these things, Henry?"

"The soldiers made me a scout, mother. I heard things. And that is why I wear these clothes."

"Do you think they will leave our people alone?"

"I do not know, mother. Some of our people help the soldiers, but some help the Boers, and that makes the soldiers angry. They want to finish the war, so I cannot say what they will do with our people."

"Well then, we will face it when it comes. Good night, Henry Mandela, we will talk in the morning. And then you will tell me the story of how you came to be a scout for the soldiers."

"I will do this, mother, but I must ask a great favor of you."

"What is it?"

"I must change my clothes, mother. If the soldiers come to the village, they will recognize me by my clothes and shoot me as a traitor."

"I will give you some clothes of my husband in the morning. He went to the mines."

"Thank you, mother. Rest well."

Susannah couldn't imagine resting well after what she'd just heard. Her chest felt tight as she lay in the dark, her eyes wide open, afraid yet hopeful, thinking of the camps Henry had described. They sounded so civilized, so comfortable, so close—perhaps even as near as Bloemfontein and her parents.

Susannah's discomfort grew as days turned into weeks. She was increasingly troubled, unnerved by the fact that the preordained order she was accustomed to did not also prevail in the village. Instead of being at the center of the village universe surrounded by subservient beings orbiting in silent obedience, she found herself living in a peripheral universe of her own making, an unfamiliar reality that did not correspond to her worldview or the deepest convictions of her faith.

She also felt like a fugitive, needing shelter but wanting to escape. But there was no escape—even to the camps—with Esmé still so sick. Despite every herbal remedy the villagers were able to concoct, the wound did not heal and Esmé did not recover. And Henry insisted they could not leave until Esmé was well enough to ride. Without his support, she knew they were not going anywhere.

Her only refuge was her faith. Yet even that rock became unstable and slippery. For the more she observed, the more the whole village enterprise seemed almost noble, not at all the embodiment of heathen ignorance and savage cruelty she had been led to believe after the Great Murder. At every turn, the dignity and graciousness of the matriarchs, the industry and good humor of the young mothers, and the respectful obedience of the children confronted her. Somehow these poor villagers contrived to be rich in good works, always ready to share their huts, their food, their meager possessions, and to exemplify the very traits she struggled so hard to emulate from the teachings of Jesus.

Was it possible God could find these villagers worthy?

But she had no sooner entertained that possibility than her image of heaven became a confused muddle of villagers commingling with her at heaven's gate. She couldn't imagine standing in the same line as them, let alone behind them, to pass into God's presence. Then again, she also couldn't imagine heaven having separate entrances for black people, or separate places for them to live, or separate fountains of life from which they should drink. But if God treated these villagers as her equal in heaven, how could she treat them as less than her equal on earth?

Her thoughts churned. If all that were true, what did it mean for her place among the villagers? To engage in village activities as an equal would mean doing as the elders and matriarchs of the village told her. But to submit to such an inverted order would completely undermine the foundations of her identity.

And there was another, more worldly issue that daily challenged her sense of propriety and kept her constantly off-balance—the villagers showed no modesty and altogether too much flesh. It was one thing to appreciate women's breasts as purely functional, but the same could not be said for male nudity. Thankfully, there was less of that to be seen, although the tiny loincloths left little to the imagination.

As the months passed, the prospect of finding De Wet's commando receded to the point where she no longer mentioned it to Henry. His lack of action, Esmé's weakness and her own inactivity all seemed to conspire to extend her stay in the village indefinitely.

It was midwinter when she finally turned to Miriam for a solution one night after they had finished their meal of samp and beans. Esmé was lying on her mat while she and Miriam sat crossed-legged near the heat of the cooking pot. The smoke blended with the aroma from the pot to create a comforting blanket of warmth and security.

"Miriam," she began in a soft voice, not looking up. "I must ask for your help."

"Yes, Susannah, what is it?"

She hesitated, still uncomfortable being addressed by her first name. At least Henry stuck to the traditional ways. "I must do something to help you in the hut and in the village."

"Yes," said Miriam. "You must."

If there was an implied rebuke, she chose to ignore it. "I mean I want to help...each day...with the work in your huts and in the village."

"What can you do?" asked Miriam.

She looked hard at Miriam, trying to discern any disrespect. Then she realized it was a straightforward question. It was widely known that the Boer women had multiple servants and reasonable to assume the servants did all the work.

"That is why I need your help," she said. "You must tell me what you want me to do. If I don't know how to do it, then you must show me." She realized a moment later that even her request for help sounded like a mandate. "Please," she added.

Miriam gazed into the embers, her expression stony. After a while she nodded. "Start with washing clothes by the stream. I will show you tomorrow."

"Thank you, Miriam," she said. "I would like that."

Her spirits lifted over the following months as her daily routine acquired purpose and distracted her from constantly worrying about Esmé. She found she enjoyed washing clothes with the village women, who sang and laughed and chattered while beating their clothes on the flat rocks beside the stream. She also learned how to crush kernels of corn to make samp, became proficient at making the fire and cooking meat and beans in the great cast-iron pot, and proved adept at sewing and mending clothes. She fetched and carried, balancing loads on her head like the other women, and learned some conversational Sotho and words to the songs the women had for every occasion.

As she reflected on her circumstances over Christmas that year, she felt strangely blessed, as though she had uncovered some essential part of herself in community with the villagers. In the stillness before dawn on Christmas Day, as she thought about the birth of her savior in a humble feedbox in a village stable, she came to think of her experience in the lowly village as her own salvation—physical salvation from the threat of British capture and spiritual salvation from the bondage of church doctrine.

She had no idea what lay ahead, but for the present it felt as though a huge weight had been lifted from her soul, as though she had been born again into a new relationship with the people around her and the savior within her.

15

A BARBED THREAD

1900

Susannah was restless as she lay in the blackness of the hut, unable to dispel a growing sense of foreboding. It had started the day two men from a neighboring village brought the news. They had been in Bloemfontein and had seen the massed-troop strength of the British and heard the talk among servants.

Something big was being planned, some big push to end the war with the Boers.

Feeling trapped and claustrophobic inside the stuffy hut, she rose quietly and headed into the night—she had to clear her head and decide what to do. The Southern Cross hung at an awkward angle overhead as she crossed the clearing in the center of the huts towards the high ground behind the village. She picked her way cautiously up the gentle slope to the crest.

Perhaps the morning sun would illuminate the way ahead. But her eyes grew heavy as she sat wrapped in the warmth of her sleeping blanket, gazing towards the southeast, her legs drawn up against her chest, her chin resting on her forearms.

She came awake with a start. Something had disturbed the peaceful rhythm of the early morning. It took a few moments to shake off the mantle of fatigue and attune her senses to the landscape. As she watched the blood-red sun pull free of the horizon, she saw a plume of dust drift across the sun's early radiance.

She squinted, wishing she had Johan's telescope. Then she heard it, a faint but steady thrum of hooves, just as a silhouetted line of horsemen emerged onto higher ground. Despite the distance and the dust cloud, the conical helmets were unmistakable. Her stomach tightened as she stared at the devil's minions steadily approaching under the flag of an alien empire. She turned, scrambled down the hill and ran into the village towards Miriam who was emerging from her hut.

"Talking to your god again, Susannah, so early in the morning?" she called out with a smile.

"The soldiers...they're coming!" she cried breathlessly, before covering her mouth with hands tented as though in prayer that her eyes had been deceived, her words spoken in error.

Miriam's eyes went wide as the smile faded. "You have seen them?"

She nodded. "About thirty, on horses."

"Ow. This is not a good thing," said Miriam. "I am afraid for you. And for us."

Henry emerged from his hut. "I heard you talk, madam. How far are they?"

"Close," she whispered. "Maybe ten minutes."

"What do you think, Henry?" asked Miriam. "What should we do?"

He shook his head. "I cannot say, mother. You must ask the village elders."

"You are the scout, Henry Mandela. Go and see the soldiers for yourself. Then tell the elders what you have seen." She turned to Susannah. "Come. You must eat quickly," she said, heading into her cooking hut.

Henry appeared in the doorway to the hut soon after, breathing hard, his forehead glistening with perspiration. "I have seen the soldiers, mother," he reported, "and spoken with the elders. They are afraid. They say the soldiers will think the village is helping the Boers."

"It is true what they say," said Miriam.

Susannah's stomach turned. "I am very sorry I brought this trouble to your village," she said.

"Trouble is everywhere in our land," said Miriam stoically. "Henry did the right thing to bring you here, but trouble has followed you."

Henry said, "I will take the women and go quickly, mother, before the soldiers see them. Where is the young madam?"

"Inside," said Miriam with a nod towards her hut. "But she is still too sick, and you will not be able to get away. They will catch you, and it will not go well for you when they see you are helping the Boers."

A deep crease furrowed her brow, as though she were trying to squeeze a solution from its folds. "I will go with them," she announced. "It's the only way. We will not get far. The soldiers will find us, but they will think I'm a maid—they will think nothing of it."

"But—" he began.

"You must stay in the village as one of our people," continued Miriam. "The soldiers cannot tell the difference between our peoples. Now go fetch the horses. Tell Jonas to pack food in the saddlebags. And make sure we have water."

Susannah felt helpless as others decided her fate. Within minutes Henry appeared with the horses and Miriam emerged from her hut with Esmé. The girl looked bewildered at having to leave the warmth and security of the hut at such short notice. Henry held her steady while Miriam clambered onto his horse in a determined if not graceful manner.

"But you promised to take us to General de Wet," Susannah blurted unexpectedly, her tone reproachful, reviving the original plan as though it had been made yesterday.

He shook his head. "I'm very sorry, madam. My heart is heavy, but I cannot do the thing I told you, and now it is too late."

She clamped her jaw, breathing hard. Henry's response was so definitive, so disheartening. Where once there had been hope, now there was none.

"This is the best way, madam. Miriam will keep you safe," he said as he handed her the reins of her horse and offered his cupped hands. Wordlessly, Susannah stepped into his hands with one foot and swung her other leg over the saddle. Then he hoisted Esmé into the saddle in front of her mother.

She looked down at him, her arm around Esmé's waist, the silence broken only by a snort from one of the horses.

"Goodbye, Henry. Thank you for helping us, for bringing us this far. And I hope you are right about my son, that he is still alive."

Then she tilted in the saddle and reached down to him with her free hand, careful to maintain her balance.

After a moment's hesitation, he reached up and took her hand in both of his. "Go safely, madam," he said. "And may the sickness of your child pass like the rain."

She held his hands, saying nothing, unsettled by an undercurrent of emotion that threatened to overwhelm her.

Miriam interrupted the moment. "Come, Susannah, we must go," she said firmly, causing Susannah to straighten up in her saddle and Henry to release her hand. "And you must do something for me, Henry Mandela."

"Yes, mother, anything."

"Take care of Jonas. Keep my boy safe."

"I will, mother."

"And make this horse move."

He grinned and gave the horse a slap on the rump.

"Goodbye, Henry Mandela from the Transkei," called Miriam over her shoulder as the horse lurched into a slow walk.

"Goodbye, mother," he called. "Go well."

Susannah was terrified.

She had escaped the soldiers at Sannah's Post, but it now seemed every Tommy in the land was trying to catch her. Miriam assured her she knew the best route and led them southwards over rolling hills and through gentle valleys, the flow of the landscape marred only by the occasional sweetly sick trace of death being carried on a shifting breeze.

"We must stop, Miriam," she said as dusk began to fall after a long, hot day in the saddle. They were moving slowly up a gently sloped hill covered in wispy grass with no natural shelter in sight.

"We should go further," replied Miriam. "I know a good valley."

"Tomorrow, Miriam. I cannot go further today... We will find your valley tomorrow."

"This is not a good place to stop," persisted Miriam. "I will go a short way to see what is ahead," she said, pointing to the hill in front of them. "If there is a better place, we will go there."

Susannah opened her mouth—the impulse to rebuke Miriam teetered on the tip of her tongue—but she said nothing as she lowered Esmé to the ground.

The boundaries of their relationship were still an evolving puzzle. She had convinced herself that Miriam was her equal before God in the peaceful coexistence of the village. But now, running for her life, when survival was her most base instinct, she found herself defaulting to the beliefs that had nurtured her through her formative years. Yet she also knew Miriam had little reason to fear the soldiers and was trying to avoid them only to protect Esmé and herself.

She sat down in the tall grass with Esmé's head on her lap. Their two horses grazed nearby, their reins trailing lazily through the grass. She tried to concentrate on their limited options, but within minutes her eyes closed and her head sagged. She did not hear Miriam return.

"Come," said Miriam brusquely, shaking her awake. "There's a farm over the hill. The house is burned and the people are gone, but it will be a good shelter. We must go quickly before it gets dark."

She stared blankly at Miriam's outstretched hand until the prospect of spending the night in a farmhouse sank in. She took the offered hand and pulled herself upright, then helped Esmé onto her horse and followed.

The farmhouse was an irregular shell with gaping holes where doors and windows had been, and broken walls supporting nothing but the night sky. She headed for the main house, but Miriam called her towards the remains of the barn, that it was a much better shelter than the house. She was too tired to argue and followed. Once inside, she lowered Esmé to the ground and cleared a sleeping area in a corner while Miriam took take care of the horses.

"The horses are tied to what's left of a plow," said Miriam returning with their saddlebags. "We must eat and sleep… Tomorrow will be another long day." She passed around some dried meat and a canteen. Esmé drank sparingly but refused the meat—she just sat and stared vacantly at her mother.

"She will get cold tonight," said Susannah. "She is already shaking."

"Then we must keep her warm... between us," replied Miriam, clearing some space for herself on the other side of Esmé.

Susannah nodded. Her world was unrecognizable—her home destroyed, her husband dead, her son missing, her daughter barely alive—and the country of her birth a cruel travesty of God's promise. Sleeping on the floor with a black woman in the burned-out remains of a stranger's barn seemed to add insult to injury, to twist the knife of despair deep into the wounded core of her being.

"I'm very tired," said Susannah as she pushed Esmé gently down and adjusted the threadbare blanket that covered her. Then she lay back, staring up at the night sky through the roofless barn, the stillness broken only by Esmé's strained breathing.

After a while she turned and wrapped an arm over Esmé's shoulders. As she did, she brushed against Miriam's arm already draped around Esmé. She stiffened. The band of comforting arms around Esmé was pleasing yet troubling, for how would Esmé know which arm was her mother's?

Her tired brain wrestled with why it was important until all thought drifted into blackness.

Susannah came awake slowly, reluctantly, her body aching after a long, cold night on an unforgiving floor. She looked around in the bleak early morning light at the unfamiliar surroundings. Esmé was restless. Her brow glistened with sweat even as her body shook. Miriam was nowhere to be seen.

She was lifting Esmé's head for a drink when Miriam appeared in the doorway.

"We must go," said Miriam without preamble.

Susannah bristled. "I'm not ready to go anywhere. Neither is my child."

"We must go," insisted Miriam. "This place is not safe."

"Last night you said it was safe! What has happened since last night to change your mind?"

"The day has come... that's what happened."

"What?"

"The day has come, Susannah. Now I see danger that I did not see before."

She gave a suppressed snort. "Ag, nonsense, Miriam. You are just seeing ghosts in this old place."

"Ghosts do not wear uniforms and ride horses," insisted Miriam. "I cannot tell which way they are moving. They seem to go this way and that way like a dog searching for a bone."

"Ag, no, dear Lord," groaned Susannah, her heart sinking as a vision of Tommy horsemen scouring the earth for her leapt to mind. "Loving Jesus, help us."

Miriam stared impassively at her. "We cannot wait for your Jesus to help us. We must go now," she said as she lifted Esmé to her feet. "Help me get her onto her horse."

The dust trails were immediately evident behind the low rolling hills. Miriam angled away from the invisible riders towards a shallow stream, where she quickly filled their canteens before urging them towards a rocky outcrop beyond. "But don't go near the top," she warned. "The soldiers will see us."

Miriam led them cautiously around the right shoulder of the rocky outcrop but then abruptly reined in her horse. Susannah came up beside her and gasped. A barbed fence stretched like a spiteful, alien presence across the benign veld about fifty yards ahead.

"Stay here," said Miriam as she dismounted. "I will climb the rocks to see if there is a way past the fence."

"But you said the Tommies will see you," she protested.

Miriam thought for a moment. "It's a chance we must take. We cannot go back, so we must find a way forward."

"Then I'm coming too," said Susannah, dismounting, determined not to leave her fate to Miriam's judgment. "Esmé will be safe for a few minutes," she added as she followed Miriam up the steep incline to the top of the rocky ridge.

Susannah saw the tower as soon as her head cleared the ridge. It was off to her left about a hundred yards away and, off to her right, a second tower loomed in the distance. The round, two-level structures rose from the earth like the devil's handiwork, with multiple ports in their walls like eye sockets from which the towers seemed to watch malevolently over all things and in all directions.

She stood up to get a better view.

"Get down, Susannah," hissed Miriam, pulling on her skirts. "They will see you!"

She ignored Miriam. The towers were so strange, unlike anything she had ever seen before, except that they appeared to support a fence that ran between them and continued beyond the towers in both directions. But she recognized the flag fluttering above the closest tower—it told her all she needed to know.

Something glinted in the early morning sunlight from the tower. As she puzzled over its significance, horsemen materialized at the tower's base, galloping directly towards the rocky outcrop. The tower had come alive and was reaching out to them.

Susannah ducked and scrambled down the outcrop behind Miriam in a tumble of dust and stones.

"Miriam," she began breathlessly, "you must—"

"The soldiers will be here any minute," interrupted Miriam, also gasping for breath. "You must hide...I will let them chase me."

"What? No! We will—"

"They saw you and are coming fast," pressed Miriam as she led the horses back around the shoulder of the rocky outcrop to where Esmé waited mutely, showing no sign of alarm. "You must stay here, Susannah. I will ride where they will see me and chase me."

"But…what about us? What will we do?" cried Susannah, her earlier resolve not to rely on Miriam disintegrating as fast as the horsemen raced toward the outcrop.

"Hide in the day…move at night…and stay strong," said Miriam, squeezing her hands. Then she mounted and kicked the horse in its flanks. The horse lunged forward, perhaps as much in fright as in obedience. Clinging precariously to the neck of the galloping horse, Miriam raced down the outcrop at an angle away from the tower and the Tommy horsemen.

Susannah gaped, her throat caked with dust and fear as the chasing horsemen thundered past the rocky outcrop. She knew they would catch Miriam. She also knew she could not escape without Miriam's help. And if she could not get away from them, perhaps she would be better off with them. Maybe these men would be different, take pity on a white woman with a sick child. They surely could not be as evil as the soldiers at Sannah's Post.

She rehearsed what she hoped would be a plausible story, took a deep breath and, with the reins of Esmé's horse in one hand, dug her heels into the flanks of her horse and moved slowly down the exposed side of the outcrop. She did not have long to wait before she saw the horsemen returning to the tower, their uniform khaki appearance broken in the middle of their ranks by Miriam's multicolored garb.

She was almost paralyzed by fear as the soldiers approached. Then, just as she thought her life's breath must surely be crushed by the grip of fear, her vision filled with the image of her heroine—Joan of Arc—a farm girl full of faith astride her horse, leading the French to victory at Orléans during the Hundred Years' War against the English, the enemy of Joan's beloved homeland, the same enemy who four centuries later now made war on her Boer people and their homeland.

Joan had been burned at a stake. Jesus had been nailed to a cross. They had not balked. Neither would she.

As the gap closed between her and the horsemen, she felt the fragments of her fear fall away, an unfamiliar courage envelop her like the body armor Joan had worn, and her heart fill with an otherworldly resolve.

One of the soldiers raised his hand and brought the other horsemen to a halt. Then the soldiers dismounted, keeping their horses between them and the rocky outcrop. Perhaps they feared an ambush. She waved and smiled, bemused by their caution, having shown none just minutes before when they chased Miriam past the same outcrop.

She stopped and waited. After a brief standoff, the soldier who had raised his arm remounted and rode towards her, his rifle prominently displayed with its butt on his hip, its barrel angled towards her.

"Good morning, young man," she called out in English when the rider was about twenty feet from her.

The soldier stopped. "What are you doing in this area?"

"I'm a hands-upper," she said. "I'm trying to reach Bloemfontein. My mother and father live there. But my daughter fell from her horse and I lost my way. I have been told we will be safe in the city until the war is over."

The soldier was silent as he appeared to consider her story. Then he spoke again, only slightly less curtly than before. "What about the black woman?"

"Ag, just a stupid maid," she said. "I told her you would help us, but she was frightened when she saw you coming so fast. She ran away before I could stop her."

Susannah held her breath as the solider looked from her towards the outcrop and around at Miriam, apparently considering all angles of the story. Then he turned and signaled to the waiting column to remount and approach.

"You're right," he said, addressing her with a tight smile. "We do have special places for people like you."

"And my maid?"

"She can go with you."

When the riders had closed ranks, he called out to one of his men. "Corporal, see that these two and the black one are on the next supply wagon to Bethanie. And give the mother a field dressing for the girl's head.

"Yes, sir," came the response.

"But keep them away from the men," added the Tommy leader. "We don't want any trouble."

16

AMERICA SIDING

1900

Henry stood in the door of the hut in mute admiration of an alien but absolute power in full flight as the horsemen swept into the village with an air of unquestionable right. His brief captivity had done little to tarnish his admiration for the majesty of the British military, especially the cavalry.

He knew the soldiers had worn red tunics when they first arrived in South Africa—it must have been a wonderful sight—but had changed to khaki to make themselves less conspicuous to Boer marksmen.

"Halt," yelled the young, slightly built lieutenant, his right arm raised. The column of horsemen formed up on each side of him in the central clearing, the sweating horses snorting and stamping after the hard ride. "Come out, all of you," the officer commanded. "Out of your huts. Now!"

Henry took Jonas by the hand and stepped out of the doorway into full view of the horsemen. He was relieved to be wearing the clothes Miriam had given him—an off-white shirt, floppy brown felt hat, dark trousers held up by suspenders—and not the khaki scout's uniform that would have betrayed him. And he was relieved to see that none of the soldiers looked familiar, although there was a black man amongst them at the end of the line closest to him.

The villagers emerged in a slow trickle and congregated behind the elders. The men shuffled forward, the women kept their distance, shielding the children who stared, their eyes wide, intrigued but afraid.

"Sergeant," called the officer, "instruct the interpreter. These people must be ready to leave within the hour."

"Yes, sir," said a stocky soldier next to the officer.

"We'll march to the railway siding at Bethanie," added the officer. "I'm sure we can find one or two more cattle cars for this lot—teach them a lesson for helping the Boers."

"Yes, sir," said the sergeant before moving to the end of the line where the black soldier waited. "You know what to tell them," said the sergeant in a low but firm voice. "Make sure they believe you."

The interpreter dismounted and walked towards the elders. Henry headed in the same direction with Jonas. He had understood the English instructions but wanted Jonas to tell him exactly what was said to the villagers in their own language.

"I bring you greetings and good news from the soldier chief," began the interpreter with a broad, toothy smile. "He has prepared a place for you...for the whole village...where you will be safe from the Boers. There will be plenty of food and work. And you will be paid for your work. But you must come quickly and bring only what you can carry—the soldiers have everything you need at the new place."

The elders groaned in collective dismay. The villagers behind them muttered in consternation.

"Where is this new place?" asked a senior elder in a querulous voice.

"Near the city the Boers call the 'fountain of flowers'," said the interpreter, smiling broadly, "Bloemfontein. But the Boer fighters have been chased away. It is safe there now."

"Why must we go so soon?" asked the elder.

"Because the Boers are coming," said the interpreter without missing a beat. "They are coming with many men. They will take all your food and burn your village."

A collective gasp coursed through the villagers.

"Why did the soldiers kill our cattle?" asked another elder.

"It was not the soldiers," said the interpreter. "It was the Boers. They wear the clothes of the soldiers to make the people think the soldiers are doing these things."

"I cannot believe what you say," said the elder. "Our people saw the soldiers kill the cattle."

"I speak the truth," said the interpreter. "Look," he said, unfolding an official-looking document and holding it high for all to see. "These are the words of the great soldier chief, Lord Kitchener. He says the Boers wear the soldiers' clothes, that it is a shameful thing they do, and that any Boer caught wearing the clothes of the soldiers will be executed...shot dead."

The elders mumbled and whispered among themselves. "What will become of our village?" asked one.

"Nothing unless the Boers burn it," said the interpreter. "It will be here when you come back after the war."

"And if we do not agree to leave?" asked another.

"The soldiers cannot let you stay here," said the interpreter. "It is too dangerous."

The elder nodded. "Leave us now. We will talk and decide."

After the elders retired to confer, Jonas summarized the exchange for Henry and reminded him that he had seen the soldiers kill the cattle. He knew them by the sound of their guns. And they had all looked exactly the same, from their domed helmets down to their identical brown leather boots.

Henry had heard enough and knew that unless he escaped he was going wherever the villagers were going. His thoughts were shaken by a bellow.

"Sergeant!" yelled the lieutenant. "We leave within the hour. No exceptions. And make sure the village cannot be used by the Boers after we leave."

"Yes, sir," said the sergeant. "I will take care of it."

Henry thought he understood the implication of the instruction but before he could formulate any kind of plan, soldiers were posted to guard each hut. There was no chance of escape and the villagers had no choice. Within the hour they were trudging out of the village, led by donkey-drawn wagons carrying the elderly and young.

An oppressive stillness descended on the bedraggled procession as it moved along the rutted track leading towards Bethanie and the railway station, a stillness interrupted occasionally by barking dogs and bleating goats trailing in obedient confusion.

Henry walked with Jonas. The dirt track was hot underfoot and the stones were sharp. They did not talk except for when the boy wondered aloud about the fate of Miriam and the Boer women.

As the sun passed its highest point, Henry looked back along the trail towards the village. He thought he saw plumes of wispy smoke. Despite his worst fears, it was hard to tell—smoke was visible in almost every direction.

The boiling steam engine, like the head of a giant black serpent anticipating a midday meal, seemed to seethe malevolently as it waited for the villagers.

Henry counted at least a dozen cattle cars plus several cars that appeared to carry soldiers, military supplies and horses. One railcar appeared fortified—guns pointed from it in every direction. He shuddered despite the heat. There was something sinister in the air. But the villagers seemed relieved as they stumbled towards the train anticipating a respite from the forced march.

On command, the soldiers fixed bayonets to their rifles and prodded the villagers towards the cattle cars at the head of the train. Each car was a dirty ochre color, little more than a rectangular box on wheels made from horizontal planks of wood held in place by corner posts and a few vertical supports. Two sliding doors opened away from each other in the center of each car as it faced the platform.

Henry kept Jonas close to him as they clambered into the first car. Then, as more villagers filled the car, he steered the boy towards the side closest to the station platform. He found a place to stand close to a horizontal crack between the car's wooden planks that offered a sliver of a view of the siding. If nothing else, he wanted to be able to see what was happening outside the train.

For the next several hours the train sat and baked under an afternoon sun that sent heat waves shimmering across the veld. The car was filthy, the air suffocating, the heat oppressive. No explanation was given and there was no water to drink. The villagers just stood in sullen discomfort, pressed together like so many sticks of kindling, smoldering.

After what seemed like an eternity, Henry became aware of activity and opened his eyes to peer through the crack. He thought he heard some shouting about a wagon and watched as soldiers stacked various provisions on the platform.

A short while later, a horse-drawn wagon appeared and stopped almost directly across from his vantage point. It seemed the rendezvous with the wagon was the reason for their long wait. No sooner had the apparently empty wagon stopped than two women sat up in the bed of the wagon—one black, one white—their identities unmistakable. He nearly called out to them but knew it would be futile and potentially dangerous.

He watched the women struggle to get the girl out of the wagon and carry her towards the train. The soldiers were loading provisions into the wagon as the women disappeared from his view. Then he heard the sound of a car door slide open and close.

"Jonas," he whispered. "Miriam and the Boer women are here." The boy looked up at him. "Miriam is here, Jonas, on the train," he repeated. The boy nodded and gave him a wan smile.

Moments later a series of shrill whistles sounded and the train lurched into motion. As it gathered speed and the jarring screech and push-pull of the cars settled into a steady mechanical rhythm, the roiling plume of soot that had initially towered above the steam engine now laid a blanket of coal dirt over the open cattle cars.

Henry closed his eyes as beads of perspiration rolled off his forehead into his parched lips. The monotony of the train's motion was oddly soothing despite the physical discomfort. He knew sitting or lying was not an option—the people were too tightly packed against each other. Besides, there was only one toilet option—at your feet where you stood, where many had stood before you. He hoped the women were supporting the girl to prevent her slipping to the floor.

Sunset brought relief from the heat but not from the oppression. His eyes were irritated, his nose blocked by the pervasive black soot and his tongue as dry as desert driftwood. As hot as the day had been, the night was bitterly cold. Children cried, adults groaned and every so often a shift of bodies signaled that someone had slipped to the floor.

He spent much of the night with his mouth pressed against the crack in the side of the car, sucking air from the outside. He got used to the taste of the soot—it was more tolerable than the smell inside the car—and drifted in and out of sleep. He was vaguely aware of the train making multiple stops during the night, of people shuffling in the darkness, of car doors opening and closing, and of the engine puffing hard as though trying to catch its breath.

In moments of wakefulness he tried to think of some plan of action for the villagers, but the gears of his tired brain refused to engage. As for himself, the only thing he knew for certain was that he would be executed on the spot if the soldiers discovered he was a scout turned traitor.

Henry stirred as the sun rose on a cloudless day. His legs ached, his lips were cracked, and his throat felt as though he had swallowed shards of coal.

The soothing monotony of the train's motion had been replaced by a harsh clickety-clack as its wheels rolled relentlessly against the cold steel joints of the tracks. And outside, the few trees he could see barely disrupted the vast canvas of dry grassland and austere scrub that stretched into the horizon.

He became increasingly disoriented as the oppressive day dragged on and the unremarkable landscape passed by. It seemed to be a journey to nowhere until, at last, he thought he recognized the low-lying hills outside Bloemfontein. He was just about to alert Jonas when the train rounded a bend and an unexpected sight caught his breath. It looked at first as though the gods had thrown down a scattering of huge white flowers on the steep slope of a desolate and craggy hill, some in clumps between the rocks and others scattered as though clinging to life in soil stripped bare of ground cover under the unrelenting sun. As the train drew closer, he realized the flowers were tents, randomly placed between the rocks on the bleak and uneven slope of the hill.

The train slowed, as though in reverence, then stopped.

There was no station or platform, just a dusty track on the side of the rail line. Car doors slid open and soldiers started yelling. He squinted through the crack in his cattle car to get a better view of what was happening. A trickle of Boer women and children came into view, shuffling like disheveled moths drawn towards the light reflecting off the white tents.

"Hey, you!" shouted a soldier, pointing towards a group of women. "Only white women at this camp. The black one must get back on the train."

He looked to where the soldier was pointing. Susannah and Miriam appeared, supporting the girl between them.

"She's my maid," replied Susannah. "To help with my sick child."

"The black one can't stay here. She must go to the camp for blacks," insisted the soldier.

"Ag, nonsense," retorted Susannah. "She stays with me, and that's final."

The soldier looked stunned. "Uh...well...we'll see about that," he stammered. "Go and report to the camp superintendent immediately."

Henry watched a few minutes more before the train lurched into motion again. He lost sight of the women as the blanket of soot once again enveloped him and the sound and smell of distress in the open cattle cars became his only reality. There was no escaping the foul oppression inside the cars or the scorching sun overhead.

Towards late afternoon the train stopped again, this time

adjacent to a desolate scene of shacks strewn haphazardly across a barren expanse of veld.

Henry stared. If this was a camp, it looked nothing like the one for the Boer women. It seemed whoever had set the white tents down for the Boers had taken even less care at this place, tossing the spare bits and pieces over the hill and out of sight, where they now lay before him.

The doors to his car opened and a crush of villagers surged towards the opening. Henry stumbled over several bodies amid the confusion of barked orders and baffled villagers before he jumped to the ground alongside Jonas. As they trudged towards the makeshift camp—a pitiful jumble of old sacking, metal sheets, mud bricks, wooden frames and a handful of tattered tents—he glanced back at the train. The serpentine creature seemed to taunt him, mocking his feeble effort to survive with a gruesome display of dead bodies visible through the open doors of the cattle cars.

Henry shook his head to dispel the images, then turned to focus on what lay ahead.

The only white people he could see were soldiers. And it seemed a strange stupor blanketed the inhabitants of the camp. Everyone seemed to move in slow motion, as if in a trance, without any obvious purpose. Even the few skinny dogs he could see were listless, their tails between their legs, their ribs stark against taut skin.

He looked for a figure of authority and caught sight of a lean dark-haired soldier a little way off. He was standing next to a signpost in the ground, smoking. Henry decided the risk of being recognized was remote and approached.

"Excuse me, sir," he began. "What shall I tell the people to do?"

The soldier looked at him blankly through sunken eyes. "Do?" he asked, flicking ash from his cigarette as his gaze swept over the new arrivals. "You want to know what the people should do?" he asked rhetorically, a wry half smile ghosting across his hagard features. "Well, my good man," he began, "that depends on what you would like to do. The possibilities are endless."

Henry looked around as the soldier had done but did not see any obvious answer to his question.

"Let's see now," the soldier continued, his tone facetious. "There's lawn tennis in the mornings between nine and eleven, cricket at noon, croquet at four, then your choice of bingo or bridge in the evening. And, after dinner, the gentlemen retire to the smoking room for cigars and a snifter of brandy." He paused. "Did I mention we serve tea and scones midmorning and afternoon as light refreshment?"

Henry frowned. Aside from tea, he had never heard of such things and was none the wiser about what was expected of the people.

But, instead of explaining, the soldier shook his head and seemed to slump. "Christ, man, how the devil should I know? I doubt even Florence Nightingale would know what to do." He shook his head. "Nobody told us you were coming. We weren't expecting so many to be sent here in the first place, and we certainly weren't expecting more to arrive almost every day. We have no tents, no material for shelters, not enough food or water, no vegetables or milk, no doctor or nurse, and no medicine for the sick."

He paused to stare at the desolation that surrounded him. "The best you can do is try to stay alive. Try to find something to build a hut or a shelter, and try to find something to eat. And there's always work to be done digging graves, loading wagons, making fences and taking care of the trench latrines. That is about all there is for you to do."

"Ow," said Henry, beginning to grasp the scope of their predicament. "What is this place called?" he asked, pointing at the sign in the ground next to the soldier.

The soldier glanced at the sign. "America Siding," he said. "And there are other camps like this with names like Virginia and Geneva for no reason I can explain."

"But what is this place?" he asked. "And why are we here?"

"Ah, yes, that's a question I often ask myself," said the soldier. "I can tell you what it's supposed to be, but I'm not sure that will explain what it is." He paused, shaking his head. "This is part of Lord Kitchener's plan to win the war," he began. "Burn the Boers off their farms and herd them into camps. There are camps for Boer women and children and separate camps for your people—men, women, and children—the ones taken from farms and villages."

It still made no sense, although Henry remembered the English family of blacksmiths in Queenstown had spoken of a country called America. "But what does America have to do with this plan?"

"Ah," replied the soldier, "your guess is as good as mine. Maybe Kitchener liked General Sherman's strategy in the American civil war. He used scorched-earth tactics to win that war. And the Americans already had a policy of forcing their native peoples onto places called 'reservations,' almost like these camps except bigger."

The soldier looked over the people huddled around early evening fires.

"One American general said the only good Indians he ever saw were dead." He shook his head. "It seems Kitchener feels the same way about the Boers and is using the same tactics—scorched-earth and concentration camps—to finish them off and end the war."

"Ow," said Henry, shaking his head and clicking his tongue. "That is a strange story."

The soldier gave a wry smile. "I agree. But it makes as much sense to me as anything else in this bloody war." He paused, then added, "And you black people are just pawns caught up in the mess, sacrificed as part of Kitchener's grand strategy against the Boers. There are black families on the Boer farms being destroyed, and black farms and villages being burned as well. That's why we have these camps for your people. Some call them refugee camps, others call them concentration camps, but whatever you call them, they have been forsaken by those who should know better, if not by God Himself."

"Ow," said Henry again, his eyes wide, trying to absorb it all.

The soldier shrugged and kicked a loose stone at the sign.

"What is your name?" he asked.

Henry hesitated. "Mandela," he said after a moment, hoping he wasn't betraying himself.

"You seem like a good fellow, Mandela, so I will give you some friendly advice." He paused, his expression stony. "People are dying like flies in the camp, especially the children, from infant diarrhea. And there's nothing I can do to save them. Don't be fooled by the name. It's a graveyard, not a siding. That tells you all you need to know about this camp."

Henry put a protective arm around Jonas and stared at the soldier.

"If you have the chance to go to the mines, take it," continued the soldier. "Go to a rich mine like Robinson Deep near Johannesburg. Plenty of gold there... and good wages. If you stay here, you will probably die along with the rest."

"I can leave this place?" asked Henry, his forehead creased in confusion.

The soldier nodded. "We want you to work for us, but you are not a prisoner. You can't go back to your farms or villages, but if you want to go to the mines, I can put you on the train."

"Ow," replied Henry, shaking his head. "These are strange things you tell me."

"Good day, Mandela," said the soldier after a brief silence. "And good luck." Then he turned on his heel, flicked his cigarette butt into the veld and walked off.

Henry shuddered as he pulled Jonas close to him. The crimson hue of the setting sun seemed to cast an ominous pall as it bled into the horizon.

17

A MOTHER'S HEART

1900

Susannah was exhausted. During the long night in the cattle car, the eyes of her soul had filled with blurred visions of clinging to the cross of Jesus as it shook and swayed for reasons she could not comprehend. It was her only refuge—as Jesus had suffered for his children, so too would she suffer for her child.

Then, just when she felt herself slipping away, the shaking and swaying stopped. She thought perhaps she had reached the gates of heaven, but the cattle-car doors were the only gates that opened. And the voice that ordered her off the train did not sound like a welcoming saint.

As she struggled towards the camp under the weight of her child, the tents in front of her assumed a brilliant white sheen in the early morning sun. She even saw a fiery red cross hovering above the ground, and for a moment her hope of salvation revived.

Just a few more steps.

The illusion did not last long. The superintendent sitting at a table inside the Red Cross tent next to the camp doctor looked belligerent, the doctor indifferent. Before there was any inquiry about her health or that of her child, the thickset superintendent gestured at Miriam with his baton.

"She can't stay in the same tent with you," he said, his tone stern. "She can be your maid during the day, but she must sleep with the other servants at night."

Susannah bristled. Insolent redneck. "Either she sleeps in my tent or I sleep in her tent," she replied. "Take your pick."

The superintendent's bloated features turned red. She couldn't tell if he was outraged by her impertinence or mortified by the alternative she proposed. Even the doctor seemed taken aback as he squinted at her through a monocle. The man's white coat and gray hair contrasted sharply with the khaki of the superintendent's military jacket, a contrast as sharp as that between the stethoscope he twirled between his fingers and the baton the superintendent slapped against the palm of his hand.

She looked from one to the other—one a symbol of authority, the other a symbol of healing—and felt equally threatened by both.

"Please, Doctor. My daughter needs your help," she said. "She is badly hurt."

The monocle fell from the doctor's eye towards his lap, its drop arrested by the attached string connected to a buttonhole in his coat. His eyebrows arched in censure as he set aside the stethoscope, idly grooming one end of his handlebar mustache while staring over his narrow nose at her. After a few moments he turned towards the middle-aged nurse standing to one side.

"Sister Kennedy," he said, gesturing off-handedly towards Esmé.

The sister who approached appeared exhausted, but her eyes were kind. She needed no direction—the messy field dressing and blood-matted hair were all too evident, the brief but gentle examination made easy by Esmé's drooped head.

"Deep laceration, right temple, badly infected," she said.

"I need to clean the wound before I can be sure, but the prognosis looks poor."

Susannah did not fully understand but added, "She was kicked by a horse. And she was violated by the soldiers."

The doctor shrugged. "This woman will need her maid for as long as it takes." He paused. Then, with an air of Solomonic wisdom, he announced his decision: "The child must go to the hospital tent. The maid will stay with the mother."

The superintendent looked relieved—someone else had sanctioned the unorthodox arrangement. "Complete your family registration first," he instructed. "Full names and the name of the farm district you came from. Then take the girl to the hospital tent. Do you understand?"

Susannah nodded and felt the tension drain from her core. She had what she wanted and now did as she was told. At a table near the tent door she gave the clerk their names, then added, "De Beer family farm, Sannah's Post," her voice quavering as absent family members came to mind.

The nurses in the hospital tent laid Esmé on a stretcher bed along one side of the tent among about thirty other stretchers, most occupied by smaller children. Although they had to wait for attention, a young nurse finally appeared with a pail of warm water to wash Esmé's wound.

"The doctor will see her in a little while," said the nurse. "You must go to your tent now."

Susannah nodded and kissed Esmé's forehead and wound, as though a mother's love was all a child needed, her tenderness an instrument of God's grace, of Jesus's own healing touch. Then she straightened up, reached for Miriam's arm and left the tent.

It seemed every tent in the camp was already filled to capacity—twelve or more in each—until they found one with space for two.

But the women already in the tent refused to share it with Miriam. To keep the peace, the superintendent found a barely usable tent just for Susannah and Miriam at the far end of the row where the most recent arrivals were located.

"This is not a good place," said Miriam when they were alone.

"What are you talking about? There are nurses and food and tents—what can be bad about that? I admit I don't like the hospital or the doctor. And I felt humiliated, but that is the Tommy way."

"The hospital beds are full, the children are too thin, and the camp smells of sickness and death."

"Ag, Miriam, what nonsense," said Susannah, her irritation flaring. "How can this camp possibly be worse than hiding on the veld, being chased day and night by soldiers?" She turned away and looked around at the empty tent. "Well, anyway, no use arguing. We are here now, and that's that. But there's nothing to do in the tent. So come, let's walk and see the rest of the camp."

The camp looked ragged, with clusters of tents scattered between rocks on a steep hill that sloped down to a flat area with a few metal buildings and the hospital. Just beyond the buildings was the railway line. And in the near distance a column of wagons approached the camp, driven by Boer women led by mounted soldiers. The wagons carried children and a jumble of household belongings. There were even cattle and sheep amongst the wagons. And inside the camp, a few skinny children chased between the tents, apparently playing some kind of game, while several old men could be seen wandering through the rows of tents.

But it was the singing that caught Susannah's attention—a mournful sound, part chant, part prayer that seemed to follow a donkey cart moving among the tents, led by a bearded old man in a black coat.

They watched as the cart stopped outside a tent. Moments later a woman emerged from the tent and tenderly laid a small bundle in the back of the cart before joining those behind the cart. The donkey resumed its slow walk, only to stop again about two tents away from where they stood. The ritual was repeated. The tent flap opened and two women and several children emerged. The group behind the wagon sang as one of the women carried a small bundle to the rear of the cart. The old man nodded and waited patiently as the woman joined the others behind the cart.

Susannah could not see what was in the bundles, but she could guess from the songs. The cart moved slowly in front of her. As it passed, she saw a tangle of small, bare, limp feet dangling over the back edge of the wagon. Without a word she gripped Miriam's arm and walked directly back to their tent.

They did not talk about what they had seen. But as she lay down on the scrap of canvas that served as her mat, she said, "God has led me to this place, Miriam. He holds my child in the palm of His hand. He will keep her safe."

Miriam stared at her.

Susannah ignored the agnostic reproach in Miriam's eyes, tried to wish away the heat and the oppression, and eventually sank into a fitful sleep.

"Everybody well?" called a politely apologetic, sweetly accented foreign voice.

The sound pierced the fog of Susannah's sleep. She came slowly awake, lifted her head and stared irritably at the intruder peering through the tent flap. The stranger wore a full-length skirt, a muslin high-necked blouse with a short man's tie knotted at her neck, and a hip-length checkered jacket.

"Oh my," said the woman. "I didn't know blacks and whites were allowed in the same tent."

"I'm her maid," said Miriam, "to help with her sick child."

"Oh, well then," replied the woman, "where is the child and why—"

"Who *are* you?" interrupted Susannah, annoyed and confused by the intrusion.

"I'm Emily Hobhouse," said the woman, adjusting her round eyeglasses, "from England. I'm here to help the Boer women and children in the camps."

"I don't understand," she said. "There are doctors and nurses here. Why do we need your help?"

The Englishwoman stepped into the tent and gazed quizzically at her and briefly at Miriam. "When did you arrive in the camp, my dear?"

"This morning," said Susannah. "Just after sunrise."

"And you have children here?" asked the woman.

"Yes," she replied. "My daughter is in the hospital tent."

The woman was silent for a few moments, as though trying to resolve a quandary. "Then you have not heard?"

Susannah flared. "Heard what? What you are talking about?"

The woman drew a deep breath and slowly exhaled. "It grieves me to say," she began, "that you need my help because thousands of Boer women and children are dying every day in camps like this, camps created by my own countrymen and run with a self-righteous inhumanity that is breathtaking."

Susannah thought she must have misheard. "But—"

"Worst of all," continued the Englishwoman, "it's the children who suffer most and die such wretched deaths. A child under age five will almost certainly die. Altogether, more than fifty children die every day."

Susannah stared at the woman. She could not even begin to imagine such a thing. The very idea of it crushed all rational response before any could even form in her mind. She heard Miriam speak.

"There are more camps like this?"

"Oh yes," said the woman. "More than forty camps already, and some for you black people as well." She paused to cough delicately into a gloved hand. "There are already more than a hundred thousand people in the camps. More arrive each day, and the death rate just keeps rising."

"And the people in the black camps, do they also die?" asked Miriam, her voice trembling.

"I'm afraid so. Conditions in the black camps are even worse. In just one month, more than four hundred die for every thousand of your people."

Miriam shuddered as her hands flew to her mouth. It was several moments before she could speak. "Do you also help the people in those camps?"

The Englishwoman looked away and slowly shook her head. "I am very sorry to say, I do not. I can't possibly pay attention to all the camps myself. Someone needs to do it, but I don't know of anybody who is trying to help the people in the black camps."

A tear furrowed the dust on Miriam's cheek, its path a slick sheen against her dark skin.

Susannah finally found her voice. "But...but I don't understand...Why do they die...Why is this happening?"

"Ah yes, well, that is the question. Why indeed does the glorious British Empire sacrifice women and children on the altar of its imperialist aspirations? I have heard many excuses offered, mostly by crassly ignorant and morally corrupt men in high places. But the simple fact is, by herding Boer women and children into these camps, Lord Kitchener believes he can force the Boer fighters to surrender."

"But why do they die?" persisted Susannah. "And why so many children?"

A wince creased the Englishwoman's refined features. "I'm very sorry to have to tell you, my dear, but the reason the children die, according to Lord Kitchener, is because of the criminal neglect of their mothers."

Susannah's features contorted in confusion. "What? What are you saying?"

"I'm saying the great Lord Kitchener blames the Boer mothers. He says you are all filthy, neglect your children and refuse proper medical attention."

Susannah reached blindly for Miriam and grasped her hand.

The Englishwoman paused and appeared to gather herself. "In fact, that great bastion of moral superiority, the empire upon which the sun never sets, has declared the Boer people racially degenerate, a polluted stock of subhuman people who have shunned civilization and believe in primitive and disgusting remedies for all their ailments."

Susannah looked blankly from the woman to Miriam. The story still made no sense. Ignoring the insult to her people, choking on emotion, she asked again, "But why do our people die? Please tell me that."

The woman sighed. "Squalid conditions, bad food, polluted water, poor sanitary provisions, inadequate medical supplies," she began. "Not to mention our complete lack of preparedness and—"

"But what does that mean?" cried Susannah.

"Disease, my dear. It means disease," said the woman in a gentle voice burdened by a grim reality. "It means measles, typhoid and dysentery—diseases that cut the children down like stalks of wheat by a farmer's scythe."

The Englishwoman looked away and adjusted her jacket and

tie, as though preparing to address a formal audience somewhere far beyond the tent. "The brunt of this unjust war against peasant farmers who just want to be left in peace," she began, "is being borne by their women and children, the innocent and the helpless. It is a shameful reminder of the depravity that results from treating our fellow humans as caricatures, as less than human, as no more deserving than animals."

She shook her head. "Some call it genocide by neglect."

Then she paused and looked directly at Susannah. "Your people die, my dear, because the British Empire does not care whether they live or die. That is the awful truth, and it will redound to our eternal shame."

"We must leave this place," said Miriam the next morning as the predawn glow began to light the tent. "Death creeps through the camp like an evil spirit. It slips among us and into the tents—even this one. I can feel it in my bones."

Susannah did not respond. Her muscles were stiff and sore, the canvas beneath her damp and foul, her thoughts in turmoil after a sleepless night thinking about what she had heard.

"Did you hear?" repeated Miriam as she sat with her knees drawn to her chin.

"I heard you, Miriam," she said wearily. "And I heard you yesterday and the Englishwoman too. What more is there to hear?"

"I've been talking to the other maids," said Miriam. "The food is not good. There is too little milk and the meat is bad. The people are hungry and many are sick, especially the little ones—they cough, grow thin, have red spots, and many have the stomach sickness. Some even have a sickness that eats their face, even the jawbones."

"Ag, Miriam, what rubbish!" she said, the comfort of silence disrupted by Miriam's idle prattle.

"The children who go to the hospital also die," pressed Miriam. "Not just the ones in the tents like we saw yesterday."

Susannah felt a surge of exasperation. "Just like that? They go to the hospital, then they die?" She forced a derisive laugh. "And why do they die, Miriam? Do the clever maids tell you that?"

Miriam was silent for a moment. "They do not know. But that's what the woman from England was trying to explain."

"I'm tired of this nonsense," said Susannah, getting to her feet. She felt grubby and sullied by the things she was hearing. Yesterday's triumph securing medical attention for Esmé now usurped by bitter disappointment, the growing sense that she had given her child up to a grotesque evil.

"I need the toilet," announced Susannah, smoothing her skirt. "Do you know where to go?"

Miriam nodded. "There are buckets on the far side close to the maids' tents. Just follow your nose."

She left the tent without a word. The sun had breached the horizon, casting a warming glow on the white canvas of the tents. She hesitated, looking left and right along deserted pathways between the tents. Despite having witnessed the column of heavily laden wagons arriving, she was surprised by the sight of furniture outside some of the tents—chairs, tables, a few sewing machines, even a piano or two. Some families had clearly escaped their burning farms with more than others. But the juxtaposition of familiar things in such an alien and unfamiliar environment only deepened her sense of dislocation as she set off down the hill for the latrine area Miriam had described.

She was glad to have Miriam in the camp with her, but she could not help being irritated by her presumptuousness. Even her reliance on Miriam was unsettling. It was not right. But then nothing in her life was right. She felt ripped from her roots—her farm, her family, her faith—and the camp didn't offer the salvation she had hoped for. She shook her head fiercely, as though to rid herself from the distressing clamor of her thoughts. She had to focus on her child, not fret about the imponderables of God's plan.

She saw the buckets lined up in a flat area below the tents. For a moment she was reminded of bees hovering over honeypots until the wind changed. It was as though some vile creature from the bowels of the earth had broken wind in her face. As she approached, the bees became flies—thick and dark like black vapors swirling around evil cauldrons of the foulest brew.

She stopped in her tracks, swaying with nausea. She did not hear the woman come up beside her.

"God will deliver us from this place," said the woman in a familiar accent, "just as he delivered the Israelites from Pharaoh. And he will give us our promised land if we keep the faith."

Susannah stared at the woman, trying to reconcile the invocation of spiritual purpose with the physical revulsion of the moment. The woman looked kind enough. She was dressed in a long-sleeved blouse with a ruffle at the neck, a dark linen skirt that almost touched the ground, and her graying brown hair was drawn back into a single braid that reached her waist. A dull silver crucifix hung from her neck.

"The buckets are better than the trenches we had before," said the woman. "Just think of the flies as part of God's plan to drive the Tommies from our land," she added in a tone devoid of humor. "Many soldiers in Bloemfontein are also sick. We think it's the flies."

Susannah looked from the woman to the buckets. The idea of the flies being any part of God's plan for her people was unimaginable, as was the idea of exposing herself to the fetid swarm long enough to relieve herself.

"Pull down your underwear and lift your skirts around your waist," continued the woman in a blunt transition from spirituality to practicality. "Then hold your nose and sit down. But be sure to spread your legs and keep your skirt up so the flies can get out." She paused. "And don't worry about anybody watching. We have all done this and seen far worse besides. And here is something to use... for after," she said, offering a handful of dry grass.

Susannah hesitated, then took the grass. "Please wait for me," she said, wrinkling her nose as she walked to the nearest bucket. She did as instructed but also closed her eyes and held her breath. However long it took was too long. She was grateful for the grass— she had not thought of that detail—and sprang to her feet gasping for air as soon as she was done. She was still swatting at flies and shaking out her skirt as she walked back to the tents with the woman.

"This is a terrible place," began Susannah as she glanced at the forlorn tents and looked around at the perimeter of the camp.

"Yes," said the woman. "The camp is a hellhole. They wanted us off our farms and burned everything, but there was no plan about what to do with us after that. This place is just a dumping ground for our people." She shook her head with evident disgust. "There is talk of another camp being set up nearby. We can only hope that one will be better than this one."

"But why do our people come here?" Susannah asked. "And why do they stay? There are no fences or guards."

The woman shrugged. "Some of our women escaped before the Tommies reached their farms and are still out there somewhere, hiding in the mountains, helping our fighters. Others were chased from their farms and then left to fend for themselves on the veld, or taken to towns and crowded into churches and schools. Most were caught and sent to the camps by wagon, train or on foot. Those who have a place to go in the towns can leave. But most of us in this camp lost everything and have nowhere to go, especially those who did not even own the land they worked. Our homes and farms are gone, and our men are at war or dead. We have no choice—we are prisoners of our poverty."

"My parents are in Bloemfontein," said Susannah, her hopes rising.

"Then you should go there. It's close."

"But my child is in the hospital," she said, her tone mournful, her nascent hope stillborn.

"Yes," said the woman, her tone flat.

"Is it true what they say?" asked Susannah.

"About what?"

"About the children dying in the hospital?"

The woman was silent for a moment. "Yes, it's true. And the mothers can only visit once a week for few minutes, even if the child is dying. And the nurses don't understand us when we plead with them—they don't speak our language."

Susannah reached for the woman's arm. It was too much to hear, too much to bear. "But why do the children die? I've heard such terrible and confusing stories."

The woman snorted contemptuously. "The doctor says we are dirty and stupid and carry disease."

Susannah closed her eyes. The Englishwoman had been right, and Miriam and the maids too. It was as inconceivable as it was unbearable. "So what do you do?" she asked, her voice thick with dread.

"We keep the tents closed and hide the children when they get sick," said the woman. "We cover them with many clothes and blankets to break the fevers. Some die anyway. And if they are taken away, we smuggle food to them in the hospital, because the nurses and doctors are starving them. But they give the children wine and brandy and whiskey, even champagne. Can you believe it! They're poisoning our children. And so they die." The woman sighed as though expelling an unspeakable sorrow. "And then we bury them," she added. "Every day there are more."

"I didn't know," said Susannah, her voice a strained whisper. "My child was sick when I got here. I told the doctor and left her in the tent with the red cross."

"I heard," said the woman. "And I heard she is very sick. I'm sorry for your child... and for you."

The fatalism of the woman's words cut like a knife through every maternal fiber of her being. She refused to concede the life of her child to such a grotesque fate, but she could feel the desperation rising, a choking hopelessness that threatened to overwhelm her unless she did something to stem the tide.

"What can I do?" she cried. "There must be something I can do!"

The woman looked at her, a faraway sadness in her eyes. "Go to her tonight. Sneak into the tent under the side—"

"But what does that help?" she interrupted. "How do I get her out of the tent? Where do I take her? I can't bring her back to my tent. And I can't just walk into the veld with my child. Bloemfontein is too far to carry her."

The woman looked away. "I do not mean you must take your child away. I mean you must stay in the tent with her. Sleep with her."

Susannah stared at the woman.

"That is all you can do," said the woman. "Be with your child at the end."

Susannah waited until the moon was high—it seemed like the right thing to do.

She and Miriam were both quiet. Everything that needed to be said had been said, and the muted voices and sounds outside the tent had long since dissipated into a tomblike quiet. Only the occasional cough and cry betrayed the presence of life in the camp, the uninhibited distress of children easily distinguishable from the subdued anguish of their mothers.

She had tried to think of every option to escape with her child, however fanciful, including stealing a wagon, hiding on the next train, or riding off on horseback. But her limited options had closed around her like the darkness, shutting out all hope of escape.

"I must take her something, Miriam, to make her feel better," she said in a forlorn tone, repeating a subject she and Miriam had already exhausted. "Anything."

Miriam sighed. "You are going to her, Susannah. That's the only thing she needs... the only thing you have left to give."

There was no more talk. The silence stretched the thread of time as the cold grip of night tightened around the tent. Susannah sat, waiting, until her need to go to her child became too much to bear.

"It's time," she said finally. She felt stiff and heavy, as though her limbs were rebelling against her planned course of action.

Once outside, a violent shiver coursed through her as the night wrapped itself around her, condensing her breath into midnight vapor. Fear squeezed her chest as she gazed at the tents standing like silent sentinels watching over the condemned. The moon hung high in the pitch-black sky, its reflection casting a ghostly luminosity onto the strange, tented landscape below.

"Will you go with me?" she asked with her back to the tent as though addressing the night. Hearing no response, she turned towards the tent. "Please, Miriam."

Moments later the tent flap was swept aside and Miriam stepped into the night.

The two women stood for a moment before moving slowly down the steep slope towards the row of administrative tents. About thirty feet of open ground separated the hospital tent from the first of multiple rows of inmate tents. Guy wires looked wraith-like in the moonlight as they stretched across the spaces between the tents, as though reaching out to each other but then diving self-consciously into the ground before they met.

Susannah stopped when she reached the last of the inmate tents. Miriam tugged her arm to move off the main path into the shadows.

"The entrance is on the other side," whispered Miriam. "So are the guards."

"Yes," she said.

The women stood in silence for a few moments. The hospital tent was straight ahead, closest to the main path.

"You must cross here and crawl under the tent on this side," said Miriam, pointing across the open ground between the tents towards the back of the hospital tent.

Susannah looked across the space. It seemed so far. Then she took Miriam's hand in both her hands and stared into her eyes, wishing for an alternative, hoping for a miracle. Miriam pulled her close, her free arm around Susannah's shoulders. "Go now," she said gently. "May your god be with you."

She nodded but stood a moment longer, comforted by Miriam's embrace the way she had been when they first met in the village. Then she stepped away and turned toward the hospital tent, still holding Miriam's hand.

"You must come to see me," she said, not looking back, her voice trembling.

"I will."

"In the morning."

"Yes."

She squeezed Miriam's hand, took a deep breath, and set off in an awkward crouch across the opening. But in her haste she forgot about the guy wires, until her foot snagged on one and she fell hard onto her chest. As she lay dazed, winded and spread-eagled in the open space between the tents, a wave of hopelessness washed over her, the taste of grit and despair bitter in her mouth.

"Anybody there?" called a Tommy voice from somewhere in the night.

Susannah went rigid with fear, certain the guards would investigate the noise. She thought of calling Miriam to help her but instead forced herself to her feet. Keeping low, she darted across the open ground, carefully avoiding the guy wires, before dropping to the ground next to the hospital tent. She took a few moments to catch her breath, then lifted the tent skirt and crawled into the dark interior.

The tent sounded like a living organism in distress—heaving, breathing, sniveling, moaning—its parts discordant yet somehow unified in their common misery. And then she was struck by the smell. It was sickly, just as Miriam had said, a sweet-sour odor that caused her stomach to churn.

As her eyes adjusted to the gloom, she crawled to an open space between two beds and cautiously stood up. She was in the aisle between rows of beds running the length of the tent, crammed together except in the open space at the entrance opposite where she stood. Some beds had two children to a bed, their small tousled heads sticking out at opposite ends.

She looked down the length of the tent, trying to picture where she had left Esmé with the nurses, then moved cautiously among the stretcher cots towards the bigger patients. The first two she came to were both lying still, one breathing hard, the other seemingly not at all. Neither had a bandaged head.

Then she saw a girl with a bandaged head lying on her side, apparently asleep. A sheet covered most of her head, but the bandage was visible. She bent over the narrow stretcher cot to confirm it was Esmé. Silent relief flooded her being when she recognized her child and detected breathing, shallow but present.

She looked furtively around her to make sure nobody was watching, then lifted one side of the sheet and squeezed in behind Esmé with her free arm draped around her waist. Lying together like two spoons was as natural as it was awkward in the narrow cot. She lay for a while, worrying what would happen in the morning, praying for a miracle and wishing she had relieved herself one last time before sneaking into Esmé's tent.

Her thoughts drifted to her family and to their farm, to her beloved Johan, whom she would see in heaven someday, and to her son William—so proud and strong, so much like his father—whom she hoped to see when the war was over, although her last memory of her beloved son was the sight of him being chased by Mandela and shot at by the Tommies.

The last image in her mind before the dark claimed her was the shrouded figure of Jesus walking across moonlit water towards her... reaching out... his hands and face as black as the night.

PART TWO

1902—1963

After the Anglo-Boer War ended in 1902, the Act of Union in 1910 united the four provinces into a single nation, and a Boer general became prime minister under a British governor general. During the two world wars of the 20th century, South Africa supported Britain against Germany, although many Afrikaners objected, others rebelled, and some even engaged in acts of sabotage.

In 1948, a whites-only election under the "separate but equal" banner of apartheid ushered in an era of Afrikaner determination to consolidate power and preserve white-minority rule. After the Sharpeville massacre in 1961, leading anti-apartheid groups, including the African National Congress (ANC), were banned as unlawful organizations. Peaceful protest turned to militant resistance, and Nelson Mandela was chosen by the ANC to lead this next phase of their struggle.

The same period witnessed the rise of global communism and the Cold War, a war that included a scramble by the two superpowers for influence in sub-Saharan Africa.

Mandela went into hiding before leaving South Africa to generate support for the armed struggle and to receive military training. When he returned, he carried a Makarov pistol and ammunition that he buried at a hideout near Johannesburg on a farm called Liliesleaf, underground headquarters of the banned South African Communist Party. The farm hideout was also where he and his comrades in the high command of the newly formed militant organization Umkhonto we Sizwe—"The Spear of the Nation"—drew up secret plans for the armed struggle against apartheid.

18

THE ALTAR OF FREEDOM

1903

General Smuts returned to camp late one afternoon, erect in the saddle of his dark gelding, but with an inscrutable expression under the brim of his well-worn felt hat.

The men were pleased to have him back. There had been a lot of speculation about the talks—whether the Tommies had finally surrendered or if they were still at war—but all they were told was that Smuts would speak to them after he had rested.

William could barely contain his frustration. After waiting so long for news of his family, there was no sign of Deneys. Aside from the general, the only other person he knew who had been at the talks and might have some answers was the general's secretary.

"What happened?" he demanded as he barged into the secretary's tent without any of the usual pleasantries.

The secretary was sitting on a campstool with his head in his hands. He looked up sharply. "Ag, man, you heard—the general will talk later."

"No, man, I mean what happened to Deneys?"

"What?"

"Deneys. Where is he?"

"How the hell should I know?" The secretary bristled at William's aggressive tone. "I saw him at the conference. But he disappeared after the treaty was signed."

"What do you mean disappeared? Where did he go?"

"Man, I just told you. I don't bloody know. His father talked about going to America or Madagascar. Maybe Deneys went with him or with his brothers."

William stared at the secretary in disbelief. "Ag, Lord...dear Jesus," he moaned and sank to his knees as his exasperation deflated. It felt as though his last reserves of strength were draining into the sand beneath him.

"What is it, man?" asked the secretary, surprised by the sudden transformation. "What's so important about Deneys?"

"My mother and sister...I haven't heard from them since the Tommies burned our farm. I asked Deneys to bring news."

"Ah, now I understand," said the secretary, his tone softening. "Deneys did not forget," he said as he reached into a pocket of his overcoat. "He asked me to give you this."

William stared at the note in the secretary's hand. Time seemed to lurch to a halt. For a moment it seemed his entire world—past, present and future—was wrapped within the folds of the insignificant-looking note. He tentatively unfolded the single sheet message penned in crisp longhand:

Dear William,

> *I'm sorry, but I don't have good news. I couldn't find any record of your mother and sister. They did not have the camp registers at the conference. Nobody knew anything of them. I'm really sorry, William.*

As for the conference, it did not end well for our people. Kitchener told us he has four hundred thousand troops in the field against our eighteen thousand. It was hopeless. I'm going with my brother to Madagascar. My other two brothers are already gone. The Tommies sent one to a prison in India and the other to a prison in Bermuda. My father is also leaving. He says he is going to America and will not return until liberty comes to our land. He wrote this poem:

South Africa,
Whatever foreign shores my feet must tread,
My hopes for thee are not yet dead.
Thy freedom's sun may for a while be set,
But not forever, God does not forget.

Good luck, William. I hope you find your family and that we meet again someday as free men. I know we will answer the call when it comes.

Deneys.

William covered his face in his hands. "Ag, no... dear Jesus," he groaned, his despair as much a prayer for relief as an accusation of divine heartlessness.

Then, just as he was about to ask about the camps, a shout went up outside the tent that Smuts was about to speak. The secretary helped him to his feet and steered him out of the tent.

He was in no mood to be sociable and stayed in the shadows as the men gathered around an ammunition box in the middle of the camp. The general emerged from his tent just as the sun touched the dark line of the horizon. Moments later, Smuts stepped onto the ammunition box, his silhouette crisp against the setting sun, and began to speak.

William quickly realized he couldn't hear well from the perimeter and moved closer, just in time to hear Smuts say "—humanly speaking, where there is no reasonable chance to retain our independence, it becomes our duty to stop the struggle." The general paused to allow his words to sink in as a groundswell of disbelief surged through the men.

Smuts waited for quiet. "We must not sacrifice the Afrikaner people on the altar of independence. We have moved to stand fast to the bitter end. But let us be men and acknowledge that the end has now come… and it was more bitter than we thought it would be." The general coughed and cleared his throat, as though choking on the disappointment of it all. "For death itself would be sweeter than the step we must now take."

Then Smuts paused, drew himself tall and, in a firm voice trembling with conviction, declared, "It has been a war for freedom—not only for freedom of all the Boers, but for the freedom of all the nations in South Africa. No one shall ever convince me that this unparalleled sacrifice that the Afrikaner nation has laid upon the altar of freedom will be in vain."

By the time Smuts finished speaking, some of the men were crying and some were praying. But others were swearing, refusing to give up the struggle—that it was the will of almighty God that they live free in their promised land. One even shouted, "Jan Smuts, you have betrayed us!"

William shook his head in dismay. It was hard enough to believe in a God who would deliver his family to the Tommies, but to believe in a God who would deliver the entire Afrikaner people to the Tommies was beyond the pale.

As the men dispersed, he drifted back to the secretary's tent and found him standing outside in the dark, smoking his pipe.

"So what now?" asked William.

"Now?" replied the secretary. "Now we are serfs of the enemy. Now we have to bow and scrape to some bloody redneck king called Edward." He shook his head and took several long draws on his pipe, reigniting the tobacco until it glowed in the dark. "And it's not just bad for us," he added as an afterthought, "the poor kaffirs got royally fucked!"

"What are you talking about?" The change in topic was jarring. "What do the kaffirs have to do with anything?"

"Quite a lot as it turns out," said the secretary. "Early in the war, the British huffed and puffed about not forgetting to be kind and generous to the natives, that one of the goals of the war was to improve their lot in life. They even promised equal rights to the blacks and coloreds if Britain won the war." The secretary shook his head. "But after they won, when they had the chance to shove it down our throats, they conveniently forgot their promises. Milner said they only had to sacrifice the 'niggers'—that's what he calls our kaffirs—and reconciliation with us would be easy."

The secretary paused to tap ash from the bowl of his pipe against the heel of his boot. William watched as the secretary repacked his pipe from a leather pouch, struck a match and held it over the pipe bowl, then drew deeply until he was satisfied the tobacco was evenly lit. It was a ritual he knew from watching his grandfather, a ritual of smoke and fire that seemed to suspend time—to evoke the past, satisfy the present and obscure the future.

"But let me tell you, De Beer," continued the secretary after a few slow draws that produced an aromatic cloud above the man's head, "reconciliation with us will not be easy." He shook his head. "Mark my words, this treaty will not sit well with De Wet and the bitter-enders. They don't want to hear what we achieved in the small print of the treaty. They know only death or glory, and they hear only one thing—that we surrendered and betrayed our freedom."

"It does not sit well with me either," replied William. "It feels like God has abandoned His covenant with us, thrown dirt on the corpse of our freedom, and walked away."

19

THE LONGING

1903

General Smuts told the men to go home. But the De Beer home lay in ruins, and William didn't know if his mother and sister were alive. He packed his saddlebags with a demoralizing sense of dislocation.

As it happened, the shortest distance between their camp and where most of the men were going was through Bloemfontein. On the outskirts of the city, a troop train full of exuberant Tommies waving and firing shots into the air thundered past the startled commando on its way south, proof positive the war was over and who had won.

When the commando broke apart, William headed directly to his grandparents' home on Zastron Street, near Grey College. After tethering his horse to the front-yard fence, he burst into the house, calling out as he headed down the hall, nearly colliding with his grandmother when she stepped out of the kitchen.

"Ma and Sissie? Are they here, Ouma? Are they safe?" he implored, grasping her frail shoulders. He knew the answer from the cry of anguish that choked her and felt the last thread of his family's connective tissue disintegrate even as he clung to his grandmother's skeletal frame.

"We didn't know until it was too late," she began, looking up at him through bleary eyes moistened by misery. "We don't know why she didn't come straight to us from the farm. And for months after the farm was burned we kept asking anyone who would listen for any news of them. And every Sunday after church we visited the camp to check the registrations." She sniffed and blew her nose. "Ag, Willie, we don't understand what happened... Perhaps they came early in the week and were already buried by the time we knew they were there."

A howl of torment erupted from deep within him as the awful certainty of his family's fate was laid bare.

"I'm so sorry, Willie," she said, pulling his head to her shoulder.

He felt her wet cheek against his, her embrace tighten as he shuddered. After the first flood of grief subsided, he asked, "Do you know where they are buried?"

She nodded. "We know, Willie... we know."

"Take me, Ouma, please."

"Today?"

"Now, Ouma. Please."

She looked at him for a moment as though to confirm his intent, then nodded. "Oupa... Oupa," she called over her shoulder. "Willie is here. He wants to go to the grave."

"Ja, ja. I heard," came the familiar and long-suffering voice of his grandfather as he appeared from a back room. "My God, it's good to see you, Willie," he said as they grasped hands. "Terrible about Susannah and Esmé, but what about you, my boy? Are you hurt? Wounded?"

"No, Oupa, I'm fine. But Ma and Sissie..." he began before choking up again.

"Ag, my boy, it's a sad business," said his grandfather as his grip tightened. "Of course I'll take you to the grave." He looked at his wife, who nodded her approval. "But we don't have our horse and buggy anymore—the Tommies took it all—so your horse will have to carry us both."

"Make him sit in front, Willie, so you can hold him," instructed his grandmother. "He's nothing but skin and bone these days. I don't want the old fool to fall off and break his neck."

William couldn't believe how unaffected the city looked as they rode through it. There were no signs of the war that had so recently consumed his people. But there was no mistaking the grotesque testament to the war when they reached the graveyard, a grim expanse of gray-brown earth interspersed with rows and rows of low rectangular mounds covered by stones paying mute tribute to departed souls. He couldn't see any grave markers. It looked as though all of creation, even God Himself, had forsaken their last resting place.

"When we heard they had been in the camp and passed on, we waited here for the next group," explained his grandfather as they picked their way on foot between the mounds. "We asked if anyone knew where they were buried. Thankfully someone did. Otherwise, we might never have found their plot."

The old man stopped unexpectedly. William thought he was trying to catch his breath until his frail finger pointed. The mound looked so stark in its ordinariness, so pitiful in its inadequacy. His mother's name was scratched into one of the larger stones. There were no thoughtful words or Bible verses, nothing to celebrate her life or mourn her passing.

His grandfather looked distressed. "We planned to come back after the war to put a proper marker on the grave."

"Where's the other grave?" asked William as he looked around him at the indistinguishable mounds. "Where's Sissie?"

"Over there," said his grandfather, pointing to a mound in the next row of graves. "There's a rock with her name on it."

William stared for a moment then sank to his knees beside his mother's mound and absent-mindedly rearranged some of the rocks. He felt his grandfather's hand on his shoulder until the pull and push of his emotion subsided, his sorrow and rage reaching some level of equilibrium.

"Where's the camp?" he asked as he looked beyond the field of graves.

"Ag, Willie, there's not much to see."

"Please, Oupa."

His grandfather nodded. After a brief stop at his sister's grave they remounted. It was a short ride and his grandfather was right. The camp looked unimaginably benign. Where he expected to see something monstrous, all he could see was a deserted, semi-arid area with little more than a scattering of white sailcloth and debris—signs of habitation but without form—that revealed nothing of the horror it had facilitated.

"Where is everybody?"

"Who knows?" said the old man, his tone tired and despondent. "It was a mess, a holding camp for thousands on their way to other camps. People were coming and going all the time. At one time there were more people in the camp than in Bloemfontein. The women and children who survived waited weeks for their men after the peace was signed. They eventually left. I suppose some went back to their farms or what's left of them. Others went to Bloemfontein. Many have nowhere to go."

William groaned. His grandfather's explanation added salt to the wound. "The damned Tommies are like an Old Testament plague. They came—wreaked havoc—then left." He could taste the bitterness rising from his gut. "But I see the ghosts of our people,

Oupa. I see the bodies of our mothers and children piled on top of each other, sacrificed for our freedom. It will forever come between us and the cursed Tommies."

"Ja, that's the truth, Willie. We can never forget or forgive. And I can't believe God will either. Vengeance will be His...unless we get the bastards first."

"I hope so, Oupa. I hope so," he said, wiping his eyes on his sleeve. "Someday our people will right this wrong. I just hope I live to see the day. And if I can help, I will, so help me God."

They rode back to the house in silence.

"I want to rebuild the farm," announced William that night. The aroma of lamb stew still hung in the air, even in the living room where they sat. It had been his first home-cooked meal for as long as he could remember. "And if I ever get my hands on Mandela," he added, "I will kill him for leading the Tommies to our farm...and for what happened afterwards."

"Ag, Willie, my boy," said his grandfather, "best to forget about Mandela. He is long gone." The old man sighed. "And I wish we could help with the farm. But we only have enough money to live on. And even that will soon be gone."

"I have no money, Oupa, even to live on." He swallowed hard. "What can I do? There must be something...anything?"

"I know one thing we can do," interjected his grandmother as she headed towards the kitchen. "We can have some tea and milk tart."

They sat in silence for several minutes, staring at the fireplace flames, until his grandfather spoke from the cushioned depths of his favorite chair. "I don't know, Willie. It's the same story everywhere. Our people have no money, no food and our farms have been laid waste." The old man paused, sucking air through his unlit pipe. "Many are going to the gold mines. The money is good, but the work is hard, and I'm too old for that."

The despair in his grandfather's voice cut a fresh wound in William's ragged emotions. "Then I will go, Oupa," he said, infused with sudden hope. "I'm not afraid of hard work. Then I can send you money. And perhaps I can make enough for the farm as well."

"Ag, Willie, I didn't mean you should go to the mines. You have only just come back to us. Besides, your grandmother will not like it—you're all that's left of our family."

"If that's where the money is, Oupa, then that's where I must go. Just tell me how I get there. Is there a special place I must go... people I must talk to?"

His grandfather looked over his shoulder towards the kitchen. "Are you sure about this, Willie?" he whispered. "You can't tell her I told you of the mines, understand."

"Ja, ja, Oupa, I'm sure," he said with a wry smile. "And I won't tell her you told me."

The old man sighed and relit his pipe, sucking hard until the draw was good. He blew several circles of smoke, fleeting targets that seemed to focus his attention.

"Getting there is the easy part," he began. "Just take the train from Bloemfontein to Johannesburg. That's where the mines are, where they found the gold reef. But it's a terrible place," he said through a haze of tobacco smoke. "Kruger calls it the devil's town."

"What's a gold reef, Oupa?"

"I'm not exactly sure, Willie. But the papers say it's like a ribbon of gold-bearing rock that runs in a curve from deep underground. And where the ribbon breaks the surface of the earth it makes a ridge of gold. They say the ridge runs for fifty or sixty miles."

"So do the miners just break the rock and pick up the gold? That doesn't sound too hard."

"Ag, no, Willie. At the start it was easy. The lucky buggers who got there first found gold in pebbles that glistened after a rain like sugar-coated almonds." The old man chuckled. "Those were tasty pickings. But the gold pebbles are long gone. Now the miners have to chase the reef as it curves down into the earth. And that means going underground, down deep shafts and long tunnels to dig the gold out with picks and shovels and dynamite. It's hard work, Willie. Dangerous too."

He nodded soberly. "I'm as strong as the next man, Oupa. And what can be more dangerous than Spion Kop?"

His grandfather fidgeted with his pipe. "But you must be careful, Willie. Johannesburg is like Sodom and Gomorrah, full of foreigners and fornicators. It's the devil's city, my boy, just like Kruger says."

"Ja, Oupa. So, anyway, where do I go when I get off the train?"

The old man pondered the question. "Well, my boy, there are many mines on the ridge and foreigners like Rhodes and Barnato—Englishmen and Jews—own almost every one. But there's at least one owner who was born here, J.B. Robinson, a friend of Kruger. People say his gold mine is one of the richest...and one of the deepest."

"You think that's where I should go, Oupa, to his mine?"

"If you are determined, Willie, then yes. Go to Robinson Deep."

20

CORDS OF SALVATION

1903

A whistle blew. With a belch of black smoke the train lurched and chugged away from the camp.

Henry glanced at the new arrivals—just another ragged group of villagers. He was about to turn away when he saw a figure he recognized, walking slowly, heaviness in every step, with a fixed stare as though resigned to the fate that awaited her.

"Mother," he called as he strode towards her. "It's me... Henry Mandela from the Transkei."

Miriam reacted as though woken from a trance. Her face immediately cracked into a wide, white smile.

"Where's Jonas?" she asked when they came together. "Is my boy here? Is he well?"

"Yes," Henry reassured her, smiling broadly. "He's well and he is with me. He is collecting firewood."

"And the people from my village?"

"They are here also," he said, expecting her to be pleased. Instead, she emitted a long wail and sank to the ground. He stared at her for a few awkward moments, not sure what to do. "I will find Jonas, mother," he said and turned away.

Miriam had barely moved when he returned with Jonas and was nearly bowled over when the boy threw himself into her arms. Henry watched as she rubbed the curly dark hair that framed the boy's face with obvious pleasure.

Then she looked at him. "And you, Henry Mandela? Are you well?"

"Yes, mother, I'm well. I saw the soldiers bring you to the train. We were on the same train. Did they catch you quickly after you left the village?"

"Yes...on the second day. Their fence and horsemen blocked our way." She sniffed. "Then they put us on the train to the camp."

"What happened to—"

"How is this place?" interrupted Miriam, looking away. "Do the soldiers make it hard for you?"

He was slow to respond, not wanting to cause unnecessary distress so soon after her arrival. "It is not a good place, mother."

She nodded, as though it was the answer she expected. "Do you and Jonas have a place to sleep?"

"Yes, mother, we made a shelter."

"Then take me there, for I am tired from the train."

A scattered chorus of *'Dumela mma...Dumela mma'* greeted Miriam as she picked her way through the patchwork of canvas and animal skin shelters, open fires and cooking pots. But he was embarrassed when they reached the shelter he and Jonas had built near the edge of the camp. They had scavenged far and wide, but their best efforts had only produced a flimsy wooden structure that provided the barest shelter. The sacking on the roof leaked and there was not enough material to cover the sides of the shelter.

"This was all we could find, mother," he said apologetically as Miriam looked over the shelter. "It is cold at night," he added. "Especially when the wind blows."

She nodded and ducked under the sacking. "Come, sit with me, Henry Mandela," she called as she settled down with Jonas on his blanket. "I saw people from our village as we walked," she said as he sat down opposite her. "Are they all in this place?"

"I think so, mother. They all got off the train at this place."

"And so? How are they?"

"I cannot speak about each one, mother, but there are some things I can tell you."

"Then tell me, Henry. I need to know."

There was no way to avoid the truth. "Many have died in this camp, mother. Some from your village also." He paused, respectful of the dismay in her features. "The soldier in charge says there are about fifty camps like this one, and that many of our people die every day."

"I heard of such things at the Boer camp," she said, rocking back and forth, shaking her head. "I hoped it was not true."

He nodded, his eyes downcast. "The soldier says there are too many of us here. There is not enough firewood for cooking, we have no vegetables or milk, the water is dirty and there are no doctors."

"What food do you have?"

"Ah," he sighed. "Mielies is all we can get... and some mieliemeal. No meat. And we have to buy our food, but the only way to pay for the food is to work for the soldiers. If we refuse to work, they charge double for the food."

"Ow," replied Miriam. "In the Boer camp they get rations for free. They refused to give me rations, but the Boer mother shared her food with me." She sniffed and looked around at the camp. "And what is the work?"

"Fetching, carrying, digging, loading wagons—whatever the soldiers say. But there is much talk of the mines. The soldier says white people place great value on the yellow rock under the ground." He paused. "He thinks it's the reason for the war. The Boers want to own the land, the British want to own what's under the land and—"

"And we just want to live on the land," she added, her tone bitter. "I tell you, Henry, one day our people will rise up in rage at what the white people are doing to our land and to our people."

He nodded. He understood the sentiment but wasn't comfortable talking about such things.

"Jonas," she said abruptly. "Take me to the people of our village. I must greet my people."

In their absence, Henry did what he could to tidy the shelter and prepare the evening meal. By the time they returned, the night air was thick with aromas drifting over the camp from multiple cooking pots. He wished he had more to offer than samp and beans, but it was sufficient. They shared a plate and ate with their hands.

His thoughts went back to the two Boer women. "I saw you and the Boer mother and child get off the train at the Boer camp," he began as they scraped up the last morsels. "What happened afterwards? Why did the soldiers put you back on the train to this place?"

Miriam was quiet for several moments. Then she sighed and began to speak. "That place was better than here, but many died there also. They have a hospital and nurses and doctors but it doesn't seem to help. She shook her head. "The Boer women believe the children die when they go to the hospital tent, although I heard the sick are fed better in the hospital than the others, that they even get some special foods that nobody else gets." She paused to wipe her eyes. "The mother took the young one to the hospital tent before she heard the stories. She wanted to take her away again, but she could not. So she went to the tent in the night to be with her."

"And then?"

"In the day I went there. I asked for her and the young one by name, but the nurses chased me away."

"Ow!" said Henry, his concern growing.

"So I waited with the other mothers. They did not mind. They knew I was the maid. After a while the nurses brought the young one and laid her outside the tent with the others who had died in the night."

"Ow!"

"Then the mother came out and sat with her child. She did not speak. After a while the wagon came and took the bodies to the place where the Boers buried their dead. There were already many buried there." She shook her head. "The space was hard to dig. Then the women sang and one read from their book. Afterwards the mother scratched some writing on a stone to mark the grave.

"I do not know why the young one died," continued Miriam. "Her head had stopped bleeding, but she had many red spots on her face and her chest."

"Ow," he muttered. "I have seen such spots on the sick. But what of the mother?"

"She was not well. At first I thought it was because of her child. But she was very hot. She had pain in her head and her stomach. And I had to help her go to the buckets many times."

The tremor in Miriam's voice caused Henry to hold his breath—he sensed the story would not end well.

"After three days her sickness was very bad. She had no more strength and did not want to go to the doctor. She just wanted to go to her god and be with her husband and children. She said there was nothing left for her on this earth. It was in the night in the tent. She held my hand as she said the prayer her people say... She did not finish."

Miriam moaned softly and swallowed hard. "We took her the

next day to the graves. One of the Boer women scratched some words on a stone by her grave."

"Ow!" he exclaimed. "I am very sorry to hear this terrible thing. I wanted to take her to her people after we escaped from the farm. But then the soldiers came to the village . . ." His voice trailed off.

They sat in silence for several minutes.

"And after she was buried?" he asked.

"When the soldiers saw I was alone—not the maid of anyone—they said I had to go to a camp for our people on the next train."

"Why this camp?"

"Nobody told me where to get off. But the missionary who named me spoke of America—he told me stories of its many peoples, of its great mountains and lakes, and showed me the name in books. So I got off the train when I saw the name next to this camp."

"Ow," he replied, astonished by the coincidence. "I am happy you came here and found Jonas. He is a good boy. He looks after the soldiers' horses. They pay him enough to buy a little food."

"What about you, Henry? Do you have work?"

He nodded. "I work as a translator. But the soldier says I should leave this place and go to the mines. He can put me on the train. And now that you are here, that is what I will do."

She looked at him with sad eyes. "The mines are not a good place. My husband went there. He did not come back." She wiped her eyes. "Are you sure you must do this?"

"It is a hard thing to know what to do, mother, but the soldier says I should go to Robinson Deep. He says the wages are good. I can earn money to take to my family in the Transkei."

She nodded. "I understand. I will go back to my village when the white people stop fighting. If it is burned, we will build it again." She paused. "When will you go to the mine?"

"I will talk to the soldier, mother. The trains pass every day."

She looked into his eyes and held Jonas close. After several moments she sighed. "Then go well, Henry Mandela from the Transkei. And stay safe."

He patted the boy on the head as he rose to leave.

"Thank you, mother. Stay well."

Then he turned and went out into the night.

Henry hated going underground. Fear and tension clamped around him every time the gates of the caged elevator clanged shut. He felt like a human sacrifice being lowered into the maws of an enormous beast—a voracious, terrifying creature living in the bowels of the earth, burrowing, chewing, swallowing and excreting gold-bearing rock—kept alive by white men in dark suits and shiny cars.

More than a hundred miners died every month amidst collapsing tunnels and deafening noise, intense heat and numbing humidity, dynamite blasts and clouds of dust. Many more were hurt or crippled. To add to the danger, there was the constant threat of being caught up in the savage underground fights between rival groups, and of beatings from white supervisors and their black boss boys. He never knew from one moment to the next whether he would emerge alive at the end of a shift.

And life aboveground was no less dangerous. Men from all over were forced to live together in cramped hostels—Zulus, Sothos, Mpondos, Xhosas and many others. Aside from the inevitable gang fights, their only relief was homemade beer and the sport of stick fighting. But even the stick fights sometimes turned deadly.

How different his experience was to what his father had described, where the miners had dug a huge hole in the ground but could always see the sky. Here, instead of a hole at the mine's center, a huge triangular iron structure towered over the compound, its great wheels of winding gears lowering the cage carrying miners and raising rock ore to the surface. Close to the headgear stood the strange-looking stamp batteries for crushing and grinding the ore, and the sheds where the crushed ore was treated and the gold extracted. And the giant wheel that never stopped turning, carrying the waste ore and water to the slag heaps—the ever-growing, yellow-brown mountains of waste that defined the landscape of Johannesburg.

He was surprised to find Boers working in the same conditions as himself—diggers just like him—competing for jobs with miners who were just as unskilled but worked for less pay because they weren't white, adding to the tension underground. But at least the Boers were kept in separate living quarters aboveground, although some lived in hovels and shanties on the outskirts of the city.

Rubbing shoulders with Boer miners reminded him of his father's flogging. He could almost taste the diamond his father had carried in his mouth that day as he climbed out of the Big Hole. And his back twitched whenever he thought of the cat-o'-nine-tails tearing into his father's flesh.

Henry stared at the rock face and blinked as sweat turned the grit in his eyes into a burning irritant. The pickax felt impossibly heavy after hours working above shoulder height in a crude tunnel of jagged rock edges, his feet constantly slipping on the wet and uneven surface.

He knew they were in the deepest part of the mine, nearly a thousand feet below the surface. He couldn't visualize what that meant exactly, but it hardly mattered. It was enough to know he was very deep under the city of gold.

It had been a hard shift. A section of tunnel had collapsed, trapping four, killing one. After helping to free the trapped miners, he had worked to clear the fallen rock and shore up the tunnel with lengths of lumber, his efforts hampered by yet another bout of coughing brought on by the clouds of dust. By the time he resumed work on the rock face, every fiber of his body felt stretched beyond breaking point.

Finally, mercifully, the boss boy gave the signal—the shift was over.

Henry and his group of workers shuffled sullenly along the labyrinthine tunnel towards the main shaft, their path illuminated by occasional lanterns flickering through the dank haze of mine air. Sounds of hammering and drilling and distant blasts reverberated through the tunnels, as though the monstrous beast had severe indigestion.

The cage was seldom on time, but he could hear it descending as he stood in the front row of the group waiting to be taken to the surface. The sound of the cage clattering and banging its way down hundreds of feet of crudely erected metal and wood framing always unsettled him. It was never simply mechanical and benign but invariably malevolent and threatening, as though impending disaster was descending upon his head in a ferocious crescendo of hard-edged violence.

As tired as he was, he instinctively tensed as the cage reached his level. Even after it finally banged to a stop, it took a few moments before he started to relax. He breathed out slowly and felt the tension drain as his body succumbed to a familiar leaden weariness. But as anxious as the men were to get to the surface, they had to wait for the miners in the cage to exit before they could board.

As the last few exiting miners stepped out of the cage, the press from behind forced him forward, and he stumbled, colliding with the last miner exiting the cage. As he staggered back, he noticed heavy drilling rods in the miner's white hands. He was about to apologize for his clumsiness when their eyes met.

Recognition was instant.

An enraged howl filled the cage as the miner dropped the drilling rods and lunged at him. Henry was slow to react and offered little resistance when the man's hands closed around his shoulders like animal traps before jerking him into the empty cage and flinging him down. As he crashed to the floor with the man on top of him, his mind flashed back to the time he had held this same Boer to the ground before knocking him out to save his life. Now the Boer had him pinned beneath his knees and was punching at him like a man possessed. As painful as the beating was, he was thankful the Boer was using his fists and not one of the drilling rods he had dropped.

"Bastard," yelled the Boer. "They're dead... because of you... I saw it all... Black bastard!"

Henry thought about trying to explain but knew there would be no reasoning with this Boer. The man's blows were almost rhythmic in their brutality, the way he imagined the German's whip had been as it stripped the flesh from his father's back. He heard his nose crack, felt the fragments of teeth on his tongue, and could taste the blood and saliva filling his throat.

"They're dead... Now you die," the Boer raged, punctuating each syllable with a punch.

He tried bucking the Boer off by thrusting his hips upwards, but the man's punches hardly missed a beat. As he felt consciousness slipping away, he became dimly aware of a brief respite in the punching. Then he saw what he had feared—the Boer had a drilling rod in his hands and was raising it above his head like a stabbing spear.

Henry stared at the tip of the rod, too exhausted to resist, and wondered what it would feel like as it skewered his chest. He watched it stop as the Boer's arms reached their full height. He locked eyes with the Boer for an instant before the rod plunged downwards.

He flinched, instinctively bracing himself for the deathblow. But in the same instant, as though a witch-doctor's magic was at work, cords of black arms materialized around the Boer and dragged him backwards. He heard a howl of frustrated rage as the Boer, still clutching the drilling rod, stabbed wildly but futilely, as though at a ghost only he could see.

Through bloodied and bruised eyes, Henry saw three fellow miners wrestle the Boer to his feet and the rod from his hands, before forcing him out of the cage. A group of black miners closed ranks in a wall of bodies around the cage, ushered in a load fellow miners, then shut the gate and gave the signal to raise the cage. He could still hear the Boer raging as the cage jolted into motion.

He tried to process what had just happened as the cage clattered its way to the surface. Only one thing he knew for certain—he had to leave the mine immediately. He had no doubt the Boer would follow in the next cage. The crazed fury he had twice experienced with the man reminded him of the explosive rage of a wounded African buffalo that would not quit until it had hunted its tormentor to the death.

He took the fight with the Boer as a sign—it was time to go home. He had been at the mine for nearly a full cycle of the seasons. And although the money was good, he no longer had the stomach for life underground. He knew when the heat came again, even if he survived the harshness of life at the mine, the dust and his coughing would be insufferable.

The cage shuddered to a halt.

21

HEWERS OF WOOD, DRAWERS OF WATER

1912–1918

The salty air of the Indian Ocean sometimes reached Henry's village of Mvezo amid the rolling hills overlooking the Mbashe River. He was home, and the rhythm of his life soon readjusted to the tempo of his village and the pulse of his Thembu people.

The relief from being far removed from the cramped confinement and urgent clamor of the mines—from the whistles, bells and blasts, the caged descent into the hot and unforgiving darkness below—was profound. But the mines had paid well, and over the years he had been appointed chief of his village by King Dalindyebo, amassed a large herd, plenty of land, and become a respected member of his community, counselor to the king and repository of the history and traditions of his people.

He had also married—several times, as was the custom—and his wives had given him twelve children. Each of his four wives had her own set of huts—one for cooking, another for sleeping, a third for storage—and each set of huts was separated from the other wives' huts, a happy and practical arrangement.

His only vexation was the coughing. It had started at the mine and become progressively worse over the years.

One of his duties as counselor was to accompany the king to important events, and there was never a doubt that the founding of the South African Native National Congress was such an occasion. Despite the discomfort of the broiling heat that enveloped the meeting hall in Bloemfontein that summer, he was thrilled to be there with his king.

The sense of expectation among the delegates was almost palpable. The national events that had brought them together in 1912 were unprecedented, as was the fact pointed out by their opening speaker, Pixley Seme, that this was the first time so many different tongues and tribes had ever attempted to cooperate under one umbrella.

"Chiefs of royal blood and gentlemen of our race," Seme continued in a somber tone, "we have gathered here to consider a theme that my colleagues and I have decided to place before you. We have discovered that in the land of their birth, Africans are treated as hewers of wood and drawers of water."

The erudition of the young Zulu lawyer was extraordinary. Henry knew of Seme's writings and that he had been to great universities in America and England, but to hear him speak was thrilling. And the decorum and civility displayed by all the delegates despite the serious theme and smothering heat was admirable. The top hats, suits, and frock coats he saw conjured images of Victorian England, as though fine English clothes were essential to enlightened culture and discourse.

He glanced at King Dalindyebo, sitting in the front row with the other paramount chiefs. Even though the Zulu chief was absent, it was still impressive to see eight chiefs sitting together in regal splendor, listening imperiously as Seme spoke of how the white people had formed what they called the "Union of South Africa," a union in which the black people had no voice and played no part in its administration.

Henry thought he understood the Union issue, but Seme's commentary was troubling. During a break he sought an audience with the king and found him outside the hall in the shade of a jacaranda tree.

"I tell you, Henry," explained the king as they sat together, "this Union is the final insult that gives the lie to the British sense of fairness we counted on. The peace treaty with the Boers and then the Union were driven by Lord Milner's belief that the white man has to rule because he is elevated so many steps above the black man... that equality between our people and the whites is impossible."

The king snorted and shook his head. "We sent expressions of loyalty to King Edward. We even sent a delegation to London to try to convince British leaders of the injustice of the Union." The king's gray head drooped. "Nobody listened. Our faith in the British was completely misplaced. It's a union of deceit against our people, Henry, built on lies and written in blood."

They sat in silence as the king poured a handful of dirt from one hand to the other as though musing over the shifting sands of fortune. The stifling heat and lament of a mourning dove seemed to add weight to an already oppressive moment. An occasional pedestrian kicked up dust around them, as though to further cloud the murkiness of human motivation.

"Why do they do these things?" asked Henry.

The king sighed. "Ah, Henry, a good question without a good answer. I can't understand the British, but it is proof they have reconciled their differences with the Boers and are united in all things, including how they will treat our people in our own land. As for the Boers, we are many and they are few. I think they are afraid to live with us, but they can't live without us. So they squash us into tiny lands to keep us separate, then herd us like animals to work in their cities and mines, far from our homes and families."

The king paused again, gazed at the dirt in the palm of his hand, then tipped his hand and watched the grains cascade to the ground. Henry sensed the king was not yet done and dared not interrupt.

"But these things happen in other places too," continued the king. "Our African peoples have been taken across the seas to strange lands and forced to be slaves." The king lifted his head and gazed into the distance. "The American people fought a great war over these things. But here our people are treated like slaves in our own land." The king drew a deep breath. "Perhaps the time will come, Henry, when our people also have to fight a great war to be free, to be treated as equals by the whites before their god... or any other god."

The king scratched his head, as though trying to dislodge a great truth. "But the whites will try to keep us apart, deepen the divisions between us, make us fight each other. So we will need a special leader for such a fight, someone who can unite us and rekindle ubuntu among our people."

The king's words gave Henry an idea. "Maybe this Congress will give us the leader we need," he blurted out before catching himself. He held his breath, hoping he had not said something stupid and offended the king.

The king nodded. "Perhaps, Henry. But don't get your hopes up. Our people are not good at this thing called national unity. You heard Seme—'the demon of racialism and tribalism among our own people is the cause of all our woes and backwardness and ignorance.'"

The king fell silent, then got slowly to his feet. "So, Henry, this is our challenge—to come together and find leaders for our people. Otherwise, our future is bleak. The Boers were never going to invite us into their kraal to sit down as equals. And now the British have made sure they never have to... unless we force our way past their wagons and inside their kraal."

Back in the hall, Henry was quickly caught up again in the thrill of being at the Congress despite the seriousness of the keynote issues. There were speeches on marriage and divorce, church and school, land and labor, and even one about African beer. And when Seme made a motion to form the South African Native National Congress, the vote was unanimous. All the delegates stood and cheered and sang hymns and songs.

Henry was especially moved by one of the Xhosa songs, a short hymn of just one verse. He was not a religious man, but the simple eloquence of the hymn moved him in ways he could not explain:

Nkosi, sikelel' iAfrika;	Lord, bless Africa;
Maluphakam' upondo lwayo;	May her horn rise high up;
Yiva imithandazo yethu	Hear Thou our prayers
Usisikelela.	And bless us.
Yihla Moya, Yihla Moya,	Descend, O Spirit,
Yihla Moya Oyingcwele.	Descend, O Holy Spirit.

Henry knew nothing of the Habsburg Empire or the city called Sarajevo, but he was fascinated that the assassination of a royal heir had precipitated a war between so many nations in such faraway lands. And although Mvezo and Dalindyebo's Great Place were a long way from the war, he knew the king expected him to be informed, especially in the wake of the Congress at Bloemfontein.

"So, what is this Great War all about?" asked the king one morning after Henry had been summoned to the Great Place. The king was pacing the floor, slapping a folded newspaper against the palm of his free hand.

"Well, my King, it seems there are two main alliances," he began tentatively. "One supported by Great Britain, the other by Germany, and—"

"Humph," interrupted the king, waving him to silence. "Just tell me one thing, Henry—are we for or against the British?"

Henry wished he had an easy answer to the king's question. Although his people had been loyal to the British during their war against the Boers, he knew some felt they were worse off than before, that they had received better treatment under the Boers than now under the British. But before he could formulate an answer, the king spoke again.

"And what do you make of the Boers fighting on the side of the British?"

"This is truly a great surprise, my King. I cannot understand their change of heart."

"And so?" prompted the king, pacing the floor. "Are we for or against the British?"

Henry took a deep breath. "My King, it does not matter whether we are for or against the British in their Great War. We must prepare for our own great war, the one you spoke of at the Congress, to be treated as equals by the whites, whether Boer or Brit or German."

The king stopped pacing and was silent for several minutes.

"That may be true, but it is no answer to my question." The king scratched his beard. "I do not care about the British and their war in faraway lands, but we have to deal with Botha and Smuts in our land." He reread the newspaper headlines, then took a deep breath, cleared his throat and regally drew himself to his full height.

"You will tell Botha that I, Dalindyebo, Paramount Chief of the Thembus, together with my best warriors will go with Smuts to fight the Germans in South West Africa. And you will come with me, Henry Mandela. This is my decision."

Henry was astonished and scrambled for an appropriate response. "The king is clever," he managed as his thoughts came together, "and a clever king is the brother of peace. If we support the Boers now, perhaps a future leader of our people might get them to open their kraal and let our people in as equals."

"Humph," grunted the king. "It is wishful thinking, but I like the idea. So tell me, Henry Mandela, where do you think we will find such a leader?"

The day after the Bolsheviks executed Czar Nicolas II and his family and just as Britain and her allies pushed towards victory in the Great War, Henry's third wife, Nosekeni, gave birth to his thirteenth child on a chilly winter morning in a thatched-roof mud hut near their village.

Henry sat patiently outside the hut, the glow from his pipe washing across his dark features in a gentle ebb and flow. He was waiting to be called after an indignant wail had heralded the moment of birth. He did not have to see what was going on—he knew the ritual well. After being washed, the baby would drink some drops made from juniper berries for good health. Then a paste made from aloe juice would be spread around the baby's umbilical cord near the navel until the cord dropped off. Some of the paste would be used to clean the baby's ears and to clear mucus from the baby's nose.

A little while later, Nosekeni emerged from the hut. He watched as she walked awkwardly to bury the afterbirth behind the group of three huts that formed her kraal. He knew the umbilical cord would also be buried there when the time came. She gave him a demure smile and nod as she reentered the hut.

Without a word, he followed her inside for the smoke ritual. He always enjoyed this part and the role he had to play. With his pipe clenched between his yellow teeth, he used both hands to light a small fire just inside the entrance to the hut. After it burned down, he dropped a few green twigs into the brushwood embers and, almost immediately, a thick cloud of acrid smoke billowed into the dim interior of the hut.

His task complete, he drew a deep, satisfied draw on his pipe and sat back on his haunches to watch as Nosekeni carefully unwrapped the baby from its blanket and exposed the nub of manhood. Then, her soft features illuminated by the glowing embers, she held the baby's hands in one hand, his feet in her other, and gently swung the upended child through the smoke. After several oscillations, she turned the baby over and swung him over the embers again, making sure his whole body was exposed to the smoke, all the while intoning softly, her lips barely moving.

Henry cherished the quiet symbolism of the smoke ritual. He imagined ancestral spirits responding to the mother's invocation, rising up through the fire to cloak the boy with their strength and protection. But the child squirmed and struggled, as though resenting the suffocating smoke and desperate to discover which blurry view of the world was the right side up.

Hah! thought Henry with satisfaction. *A feisty child, a troublemaker if ever I saw one.*

He named the writhing infant Rolihlahla—"Shaker of Trees."

Seven years later, on his first day of school in a one-room schoolhouse over the hill from his village, proudly wearing a pair of his father's trousers cut off at the knees and cinched around his waist with a piece of string, Rolihlahla's teacher would give him an English name—as was the custom—and call him "Nelson."

22

DIVIDED LOYALTIES

1914

William hated the mine—the heat, sweat, blasts and fights, the constant stench of fear and despair as miserable men tore at impervious rock like rats scratching for food. And he'd had enough of the black faces with orbs of white glaring in sullen resentment at their fate.

Although he was now a supervisor and accustomed to the routine, he still had to go underground every day into one of the deepest mines in the world. And every time he rode the cage and the door opened he half expected to bump into Mandela. He still cursed when he thought of the fight—he had so nearly finished it that day.

It was hard to believe that was twelve years ago. He had scoured the compound, searched the hostels, watched every shift change, but it seemed Mandela had disappeared into thin air. The only trace of him had come from the mine register thanks to a sympathetic clerk. The man had remembered the well-spoken black miner with the tuft of white hair above his forehead and had confirmed the entry in the register: "Mandela, Henry. Mvezo, Transkei (Xhosa)."

His sole refuge was Anna. It had been a hard decision when Izak, his closest friend at the mine and Anna's brother, first invited him to their family farm near the Sterkfontein Caves, northwest of Krugersdorp. He usually spent his precious time off work going back to his own farm at Sannah's Post and visiting his grandparents in Bloemfontein. But that was before he met Anna. Her mother had insisted that Anna had not yet filled out after being in the camp where her sister died, but Anna had looked wonderful to him from every angle.

His weekend visits became frequent and Izak proved an able facilitator. After church they would stroll together below the farmhouse and across a shallow stream into the walnut grove beyond. It was shaded and secluded, and Izak invariably managed to find his interest drawn to a different area of the grove.

The progression had been excruciatingly restrained—a furtive glance, a shy smile—until one Sunday their hands inadvertently collided as they walked in the grove. He had been mortified by his clumsiness but thrilled when Anna clasped his hand. Hand-in-hand they had walked until he found some rocks at the edge of the stream to sit on, with Anna sitting a little below him. They were talking of families and children when Anna had turned to look up at him just as dappled rays of sunshine drifted across her radiant features, illuminating the soft moisture of her lips.

Without thinking, he had bent down and kissed the corner of her mouth. She had instinctively pulled back but then turned more fully towards him. He had been afraid to make another move until she nodded and smiled. He had cautiously bent forward and, when she did not recoil, their lips had come together in a featherlight moment of awkward intimacy.

But just as he started to believe his life's path had found true north, an unexpected sacrilege stopped him in his tracks. Two of his heroes from the Second War of Freedom—General Botha, now the Union's Prime Minister, and General Smuts, the Union's Minister of Defense—agreed to support Britain in her war against Germany. Smuts said it was a matter of duty and honor and that they would show their support by invading German South West Africa.

William saw it differently, as a matter of treachery and dishonor to take them into a war against the only people to have supported their fight for freedom against the British. And to take them to war on the side of Britain only added insult to injury. It made him sick to his stomach every time he saw the Union Jack flying over South Africa or was forced to sing "God Save the King." At every opportunity he sang the alternate version:

God save our noble king,
Wash him in paraffin,
And set fire to him.

To expect him to wrap himself in the Union Jack and fight on the same side as his most bitter enemy was too much, a bridge too far. Had not Smuts himself told them how their surrender to the Tommies was more bitter than they could ever have predicted? And had not Botha gone to Germany to accept eighty thousand pounds from the German people after the war? The newspapers had showed him on his knees thanking the man who gave him the money. Yet now they were supposed to turn around and shoot the same German out of duty to the King of England.

He would not do it—he could not do it.

Above all, if he now fought for the Tommies, it would be like forgiving the British for their barbarism against his family and his people. He could not imagine stepping over the barrier of children's bodies, including his sister's, to take up arms for Britain in the name of honor and duty to the king of England.

The call for commandos to bring their "pipes and matches" to a reunion was unmistakable—every right-minded Afrikaner understood it was a call to armed rebellion. And when General de Wet stepped forward to lead the rebels in the Orange Free State, William did not hesitate. At least one of his former leaders remained true to the covenant. But Anna did not take the news well. Not only were her parents implacably opposed to the rebellion and determined to remain loyal to Botha and Smuts, but if he joined the rebellion he would no longer be welcome in their home.

It was a difficult parting. Denied a comforting word as he rode slowly out of the farmyard, he was lost in a whirlwind of conflicting loyalties, determined to be faithful to the cause of freedom, yet disorientated by the wrenching banishment from Anna's family. He turned in his saddle just in time to see her disappear into the farmhouse.

He felt rather foolish as he pressed ahead. He had a horse and some food, but no rifle and ammunition—no pipe and matches—for the fight he was joining. But his despair was short-lived when, less than a mile from the farm, a rider suddenly appeared around a kopje at full gallop, heading straight towards him. Moments later the wide-eyed horse thundered to a halt a few yards away in a cloud of dust and lather.

"I took the shortcut," said Izak breathlessly. "Here, man, take my Mauser. You can't fight the bloody government without a gun."

"Where the hell did you get this?" asked William as he reached for the rifle. "We were supposed to hand over our guns when we surrendered."

"Ja, man, I know," said Izak with a grin. "I gave the Tommies a buggered-up old Enfield but kept my Mauser." They laughed.

"My God, Izak, thank you. I felt damn stupid riding off on commando without a rifle."

"Ja. Looked damn stupid too," he said with a chuckle as he handed over a bandolier of bullets. "Be strong, William. Anna says she'll wait for you. And if you see Botha or Smuts, take a shot for me—either one will do. Now I have to get back before I am missed." With that he wheeled his horse and was gone.

William sat for a while as Izak disappeared through a stand of trees. He felt lighter in the saddle despite the extra weight of the rifle and bandolier. Then he turned, set his hat firmly on his head and urged his horse into a canter for the two-day ride to join De Wet. He was confident the general would set the example of how to stand tall against the treachery of Botha's government.

Towards the end of the second day, he came across an astonishing sight. Strewn across the veld was a trail of dolls, clothes, pretty hats and rolls of dressmaking material. When he finally caught up with the source of the discarded items, he realized the goods were falling off the wagons of De Wet's rebels, wagons filled beyond capacity with loot. The high-minded rebels were plundering to support their cause, nothing but petty criminals wrapped in the flag of patriotism.

The last pillars of his world order crumbled. First Smuts and Botha, now De Wet—all unworthy. He felt completely disorientated. Every familiar thing had either been ripped from his grasp or had proved illusory.

When De Wet's rebels headed towards Mushroom Valley, William kept riding until he reached his farm at Sannah's Post, less than fifty miles away. A few days later he heard De Wet had been defeated by government forces and jailed. The rebellion had lasted about three months, a disaster that had ended in ignominy.

As always when he returned to the farm, he paid his respects to his father and spent a few minutes clearing the weeds and grass around the memorial under the willow tree. But the farm did little to lift his spirits, the fallow fields and deserted paddocks a bitter reminder of the war and the emptiness of his life. His only consolation was Solomon, his farm headman. By some miracle he had survived the war and returned to the farm with his family. At least somebody from his past was faithful.

One morning, as he sat under the willow tree thinking about his life and the war that had changed everything, he felt himself slipping into despair, into a darkness that seemed to blanket his soul and extinguish his spirit. He shuddered and reached for the willow tree, its downcast limbs offering an anchor even as the melancholy tree seemed forever engaged in a forlorn search for its own roots.

Get a grip, William, he thought angrily. *Enough! Time to move on, to rebuild, and to start a new family at Sannah's Post.*

He would tell Anna's family he had changed his mind about joining the rebellion, that he had found it impossible to take up arms against his former comrades even though he thought they were wrong to support Britain in the Great War.

At least the last part was true.

23

DEATH IN THE AIR

1922

The drone of the aero engine muted the harsh staccato of the machine guns. William didn't recognize the sound at first, but there was no mistaking the explosive destruction of heavy-caliber bullets ripping through the small building, the sound of shards of glass and splinters of wood and brick scything through air inside the Benoni strike office.

He instinctively reached for Anna to shield her and pull her to the ground as terrified miners dove for cover. There was so much noise he never heard whether she cried out or not, but he felt a wet warmth between his fingers as he pulled her down. And when he turned her over to face him, her eyes were wide with fright and shock. A trickle of blood meandered from the corner of her mouth.

"Oh my God! Anna... Anna. Ag no, loving Jesus, please..."

She blinked, her wide eyes staring through him to some far-off place. And in a small voice brittle with pain and fear, she murmured, "Lord, forgive me my sins... Lord, forgive me my sins... Lord... forgive me..."

"Please, God," he beseeched. "Please... dear Jesus... please—"

"Look out! Look out!" yelled Izak. "He's coming again."

Izak's jarring warning tore his attention away from Anna. He looked to where Izak was pointing through a window. The yellow biplane was banking sharply and, as it straightened out, its stubby nose pointed directly towards them.

God help us, he thought as he stared, expecting at any moment to hear the chatter of machine guns as the biplane swooped down like a bird of prey. But what he saw instead filled him with an undefined dread. For a moment it seemed the bird had laid an egg in the sky... or taken a flying shit.

"Bomb!" screamed Izak. "Everybody down... Get down!"

All he could think to do was protect Anna with his body. The last thing he heard as he crouched over her was a whistling sound, then an ear-shattering blast and momentary sense of violent weightlessness as he was flung into the air. Then nothing—just complete silence as time seemed to pause before the gates of eternity.

Sunlight was filtering through the settling dust from the roofless building when he recovered his senses. He gazed around him through grit-encrusted eyes and found himself sitting against a pile of rubble that had once been an outer wall. Muted sounds of distress reached his still-ringing ears as he watched khaki-clad soldiers moving through the destruction with bayonets fixed to their rifles.

"My God," Izak was saying, "Smuts used the bloody air force against us. Jesus, William, there are bodies everywhere." He felt Izak's hand on his shoulder. "Are you okay? And where's Anna?"

He barely heard Izak as he stared at the beloved figure lying under a section of roof beams shaped like a cross. He blinked hard, hoping he was hallucinating. When his eyes cleared, he saw a soldier with his bayonetted rifle almost at Anna's side. His mind flashed to the image of Jesus crucified, a Roman soldier about to stab him in the side with his spear.

"No, no, get away...Don't touch her...Hands off!" he shouted as he scrambled to his feet and stumbled through the rubble towards Anna, ignoring the rifle as the soldier spun to meet the unexpected challenge. He could barely see through his tears as he crashed to his knees in the rubble beside her.

"Anna...loving Jesus," he cried as he tried to lift the beams off her body. "Help me, someone...please." He heard Izak cursing behind him, then felt him lift a section of the beam. Without a word, the soldier dropped his rifle, took hold of the other end of the beam, and together they lifted the beam off Anna and set it down to one side.

William stared at Anna's lifeless form—the fixed gaze of her eyes, her gaping mouth, the mess of flesh and fabric that marked the exit wound in her chest—and shuddered as a wave of emotion crashed over him.

"You know the woman?" asked the soldier after several moments, his tone respectful, his accent familiar.

William nodded. "My wife," he stammered.

"Ag, I'm really sorry, man," said the soldier. "I was just following orders."

"Smuts's orders," spat Izak.

The soldier nodded, his eyes downcast.

"I fought with Smuts," added William bitterly, wiping his eyes and nose on a sleeve of his torn coat. "He was my hero...Now he does this." His chest heaved as he glared at the soldier. "You can tell Smuts I'll kill him if I ever get the chance."

The soldier nodded. "Ja, man, I understand," he said. "But be careful boasting about killing Smuts. My commandant says many strikers will be charged with high treason. Some will be executed."

"I'll tell Smuts to his face," replied William fiercely. "And, if needs be, I'll die a patriot's death."

"Ja, man, I hear you. Just don't be stupid. But I tell you this," he added lowering his voice, "after today, Smuts won't be our leader much longer. We've counted about thirty strikers dead, sixty army and police, and at least forty civilians. Just in this place I counted three young people and three women dead... including your wife." The soldier swallowed and shook his head. "And these are our own people, not Tommies or kaffirs."

The soldier was still shaking his head as he moved off to complete his macabre census.

The next few hours were a blur. To think about what Smuts had done was one thing. But to think about Anna's lifeless body was another thing entirely. He couldn't imagine trying to take her all the way back to Sannah's Post to be buried. When Izak suggested his family's burial plot on their farm near Krugersdorp, he simply nodded in mute assent.

Izak drove the one-horse wagon at a gentle pace. The hypnotic rhythm of the horse's hooves deadened William's emotions and freed his mind to try to make sense of what had happened.

The visit to Izak's home in Benoni had seemed like a good idea—he and Anna had needed a break from the farm. Still, he should have known better than to accept Izak's invitation after what happened the last time, several years before.

"Remember Selborne Hall," he prompted as they passed beyond the slag heaps and shantytowns of the mines, recalling the violence of that night.

Izak seemed relieved by the chance to talk. "Ja, that was a helluva meeting," he said with a wide grin. "Malan's speech was inspiring. And the cheers when I tore down the Union Jack." He chuckled, his eyes bright. "I tell you, William, for a moment it felt like I was tearing up the peace treaty and turning back the clock, restoring our freedom. God, it felt good!" He laughed. "And then the chase through the streets of Jo'burg to our clubhouse. Man, that was a close thing. I still can't believe we got out before the Tommie-loving buggers burned it down."

"So what happened after that? I remember you going on about how true Afrikaners were threatened from all sides, that we had to do something."

Izak turned a quizzical gaze on him and looked around before speaking, although it was obvious nobody else was within earshot.

"Have you ever heard of Die Broederbond?"

He shook his head.

Izak nodded. "You can never tell anybody what I'm going to tell you, William. Understand?"

He shrugged and nodded. "Ja, okay, man. So what's the story?"

"We formed a secret society, a brotherhood of true Afrikaners," said Izak, his eyes bright with zealous enthusiasm.

"To do what?"

Izak's face lit up. "To save our people—our language, our culture, our history—to save the heart and soul of Afrikanerdom!"

William nodded but said nothing for several moments, the quiet broken only by the rhythm of the horse's gait as it plodded along the dirt track. "So what does this brotherhood of true Afrikaners do?" He tried not to sound skeptical, but saving the heart and soul of Afrikanerdom sounded a bit melodramatic.

"Our leader, Henning Klopper, is a great man," said Izak. "He says our first task is to help our people recover from the war. Most are dirt poor, living and working as squatters and laborers. We have to change that. So we help our people buy houses, start businesses and receive fair wages—that sort of thing. And we want our children to be taught in Afrikaans, not just in English, and to have

Afrikaans recognized as equal to English. You know what happened to my neighbor's son the other day at school?" Izak asked rhetorically. "He was caught speaking Afrikaans. They made him sit in the corner of his classroom with a big sign around his neck that said, 'I am a donkey. I must not speak Dutch.' And then the boy had to write a thousand lines, each one the same—'I must speak English at school.'" He paused and shook his head. "This sort of thing, this racialism, happens every day to our people, William. In shops, in banks, in schools, everywhere."

Izak flicked the reins. The horse twitched but didn't change its pace. "I tell you, William, we're so dominated by the damn English that Afrikanerdom is on the brink of extinction. Sometimes I think the kaffirs are better off than we are," he added. "At least they don't know any better and don't expect to be treated as equals."

Then he beamed unexpectedly, as though the daybreak of salvation was about to burst through the dark clouds of oppression. "But the Brotherhood will change everything, William. We will take over the government and get rid of Smuts, replace him with a true Afrikaner."

They were approaching the ring of low, flat hills that separated Johannesburg from Krugersdorp. The horse was laboring. The air ahead was crisp, the sky clear—a typical Highveld day. Behind them, smoke and fog hung over Johannesburg like a solid gray mantle from so many open fires and coal stacks.

William's thoughts returned to Anna. "So was the bloodshed in Benoni part of some great plan by your Brotherhood?" he asked, gesturing with his head towards her body, his tone raw with emotion.

Izak seemed stung by the suggestion. "No, man, I swear. It started as a strike to protect white miners. The owners wanted to replace us all with cheap labor—with kaffirs. So we couldn't let them break the strike. But things got out of hand. By the time you and Anna were on the train from Bloemfontein, we were already in the streets with guns and grenades. There was looting and rioting and the black compounds were being attacked. Shit, William, it was chaos! We were fighting for our lives and for our jobs. And then someone called for the overthrow of the government, to form a people's republic dedicated to the white race. I tell you, William, there was talk of a bloody revolution, just like the one in Russia."

Izak paused, his mouth ajar, as though the anarchy could not be contained. "That's when Smuts went crazy! He called out the whole damned army and declared martial law."

"And you seriously thought we'd be safe at the strike headquarters in Benoni?" replied William, shaking his head in disbelief.

"Ag, Jesus, William, I had to take you somewhere from the station, and I had to be there because I'm in the union. And yes, I did think you and Anna would be safe in a brick building." He wiped his nose on his sleeve. "But as God is my witness, William, I never thought Smuts would drop a fucking bomb on us!"

The pages of the pastor's Bible rustled in the autumn breeze.

Aside from the quiet weeping of Anna's mother, the family stood in mute disbelief around the small plot just off the road leading to the farmhouse. The deep shadows cast by a stand of nearby gum trees seemed to darken their despair. William stood slightly apart, between Izak's family and the bearded pastor in his black frock coat. The farm headman and two housemaids stood off to one side, their heads bowed.

The pastor was the same one who had married them eight years before. He seemed at a loss for words and sought refuge in a familiar text. "Now we see things imperfectly," he began, "like blurred reflections in a mirror. But on that glorious day when the Lord calls us home, on that day we will see everything with perfect clarity." He paused to look into the grief-stricken eyes of Anna's parents and family members, as though imploring them against their better judgment to be comforted by God's promise. "All that we can know now is partial and incomplete," he continued, "but on that day we will know everything completely, just as God knows each of us completely."

William had heard variations of the theme before. It left him unmoved. It was no answer to talk of the mystery of God's plan. How could the plan of a loving God include the slaughter of the innocent? It made more sense to talk of God's judgment against the people for their lack of faith, their disunity, their betrayal of the Covenant.

As he looked into the grave, his thoughts turned to what Smuts's secretary had said after they lost their war of freedom against the British—how they were standing over the grave of their republics, staring at the corpse of their freedom. He shook his head. And now he was staring at the corpse of his wife. Dreams should not end in a grave while there was still breath to move forward, to fight another day. Perhaps Izak was right. Perhaps the time had come for a brotherhood of true Afrikaners to take action to save their people and restore their covenant faith.

The final prayer offered, he stood for several moments gazing into the awful dankness of Anna's final resting place, trying to pierce the dark despair of the moment, to discern a way forward. Then he reached out and slowly opened his fingers. The handful of dirt tumbled onto the coffin below, making a series of soft, inconsequential sounds against the wood.

Earth to earth, ashes to ashes, dust to dust.

William turned and walked away.

24

THE GREATEST GIFT OF ALL

1918–1932

The drumbeat crashed against Nelson's ears as he sat on his robe with his legs spread out in front of him, wearing nothing but a sacred necklace woven from the hair of a cow's tail. It felt as though every nerve ending in his sixteen-year-old body had been burned raw by the blazing sun, a sensation only slightly mitigated by the animal fat spread over his head and body.

Four initiates sat on his right and about twenty on his left, including his good friend Justice, son of the regent. They were all naked, all terrified, their eyes fixed with morbid apprehension on the central hut in the dusty semicircular compound.

A gasp coursed through the initiates as the gleaming metal head of a spear appeared suddenly in the doorway of the hut. Then the *incibi* stepped out of the hut with a flourish, the ebony patina of the spear's shaft an extension of the tribal surgeon's arm.

In one powerful movement the *incibi* thrust the spear high above his head and, in a defiant chant, called out, *"Bayete a-a-a Dalindyebo, bayete a-a-a Dalindyebo,"* as though daring the assembled dignitaries to challenge the invocation of so great a lineage of Thembu kings. And with each syllable the *incibi* stomped with exaggerated strides as he advanced towards the initiates, the exotic animal skins that cloaked his body sweeping a cloud of dust into the air around him, the beads and bells tied to his ankles crashing together like off-key cymbals, shattering the stillness of the little village nestled in the coastal plains not far from the Indian Ocean.

Slack-jawed and wide-eyed, Nelson stared and tried to concentrate on just two things—to be brave by not crying or flinching when the *incibi* severed his foreskin with the spear, and to loudly declare his manhood at the very moment the deed was done.

Out of the corner of his eye he watched as the *incibi* moved quickly from one initiate to the next. He saw the spear's blade flash and heard his friends cry out, although it was hard to tell if they were cries of pain or declarations of manhood. Then, in a blur of movement, the perspiring *incibi* was in front of him, kneeling between his legs.

It happened so quickly he was more astonished than scared. In what seemed like a single sensation, he felt a tug on his penis and a searing pain. Almost choking in agony, he finally found his tongue and called out "*Ndiyindoda*"—I am a man.

He was dimly aware of the *incibi's* assistant attaching his severed foreskin to a corner of his initiation blanket as the *incibi* moved to the next initiate. But it was done. He had survived, even though his wound was more painfully disabling than he expected, his declaration less manly than he intended.

He slept uncomfortably that night. Not only was the hut filled with smoke believed to promote healing, but the tribal attendant forced him to sleep on his back with one leg straight and the other bent at the knee. And then, around midnight, the attendant woke him and told him to go out into the night and bury his foreskin—to prevent wizards using it for dark deeds and to symbolize burying his youth. Looking like a tortured ghost—his body painted in the white clay of purity, his penis wrapped in a healing leaf—he reluctantly left the warmth of the hut and walked awkwardly into the cold and dark.

He found a small area among some trees and dug a hole in the dirt with his hands. He sat for a few moments—the dirt hole between his knees, the bloodied foreskin between his fingers—trying to grasp the gravity of the moment. But he was too tired, and the pain too great. He dropped the tiny ring of flesh into the shallow grave, covered it over and stumbled back to the smoke-filled hut.

In the days that followed, he spent time alone thinking about what it meant to pass into manhood. Then, on the day of their reemergence into Thembu society, their initiation huts and blankets ceremoniously burnt to sever all connection with their childhood, the initiates washed away the white clay, replaced it with red clay, and enjoyed a feast of roasted meat and tribal beer.

Nelson couldn't believe he was already a man. It was only 1934 and he had already taken a giant step towards his dream of following in his father's footsteps as counselor to the Thembu king.

He sat aglow in pride as the main speaker at the ceremony, an important chief and a son of Dalindyebo, began to speak. He anticipated the chief would shower the initiates with all the traditional platitudes about manhood and marriage, acquiring property and wealth, nurturing children in traditional ways, respecting tribal elders and customs, and making sure their mothers' cooking pots were never empty.

Although the chief started out as expected, an almost tangible tension descended upon the gathered crowd as his speech took an unexpected turn. Nelson's glow of pride dimmed as the crowd grew silent. He looked around but saw only rapt attention to the chief as he spoke.

"There sit our sons, young, healthy, and handsome, the flower of the Xhosa tribe, the pride of our nation," the chief was saying. "We have just circumcised them in a ritual that promises them manhood, but I am here to tell you that it is an empty, illusory promise, a promise that can never be fulfilled. For we are Xhosas, and all black South Africans are a conquered people." He paused to blow his nose with his fingers before continuing. "We are slaves in our own country, tenants on our own soil. We have no strength, no power, no control over our own destiny in the land of our birth." He pointed at the initiates. "They will go to cities, where they will live in shacks and drink cheap alcohol, all because we have no land to give them where they could prosper and multiply. They will cough their lungs out deep in the bowels of the white man's mines, destroying their health, never seeing the sun, so that the white man can live a life of unequaled prosperity."

What madness is this? thought Nelson. *I am a member of the Madiba clan, related by birth to the great Thembu king Ngubengcuka, a slave to no man!* He looked around, expecting others to be outraged, but nobody protested and the chief was not finished.

"The abilities, the intelligence, the promise of these young men will be squandered in their attempt to eke out a living doing the simplest, most mindless chores for the white man. These gifts today are worth nothing"—his voice rose in anger—"for we cannot give them the greatest gift of all, their freedom and independence."

A murmur swept through the ranks of the tribal elders, stilled only by the chief's invocation of the Xhosa god.

"I well know that Qamata is all-seeing and never sleeps, but I have a suspicion that Qamata may be dozing. If this is true, the sooner I die the better, because then I can meet him and shake him awake and tell him that the children of Ngubengcuka, the flower of the Xhosa nation, are dying."

The chief looked out over the stunned crowd, shook his head with a look of terrible sadness, then walked slowly back to his place with the elders.

Nelson had never heard such talk. This foolish old chief was spoiling his glorious celebration of manhood. But could it be, despite tales of ancestral courage and leadership he had learned since his earliest days, that his people were conquered, slaves in their own land, without control over their destiny?

He wished he could talk to his father, but those days had passed. His father had long ago been stripped of his status and wealth by a white magistrate after defying an order to appear in court—it was a tribal matter that his father believed he had the right to deal with himself as a Thembu chief—and had died one night from a lung disease.

He still remembered finding his father on the floor of his mother's hut, coughing uncontrollably, and the distress of his mother and his father's youngest wife as they had tried to make him comfortable. He had watched as his father sat, silent and unmoving, for several days. At the end he had asked for his pipe, calmly smoked for a while, and then exhaled for the last time. His lifeless fingers had clutched the lit pipe—its smoke had hung like a shroud over his body.

That was seven years ago, when he was only nine years old. He still remembered how he had felt after his father died, cut adrift from the one person who had given definition to his life.

Then it struck him—perhaps his father was speaking to him, still defining his life from beyond the grave. Had the chief not spoken of the flower of his people coughing their lungs out deep in the white man's mines, and had his father not done exactly that?

Had the chief not spoken of shaking Qamata awake, and had his father not named him Rolihlahla, shaker of trees, troublemaker? Perhaps his father was urging him to make trouble, to shake his people until they took control of their destiny and could pass on to their children the greatest gift the old chief had spoken of—the gift of freedom and independence.

But if there was destiny in a name, then his English name—Nelson—now seemed like a bad omen. For Lord Nelson had been shot to death during his most famous victory at the Battle of Trafalgar.

25

FROM THE ASHES

1938

At last, thought William as he stood on a street corner reading the newspaper, his people were turning back to God. The article said two ox wagons, named the Piet Retief and the Andries Pretorius, had left from the heart of Cape Town six hundred miles away to recreate the great wagon trek of his people one hundred years before on their quest for freedom from British rule.

The wagons were dubbed "freedom wagons" and more had joined along the way.

After arriving in Bloemfontein, some of the wagons would go to Pretoria to the site of their new monument. Others would go to Blood River to the site of their great victory over Dingane on December 16, 1838. And the whole event would be celebrated on the centenary of the Battle of Blood River, the day of their covenant with God.

He had arrived in the city the night before, just in time to see a relay of flaming torches carried through the streets by young Afrikaner boys, torches carried all the way from Cape Town. A local pastor assured a rapturous crowd that the fire of nationhood was a gift from God, a burning torch that would never be extinguished.

The only discordant note was news that the English-dominated city council had refused to rename city streets after Afrikaner heroes, as other cities and towns had done along the wagon route. Word had spread that the people were going to pull the wagons through the streets in protest.

As the crowd grew, all wearing the traditional clothes of their culture—women in long dresses with lace scarves, braided hair and bonnets; men in corduroy breeches with long coats, long beards and soft felt hats—he felt himself caught up in a surge of euphoria, as though a nourishing rain was coursing through his parched spirit after years of desolation, promising renewal, perhaps even rebirth.

He glanced again at the newspaper. Another article caught his eye quoting a speech in Cape Town by a man named Henning Klopper, the trek leader:

"This movement is born from the people. May the people carry it in their hearts all the way to Pretoria and Blood River. Let us build up a monument for Afrikaner hearts. May this simple trek bind together in love those Afrikaner hearts that do not yet beat together. We dedicate these wagons to our people and to our God."

He closed his eyes and felt his heart pound. Images flooded his mind's eye of what a monument to the lives of those he had lost might look like. He couldn't quite imagine it, but he knew in his heart it would be glorious and forever honor the struggle of his people, a struggle that included his grandparents, slaughtered by the Zulus, his father, shot by the Tommies, his mother and sister, sacrificed in the concentration camps, and Anna, gunned down by fellow Afrikaners.

He felt a wave of emotion rise through his core, but just as it was about to crash over him, people around him began to cheer.

He blinked. When his vision cleared, he saw three covered wagons moving slowly up the street towards him with a group of men pulling the first wagon, women pulling the second, and children the third. More wagons were coming behind, cheered on by the crowd. And all around him the people were singing the new anthem—the call to sacrifice.

He began to sing along, his voice cracking with emotion:

Ons sal antwoord op jou roepstem,	We will answer to your calling,
Ons sal offer wat jy vra:	We will offer what you ask:
Ons sal lewe	We shall live
Ons sal sterwe	We shall die
Ons vir jou, Suid Afrika.	We for you, South Africa.

As he sang the last line, he felt a sudden compulsion to help with the wagons and stepped into the street as though pushed by an unseen hand. He moved towards the first wagon, but there were already so many men pulling that his only option was to go around the back to push. He found a spot just inside the right rear wheel and quickly settled into the rhythm of men pulling and pushing the wagon.

In the middle of the next city block the wagon suddenly stopped. As he looked around to see why they had stopped, he saw a woman step into the street and walk towards the back of his wagon, untying her bonnet as she approached. He was about to wave her back to the second wagon when she looked at him and smiled. Her braided hair had come loose, cascading in light-brown swirls over her slender shoulders. Her blue eyes, set amidst a sprinkling of freckles, seemed to see right into his heart as she walked up to the wagon wheel where he stood. She was much younger than him—he guessed by at least twenty years—but she met his gaze with an directness that was disconcerting.

Then she did an astonishing thing. Without taking her eyes off him she kissed the steel rim of the wagon wheel right in front of him, then reached down to the axle and wiped off some grease with her fingers. As she stood up, she smeared her cheeks with the grease and smiled.

Without thinking, he reached for a blob of grease on her cheek and wiped it off with his finger. Their eyes met and held as he slowly smeared the grease onto his own cheeks. He saw her eyes flick to his cheeks and widen with amused inquiry. As their eyes held, he felt the blood drain from his face, the breath from his lungs, as though she were drawing his life force into union with her own, a union of shared roots and a covenant faith.

He smiled tentatively. Then, giving voice to an impulse that welled irresistibly to the surface, he blurted, "Come with me!"

The woman looked at him for several moments, eyebrows arched, her smile frozen. "Where to?"

"Blood River," he said. The words were out before he caught himself. He was about to apologize for offending her when she nodded and smiled again.

"I will tell my guardian I'm going with the wagons. We'll see how it goes." Then she turned, retied her bonnet and started back towards the crowd.

"What's your name?" he called as she walked away.

She half turned and, without breaking stride, called out, "Maria."

"I'm William," he shouted as she disappeared into the crowd.

And I must be mad! he thought as he dropped his head and stared blindly at the wagon wheel, his thoughts swirling in a maelstrom of confusion through the harsh reality of the last decade of his life.

It was a nightmare that had consumed his days and tortured his nights. The newspapers had been so full of stories about the Crash and Depression that he had begun to think of the Depression as a shape-shifting creature that had escaped the Crash and then roamed the surface of the earth, a voracious beast devouring all hope and aspiration in its path.

He had been unable to define it but had known the smell and taste of it. It had seemed to pervade the air he breathed, the food he ate, the soil he tilled, sucking life's essence from all living things. Every fiber in his body, even the marrow of his soul, had seemed to shrivel and atrophy as the landscape of his life had distorted into a wasteland.

It had been hard enough when he and Anna had tried to rebuild the farm, but after Anna died things had been so much harder. And after Anna's father died in his sleep, her mother had lost the will to live and died soon after. Their deaths had scraped the barrel of his emotional reserves, leaving him with nothing more to give or to lose. He had shuttered their home in Bloemfontein and retreated to the barren refuge of the farm.

The only good thing he recalled from those years was the defeat of Smuts in the 1924 general election. It had been some consolation that the traitor had received his just desserts—thrown out of office and onto the streets where he had so callously shed the blood of innocent Afrikaner workers, women and children—and Anna.

But the euphoria had been short lived.

The ultimate indignity of those years had come to him in a black Ford sedan one Sunday afternoon in 1929 as he sat on the porch. The men had told him they were working for the Carnegie Corporation of New York investigating the problem of poor whites in South Africa. He had protested he was no such thing, but the truth had been impossible to hide.

One of the men—a fellow Afrikaner named Malherbe—had

told him that the problem of Afrikaner poverty was widespread and extremely serious and he was lucky to have a roof over his head—that many thousands of Afrikaners were living as paupers in mud and stone shelters unsuitable for human habitation, whose children didn't even have proper food and clothes. Almost as an afterthought, the man had added that many were going onto the African reserves to work for the natives in exchange for food.

William had promised himself he would never sink that low—a promise he had been unable to keep—and given thanks that he was childless, grateful he and Anna had not brought children into such a world, to be among a people so destitute as to be the subject of an American commission of inquiry.

He had tried to resist the morbid gloom that had crept over him as the years unfolded, but there had come a day when the wretchedness of his circumstances fused with the desolation of his soul, when getting out of bed had seemed pointless and surviving the day irrelevant. The home he had worked so hard to restore had turned shabby, his threadbare clothes had gone unwashed and his meals had become more meager, irregular and unappetizing. His once sturdy, work-hardened physique had shrunk until he had been able to feel his bones through a paper-thin layer of skin.

Even his headman had noticed the change. "Master must eat," Solomon had said one evening when he came to the house with a slice of beef and roast potatoes on a plate. William had refused at first but had eventually accepted the food on condition he could help Solomon work his plot of land. He had hoped the work would inspire him to work his own land, and that his neighbors would not notice.

Sundays had been especially difficult. He had felt compelled to go to church but had taken no comfort from the sermons and had been embarrassed by the charity. It was an open secret that the men in the black Ford had visited him and that he worked for his headman for food.

But it was during a Sunday service about covenant relationships that he had heard about the centenary recreation of the great trek of his ancestors from the Cape. Before the last hymn was sung, he had made up his mind to see the event for himself.

Miraculously, when all hope seemed lost, the freedom wagons had come to Bloemfontein and Maria had come to him. And in that moment, as their worlds converged across the wagon wheel, his downward spiral into hopelessness was arrested, the despair in his life quieted. Even if it was all a delusion, the solace of the moment felt real. He would know soon enough whether it might last.

With a sudden jerk, the wheel began to turn.

At every farm, village, town and city it was the same—the humble wooden wagons were treated with a reverence bordering on worship, as though they represented the promise of God carrying the Ark of the Covenant to its sacred destiny.

William had never known anything like it. The songs, the anthem, the message all melded into a single, sanctified whole. It felt like a revival, not just of his spirit, but of the soul of his people. And at every stop the trek leader, Klopper, made the same point— the trek was not the work of man but of almighty God, the same God who had given them victory at Blood River and who would bless their efforts if they would only renew their covenant faith with Him.

William finally remembered where he had heard Klopper's name before—he was the leader of the secret brotherhood of Afrikaners Izak had spoken of after Anna died in a hail of bullets. It seemed like a sign from above—divine coincidence—and gave him much to think about as he took turns with the other men driving the teams of eight oxen pulling each wagon.

But one thing occupied his thoughts above all else—Maria's presence on one of the wagons. What he had feared might be a delusion had materialized in flesh and blood. Although they had not had an opportunity to spend time together in private, it was enough to know she was nearby. And when Klopper's wagons continued to Pretoria, he and Maria made sure they were on the wagons headed for Blood River.

As thrilled as he was to be part of the great event, it was frustrating to have so little time with Maria—just a few stolen moments when they stopped to rest the oxen or during evening meals when the group cooked around an open fire. But although their moments together were brief, all the covenant talk convinced him that God had brought them together to share the covenant journey, perhaps even life's journey.

It had been so difficult with Anna. Her mother had warned him that she might not be ready, that she might need time after what had happened at the concentration camp. He had tried to be patient, but when frustration led to forcing, it had been like a steel trap closing on their union. He hoped it would be different with Maria—at least she had been spared from the camps.

When he turned his gaze outward, the spectacle of the Drakensberg took his breath away. His father had described mountains that looked like castles and bells, a cathedral and even a rhino's horn. And so it was. The spires and peaks seemed to pierce the sky above, and all around ice-cold water cascaded down rocky crags into crystal-clear pools. It was hard to imagine his grandparents crossing such a formidable natural barrier a hundred years before—dismantling and carrying their wagons across rivers too deep and passes too sheer for their oxen, using tree branches in place of rear wheels as brakes down the most precipitous descents—trying to reach a land they hoped to call their own only to be deceived and butchered by Dingane and his warriors.

When they finally stopped at dusk one evening on a hill overlooking Blood River after several weeks on the trail, the battle site looked eerily benign. The bucolic scene set amidst low-lying hills was so peaceful it was difficult to picture the pivotal battle that had raged in the fork of the river and the dried-out tributary. But he had heard the story so many times he could almost hear the army of warriors beating on their shields before the battle, their fearsome war cries as they charged down the gentle slope, the desperate defense of the wagons by a few hundred farmers, and the screams of the warriors as they ran into an impenetrable fusillade of bullets and cannonballs.

Through the smoke and dust, he could see his father as a young boy frantically loading balls and shot, scrambling to control frenzied cattle and horses, the chaos of battle raging around him, and then the desperate horseback charge against the warriors until finally, mercifully, the guns fell silent. And in the dread silence that followed, he imagined a mass of tangled bodies lying around the wall of wagons and floating in the hippo pool, as though the wrath of God had struck down the pride of Dingane's army before it bled out into the river.

When his mind cleared, the images of violent and bloody battle were replaced by a field covered with prairie grass pirouetting silently in a gently swirling breeze. The only sign of life was a small group already gathered at the place where the laager of sixty-four wagons had stood against the Zulu onslaught. As the sun dipped below a shroud of low clouds that looked like a blanket of charred embers over the distant hills, he could see torches that seemed to bathe the area in a sacred and purifying light—the fire of nationhood. A gift from God, as the pastor had said in Bloemfontein.

The arrival of the wagons was greeted with hymns and the anthem. Even the efforts of sweating men, heaving oxen and preparations for the evening meal seemed consecrated by the circumstances. And as he sat close to the campfire near Maria that night, listening to stories of heroism and sacrifice, courage and treachery, he experienced a deep sense of restoration, of belonging, of being part again of a people chosen by God.

His last thoughts as he drifted to sleep beside a wagon were of Maria and the call of the anthem—we shall live, we shall die, we for you, South Africa—and somehow the two became one, his commitment to the one a commitment in equal measure to the other.

William stirred as the glow of dawn cast a promise of summer heat across the rolling hills. A hint of grilled meat from the evening meal still hung in the air as he ambled down to the river to wash his face in the frigid water.

He found himself thinking again of commitment and covenant as the thread of last night's thoughts wove its way back through his subconscious. And the more he thought about it, the more convinced he became, until the idea of Maria sharing his life was so insistent it seemed the voice in his head was the voice of God. But he felt shabby, unclean, unworthy, in dire need of a good wash, especially if he was going to ask Maria to be his wife in the presence of the Almighty.

He hesitated at the water's edge to make sure he was alone and out of sight of the encampment, then stripped off his clothes and plunged into the hippo pool. For a moment it felt as though he were being baptized again, reborn into a new relationship with his

Creator. A moment later he was struck by the thought of bathing in the blood of Zulu warriors. He shuddered, washed himself down as quickly as he could, and was just about to step out of the water when he heard a singsong voice from above.

"Good morning, my man, there is coffee in the can."

He smiled as he recognized the familiar tune and looked up in time to see Maria jumping down the shallow bank of the river. Her hair and skirts flew as she ran towards the water's edge where he bathed. He instinctively squatted down into the pool until only his head and shoulders were above water.

"Please, Maria. It's freezing. Please turn around so I can get dressed."

He saw her smile as she picked up his bundle of clothes. "Come and get them, dear William," she said mischievously, laughing as she backed away from the water's edge.

His eyes went wide. "Maria! God will hear you—and someone will see," he hissed, trying to shush her and struggling to keep a straight face.

She laughed again. "Ja, I know, my dear wet William. And I hope it's me."

"Maria!"

"Ag, okay, okay, spoilsport." She dropped the bundle and turned around. "But you can't blame a girl for trying."

He reached for her as soon as he was dressed, spun her around and, in a voice he did not recognize as his own, said, "Now that you've seen me naked, you have to marry me, Maria. It's the only decent thing to do."

She took a step back. "What did you say after the 'naked' part?" she asked, her eyes sparkling, her smile warm and generous.

"It's true, Maria. I have to save you from the sin of lust," he said, trying to sound serious.

She threw back her head and laughed, a joyous and unrestrained eruption he was sure would wake the whole camp.

"So will you, Maria?" he said, dropping to his knees. "I don't have anything to give you, but the nothing I have is all yours."

She laughed and cupped his head in her hands. "I thought you would never ask, you silly man." Then she sank to her knees, kissed him lightly on his cheek, and said, "I will, William. I will!"

He stared at her. "Really? Maybe that pastor who came with other wagons can marry us right here, at Blood River."

"He will," she said, smiling radiantly. "His name is Malan. And I already asked him." Then she laughed again and kissed him on the other cheek.

He grinned through his ragged beard, took her in his arms, dragged her to her feet and danced an awkward polka, tripping and stumbling as he swung her around him. After a few moments of abandon, he stopped to catch his breath.

"I only wish I had something better to wear," he said as cold water dripped from his wet hair.

"Don't be silly," she said. "I'd marry you if you wore a sack. Besides, my dress isn't exactly from a wedding shop."

"At least you look proper. I look like I've spent a month on commando being chased through the bush by a flying column of Tommies."

She laughed. "You'll do just fine." Then she knelt on a riverside rock to splash her face.

"Are you sure about this?" he asked from behind. "About marrying me. I'm much older than you and we hardly know each other."

"Ag, who cares about age. And maybe it's just as well we don't know too much about each other," she said with a smile as she straightened up and smoothed down the folds of her dress. "I'm sure we both have our faults. But just think of it as an arranged marriage—arranged by God. We will reveal ourselves to each other over time, just as God will reveal Himself to us in the fullness of time."

He beamed. "Ja. And to think we found a pastor to marry us in the middle of nowhere." Then he paused and his brow creased. "Strange thing is, I think I've seen him before. Even his name sounds familiar."

"As long as he's not the same pastor who married you the first time—that would be sad." Then she turned and headed back up the embankment to the wagons.

The sunrise ceremony was two events—a baptism and a wedding.

A couple's baby was baptized with water from Blood River using a copper chalice brought from France by their Huguenot ancestors.

Next was their wedding. Pastor Malan nodded and called them out of the small circle of kindred spirits.

William and Maria stood side by side before him, facing the battle site and the rolling hills in the distance, the sky a vast indigo canvas with just a hint of whitewash at its fringes. William felt as though he was finally home after a long exile adrift on a sea of uncertainty, washed ashore and warmed by the embrace of his people, their covenant faith like a salve to the open wound of his soul.

He tried to pay attention as Malan contrived to mix themes of baptism and marriage into a sermon about covenant relationships, that just as William was the groom and Maria the bride, so too was Christ the groom and true Afrikaners the bride, baptized into nationhood in the river of blood. It was when the baby cried that his memory was jarred and he recalled where he had seen the pastor with the round face and glasses—Selborne Hall at the meeting he had attended with Izak and Anna. He was Dr. Daniel Malan, the fiery nationalist speaker who had applauded when Izak tore down the British flag and ripped it to shreds.

William was so distracted by the memory that he missed the cue to recite his vows. A sharp elbow from his bride brought him back to the present. Then it was done, and Malan spoke the cherished words.

"I now pronounce you man and wife. You may kiss the bride."

And he did...on her lips...their first kiss.

26

THE OX-WAGON SENTINEL

1939–1944

"I'm sorry we couldn't find the grave," said Maria as she carried the box of provisions into their kitchen pantry. "There were just too many rocks and bushes at that terrible place with the baboon-faced rock. But perhaps we can make a little memorial for them under the tree just like—"

"It's from Izak!" interrupted William. The handwritten envelope had been burning a hole in his coat pocket ever since he picked up their mail at the post office on their way through town. "I can't believe it. I haven't heard from him in nearly fifteen years, since Smuts was thrown out of office in '24."

"Who's Izak?"

"Oh...yes," he responded awkwardly as he sat down at the kitchen table—he had not yet told Maria everything about his life before they met. "He's Anna's brother. We were at the mine together. He was with me when she died. I think Izak became a big shot in the union."

"Well, what does he say?" asked Maria, wiping the dusty kitchen table with a cloth as she sat down opposite him. "Read it so I can hear."

He turned to the first of two pages. "He wrote it the day after Christmas. Hard to believe 1938 is already past." He started to read aloud.

Dear William,

I just had to write. It was unbelievable. If I'd known it was going to be such a big event, I would have written and told you to come. But standing in the middle of the crowd I thought of you.

"What's he talking about?" Maria's tired voice was tinged with impatience.

"I've no idea," said William, "but I'm sure he'll say."

There were over a quarter of a million of us. It was like a sea of people, all waiting and watching the fires that were set on the hills around Pretoria. Then the torchbearers arrived and thousands more joined them and they all marched to the top of the hill and threw their torches onto a huge bonfire.

"He's talking about the ox-wagon trek," cried Maria, her eyes widening. "The one that went straight to Pretoria when we went to Blood River. He must have been there, at the celebration of the new monument in Pretoria!"

Their eyes met in delight at the unexpected firsthand account of the great event.

When the wagons arrived, the oxen were outspanned—we weren't going to allow filthy beasts to defile our monument. So teams of men pushed and pulled the six wagons to the top of the hill, escorted all the way by horsemen, looking just like commandos from the old days. After the wagons were in place, descendants of our leaders laid a foundation stone for the new monument.

We cheered and sang and prayed and listened to all the stories about our struggles and victories, our friends and enemies, our hopes and dreams. And every so often a speaker would shout "Freedom" and everyone would chant "Freedom" in response.

I tell you, William, the day will come when we take back this land of ours—all the talk is about becoming a republic again. But you must do your part. You remember that secret society I told you about? Well, it's growing fast. There's a farmer in your area, Colonel Laas. You must talk to him.

Anyway, my parents both passed and I'm still very sorry about what happened to Anna, but I hope you are well.

Be strong and believe.

Izak

William sat back, his eyes luminous. "I wish I'd been there, Maria. It sounds as though God Himself was in amongst our people."

"You were exactly where God meant you to be, my dear husband. But you must write back," she added, "and tell him we married in the shadow of the wagons right next to Blood River."

He looked at her and grinned. "Ja, I will. It was perfect, Maria. I thank God for making it so."

"It was," she said with a shy smile. "And our wedding night too... The pain, then the pleasure... Lying under the stars... the Southern Cross hanging over us. It felt like Jesus himself was blessing our marriage."

"You mean spying on us as we lay together," he said with a wink.

"William! That's blasphemy!" she said, laughing joyously. "But you really must write back."

"I'll write in the morning. But first let's find a bed... Dinner can wait," he said, his throat suddenly dry as his thoughts returned to their wedding night.

The name of the new organization was provocative—Die Ossewabrandwag, or "OB" for short.

All William knew as he waited for Colonel Laas to speak on that bleak day in early 1939 was that the OB was a sort of guardian group to protect the spirit of the ox-wagon trek. It was not secret like Die Broederbond but was politically connected to it in ways he did not fully understand.

The twenty men crowded into his living room quieted as the colonel cleared his throat. "Less than two months ago we laid the foundation for our Voortrekker Monument in Pretoria," he began. "The monument honors the sacrifices of our forefathers as they tried to carve out a homeland in the African wilderness. And it celebrates their famous victory over the Zulus at Blood River."

He paused to straighten his tunic, the crisp brown uniform of the South African Defense Force adding an aura of official sanction to his words.

"But we must do more than honor the past. We must make sure their sacrifices were not in vain—Retief and his men, the innocents slaughtered in the Great Murder, our fighters who died in battle against the Tommies, our women and children who perished in the camps—and that their dreams of freedom stay alive. We must not only protect the flame of nationhood, we must fan it into a raging fire, a fire that consumes our enemies."

William could feel his fervor rising. There were several grunts of approval and a few handclaps.

"And we know how to do it," continued Laas. "Hitler has shown us. He's our inspiration for the fight to come. He has taken the German people from being oppressed and surrounded by their enemies in 1919 to the brink of greatness. And it's only 1939! Who knows what he will achieve in the next twenty years."

Laas strode back and forth several times. He seemed to be gathering himself.

"Afrikaners!" he boomed. "We must do the same for our people. We too must cleanse our ranks of all who are not true Afrikaners. We too must have our storm troopers to take the fight to our enemies. And we too must have our own fatherland, our republic." Then he stopped pacing and faced the enthralled group. "As one of our churchmen has said, Hitler has given the Germans a calling, a fanaticism that causes them to stand back for no one, and it's only by such holy fanaticism that the Afrikaner nation can achieve its calling."

William liked the idea of holy fanaticism. He wasn't exactly sure who their enemies were, but he liked the colonel's zeal. This was fighting talk.

"Count me in, Colonel. What's the plan?"

"Training first, De Beer, then action. You will hear from me. In the meantime, all of you, keep your pipes clean and your matches dry."

"Hitler is just a nasty little man surrounded by jackbooted bullies," said Maria one morning as they worked in the barn separating buttermilk to make cheese. "The idea that he could be the savior of Western civilization is absurd. And to believe he will help us get our republic is just as crazy as the Xhosa believing the Russians would save them from the British."

"You're wrong, Maria. Hitler's a great man who saved his own people. Even the king's brother—the one who abdicated—admires him and had tea with him in Germany. We can learn from Hitler, use his methods. He can help restore our dream for our own fatherland. What's so wrong about that?" He paused, breathing hard. "I know you don't like Laas—you've made that painfully clear—but the OB is bigger than Laas. Can't you at least support our efforts?"

"No, William, I can't," she said, smacking her ladle on the side of the urn. "Laas and the OB are too bitter and twisted to see anything clearly. And the OB's obsession with Hitler goes too far. For heaven's sake, William, the OB emblem looks just like the Third Reich emblem, and your Greyshirts look just like Hitler's Brownshirts. And all the marching and shooting and bomb-making! I just can't believe God wants His people to behave that way. Jesus said the meek will inherit the earth, not the arrogant and hateful like Hitler and Laas."

She glared at him, then turned to skim some unwanted specks off the buttermilk.

He knew better than to argue with her about what Jesus might have said two thousand years ago. He was not surprised by Maria's sentiments. Her dislike for Colonel Laas had been evident ever since the meeting at their home. She hated the way Laas hovered at the OB gatherings she had attended, always watching everyone with hawklike intensity. And it became worse after the government denounced the OB, stripped Laas of his rank and barred any officer in the armed forces from joining the OB. Instead of being deterred by the government's action, Laas had been emboldened—it had merely helped him define who their enemies were and to put a face on those who were true Afrikaners and those who were not—and had further distressed Maria.

"But Jesus *was* a man of action," countered William. "After all, he threw unbelievers out of the Temple. There's nothing meek about that. God is surely on the side of true Afrikaners against the unbelievers of our time. Can't we agree on that?"

"Ag, William, listen to yourself," she said, turning back to face him. "Who decides who is a true Afrikaner and who is not? The idea is absurd. And worse, it's dangerous. For heaven's sake, that's the way Hitler talks. The things he says about racial purity make my skin crawl. After all, how pure is the Afrikaner race? We all know families of mixed blood going back to the days when our ancestors first settled at the Cape."

"But those are two different things, Maria. Being pure and being true are not—"

"And what about the Jews?' she continued, pointing the ladle at him. "The Bible says they're God's chosen people. And we believe we're also God's chosen people. So how is it we suddenly have so much faith in Hitler and so little in God? What about our covenant with God at Blood River, the centenary trek that was supposed to bring us together as a people to preserve God's promise for our future?"

"Ag, Maria, speeches and monuments and wagon treks are all very well. But God helps those who help themselves. We must fight for our freedom, for our culture, for our future. And Hitler has shown us how it can be done."

Maria shook her head in dismay.

"This is total war, Maria, a fight for our survival as a people. And if God is for us, who can be against us?"

News of the war was breathtaking. Hitler's blitzkrieg of tanks, artillery, dive-bombers and ground troops seemed unstoppable.

William rejoiced in Hitler's successes—surely the salvation of Afrikanerdom was not far behind—but he was disappointed that the OB seemed marginalized. Laas did not appear to have a plan despite all the talk of heroic action, and he himself had done nothing except attend OB meetings and training sessions. Then everything changed when the Royal Air Force held its own against the Luftwaffe during the Battle of Britain. Almost overnight two central convictions of William's worldview were shaken—that Germany was about to win the war and that America would stay out of the war.

The evolving fortunes of the war were not lost on Maria. "Read his speech, William," she insisted as they sat on the porch one afternoon, gesturing at a newspaper report of Churchill's speech to the House of Commons. "Churchill and Roosevelt are cooking something up. See...here. After he speaks about how so much is owed by so many to so few, then he talks of how the British Empire and America will join together and, like the Mississippi, roll in a full flood that no one will be able to stop."

She paused and looked at him, her eyes bright with conviction. "And it will roll, William. And it will be unstoppable, especially if Hitler invades Russia, as he said he would in that silly little book of his that the OB seems to think is the bible for all human struggle."

William felt his frustration turn to despondency, as it invariably did when he locked horns with his wife over the war. The porch felt less sunny, the air less warm, the company less cheerful. But before he could respond, the atmosphere turned even darker.

"You're on the wrong side of history, William," she continued. "For heaven's sake, over three hundred thousand of our boys, English and Afrikaner, are fighting in the desert against Rommel, in the sky against the Luftwaffe, and in the hills against Mussolini. Our Sailor Malan in his Spitfire has shot down over thirty German planes, and Smuts is a field marshal in the British army. *These* are our people, William, not your pathetic little group of OB fanatics. You should be cheering for our troops, supporting our fight against Hitler, not denouncing their efforts and doing your best to sabotage them.

"You are repeating the same mistake you made during the Great War when you rode off to join De Wet's rebellion against the government's decision to support the British," she added, her voice rising. "That rebellion ended in failure and imprisonment for the rebels, even execution for one of their leaders. Our own people shooting and killing each other! It was shameful, William, a civil war amongst our own people."

"I didn't shoot anybody," he responded testily. He could feel his temper rising to meet his wife's passion.

"But you *wanted* to, William. You told me so many times. And, but for the grace of God and the stupidity of the rebels, you might've killed someone or been killed yourself! This OB rebellion will suffer the same fate as that last rebellion—mark my words—and this time you might actually kill someone. Why else do you practice all the shooting and bomb-making with that idiot Laas?"

He flared. "I'm not going to kill anyone, Maria, and you're the one who's on the wrong side of our people's history. Smuts betrayed our cause during the Great War and now he's doing it again in this war." *And he killed Anna*, thought William bitterly. "We're being forced to fight for our greatest enemy against our greatest friend. How can that be right? If we are God's people, how can we fight for the very people he has set against us?"

"Ag, William," she sighed. "All I know as a Christian is that fighting Hitler is the right thing to do, and that relying on him for the salvation of our people is pure heresy and complete nonsense."

He could only shake his head. The wedge between them was being driven deeper by the day. He loved her, but he could no more abandon his beliefs than abandon his roots. He rose slowly and stepped off the porch. The familiarity of the paddock and mute contentment of his cattle offered a welcome refuge from the rancor on the porch.

The strain with Maria deepened when word filtered through that a fiery new leader would replace Laas at a ceremony at Majuba presided over by the chairman of Die Broederbond. William knew he had to be there. Besides, he had always wanted to visit the site of the Boers' great victory over the British during their First War of Freedom in 1881.

The OB's new commander general, Hans van Rensburg, was everything William hoped he would be—fearless, resolute, determined—his speech on top of Majuba an uncompromising call to arms, the gauntlet unyielding.

"Afrikaners!" thundered Van Rensburg. "The war in North Africa calls for new cannon fodder. The Empire wants more of our Boer blood to be spilt in the desert sand under the shadow of the Union Jack." The roar of protest from the men gathered around was immediate. William could feel his blood rising, even as he imagined his fellow Afrikaners dying in the desert against Rommel.

Van Rensburg waited for the men to settle down. "Our path of suffering is just beginning, but we will tread it step by step, man for man. And if we must go to prison or face a firing squad to prevent spilling more Boer blood on behalf of the damned British Empire, then that is what we will do. That is an honorable service to the Afrikaner *Volk*." The applause was deafening. "OB...OB...OB," the men chanted, until Van Rensburg quieted them with his outstretched hand.

"People talk about democracy. One shouldn't speak ill of the dead. But I don't care what you call the system—the end is the

Afrikaner nation. If the choice is between democracy and Afrikanerdom, then the choice is clear." With that, the brawny man thrust his right arm and hand straight out, angled upward.

The men leapt to their feet cheering, "OB...OB...OB," their right arms held high in a reciprocal salute.

That evening, as they sat around a wood fire on top of Majuba, Van Rensburg outlined his plans to sabotage Smuts's war effort. They would blow up railway lines, power lines, telephone lines, utility stations, post offices, banks and shops. Specific targets were proposed, including a ship in Durban harbor they would sink to stop the troop ships leaving port.

And they would bomb the Benoni Post Office.

William didn't hesitate—the words were no sooner out of Van Rensburg's mouth than he volunteered for the Benoni target. The symmetry was irresistible—to strike back at Smuts for what he had done to Anna in Benoni.

Then came the call for the elite storm troopers—*Stormjaers*—to step forward to receive their orders. Total commitment was the expectation. There was no exception and no going back. The cause was more precious than life itself. A public display of loyalty was required.

William stepped forward. He had no doubt he stood where the destiny of his people needed him—at this place and time, at the point of ultimate commitment. Grim-faced men surrounded him on the uneven crest of Majuba, their features ominous in the flickering flames of the wood fire as the last light of day faded behind distant hills. And as he looked around him, he imagined the disciples of Jesus gathered together at the Last Supper, their grim expressions testament to the struggle to come against the Roman Empire.

William's jaw tightened as he stared at the man pointing a pistol at his chest and holding a Bible in his free hand. And he was acutely aware of a second man behind him, pressing a pistol against his back. He slowly extended his right hand and placed it on the Bible. The pistol at his chest jabbed his sternum. He took a deep breath and began to speak, each word precious between his lips.

"Of my own free will I solemnly promise before almighty God that I submit without reservation to the demands my people's divine call require of me. My higher authority will find me obediently faithful, and all commands I receive will be carried out promptly and kept secret."

He paused to swallow and glanced at Van Rensburg. He felt the barrel of the pistol dig into his chest again.

"May the Almighty grant that I shall be prepared to sacrifice my life for the freedom of my people. And may the thought of betraying the cause never occur to me, knowing that I will be subject to the vengeance of a storm trooper if I do."

He paused again, concentrating on the all-important last part of the oath. He took a deep breath. This was the moment. The pistol at his back prodded him to finish.

"May God grant me the courage to call out with my comrades, 'If I advance, follow me...If I retreat, shoot me...If I die, avenge me...so help me God.'"

27

THE FAULT IS NOT IN THE STARS

1941–1944

"We had to escape," said Nelson with quiet intensity. "It was the only thing to do."

The elderly white driver looked anxiously into her rearview mirror at the two backseat passengers. Despite having offered them a ride, Nelson recognized the concern in her eyes—to be alone with two young black men in the confines of her car for a ten-hour journey to Johannesburg.

He glanced at Justice, his stoic features dimly illuminated by the headlights of a passing car, and then at the landscape outside, an endless expanse of darkness that seemed void of life until it leapt upwards into a night sky illuminated by random brilliance.

"But I am very sorry to have angered your father," added Nelson. "He has been good to me since my father died, and I could not have wished for a better guardian."

Nelson fell silent as a narrative of their flight took form. "Our story is like something out of Shakespeare," he mused after a while. "The king arranges marriages for his son and ward, his son to marry a nobleman's daughter, his ward to marry a priest's daughter, except that the priest's daughter is in love with the king's son, neither groom loves the brides chosen for them, the king refuses the entreaties even of his queen, and so, on the eve of the wedding feast, with the bridal dowries already paid, the grooms secretly sell two of the king's prized oxen and use the money to run away to a city of gold."

Justice laughed. "When you put it like that, our story sounds poetic, almost heroic."

Even the lady driver chuckled.

The two fell silent as the black sedan sped through the night at a steady sixty-five miles per hour.

"But I will never finish my studies at Fort Hare after this," reflected Nelson. "That is too bad. I really wanted to get my degree...be a court interpreter...then counselor to our next king. And I'm sorry you were not there with me. I really enjoyed university life—so many good friends and good professors, the football and dancing, and the cross-country running."

"And the girls," added Justice with a snigger.

"True...true," he conceded. "The girls were wonderful."

The two men laughed. The lady driver smiled.

"There was so much to do," continued Nelson. "I was even in a play about the assassination of Abraham Lincoln—I played Booth, the assassin—and I will never forget when the prime minister came to Fort Hare."

"Smuts was at Fort Hare?"

"Ja, at the graduation ceremony after my first year in 1939. It was very exciting to have such a famous man come to speak to us in person. He spoke about the war and why South Africa should support Great Britain against Germany." He smiled. "And Louis Botha, the same one who had been a Boer general with Smuts, he actually came to open the university in 1916 when he was prime minister."

"What?" asked Justice incredulously. "What did the Boers hope to achieve with a black university based on an English education?"

"Ja, good question. Who can say what their motives were? But the British, that's another story. Their missionaries taught our students, but their armies made war on our people. And to make sure we could not rise again, they sent many of our chiefs and leaders to Esiquithini."

"Not only Xhosa chiefs," replied Justice. "They sent Zulu chiefs to the island as well."

The two fell silent again, staring out into the inky darkness.

"What do you know of the island?" asked Justice after a while.

"Only that it's a terrible place, a place for the unwanted, for lunatics and lepers, criminals and troublemakers. And that it's flat and desolate," added Nelson, "just a few miles from Cape Town, surrounded by ice-cold seas and hungry sharks. They say escape is impossible."

A mood of silent reflection settled over him as the car sped on through the night towards the City of Gold. He recalled the Xhosa poet-warrior Makhanda ka Nxele, sent to the island by the British, had promised to return to liberate his people but died trying to escape.

The people had waited in vain for something that would never happen—*Ukuza kuka Nxele*—a forlorn hope. Could anything be more pitiful than a people's hope of freedom being trapped on an unforgiving island prison surrounded by a cold and cruel ocean?

Nelson could hardly believe how much had happened to him over a few short years as he sat on a bench in the Men's Social Center in Johannesburg with about two hundred others on that Easter Sunday in 1944. They were all waiting for the main speaker at the first public meeting of the African National Congress's Youth League.

He smiled as he thought of his first years in Johannesburg, the innocent and unsophisticated first steps of a country bumpkin experiencing city life for the first time. Perhaps it was Qamata's doing, or just being in the right place at the right time, but he had been swept along at a pace as dazzling as the city lights at rush hour, through a series of fortuitous connections into associations that had shaped his life, including a position in the Youth League.

It was all so improbable.

His thoughts were interrupted by enthusiastic applause as Anton Lembede, the dynamic and articulate Zulu activist, rose to speak. His double-breasted gray suit seemed to swallow his slight physique, but his narrow head and luminous eyes framed by round glasses rose above the suit like a beacon determined to illuminate every dark corner of ignorance and bigotry.

Lembede's remarks carried easily to the back rows: "The majority of whites regard it as their destiny as a chosen and superior race to dominate people of color," he began, his voice resonant with authority. "In some countries the oppression is naked; in our country it is clothed in the trappings of trusteeship—that the whites are duty bound to manage our lives for our benefit and in our best interests. Do not be fooled," he warned. "Trusteeship is eyewash, an empty platitude, intended to pacify us into believing that our oppression is actually a pleasant experience under well-meaning Christian and democratic rule."

Nelson was transfixed. Lembede seemed to be speaking directly to him, as though willing him to recognize the truth of what he was saying. But what followed was a little esoteric—about how the African people regard civilization as the common heritage of all mankind, whereas the whites divide the world into multiple individual entities in constant conflict. But then he brought the point home:

"This war across the seas is just such a conflict among whites. We are told that South Africa is fighting against oppression and for freedom. The blood of our youth, both black and white, is being shed to free white people in Europe, yet nobody fights to free black people in Africa. Do not be fooled," he warned again. "When the whites are finished with their war for freedom in foreign countries, they will still deny us freedom in our own country."

A murmur of disgruntled assent coursed through the audience as Lembede continued, his voice strident: "But we cannot rely on the good graces of the whites to grant us our freedom. We must determine our future by our own efforts—we must free ourselves. It is not our fate to scurry about under the legs of the white man, creeping around in our own land to eke out disgraceful lives ending in dishonorable graves."

Lembede paused until the crowd had quieted. Then, in a stage whisper that quickly rose in intensity, he admonished, "The fault is not in the stars but in ourselves that we are underlings. We are the masters of our fate."

The audience stood and applauded. Many held hands. Some cried. Nelson cheered along with his friends Walter Sisulu and Oliver Tambo.

Lembede applauded with them, then waved the audience to silence. "It is the divine destiny of the African people to be free," he affirmed. "The cause of Africa and of our people must triumph, and it will triumph!"

As Nelson lay in bed that night in his cramped township room thinking about Lembede's speech, he was reminded of a poem by the Xhosa poet Mqhayi, written to mark a visit to South Africa by the Prince of Wales in 1925.

You sent us the truth, denied us the truth;
You sent us the life, deprived us of life;
You sent us the light, we sit in the dark,
Shivering, benighted in the bright noonday sun.

And still we sit in the dark, shivering, benighted, deprived of life, denied the truth, thought Nelson, recalling with pride how the humble Xhosa poet had spoken truth to power, just as Lembede had done.

Whenever he thought of Mqhayi, he remembered the day the poet had visited his boarding school and strode imperiously across the stage in a leopard-skin cloak with matching headpiece, stabbing the air with his assegai, raging against the influence of foreigners and the false gods of the white man, and all in the presence of their English headmaster. At the climax, he had launched into a magnificent poem about the stars and constellations and nations of the world, and then, dropping to one knee at the front of the stage, had concluded in a deep, rasping voice: "Now, come you, O House of Xhosa. I give unto you the most important and transcendent star—the Morning Star—for you are a proud and powerful people."

The poet's words had made him feel invincible, like one of a chosen people.

28

THE FACE OF EVIL

1944–1945

The bomb was a simple device—five sticks of dynamite wrapped together with a thirty-minute fuse—just as they had been taught.

William assumed his fellow saboteurs, Julien and Hennie, were members of a local OB cell, but he never asked and they never said. They considered using a timer but chose a fuse instead. It seemed symbolic of their cause—there was no going back after it was lit.

He had carried out his reconnaissance task earlier in the day and identified the small recess at the entrance to the post office in Benoni as the best place to leave the rucksack. He would keep watch from an alcove in the building across the street, although they expected the area to be deserted on a Sunday morning.

At the agreed time, Julien and Hennie ambled along the sidewalk, the rucksack casually slung over Hennie's shoulder, until they reached the post office. The street was quiet, as expected. But William hadn't anticipated such a paralyzing sense of unease, exacerbated by the Sunday morning silence, as though eyes were watching their every move—perhaps even the eyes of God.

After a quick glance at him to confirm all was clear, they lit their cigarettes and casually smoked for a few moments. Then Julien stepped behind Hennie, opened the backpack and reached inside with the burning cigarette. After a moment he carefully lifted the backpack off Hennie's shoulder and laid it gently against the post office door. The two men looked at him for confirmation that all was still clear, then began to walk away, still smoking, maintaining their nonchalant demeanor and pace.

He knew he was supposed to walk away in the opposite direction, but he delayed, morbidly fascinated by the dramatic event he anticipated in just a few moments. Then, just when he decided it was time to move, a car approached and he retreated into the alcove. He watched Julien and Hennie turn their backs as the car drove past, and relaxed as it receded into the distance.

But again, instead of moving away, he looked at his pocket watch, trying to calculate how much time was left. When he realized the blast was due any second, he knew he had to move fast. He was about to step out of the alcove when a young man appeared as though from nowhere only yards away, walking diagonally across the street towards the post office.

In the few paralyzing moments it took to decide what to do, the man reached the other side of the street, directly in front of the post office. William's frantic shout reached him just as he stepped onto the sidewalk. The man turned to look at him, his expression friendly but quizzical, just as the bomb exploded.

The fireball completely enveloped the man before hurling him forward like a rag doll into the street that almost immediately disappeared in a burst of shattered glass, bricks and dust. William felt himself being thrown back into the alcove. His head hit something hard and everything went dark and silent.

After a while—he didn't know how long—reason returned

through layers of murky confusion, like a swimmer struggling to the surface of a dark pool. All he knew for certain was that he was still alive. He struggled into a sitting position and stared at the man lying facedown, eyes wide open, fixed and unblinking, the letter in his hand about to be enveloped by an expanding pool of blood.

He knew the man was dead just as surely as he knew the last image those eyes had captured were of him, his killer, an image the man had taken directly to God.

William got to his feet, his senses still reeling from the blast and the reality of violent death. The only thing he could think to do was get away from the post office as quickly as possible. Giving no thought to the rendezvous with Julien and Hennie, or to his suitcase back at Izak's house, or to their plan of escape, he ran down the side street closest to his lookout alcove. His only thoughts as he ran were of the blast and the body lying in the street, and that the man must have walked up the same side street, invisible until it was too late.

He fumbled through his pockets as he ran, taking inventory of what he had with him, hoping to find anything that might help him get away. The only useful thing he found was in his rear pant pocket—his return train ticket—and, miraculously, his escape plan fell into place.

Maria sympathized when he described the vicious robbery on the way to the train station by a group of black mine workers—how they beat him, ripped his clothes and made off with his suitcase. But while she seemed to accept his explanation and appeared to put the matter out of mind, the bombing was front-page news.

Reports of the police investigation filled his days with dread and his nights with demons. Every unexpected sound rubbed the raw nerve of his fear and guilt. There were times he felt like Jesus must have, alone before being betrayed, expecting at any moment to hear the footsteps of the guardians of society and be pointed out by an accusing finger.

As the weeks wore on, he led Maria to believe his state of despair was a response to the scale of Hitler's reversals on every front and to America's entry into the war. But he lived in constant fear his terrible secret would be discovered. And, on an otherwise uneventful day, he thought the moment had come.

"Look, William, look!" called Maria excitedly as she entered the kitchen with the morning paper. "The police caught the Benoni bombers."

He nearly choked as his throat clamped shut. He imagined his name in the papers, his secret revealed, his wife betrayed and his life condemned.

"The report says two men have been tracked down and captured." Her voice was filled with triumph. "Isn't that good news?" And after a moment, in a more solemn tone, she added, "I'm sure there is a special place in hell for such people."

Inexplicably, his name was never mentioned at the trial of the bombers. He silently gave thanks every day for his anonymity. But when the government called for the ultimate penalty, he was convinced Julien and Hennie would implicate him in the plot. Yet even after the judge handed down the death sentence, there still was no mention of his name. He had not been betrayed—their oath as Stormjaers had prevailed.

The very next day, two policemen arrived at the farm.

He saw them coming. It seemed his reprieve was short lived. He thought of trying to run or of using his rifle, but that would be the end of his life with Maria. He took a deep breath, opened the door, and waited on the porch with Maria at his side as they approached.

"You are William de Beer?" asked one of the policemen.

"Ja," he said amiably. "So what's the problem? Has my Brahman bull got amongst the neighbors' cows again, eh?" He forced a laugh.

"You are under arrest," announced the policeman.

"What?" cried Maria. "What for?"

William held his breath—life as he knew it was surely over.

"For being a member of the OB and a supporter of Hitler. We have orders to take you to the detention center at Koffiefontein."

"What?" He thought he must have misheard.

"You heard me," said the policeman. "For being a member of the OB and a supporter of Hitler."

He only just managed to turn a laugh into a cough. "That's it?" He feigned indignation. "Just for being a member?"

"Orders are orders." The policeman was polite but firm. "You're on a list of troublemakers. Smuts wants you put away so you can't interfere with the war effort."

William sensed Maria stiffen—her dismay almost palpable.

"How long?" he asked the policeman, ignoring his wife.

"Can't say," said the policeman. "But at least as long as the war lasts."

The bombing was never mentioned. It was hard to imagine a prison sentence could feel so much like an acquittal, as though he had passed through the valley of the shadow of death and back into the sunlight of life.

He was allowed to pack a few things and to have a private moment with Maria. But he received no fond farewell from his wife. Instead, she kept her distance, her expression of displeasure so fierce he decided discretion was the better part of valor and left without a word.

The internment camp turned out to be less a prison than a boarding school for old friends, with curfews, strict rules and decent food, although it was disconcerting to be rubbing shoulders with more than a thousand Italian and German prisoners of war.

The OB inmates used the camp as a learning opportunity, even referring to it as the "Boer University." One of their comrades, John Vorster, had a degree in law and was the youngest OB chief general at just twenty-seven years old. Vorster was a firebrand who raged in his lectures to the Boer inmates about the right of Afrikaners to control their own destiny, about being forced to fight in England's wars, and how "the devil of race hatred" was supposed to be dead after Afrikaans was recognized as an official language equal to English. "But," he demanded, "how can there ever be racial peace between us and the English if true Afrikaners are humiliated every time England is at war?"

William's fervor was aroused by Vorster's rhetoric. He burned to prove himself worthy among his OB comrades but kept secret his role in the Benoni bombing for fear the story would leak to the camp guards. But he did share his family story with Vorster—his father at Spion Kop, the Tommies at their farm, his mother and sister at the concentration camp, and the treachery of Mandela.

He left Vorster in no doubt of his resolve to avenge his family's suffering, even if it was the last thing he did on this earth.

By the summer of 1944 the Allies were moving towards Berlin on the western front, the Soviets were pushing back into Germany on the eastern front, and members of Hitler's inner circle had tried to assassinate him. And when the Allies finally reached Berlin in the spring of 1945, the war was all but over. Partisans executed Mussolini, Hitler committed suicide and Germany surrendered. A few months later, Japan was forced to do the same after the Americans dropped two atomic bombs on the tiny Pacific island.

The war over, William was allowed to return to the farm. He was relieved to be home and sobered by the outcome of the war. But then came reports of terrible things the Nazis had done. Although he had no great love for the Jews, he preferred not to believe the stories. If the Nazi concentration camps were anything like what people were saying, he thanked God his mother and sister had not been sent to such camps.

"It's shameful, William—the concentration camps—truly shameful," said Maria one Sunday night after dinner as she read the newspaper while he sat staring at the embers in the fireplace.

"Ag, Maria, you can't believe everything you read in the newspapers." He got up and added a log to the fire. "I'm sure they're exaggerating. Besides, bad things happen during wars—that's the nature of war."

She shook her head. "That's the nature of evil, not war. The end never justifies the means, William," she said as she sniffed and blew her nose. "God forbid we ever become like them—nothing but thugs and murderers, truly evil."

29

THE FORTRESS

1948

The election result was a miracle. Nobody had predicted Dr. Daniel Malan would beat Smuts and form a government of true Afrikaners. It was as stunning as Churchill being thrown out of office after winning the war against Hitler.

Even the choir that Sunday was caught up in the excitement and sang as though manna from heaven was their daily bread, the rapture imminent. As Malan had told them, their Afrikaner history was "the greatest masterpiece of the centuries," their nation a "miracle behind which must lie a divine plan," their identity as a people "not the work of men but the creation of God."

William had even more reasons for celebrating. The pastor had told him in private that Die Broederbond was behind Malan's victory and the genius of the apartheid platform. It felt like a vindication of his feelings about Smuts and somehow eased his guilt over the Benoni bombing. And he cherished the fact their new leader was the same Malan who had joined him to Maria in marriage at Blood River—it felt like a special blessing, a personal connection to God's plan for their country.

Back on their porch after church, the bucolic scene belied the euphoria of the moment. A hint of damp manure hung in the air as a luminous but cool sun flooded the farmyard and porch. The family dog lay at Maria's feet with its black muzzle on the edge of the top step, the burnished red-brown coat stretched taut over the Rhodesian Ridgeback's ninety lean pounds. A cow bellowed, immediately joined by several others, perhaps in disapproval of two combative roosters. The ridge of hair on the dog's back twitched in irritation.

"What's this 'apartheid' the papers talk about?" asked Maria, looking up from the newspaper. "I always thought it meant keeping our people from marrying the English, to keep us separate and prevent the horrors that result from such mixed marriages."

"Ja, that was true before, but now it means something else." He reached for his pipe. "But why don't you read what the papers say?"

She scanned the paper. "Malan says apartheid is a chance for each race to uplift themselves on the basis of their own language and culture, in their own place, according to their own abilities. He says it solves the problem of what to do with all the blacks and the coloreds and the others that outnumber us ten to one… that we can't have political equality if we want to survive." She paused to turn the page. "He also talks about being separate but equal, like America, because if we surrender to race mixing, that will be the end of us as a people." She stopped reading. "It almost sounds like a good idea. What do you think?"

William patted the dog's back as he gathered his thoughts. "Here's how I see it, Maria." He paused to sip his tea, wishing he had a biscuit or a rusk to dunk.

"Do you remember what Malan said about the ox-wagon trek after he married us at Blood River?"

She shook her head. "He said a lot of things. I was thinking of only one thing."

William smiled. "Malan saw Blood River as a symbol of victory in the battle to come in the cities—the battle against the blacks for jobs—and that freedom for our people means not just becoming a republic but the freedom to preserve ourselves as a white race in this land."

"And so?"

"Well, at Blood River our few hundred beat Dingane's hordes by circling the wagons, keeping the gaps small, using the wagons to protect our cattle and belongings, and shooting down the Zulus when it seemed they would sweep over us and destroy everything."

"Yes. God was truly on our side that day."

"Ja, and Malan is saying this is our Blood River, our time to circle the wagons. We have to keep the blacks, the coloreds, the Indians outside our wagons—they are too many, we are too few. It's our only hope to protect our people, our jobs, our schools, our homes and our culture. Our survival depends on it."

He was surprised by his fluency. It was the first time he'd tried to pull all the pieces together. But judging from Maria's expression, she was not entirely persuaded. Then the final piece fell into place.

"Besides, Maria, you remember what pastor told us this morning, that the blacks have their place, that the sons of Ham are destined to be hewers of wood and drawers of water?" She nodded. "And do you remember the passage he quoted from Scripture?"

She answered without hesitation. "'From one man He made every nation of men and he determined the times set for them and the exact places where they should live.' Book of Acts, Chapter Seventeen."

"Ja, exactly, Maria. That's what God wants and what we must have—that all our different peoples have their own places to live. And because we are so few, we have to make sure we keep the other peoples in their places, separate from us. That's what apartheid means for us and for our people."

He paused to light his pipe, his thoughts swirling like the hot smoke in the bowl of the pipe.

She was silent for a few moments, her brow creased. "But that's nothing new, William. We have been living separate lives in separate places ever since Van Riebeeck landed in the Cape in 1652."

He nodded. "It's not that it's new, Maria, but now we have the power to make it permanent—in all things—to make sure that nobody can breach our circle of wagons, that nobody can take our land and our freedom away from us. Ever!"

He sucked on his pipe and blew a perfect circle of smoke. "And God is on our side, Maria, just like He is on the side of the Jews." He paused to blow another circle of smoke straight through the center of the previous circle. "Just like that, Maria—two perfect circles—that's the way the Almighty works." He smiled with satisfaction. "Just think of what has happened in the last two weeks. On May 14 the Jews declared their independence in the Land of Israel, and on May 26 true Afrikaners finally came to power in our own land. Are these not signs of God's blessings upon His chosen people?"

She stared at him for several moments, then picked up her knitting. He dropped the subject to give her time to think while he busied himself with their dairy herd, even though it was a day of rest. Solomon fetched and carried and slopped out the barn as usual, although he moved slower these days and his hair was graying around the temples. Even after the chores were done, William stayed out of the house until she called him to dinner.

"Anything else you saw in the newspaper?" he asked, making conversation as they sat at the kitchen table after they had eaten.

"Ag, William, there's lots of talk about black peril and red menace—city talk that makes me nervous. And something about black unions stirring up trouble, promoting a thing called socialism and mass struggle and majority rule, led by communists and blacks trained in Moscow."

He shuddered. "I've heard of this communism thing, Maria. It's dangerous. It comes from the Russian Revolution, and we all know what happened to the poor czar and his family." He paused. "It sounds to me like the black peril and the red menace are two sides of the same coin."

She sat for a while shaking her head. "All this talk makes my head spin," she said, disturbing the dog as she pushed back her chair. "I'm going to make another pot of tea. I only hope the kettle boils before the revolution comes."

He settled back, picked up the newspaper, and was surprised to read that the Voortrekker Monument in Pretoria was almost finished. A photograph showed a huge square structure over 130 feet high surrounded by 64 granite wagons—the wagons of Blood River.

"I didn't realize the Monument opens next year already, Maria," he said when she sat down with their tea. "It says here that below the Hall of Heroes is the Cenotaph, a stone coffin made of red granite, the symbolic tomb of Piet Retief and his slaughtered comrades. And at exactly midday on the sixteenth of December every year, the day of our victory over Dingane, the sun shines through a special hole in the roof of the Monument, down through a big round opening in the floor of the Hall of Heroes and down onto the Cenotaph below, where a circle of sunlight illuminates the inscription on top of the coffin—'We for You, South Africa.'"

He looked at Maria, his eyes bright. "Can you picture it, Maria? The light of the world, the finger of God, reaching down, touching and blessing our people."

She sipped her tea and smiled. "Yes, I can picture it, William. It seems the same finger has reached down and blessed our marriage."

"Huh?" he grunted. "What are you talking about?"

She smiled again. "God has answered our prayers, William." She paused, enjoying his confusion. "I am with child."

William came awake fearfully, to visions of the Great Murder, of Zulu warriors stabbing and slashing, to sounds of mothers and children screaming. But as soon as he sat up, the vision dissipated, except for the screaming.

He looked around the room, blinded by the dark, bewildered by the sound, his eyes adjusting slowly to the light from a sliver of pale moonlight through the bedroom window. He reached for Maria. She was not in bed. Then it registered—the screams were hers and coming from the far side of the bed.

"Oh my God! Maria!"

He scrambled across the bed and looked down. In the dim light he saw her lying on her back clutching her swollen belly, her legs apart and pulled up, her nightdress almost past her swollen breasts.

"What is it, Maria, what's wrong?"

"The baby! It's stuck—it can't come out." She screamed again, a long despairing wail of pain, begging for relief. "Oh my God, William, my insides are tearing. Dear God. Do something, William! Please, God!"

He reached for the kerosene lamp and matches on her bedside table. Hands shaking, he needed two strikes to get it alight. The flickering light illuminated the sweat on her body, her long hair in damp cords around her face, the dark tangled mess between her legs in stark contrast to her pale skin.

"I can feel the baby's head—it's in the wrong place," she gasped through clenched teeth as she guided his hands. "Here...and here." She cried out as he pressed. "You have to turn the baby...so its head is down."

He swallowed hard. He knew what to do with cattle—reach deep into the mother and turn the calf—but he couldn't imagine doing that to Maria. It surely had to be done from the outside. He pushed and squeezed her belly as hard as he dared, trying to force the baby's legs one way, its head the other way. Maria screamed and wept, at times stopping his hands, then pushing with him, until she suddenly went limp.

William stared at her face, horrified, fearing the worst. Then he ran from the bedroom. He could hear the dog behind him scrabbling for traction on the wooden floor trying to keep up with him. He grabbed his shotgun from its rack in the hall, sprinted out the front door and leapt to the bottom of the porch steps, firing both barrels into the sky as he landed. The dog barked frantically and the chickens and roosters immediately added to the cacophony of alarm. Then William raced back up the porch steps and into the kitchen.

Maria was still motionless when he returned to the bedroom with a jug of water and a towel, the dog trailing obediently behind. But at least he could hear her rasping breath. He heard heavy footsteps on the porch steps, then Solomon's voice.

"Master? I heard the gun. Does master need help?"

"Come, Solomon, quickly. To the bedroom," he called out as he covered Maria's lower body with her nightdress. Moments later Solomon was at his side.

"Ow," said Solomon when he saw Maria on the floor. "Madam is hurting with the child?"

"Yes. Help me get her onto the bed. Take one side...under her leg and shoulder. Try to keep her straight."

Maria groaned as she was lifted onto the bed. William arranged the pillows as best he could under her head. Then he looked at Solomon across the bed.

"We need a doctor, Solomon, quickly. But the one at Sannah's Post is in the Cape with his dying father. The pastor told us at church."

Solomon nodded. "I know a doctor, master."

"I'm not letting one of your witchdoctors touch my wife, Solomon. Are you mad?"

"No, master, he is not a witchdoctor. He has certificates and photographs from across the seas."

"A white doctor—why didn't you say so?"

"No, master, a black doctor. His name is Moroka."

William stared hard at his headman. "Ja, well, Solomon, I'm not carrying my wife to Bloemfontein in the middle of the damn night to see some black doctor I've never heard of."

"He's not in Bloemfontein, master. He is near here, in Thaba 'Nchu."

William's eyes narrowed. "Moroka...Moroka...I've heard that name. A chief by that name helped our people many years ago."

Solomon beamed. "Ja, master. Doctor Moroka is the great-grandson of that same chief. He treats whites and blacks. People say he's a good doctor."

William shook his head. "Ja, well, anyway, I'm not going to go and sit with my hat in my hand waiting on a black man to treat my wife."

Maria groaned and dug her fingernails into his forearm. Her face was ashen even in the low light, her breathing shallow, strained. Her bloodshot eyes pierced the gloom and seemed to bore into his, pleading for relief from any quarter.

He took a deep breath. "Fetch him, Solomon. Tell him to come quickly. Tell him the child is the wrong way around...that I'm afraid for the mother...and for the child."

He sat on the bed holding her hand after Solomon ran from the house. All he could think to do as he waited was to dribble water into her mouth and to wipe her brow with the towel.

And pray.

With the sun came the doctor, a big man with a big smile despite the dog that barked at the sight and smell of the stranger. William had his hands full restraining the dog until Solomon took the animal by the collar and left the room.

"The child's head—" began William.

"I know," said the doctor, taking Maria's wrist to check her pulse. "Solomon told me."

Nothing more was said as the doctor took off his coat and got to work. As much as William wanted to leave the room, he wasn't about to leave Maria alone with Moroka. But he wished he had not been present to see the huge black hands on his wife's pale belly and, above all, he wished the man hadn't seen Maria in all her nakedness.

He hoped Maria would remain oblivious as Moroka pushed and twisted, trying to rotate the baby, but the manhandling was so intense that she became agitated and lifted her head. She stared in confusion at the black man kneeling between her legs, then screamed. He couldn't tell whether in fright or pain.

"Do not be afraid, madam. I am Doctor Moroka. I have done what I can. Now it's your turn," he said gently. "The baby wants to come out...to see who has been pushing him around."

Maria smiled weakly. Then, gritting her teeth and holding William's hand on one side of the bed and Moroka's on the other side, she pushed and cried out, then pushed again. Within minutes the baby's head emerged. Then more pushing and more pain, until at last, the tiny being was forced from the cozy safety of her womb into the doctor's hands.

Moroka grinned as he held the baby upside down. "A healthy boy," he announced as he slapped the tiny bottom and cut the umbilical cord.

The baby cried. Maria cried, then laughed. William gaped.

The doctor laid the baby on Maria's chest, helped him latch onto her breast, made sure she was comfortable, and chortled with pleasure.

"Your baby is at least nine pounds," said Moroka with a broad smile. "He will be a strong man when he grows up. Feed him now and then bathe him later in a basin of warm water. And rest. I will come back again before the sun goes down."

Maria nodded, her eyes bright with pride and relief.

"Thank you," said William as Doctor Moroka threw his coat over his shoulder and left the room.

30

THE RED SCARE

1956–1960

The arrests started in the early hours that December morning, a nationwide effort to arrest everyone thought to be plotting to overthrow the government by force.

"It was inevitable," said Nelson as he sat with Oliver Tambo and watched more and more community leaders being brought into the police station. "Our Freedom Charter must have been like a red rag to a bull. Even we knew our charter of people's rights would be revolutionary."

Tambo nodded. "Ja, and any kind of social justice is a form of communism in their eyes. Trouble is they already know that many of our friends are communists." He shook his head. "So our association with communists is a difficult issue for us."

"What do you mean?" asked Nelson.

"'Communism' has become a dirty word in the West," Tambo began, "the basis for accusing people of all sorts of treasonous activities and putting people in jail." He paused. "Just the other day I read about an American politician, McCarthy, who accused all sorts of Americans of being communists, of being disloyal to America. Even Charlie Chaplin."

Tambo drew a deep breath and slowly exhaled. "It's one thing for Afrikaners to make arguments about their rights over us based on a distortion of their Bible and their so-called covenant with God. These arguments sustain their struggle against our people but fall on deaf ears outside South Africa." He paused. "But imagine the support they'll get from America and Britain if they can portray their struggle against us as part of the West's struggle against international communism. What better way to disguise their oppression of our people than cloak it as a struggle against communism?"

Nelson rolled his eyes. "I can only imagine what they thought when Sisulu visited the Soviet Union, spoke on Radio Moscow and celebrated the anniversary of the October Revolution."

"Ja, that was quite something," agreed Tambo. "But revolution is happening everywhere," he continued, "in China, India, Indonesia, Vietnam, Korea and other parts of Africa. The struggle against the imperialism of the Americans, British, French and Dutch is shared by many peoples who resist the idea of the supremacy of whites over other races."

"And we suffer," added Nelson, "because we resist the efforts of America and her satellites to drag the world into the rule of violence and brutal force—into the rule of napalm, hydrogen and other bombs that kill millions to satisfy the criminal and greedy appetites of the imperial powers."

The two men fell silent as more of their comrades were hustled into the police station. It was going to be a long day. And it looked as though they would be spending Christmas in jail that year.

"So, here we are," mused Nelson reflecting on their situation. "High treason. And the penalty is death." He shook his head. "I tell you, Oliver, there is no easy walk to freedom, anywhere."

"It's him, Maria," yelled William, "from Mvezo in the Transkei. It's him!" He was stomping around the porch, dancing with glee, when Maria emerged through the screen door wiping her hands on her apron.

"So you keep saying, William. But who are you talking about? And please stop shouting."

He thrust the newspaper at her. "See the photo from the Treason Trial," he said, jabbing at a grainy image with his finger. "And read the story, Maria. I tell you—it's him."

She took the paper from him without a word and sat down.

"Nicolas," she called over her shoulder. "Come sit with your mother."

Moments later, a stocky six-year-old pushed through the screen door and squeezed into the chair with his mother, frowning as he watched his agitated father pace up and down the porch.

After a while she looked up from the paper, quizzically. "But it's 1956, William. That can't be the same Mandela from the mines. That was fifty years ago. This one is too young."

"Ja, of course it's not the same Mandela, Maria. I'm not stupid. Didn't you read the story?" He tried to control his exasperation. "It says this Mandela is from Mvezo, just like the entry in the mine registry. That one's name was Henry. This one's name is Nelson. Look," he said, pointing at the text. "It says his father—Henry Gadla Mandela, from Mvezo, in the Transkei—was counselor to the Thembu chief. This one is his son!"

He sat down and took a deep breath. The promises he had made after the Second War of Freedom—to rebuild the farm and to find Mandela—were suddenly as fresh in his mind as the day he had made them. And while the farm had recovered with Maria's help, the quest for Mandela had slipped inexorably from his grasp as the years became decades—until now. In an instant, every buried memory of those terrible events flooded his mind.

Maria folded the newspaper slowly and looked at him. "So what if it's the son?" she said. "What's that to us?"

He stared at her, trying to formulate an answer. "I don't know exactly, Maria. But the Bible tells us the sons will pay for the sins of their fathers, so this Mandela must pay for what his father did to my family."

She nodded slowly. "The Bible says a lot of things, William. But you're right," she said, pulling Nicolas closer to her, stroking his fair hair, "it does say that. And that's what worries me. The same passage also applies to your son."

The Old Synagogue in Pretoria, converted into a court of law for the Treason Trial, bore silent witness to the austere majesty of two peoples who believed they were chosen—the Jews to serve, the Afrikaners to rule.

In stark contrast, the Freedom Charter was portrayed as an unholy covenant, conclusive evidence the accused not only wanted to overthrow the government with violence but to replace it with a communist state. Of the one hundred and fifty-six defendants originally charged, ninety-one remained to face charges of high treason when the trial finally began in 1958. Among them were fifty-seven blacks, sixteen whites, sixteen Indians and two Coloureds.

Two years later, at the end of another long day in court, Nelson despaired. "The damn trial starts and stops," he complained to Tambo. "From one day to the next we never know what's going to happen. I spend my days in court and my weekends with you trying to salvage our legal practice. At least they have let another sixty of us go—just thirty left now."

"Yes," said Tambo as they boarded the bus for the uncomfortable journey from Pretoria back to Johannesburg. It had been an especially challenging day, with the ANC president, Chief Albert Luthuli, in the witness box testifying about the ANC's policy of nonviolence. "But apparently we thirty are especially violent and revolutionary."

Leaden weariness settled over the group like a sodden blanket as the bus headed through the city towards the main road to the south. But they had no sooner reached the main road than their torpor was unexpectedly disturbed.

"Look!" shouted one of the men, pointing. Heads jerked and swung in unison towards the windows as a convoy of military vehicles raced past them on the road to Johannesburg.

"Something's going on, comrades," said Nelson. "Something big."

Sisulu met the bus in Orlando Township. "There's been a shooting at the Sharpeville police station," he said in a rush as Nelson and Tambo stepped off the bus. "It was a passbook march—maybe five thousand protesters, maybe more. Nobody is sure what happened. It started peacefully, but then the police started shooting. I hear maybe sixty dead and many wounded, women and children too. Army and police are everywhere."

It was March 21, 1960.

Good God, thought Nelson. *Perhaps this is it. Perhaps this will push us over the precipice!*

"We must seize the moment," he insisted as a small group sat around the kitchen table in Sisulu's home that night. "This issue is the flashpoint that could make the whole apartheid system untenable."

Sisulu nodded. "I agree. And the British prime minister just spoke in Cape Town about the wind of self-government blowing through Africa. But we must be careful, comrades. We don't want the wind of change to become a gale of oppression blowing the other way, back in our faces—"

"Comrades," interjected Nelson fiercely, rising from his chair, "the time to be careful, to be diplomatic, to deal in good faith, has passed. Our country is bleeding, our people are dying—the butchers roam the streets, invade our homes and kill our children!"

"What are you saying?" asked Sisulu in a hushed tone.

"I'm saying it's futile for us to continue talking nonviolence against a regime whose only reply is savage attacks on an unarmed and defenseless people." He was breathing hard but he had said it—given voice to the heresy. He could sense the idea swirling around the table, demanding to be considered.

After a while Sisulu cleared his throat. "You may be right, Nelson, but if we resist, we should prepare for a heavy-handed response." He paused. "Oliver is key. We must get him out of the country. We need someone like Tambo outside who can be our voice."

Nelson nodded as he settled down. "Good thinking. But it will be the end of Mandela and Tambo. And that is a sad thing. We had high hopes for our law office serving the needs of our people." He shrugged in resignation. "But there is a season for all things, comrades, and I have a strong feeling a season of great change is upon us."

"That's what worries me," mused Sisulu. "There's a rumor the regime will declare a state of emergency."

"Martial law?"

"Yes. Their power is absolute and they will use it to arrest our people en masse. They will come for us too."

Nelson nodded and was silent for a moment. "I don't like the sound of it, Walter. But I'm already on trial for treason. What more can they do to me?"

31

OATHS REVIVED, JUSTICE DELAYED

1960−1961

William recognized him the moment he stepped out of the car—the same bulldog demeanor of the OB commander he remembered from the detention center. And he made no effort to disguise his pleasure at seeing his old comrade again, even though Vorster was now the minister of justice.

"My God, John, it's good to see you again," he said as he pumped Vorster's hand. "You've come a long way since Koffiefontein, Mr. Minister."

Vorster smiled as he took off his suit coat and loosened his tie. "Ja, but we've all come a long way since those days," he said, looking around at the paddock and fields beyond. "Nice place you have here, De Beer. Good farming country," he added.

William smiled, pleased by the compliment. "So what brings you this way? Am I in trouble?" he asked, laughing awkwardly. The only thing he could think of was the Benoni bombing, but the Malan government had pardoned Julien and Hennie after it came to power in '48, so he was pretty sure it was not about that.

"Come," said Vorster, "let's talk on your porch out of the afternoon sun."

William called through the screen door for Maria to make tea and come meet a friend from the old days.

"I'm here on official business, De Beer," said Vorster after they had settled into two of the porch chairs. "It's the referendum," he added in a tired voice. "The opposition is campaigning hard against us becoming a republic. It's going to be close." He yawned. "Sorry, De Beer. It's been a long day. But let's wait for your wife—she should hear this too. And any children you have who are sixteen. We lowered the voting age for this one."

William nodded. "My wife will be out in a minute. But my son is too young—we struggled to have children. It's a long story."

Almost on cue, Maria emerged with a tray of tea and rusks, followed by Nicolas. He introduced her with some trepidation but was relieved when she remained courteous even when the OB and Koffiefontein were mentioned. She politely served the tea and then sat down with Nicolas.

The dog sniffed at Vorster, then ambled off to investigate the strange car in the yard.

"Ja, well, it's nice to meet your family, De Beer. And the rusks are very nice." He smiled at Maria. "So, the referendum is almost upon us," he began. "I'm visiting as many of our people as I can in this area. The plan is to get out the vote and to make sure our people vote yes in October."

Vorster paused to sip his tea. "After generations of struggle our people finally have a chance to shake off the blanket of colonialism and imperialism that has smothered us for so long. If the yes vote wins, we will be free to govern ourselves and to chart our own course. No more bowing and scraping to kings and queens of the British Empire."

"Will we still be part of the Commonwealth?" asked Maria.

"No," said Vorster. "Too many foreigners want to tell us what to do—how to run our country and how to treat our non-whites. We will be done with the Commonwealth after we become a republic."

"So it's about apartheid then?" she asked. "The referendum, I mean. The blacks can't vote so it's really about keeping South Africa white, isn't—"

"Maria! Let the minister speak. Ag, sorry, John."

"No, that's all right, De Beer. Your wife is right, except the world doesn't understand apartheid. They make up all sorts of nonsense and condemn us as racists."

"But they understand Sharpeville, Mr. Minister," countered Maria. "They're not making that up."

The assertion hung in the air like a bolt of lightning before the crack of thunder.

"Maria!" exploded William, shocked by his wife's impertinence.

Vorster intervened. "Steady, De Beer. Your wife asks good questions. Again, the liberal media made a meal out of Sharpeville. The truth is the police were surrounded by a mob of thousands. There was a scuffle...some stones were thrown...and when one policeman lost his nerve and pulled the trigger, the rest panicked and started shooting."

Vorster paused as Solomon shuffled past with a milk pail in each hand, his back bent with age and toil, his head a thicket of gray above eyes that seemed forever fixed on a distant shore—a shore he never expected to reach. Vorster cleared his throat then sat forward and fixed his stern gaze on Maria.

"You must remember," he added, lowering his voice, "Sharpeville was just two months after Cato Manor, where nine of our policemen—four whites and five blacks—were stoned and hacked to death by a black mob. They were mutilated and their private parts stuffed into their mouths." He paused. "Forgive me for being so graphic, missus De Beer, but you can imagine what went through the heads of the Sharpeville police when they were surrounded by thousands of blacks and some began chanting 'Cato Manor! Cato Manor!' The shooting was unfortunate, of course, but you can understand why the police panicked."

Maria shrugged. "If the minister will excuse me, I need to prepare our dinner. William, you may ask the minister to eat with us...if you like." Then she stood up, as did Vorster as a courtesy. "Nicolas, come. You can help me in the kitchen."

The screen door banged shut as they went inside. The dog trotted back up the porch steps and settled at William's feet.

"Sorry about that, John, but my wife will vote yes when the time comes. You have my word."

Vorster yawned again. "Good. I can't stay for dinner, De Beer, but I'm sure I can count on you. There's a lot going on behind the scenes that makes the vote very important for our people."

"Anything you can tell me?" he asked.

Vorster looked pensive. "Sharpeville was a turning point, De Beer. Our sources tell us the ANC and others will use more and more violent tactics against us. After Luthuli replaced Moroka as president of the ANC, we thought things might settle down a bit. But there have been violent revolutions all over Africa the last few years. We'd be fools to think it can't happen here."

"Moroka? President of the ANC?"

"Ja, he's a doctor, believe it or not," said Vorster. "Lives in these parts, near Thaba 'Nchu, I think."

William gaped as an uncontrollable fury raced through his gut and into his throat. He coughed to cover his rage.

"You know him?" asked Vorster, frowning.

He swallowed hard. "Ag, uh...no, John," he stammered. "There was a Chief Moroka in this area many years ago. Just wondered if they were related."

"Humph!" exclaimed Vorster. "Anyway, we have to be proactive against the ANC, hit them hard before they can organize. But if we're still part of the Commonwealth, there will be too many eyes on us. We need to be free to do what we have to do—to take care of agitators like that Nelson Mandela from the Treason Trial. I tell you, De Beer, that one's a real troublemaker. It's definitely gloves off with him."

William's jaw tightened. "The father destroyed my family and now the son wants to destroy our people. You must stop him, John, whatever it takes."

Vorster nodded. "Ja, we're working on it. We're keeping an eye on Mr. bloody Mandela and his friends. Even though they're on trial for treason, they're free to go home every day and on the weekends. So we watch day and night for the right moment. It will come."

"It can't come too soon for me."

"I hear you, De Beer. And I remember what you told me at Koffiefontein about your family's suffering." He paused, then turned and looked around him. "Walk with me, De Beer. Show me the paddock there on the far side behind the trees."

When they were past the trees, close to the paddock, Vorster spoke again. "Our future is uncertain, De Beer. We don't know how the people will vote in the referendum, and we don't know how the judges will rule in the Treason Trial. But regardless, it won't be the end of our struggle. We have a long road ahead against the communist onslaught. We need all the resources we can muster for the fight to come."

William nodded, then followed as Vorster walked a little further until the trees obscured them from the farmhouse.

"Listen to me, De Beer, and this is for your ears only," he said, his tone a forceful whisper. "In my heart, I'm still a commander of the OB. Our enemy has changed, but the goal is the same—the survival of the Afrikaner nation—just as Van Rensburg said on Majuba that day."

William stood tall, remembering his oath of commitment on top of Majuba. "Yes." His gravelly whisper matched Vorster's. "I promised then before almighty God to answer the call. Nothing has changed. I'm still prepared to sacrifice my life for the freedom of our people."

"And to obey all commands, to carry them out promptly and in secret?" pressed Vorster, looking intently at him.

He nodded vigorously. "Yes, absolutely, so help me God."

Vorster's smile was tight. "I know about Benoni, De Beer. Perhaps you have one more mission in you, even at your age. Private citizens like you can sometimes do things that we in government can't do, or can't be seen to do."

"What do you want me to do?" he asked, his brow furrowed. He had no idea where this was leading.

"I don't know yet, De Beer. But you have a history with Mandela. And the way things are going, I'm sure the opportunity will arise." Then he extended his hand, his grip firm, his expression resolute. "I know how to reach you. In the meantime, comrade, keep your pipe clean and your matches dry."

Then he turned and was gone, the black sedan throwing up a cloud of dust as it disappeared down the farm road.

William read the newspaper in disbelief. Nothing made sense. Even the sounds of the farm outside the kitchen and of Maria behind him preparing their meal seemed alien, disconnected from the world he thought he knew.

"My God, Maria. I don't bloody believe it! How can the damn fool judges accept the ANC is pro-Soviet, that it advocates violence and wants to overthrow the state, yet not accept that Mandela and the others are guilty of high treason?"

He shook his head, as though to dispel a nightmare. After all the years of trial, it was over, just like that. Not guilty. The defense didn't even have to finish its closing argument. He slammed his hand down on the kitchen table.

Maria gasped behind him and dropped her kitchen knife. "Good heavens, William. You gave me such a fright," she said as she stooped to retrieve the knife. "But I'm sure the judges know what they're doing."

"Ha!" he fumed. "Not this lot, Maria. Damn judges are worse than a bunch of senile ostriches with their pea-sized brains buried in the sands of the Kalahari. It's absolute bloody rubbish!"

"William, don't talk like that!"

"It's true, Maria. My God, how much evidence do they need—a signed statement from Khrushchev? Everybody knows the ANC's Freedom Charter is nothing but a communist manifesto."

She said nothing as she added ingredients to a lamb stew and boiled the potatoes. Nicolas was outside, shooting at old coffee cans with his pellet gun.

"So Mandela and his bloody communist friends go free, treated like heroes by their supporters. I can't believe it!"

"Well, if they're not guilty they must be set free, William. That's the way the law works."

"Don't tell me how the law works, Maria," he replied, his temper rising. "They're as guilty as sin and everybody knows it."

"Ag, really, William. You believe everything the government tells you, and then repeat it like a parrot. The state's evidence relied on nonsense like who was invited to certain weddings, and restaurant signs for soup with meat and soup without meat. It's a fantasy, William. It's embarrassing."

He bristled. "There's nothing embarrassing about fighting communism, Maria. And it's no fantasy the damned ANC wants to overthrow the government."

"Ja, Ja, William, so they keep telling us," she replied. "But tell me, dear husband, does a communist have his soup with meat or without? I need to know so I don't turn you into a communist by mistake. And perhaps we should check on Solomon's soup—we may have to hand him over to stand trial for treason."

William thrust himself back from the kitchen table and stood up. His wife's stubbornness was exasperating. But just as he was about to get some fresh air, the aroma of lamb and vegetables filled his senses. He sat down again and picked up the newspaper, holding it as though defiled by its touch, repelled by the news it conveyed.

"The police should just lock them up and throw away the key," he said after a few moments. "Or better still, hand the buggers over to true Afrikaners. We'll take care of them."

"And take the law into your own hands?"

"If that's what it takes, Maria, then yes—take the law into our own hands."

She turned to face him. "And become thugs and murderers, William, just like the Nazis?"

"Maria, what don't you understand? They're closing in on us from all sides. This is our Blood River, just as Malan told us. We have to close ranks, pull the wagons tight, plug every hole. Otherwise, they'll overwhelm us with their majority rule and communist ideology. Why can't you see that? Everything our people have fought and died for will be lost."

She nodded, then turned to stir the stew. The sounds of old Solomon cajoling the cows into the barn for the night drifted in on the warm autumn breeze. Then she began to speak, her voice quiet, her conviction plain.

"Act justly, love mercy, and walk humbly before God. That's what God wants from you, William. It's what my mother taught me and what I'll teach Nicolas." She turned to face him. "But you seem to have lost your sense of right and wrong, your ability to show love and kindness. And you trust your judgment instead of God's." She shook her head. "The end never justifies the means, William. God expects you to do what is right in his eyes, not what politicians like Vorster say is right in their eyes."

He stared at her, trying to control his resentment at being chastised. He had heard the homily before, but this was not the time for a sermon—it was time for action.

"God gave us victory at Blood River for a reason, Maria. Our cause is just. And now you want to surrender to these godless communists just because some idiot judges can't see the writing on the wall?" He glared at her. "Well, I say not over my dead body. We can never forget what has gone before, just like the Jews can never forget their history."

She looked at him with an inquiring tilt to her head, as though trying to recognize someone she thought she knew.

"So, William, let me see if I understand. You look to the Jews as a spiritual model of our fight, and to the Nazis for a practical solution to our problem. Did I get that right?"

He shook his head in mute dismay. Before he said something he knew he would regret, he turned and left the room.

Dinner be damned, lamb or not.

32

THE SPEAR OF THE NATION

1962

Nelson's stomach rolled with every lurch of the small airplane. An unseen hand seemed determined to hurl the flimsy intruder through the dense fog into the mountains that he knew were close enough to touch. His life, or at least its recent past, flashed with brilliant clarity across the screen of his mind as he anticipated smashing into a mountain long before he reached Tanganyika in East Africa.

It had been brutal after the state of emergency was imposed, as if a beast had been let loose to avenge the result of the Treason Trial and to ravage the aspirations of his people. The ANC had been banned, over twenty thousand people arrested, and a new campaign of terror and repression unleashed by the regime.

The decision to take up arms had not been easy, but he had no reservations about the new phase of the struggle. Although he had insisted during the Treason Trial that nonviolence was an inviolate principle, not an optional tactic determined by conditions on the ground, he believed exactly the opposite—that nonviolence was a tactic to be employed or abandoned depending on the circumstances. Yet many comrades in the ANC were still committed to nonviolence, including their president, Chief Luthuli.

The compromise had been to create a new organization to conduct an armed struggle, blessed by the ANC but not formally part of it—Umkhonto we Sizwe—the Spear of the Nation. And he was its first commander, flying as blindly into his new role as the pilot was flying blindly into the heart of Africa, the magnificence of Victoria Falls replaced by the malevolence of mountains crouching in ambush behind a screen of fog.

At one point the airplane banked so sharply to avoid the mountains that the stall warning blared into the tense silence of the tiny cabin. He felt his sphincter tighten as his fingers dug into the armrests.

"This is the end of us," he mumbled, his eyes squeezed shut as though to shield himself from the impact. But just as he resigned himself to sudden death, the airplane emerged from the fog into brilliant sunlight.

He exhaled slowly as the tension drained from his body. It seemed to be a good omen—after decades of darkness, suddenly the light. His mission—to raise funds, obtain weapons, arrange training and gain support for their struggle—was still on course.

He smiled grimly to himself. "The struggle is my life," he had written in an open letter to the media, despite his passionate romance with Winnie. It had sounded noble on paper, but he felt a knot in his stomach as he thought about it. He was a husband and father. He had never been a soldier, or fought in a battle, or fired a gun. Yet he was tasked to start an army, and an underground army at that. To prepare, he had read everything he could find on how to create, arm and train a guerrilla fighting force—including *Commando* by Deneys Reitz and *The Revolt* by Menachim Begin—and about the tactics of Mao Tse-tung, Che Guevara and Fidel Castro. But reading was one thing, *doing* was quite another.

He smiled as he recalled his life as an outlaw, especially the time he spent at the Liliesleaf farm outside Johannesburg, where he had lived and worked under the guise of a houseboy and caretaker. But he had moved frequently and used various aliases and disguises—chauffeur, gardener, manservant—and been dubbed the Black Pimpernel for the way he would appear in public and then vanish before the police could catch him. He liked the association with the fictional Scarlet Pimpernel of the French Revolution, saving the innocent from execution during the Reign of Terror. But there was nothing fictional about his efforts to protect the innocent from this regime's reign of terror.

He gazed down as the early autumn landscape passed beneath the airplane. He imagined a time before the Europeans arrived, when wild animals and native peoples had lived and moved freely under the canopy of Africa's vast skies. And he thought of the colonial imperialism of the British Empire and the religious nationalism of the Afrikaners, how these alien and competing forces had shaped his life, his people and his country.

He closed his eyes. He knew only too well the old cliché that "One man's terrorist is another man's freedom fighter." But if the regime had lacked sufficient evidence to hang him during the Treason Trial, there would be no shortage of evidence during the next trial—cliché or not—assuming it bothered with a trial.

He was startled when the airplane's wheels bounced and skidded on the runway.

He opened his eyes.

He had crossed the Rubicon.

The die was cast.

William stood on his favorite hill overlooking the farm, spread his arms out wide and shouted, "We shall live, we shall die, we for you, South Africa!"

It was hard to believe the rebirth of his people into nationhood had finally come to pass after generations drenched in blood and tears—from the Great Trek to the Great Murder, through two wars of freedom and the suffering of the concentration camps, to the destitution of scorched farms, brutal mines and oppression as poor whites in a land promised to them by God.

The "Republic of South Africa" had such a sound to it, as unshakable as the Monument in Pretoria, as unyielding as the wagons of Blood River, as unalterable as the Word of God. They had only prevailed by standing together against aliens and foreigners, through their solidarity as a people and their faith in God. And so it had to be if they were to survive this latest threat—shoulder to shoulder, their faith strong, their wagons tight—for they were too few and their enemies inside and outside South Africa were too many and too strong.

He looked down from the hill and lowered his arms. He could still picture exactly where he and Vorster had stood the day they had talked. The referendum six months later had been close, but the yes votes had won. And although it was a bitter blow when Mandela and the others were acquitted at the Treason Trial, at least the ANC had been banned and a state of emergency declared to deal with the violence after Sharpeville. The crackdown had helped quiet the rage he still experienced whenever he recalled that Moroka, a leader of the detested ANC, had seen his wife in her most vulnerable moment, touched her in her most intimate place, and delivered their most precious son.

All in all, 1961 had been a big year. But trouble was in the air, perhaps carried on the "wind of change" the British prime minister had spoken about in Cape Town. He could feel it, almost taste it, and was convinced it was only a matter of time before he heard from Vorster, especially now that Mandela was back on the street—the Black Pimpernel—a communist agitator and the worst kind of troublemaker.

Nelson was relieved when his flight touched down in Addis Ababa. It had been a difficult trip, filled with highs and lows. He was looking forward to a complete change of pace and environment—six months of training with the Ethiopian army, blessed by the emperor himself, Haile Selassie.

His personal trainer taught him how to make and detonate bombs, to aim, load, and fire a mortar, to deploy and detect landmines, and to use a Kalashnikov automatic rifle as well as a Makarov pistol. He especially appreciated learning guerrilla techniques, including camouflage and concealment, use of terrain to screen troop movement, selection of firing and observation positions, recognition of ambush locations, camp craft and defensive techniques, and how to survive in the field without access to food and water.

He immersed himself in every aspect of his training, but after only three weeks, just when he was beginning to feel more like a guerrilla leader, he received a telegram from Sisulu. He was needed in South Africa. He had to return immediately to resume command of the armed struggle.

As disappointed as he was to cut his training short, he was thrilled with his parting gift from the colonel in charge of his training program—the Makarov pistol he had been trained to use, together with two hundred rounds of ammunition, first fruit of his efforts to acquire weapons for the armed struggle.

His ancestors had fought their wars with wood and bone and cowhide. He would fight their next war with steel and bullets and bombs.

33

THE BLACK PIMPERNEL

1962

"Come, son—it's time for your first commando," said William, looking down at his twelve-year-old son as they stood at the paddock fence enclosing their three horses. The brisk midwinter morning produced puffs of misty condensation from his breath as he spoke, an effect more than matched by the vigorous snorts of the horses clearing the night chill from their nostrils.

"Really, Pa? Where to?"

"To find Mandela."

"Mandela? The one Pa calls a terrorist?"

He nodded, smiling.

"Where is he, Pa?"

"At a farmhouse near Johannesburg. But this is a very big secret, my boy. You can't tell anybody—not even your mother. Understand?"

"Ja, Pa. If you say so, Pa."

"I do say so, my boy. All your mother needs to know is that we're going to the Monument and Majuba and Blood River. We might also visit your Uncle Izak on his farm. I hear he's very sick and may be close to the end. And we're going to ride all the way there and back. It's not a real commando unless we go by horseback and sleep under the stars."

The idea of doing something like this had been growing for some time. As proud as he was of having a son, it gnawed at him that he couldn't do all the father-son things he would have done if he had been a younger man. But this was something he could still do—sit on a docile horse and sleep on a blanket—and the idea of taking his son on a commando had a nostalgic appeal he found irresistible. And to have Mandela as a target made the adventure all the more compelling.

"But how do you know where to find him, Pa?"

"Ja," he chuckled. "He's a tricky bugger. Even the police can't catch him. He just pops up out of nowhere, makes trouble for our people, then disappears—that's why they call him the Black Pimpernel. But I know a man who does know where to find him, whose job it is to know exactly where to find him."

"So why haven't we caught him yet?"

"Well, he's always on the move. Right now he's out of South Africa visiting his communist friends. But when he comes back the police will be waiting to catch him...unless we get to him first."

He winked conspiratorially and drew a deep breath. The air still carried the rich sweetness of last night's rain, the smell of hay and cattle rinsed and refreshed. The horses had ambled closer to be nuzzled and fed their daily apple treat, the brown stallion skittish as usual.

"Will you shoot him, Pa?"

William looked from Nicolas to the stallion.

"Mandela, I mean," said the boy.

William grinned for a moment, then his jaw tightened. He could feel the answer rising from the center of his being, as inevitable as any other would be unforgivable, a betrayal of his family, his people and his God.

"Well, son," he began earnestly, "let's just say it's unthinkable for me to go on commando without my Bible and my Mauser." He paused and took a deep breath. "And if God delivers the enemy of our people to me...then so be it...I will pull the trigger." He was tempted to tell the boy the whole family story but decided the time was not right. He hoped when all was said and done that his son would realize his father was more than just a pipe-smoking repository of old war stories.

He gazed out over the paddock and watched Solomon herd the cows towards the barn. He felt sorry for the old man—it was too bad his son had got himself mixed up with the mine workers' union in Johannesburg and had been beaten and imprisoned by the police.

He lifted his gaze towards the far-off hills. It had been a surprise when the postmaster in Thaba 'Nchu, also a former member of the OB, pulled him aside to say he had a private message from Vorster. Mandela was due back in the country at the end of July. He was expected to head straight for his hideout on a hobby farm called Liliesleaf just outside Johannesburg in the suburb of Rivonia. The postmaster had given him a hand-drawn map of the area and said, "John says remember Majuba, and don't forget your pipe and matches."

He looked down and tousled the unkempt brown-blond mop that all too often hung in his son's eyes.

"But remember, my boy, you can't tell anybody about this. Not your ma, your best friend, your teacher, not even the pastor. Nobody. Okay? You promise?"

"Ja, Pa. I promise...I promise."

He had planned his son's spiritual education ever since the

boy was born two years after Malan won the election in '48. In the decade that followed, the plan had matured into a kind of pilgrimage. But now, with Mandela more than just a name in the story, it had become something much more—the opportunity to fulfill a sacred promise.

He knew Maria would not approve of the journey into the past even without knowing about Mandela. He tried to choose his moment—after a nice dinner as they relaxed in the living room in front of the glowing fireplace. But the roast chicken and cozy setting did nothing to help her digest the idea.

"Ag, William," she replied, her tone despairing, "how can you even think of it—to go chasing ghosts all over the countryside with our son? For heaven's sake," she continued, "you're almost eighty, and Nicolas is only twelve. It's a ridiculous notion by a foolish old man."

He nodded. She was right, of course. Always the sensible one. But this was not the time to be sensible. He took a moment to relight his pipe, sucked hard for a few moments to establish a good draw, then waited until the smoke and evocative aroma had bridged the space between him and his wife.

"You know, Maria, I remember when my father told the family he wanted to go fight with General Botha against the Tommies. We were all sitting around the family table. Everyone thought he was mad, my mother too—a seventy-year-old going off to fight the British on the other side of the Drakensberg. Besides, there were more than enough Tommies to fight closer to home. It made no sense." He paused to make sure he had her attention. "You know what he said, Maria?"

She looked at him with tired eyes. "Do tell, William. What pearls of wisdom did your father come up with that got him killed at Spion Kop?"

He winced, as much at the memory of his own role in his father's death as to shake off his wife's insensitive remark.

"I remember almost every word, Maria. He said he was there when Dingane clubbed his father to death...when the warriors butchered his mother and sister in the Great Murder...when they fought to the last bullet against the Zulus at Blood River...and when they celebrated their covenant with God after the victory. He said he had made a vow to go back to where his family had died to honor the sacrifice they had made."

Maria closed her eyes as though shielding herself from the images he invoked.

"This is something I have to do, Maria. I have to share these things with my son while I am still able to get out of bed and onto a horse. I must show him the signposts of his life so he understands the road our people have travelled and can find it for himself once we are gone."

"What's a 'violation,' Pa?" asked Nicolas in the half-light of their campfire. "What you said the Tommies did to your sister?"

He shook his head. "Ag, son, there are some things I cannot speak of, things that godless men do to women—ugly, terrible things you will understand when you're a man. And when that day comes, you will share my anger."

He fell silent as he poked at the embers with a stick and reflected on that time so long ago, still so vivid in his memory. As the fire flared, so did his anger.

"But I saw it happen, my boy, up close through this same telescope I brought with us. I was too far away to stop it. But Henry Mandela, the father of the terrorist, he was there. He just sat and watched." He shook his head in disgust. "That was after he spied on our farm and led the Tommies straight to it. And then he led their chase after me—tried to kill me—before he helped the Tommies burn our farm to the ground and slaughter all our animals."

William took a deep breath and slowly exhaled. "There has not been a day in my life when I have not thought of the things I tell you, my boy. They burn in my heart just as surely as these red-hot coals would burn in my hand if I picked them up. I have no choice but to hold these things in my heart, where they continue to burn day after day, every day of my life."

In the silence that followed he reached for the Mauser lying against his saddle, made sure the five-shot magazine was full, then used the bolt action to chamber a round. Satisfied, he set the rifle aside.

"I'm ready, my boy," he said. "From here we'll make a big loop, first towards Krugersdorp along a route that will take us west of Johannesburg. Then we'll head towards Mandela's hideout. From there we'll go north to the Monument, near Pretoria, then east to Majuba and Blood River, then south around the foothills of the Drakensberg back to the farm."

Nicolas nodded as though in approval.

"Anyway, that's the general idea. But we're flexible, right son? We make whatever plans the situation demands. Hit and run—like a leopard in the night—just like we did against the Tommies in our war of freedom." He poked absentmindedly at the coals for a few moments.

"Who knows what will happen if we find Mandela?" he added before tossing the stick onto the embers.

Three days later they were riding through the northern suburbs of Johannesburg towards Liliesleaf. He hoped they would not look too out of place among the mansions, country estates, and thoroughbred horses, and was relieved to have the postmaster's hand-drawn map to guide them.

Their first reconnaissance pass on Saturday afternoon skirted the front side of the impressive single-level manor house with its tall roof, white-washed walls, and a large bay window overlooking an extended lawn and above-ground swimming pool. They rode in a wide circle on the way back, past an enclosed chicken coop and a complex of outbuildings at the back of the manor house that looked like servant quarters. He guessed the property to be about twenty-five acres, based on features he took to be its boundaries.

They saw a few other riders in the rolling landscape among the impressive estates with their neat paddocks and well-groomed horses, but they attracted no obvious attention. And when they came across an unused paddock close to Liliesleaf, William decided it was a good place to leave their horses. A mound of old hay in the paddock provided a ready-made blanket of cover to hide their saddles, and a nearby stand of trees a convenient screen to answer the call of nature.

He headed for the trees while Nicolas took care of the horses.

"Does Pa want the Mauser now?" asked Nicolas after removing their saddlebags.

"Of course, my boy. A commando is no use without a rifle," he called over his shoulder. "It was good enough against the Tommies, and it will be good enough against Mandela."

Nicolas carefully removed the heavy rifle from its saddle holster, engaged the safety catch as he had been taught to do, then waited like an armed sentry until his father returned before handing him the rifle.

After hiding their saddles under the hay and making sure the paddock gate was secure, William slung the rifle strap over his shoulder so the rifle's stock hung under his armpit and the barrel pointed at the ground. Then he threw his long winter coat over his shoulders to cover the rifle and picked up his saddlebag.

"Take care of your business in the trees, my boy. There'll be no chance after we're in position," said William with a wink and nod. "And don't worry," he added as Nicolas set off to do as he was told, "I'll wait right here until you're done."

After Nicolas returned, William led them on a circuitous route to intersect the tree-lined dirt road leading to Liliesleaf. It was almost dark by the time they reached the row of tall poplars that lined one side of the road to the farmhouse. Moving carefully from tree to tree, staying in the shadows, they reached the last few trees where the road turned sharply towards the house.

William signaled Nicolas to drop to the ground and wait.

Ahead of him the dirt road dipped to a parking area between the back of the main house on his right and the servant quarters on his left, including a thatched roof cottage on the far left closest to where he lay. From his position, the terrain sloped down to the house and, on his left, it sloped down from the cottage to the back of the house. He couldn't see the back door of the house—it was obscured by a section of the house closest to him—but he knew where it was from their reconnaissance ride and that a large electric light hung over the door.

He needed a good vantage point—an unobstructed field of fire covering the area between the house and the servant quarters. He tried several positions until he found a good one behind a poplar tree and some low scrub and winter grass that lined the roadside.

The ground felt hard beneath his bony frame—it reminded him of the rocky crest of Spion Kop where his father had fallen to a Tommy bullet. He adjusted his position until he had a clear view through the scrub down the middle of the dirt road to the main house and the servant quarters on his left. He made sure he was well camouflaged—anyone driving up the road from the house would be heading straight at his position before passing within inches from where he lay as the road swung away to his right along the line of poplar trees and disappeared out of sight.

Satisfied, he signaled Nicolas to move closer.

He couldn't imagine Mandela staying in the main house but could see him crossing the open area between the servant quarters and the house. He knew he was guessing, but he needed some kind of a plan. And if Mandela did show up, then the area between the two structures was the most likely place for a clear shot.

He took a moment to clean the open groove of the rear-sight notch with the edge of his thumbnail and to make sure the rear ladder sight of the Mauser was set flat for such a short-distance shot. He wouldn't need more than one of the five rounds in the magazine.

He was ready.

34

LIFTING UP THE SWORD

1962

William shivered. It was a cloudless night under a canopy of frigid stars. And as each bone-chilling hour passed, he became increasingly ambivalent about the wisdom of what he was doing. Even the Southern Cross, hanging askew, seemed skeptical about his endeavor.

Nicolas was sound asleep in a fetal position, his head cradled in the crook of one arm, his free hand stuck between his knees for warmth. There had been very little activity at the house and servant quarters, aside from lights being turned on and off and occasional muffled voices.

His eyes grew heavy as the night wore on and the imperative of sleep tightened its grip on his leaden senses. He tried to fight it, to stay vigilant—Mandela could arrive at any time—but he knew he was drifting. His last sensation before sleep won the battle was the reassurance of the rifle stock against his cheek.

It seemed like only moments later when insistent tugging at his elbow dragged him from the depths of sleep. He came awake reluctantly, distracted by the ache of discomfort. Nicolas was on his knees, pulling at his sleeve with one hand and gesturing frantically with the other, pointing along the road to their right.

A large sedan, its headlights off, was moving slowly towards them as the first light of dawn stole across the Liliesleaf compound.

William felt a jolt of energy surge through his aching joints, rekindling his instincts as a commando fighter. He kept his head down and signaled Nicolas to stay low. The crunch of gravel beneath tires was crisp as the stealthy black silhouette passed in front of them before turning away towards the house. It stopped in the middle of the driveway close to the house, its rear facing them about thirty yards away.

He raised his telescope to peer through the rear window into the dark interior of the car. He couldn't see a thing. Then he heard a car door unlatch, and the interior of the car flooded with light. He adjusted the telescope and two faces sharpened into focus—two men facing each other. The white face on the driver's side he didn't recognize, but the black face on the passenger side was unmistakable—the bulldog features with short black hair and a stubbly black beard he had seen in photographs.

"It's him," he hissed as he set the telescope aside and raised the rifle, adjusting his position to aim at the passenger side of the car. To stabilize his firing position, he twisted the rifle strap around his left forearm, cradled the rifle's forestock in his left hand, dug his elbows firmly into the ground, spread his legs wide—his left leg bent slightly at the knee, his feet turned out flat, his waist kinked to the left—and pressed the rifle's butt into his right shoulder. The adjustments were instinctive. Within seconds he was ready.

Moments later the white man got out of the car. He was smartly dressed, with a sport jacket over long dark pants. He moved to the rear of the car and opened the trunk. Then the passenger-side door on the left of the car opened. The dark figure that emerged into view towered above the roof of the car. He was dressed in green or brown military fatigues with short sleeves and long pants. He stretched his arms and back before looking around the compound.

For a moment William was mesmerized by the imposing figure of the notorious terrorist. Then he lowered his head, aimed with his right eye, slowed his breathing and tried to relax. The rifle barrel dipped as he breathed in, and rose into alignment as he exhaled. At the perfect moment—when the metal blade at the front of the open sights aligned with his target and the notch in the rear sight—he would squeeze the trigger. But though he could see his target clearly enough, the deep shadows of his firing position blurred the alignment between the rifle's front and rear sights.

In the time it took to recognize it was a risky shot under marginal light, the white man stepped in front of Mandela as he moved to the passenger side, carrying a duffel bag and small suitcase. The two men then moved around the front of the car towards the main house and disappeared, their passage into the house marked by the sound of the back door opening and closing.

William exhaled as the moment passed. He was surprised how hard and fast his heart was beating. He took several deep breaths to calm himself.

"That was close, my boy. We nearly had him." He let out a deep breath and shook his head. "But we'll get another chance, you'll see. We just have to be patient."

"You sure it's him, Pa?" whispered Nicolas.

"Ja, I'm sure. That bloody terrorist's face has been all over the newspapers. And he looks like his father, except he's bigger and doesn't have that patch of white hair above his forehead like his father."

The two fell silent as the predawn stillness embraced the farm compound.

"What kind of car is it, Pa? It looks fancy."

William raised his telescope and scanned the back of the car with its sharp rear fins, the name of the car maker and model clearly visible in chromed cursive lettering on either side of the white on black Johannesburg license plate.

"Ah, there it is," he said without taking his eyes from the telescope. "An Austin Westminster Overdrive. Ja, really," he mused, lowering the telescope. "That's a hell of a fancy car for a bloody communist. Damned terrorists drive a better car than we do."

Nelson was agitated. The border crossing and return to Liliesleaf had been uneventful, but debriefing his comrades was challenging.

"We've lost the initiative," he began as the group convened around the kitchen table in the main house. "We've been discredited among potential friends in Africa who can't understand our nonracialism and association with white and Indian communists. One leader I met tore his copy of the Freedom Charter off his wall when he heard that our white comrades helped write it. We have to make a change... show the world that Africans are the true leaders of the struggle."

"How do you propose to do that?" asked Kathrada. "We Indians have been among your closest friends and allies from the start. Don't tell me you want to turn your back on us now, shed multiracialism like a snake's skin after it has served its purpose and no longer convenient."

The group sat in stunned silence. These were controversial issues that went to the heart of the struggle.

"It would be hard to reinvent ourselves now," interjected Sisulu. "The Indians and Coloureds face many of the same issues as we do. And we have a formal alliance with them through the Congress."

"Ja," replied Kathrada. "And you can't just ignore the role Indians played in the conception of the Freedom Charter."

"Or that whites like Joe Slovo are part of the high command of Umkhonto," added Sisulu. "It's the spear of the *whole* nation, not just of one group. Our struggle has never been based on the color of anyone's skin."

Nelson scratched his head as though trying to extricate a solution from a thicket of competing interests and interwoven strands.

"I understand it will be difficult, but we have to make a change," he insisted. "The fact is we're not seen as truly Africanist. Potential allies think our president is a white stooge and that the ANC is a tail being wagged by a white communist dog. Some even think Umkhonto is the brainchild of the communists to use blacks as cannon fodder against the white regime. We must find a way to reassert the role of Africans as leaders of the struggle."

To head off further dissent, he added, "I will travel immediately to report to Chief Luthuli and get his views. Then I will visit the Indian Congress leaders in Durban to explain the situation."

To his relief, the group agreed with the idea. But security was a problem—the newspapers had been reporting the return of the Black Pimpernel.

"We have to assume the security police are already looking for you, Nelson," argued Mbeki. "And they probably know exactly how you crossed the border—with Cecil in his shiny new car. I am afraid for you and afraid for what your capture would mean for our struggle."

"I agree," said Kathrada. "It's too risky to drive hundreds of miles on a public highway. Your face is too well known—the photos of you with that beard of yours are all over the place. Why not wait until more secure travel plans can be made?"

"I hear you, comrades, but time is of the essence. I must speak to Luthuli as soon as possible—the credibility of our struggle is at stake. Besides, who's to say I'm any safer here than on the road?"

"At least shave off the beard," urged Kathrada. "Change the way you look. Don't make it so easy for the police to spot you."

Nelson shook his head. "No, the beard stays. I like the way I look—it's who I am."

With that, the matter was settled. But it would be a long drive to the coastal city of Durban and then north to the chief's village in Zululand—perhaps as long as nine or ten hours. And certain plans had to be made before he could leave. It would take at least one more day to organize.

In the meanwhile, it had been sixteen months since he had last seen his wife and children. He made arrangements for Winnie to visit in the morning.

It was a long, cool day at Liliesleaf. The bright sun flattered only to deceive. Occasional activity broke the monotony—black workers interacting with a white woman over window cleaning, flower planting and vegetable gardening.

Sometime in the late afternoon, a group of six men, including Mandela, emerged from the main house and crossed to the cottage.

There was no chance of a shot.

"Pa, what's our plan after you shoot Mandela?" asked Nicolas as the men disappeared into the house.

William was taken aback by the question. He had to think for a moment before answering. "After I take the shot, you run like hell and fetch the horses. I'll shoot at anything that moves—man or beast—keep their heads down as long as I can. Then we ride, my boy, we ride like hell. If anybody chases us, we head for Uncle

Izak's farm. I know a good place to hide—a secret place where I kissed my first girlfriend."

Nicolas grinned.

"But I can't see Mandela's friends chasing us," he added. "The police would arrest them and cheer us on!"

He realized he hadn't anticipated actually getting a shot at Mandela. It had seemed like no more than a fanciful father-son adventure. But he now knew it was not so fanciful after all. He closed his eyes and added one more element to the escape plan he had just conjured up for Nicolas—a silent prayer that Maria would never discover just how adventurous her son's pilgrimage had been.

As dusk began to cast long shadows over the bucolic setting, he wondered how much longer they could maintain the vigil. Nicolas had napped on and off during the afternoon and was obviously hungry and uncomfortable. As he considered their options, Mandela emerged from the cottage carrying a bundle under his arm and something in his hand that gave off a dull glint.

William reached for the rifle, shook Nicolas and pointed.

Mandela had stopped to look around. He seemed indecisive, to be considering his next move. Then he walked away at an angle towards the servant quarters' kitchen before disappearing behind the structure.

"He's up to something," hissed William. "Follow him, my boy...quickly. See what he's doing. Go around behind the servant quarters and the chicken coop. But don't scare the chickens. And don't get too close."

Nicolas darted off like a fox, moving from cover to cover, on a path through the trees towards the far side of the cottage. He was no sooner out of sight than William wanted to call him back. He closed his eyes and said a prayer, as much for Nicolas's safety as for forgiveness for sending his son chasing after a notorious terrorist. This could end very badly for both of them. He lay immobile, frozen in self-reproach, his stomach churning beneath him, until he finally saw Mandela emerge from the shadows.

He held his breath, half expecting Mandela to be dragging Nicolas by the hair. But the boy was nowhere to be seen. Then, just as Mandela disappeared through the door of the cottage, Nicolas materialized through the trees, breathing hard, flushed with excitement.

"My God, Nicolas, you gave me a fright. What took so long? What happened?"

"He went to the servants' kitchen, Pa. From there he walked towards the chicken coop on the far side of the farm. I watched from the trees near the chicken coop."

"Ja, ja, my boy, good. But what did he do?"

"He buried the bundle he was carrying, Pa."

"What?"

"He buried it."

"You're sure?"

"Ja, Pa. I saw him do it."

"Where?"

"On the other side of the chicken coop."

"With his hands?"

"With a shovel."

"And was he trying to get rid of it or hide it?"

"I think he was hiding it, Pa. He seemed to look for the best spot and then dug a deep hole—that's what took so long. He kept looking around like he wanted to make sure nobody was watching."

"Did you mark the spot? Do you think you can find it?"

"Ja, I think so. It's near a big tree I saw."

"How far?"

"I dunno, Pa, but not far from the servants' kitchen. Maybe forty or fifty paces from there. And then—"

William chuckled. "Buried treasure, hey?" He was so engrossed in the boy's story that he didn't notice Mandela reappear until Nicolas broke off his storytelling midsentence and pointed frantically, stabbing the air with his forefinger.

"Pa...Pa...there...Just past the cottage," he whispered, breathless with urgency.

William grabbed the Mauser and quickly adjusted his position. All he could think of was to control his suddenly accelerated breathing and ignore the pounding in his chest. The natural light was low, but the electric light above the back door of the house cast some light as he tracked the profile of Mandela moving across his field of fire from left to right.

Then, for no apparent reason, Mandela stopped walking and, like an animal sensing danger, lifted his head as though to catch the threatening scent in the air. He looked to where he had buried his package, then up the road towards where they lay. The coal-black features seemed to glare defiantly, the severe parting in his black hair creating a gleaming line of bare scalp in the low light, a line that appeared to point an accusing finger straight at them.

William didn't second-guess his quarry. He lowered his eyes to the sights and wrapped his finger around the trigger. His breathing slowed—the rifle barrel began to rise and fall in smooth, measured movements, coming into steadier alignment with his target with each breath. And the light was just good enough to sight the rifle. He decided to take the shot—not too difficult at thirty yards.

Mandela's chest dwarfed the front sight of the rifle as his head rotated slowly as if he were scanning the tree line, his arms hanging loose, his chest unmoving—a perfect target.

William exhaled slowly as his right forefinger tightened against the trigger. The sights aligned with Mandela's chest. The slack in the old trigger mechanism yielded. He held his breath to maintain the rifle's alignment.

That's good... Right there, you bastard... For my mother and sister... our farm... our people...

He squeezed the trigger, anticipating the explosion of gunpowder, the sight of Mandela crumpling to ground, the satisfaction of long-delayed retribution. But it was as though the world just froze in place. Nothing happened—just an unyielding trigger, an unbroken silence and an unperturbed Mandela.

"What the devil?" fumed William under his breath as he glared at the mute rifle and then at Mandela, who turned and continued walking towards the house.

"The safety, Pa, the safety—"

"Ag, damn... damn... damn," he swore as he fumbled to rotate the small winged safety catch on top of the bolt sleeve over to the left before swinging the rifle back towards his target. He was just in time to catch a glimpse of Mandela's back before the dark figure disappeared. They heard the back door slam against its frame, the reverberation like a hammer blow confirming the failure of their latest effort.

William slumped over the rifle, breathing hard. "Jesus, Nicolas... he was as good as dead. Goddamned safety! How the devil did that happen?"

Nicolas looked crushed. "Yesterday, Pa. When I gave you the Mauser," he began, his voice trembling. "I'm sorry, Pa. I put the safety on..."

William glared at his son. Tears already glistened through the boy's eyelashes. "Ag, my boy, don't worry," he said as he stifled a rebuke and laid the rifle aside. "I never used the safety on commando. It didn't cross my mind to check. But you did the right thing, my boy. It's my fault the bugger got away."

Nicolas stared at the house, looking thoroughly dejected.

"Tell you what, my boy, all is not lost," he said with a forced smile. "Let's dig up that treasure of his. We'll wait until it's pitch-dark and then make our move. Okay?"

Nicolas nodded, his features brightening.

"Do you think you can find a shovel?"

The boy nodded again. "I saw one behind the chicken coop."

"Good. In the meantime, let's have some more biltong."

Nicolas was as good as his word, although it took longer than expected before he emerged from the shadows and handed him the bundle. It was surprisingly heavy, wrapped in thick cloth or perhaps clothing.

He looked inquiringly at his son. "Is that all?"

Nicolas reached into his coat pocket and withdrew a round object that emitted a dull shine, even in the darkness.

"What's that?"

"A tin plate, Pa."

"A plate?"

"It was in the hole covering the bundle, Pa. The hole was about five feet deep. The bundle was at the bottom of the hole with the plate on top of it."

"Ag really, hey. So, it seems our Mr. Mandela is quite a clever terrorist. We used to do the same thing on commando—the plate helps keep things dry. Did you replace the dirt, my boy, cover up the hole so it looks undisturbed?"

"I did my best, Pa, but it was dark. And I did not want to wake the chickens."

"Hmm," mused William as he unwrapped the bundle. "Let's see what treasure our terrorist friend took so much trouble to hide."

Beneath the outer layer, his hands closed over one irregularly shaped object wrapped in aluminum foil and a second square object wrapped in light cloth. He experienced an unexpected flashback to his time as a saboteur and flinched as he recalled the blast of the Benoni bomb. He half expected the package in his hand to explode, but nothing disturbed the dark silence that surrounded them.

He realized he had been holding his breath and slowly exhaled. The cloth around the square object felt familiar, like the cloth he had used to clean his Mauser at Spion Kop. As he unwrapped it, the object separated into four smaller boxes.

He looked at his son.

"What is it, Pa?" whispered Nicolas.

"Shush," he said as he laid the boxes on the cloth. He picked up one of the boxes and opened one end. He was pretty sure he knew exactly what the box contained as he turned it upright and allowed the contents to spill into his hand.

"What is it, Pa? What's in the box?"

"Shells."

"Shells, Pa? From the sea?"

William chuckled. "No, my boy. Definitely not seashells."

"What then, Pa?"

"For a gun, my boy. These shells are for a gun." He passed a handful to Nicolas while he ran his other hand over the remaining boxes. "Four boxes, probably fifty rounds to a box."

"That's a lot, Pa," said Nicolas, reaching for the second package.

William blocked his son's hand. "Patience, my boy," he cautioned. "I will unwrap it," he said as he slipped his fingers under the flap of foil and slowly peeled it back. It took only seconds to unwrap the foil and orientate his hand over the dark angular object in a way that immediately identified it for what it was.

"What is it, Pa?" implored the boy.

"It's a pistol."

"A gun, Pa?"

"Ja, a gun, my boy. We've found Mandela's gun!"

He turned the pistol over in his hand and smelled the barrel. It had definitely been used but was well oiled. He couldn't tell whether it was loaded, or whether the safety was on, and didn't want to risk manipulating the unfamiliar weapon for fear of inadvertently firing a shot.

"Here, my boy, but don't touch the trigger," he said as he handed the pistol to Nicolas.

William rewrapped the shell boxes in the cloth and forced the package into his saddlebag. Then he took the pistol from Nicolas, rewrapped it in the foil, and found a separate spot for it in his saddlebag.

"Stuff the plate and that bundle of clothing into your saddlebag, son. We can't leave any trace behind. Now we must get some sleep—that's quite enough excitement for one night."

"Ja, Pa," said the boy as he took care of the treasure, then found a spot and squirmed until he settled and succumbed to the night.

William sat staring at the darkened house, thinking about his father, mother and sister, and about Mandela's father and Mandela himself.

Mandela! God in heaven, he thought, *it was such an easy shot. Bloody safety!*

He silently cursed the missed opportunity. This wasn't just personal anymore. His people were at war with communist terrorists who wanted to destroy everything they had worked so hard to achieve. And Mandela was one of their leaders! He would give the mission one more day. He only needed one shot.

He slept fitfully, thinking of what might have been, before stirring to the sounds of a new day. He watched the sun rise and waited patiently for Nicolas to wake.

"Lazy buggers must be sleeping in," he said after the boy stirred.

They spent most of the day on their stomachs, watching and waiting, occasionally eating dried fruit, the monotony only briefly interrupted when Nicolas crept away to check on their horses.

"What do you think he was going to do with the gun?" asked Nicolas when he returned.

"He's a damned terrorist, my boy. You remember the bombings last December, on the Day of the Covenant, and all the bombings since then? Mandela and his terrorist comrades are doing it. They want a revolution and Mandela is one of their leaders. That's why he had a gun, my boy—to kill us with it!"

Nicolas stared, blinking several times.

"Do the police know about this, Pa?"

"Ja, of course, my boy. They know all about it, but they haven't been able to catch the bugger. And when they do there'll be another trial, and who knows what the damn fool judges will do? He should hang, but they might let him go just like last time."

Aside from the movement of a few servants, the only activity at the farm compound was the unexpected arrival of a car. A well-dressed black woman stepped out of the car with two young children. Then Mandela appeared and swept both children up in his arms before the woman threw her arms around him. After a few moments together, they all disappeared into the cottage.

"Who are they, Pa?" whispered Nicolas.

"I'm not sure, my boy," he said, scratching his beard. "Looks like family."

"So what now, Pa?"

"We wait, son. We wait and see."

Not long after Mandela's visitors left, a white couple emerged from the main house and strolled around the house, inspecting the gardens.

"Who are they, Pa?"

"Ag, I don't know, my boy. But they behave like they own the place. Probably commie traitors—I should shoot them too."

"But Pa, you can't shoot people just because you don't like them."

He looked sharply at Nicolas. "We're in a war, my boy, a war for the survival of our people. Any friend of our enemy is our enemy too. Never forget that!"

"Ja, Pa," said Nicolas contritely. "Sorry, Pa."

35

FRIENDS AND ENEMIES

1962

Nelson packed light, but he was determined to take his commander-in-chief khaki outfit. He wanted people to see him as a real guerrilla leader. But he could hardly present himself as a credible leader of the armed struggle without being armed.

He made a mental note to dig up the pistol he had just buried. He had not expected to be travelling again so soon after his arrival.

The visit by Winnie and the children had been difficult. She had tried to be brave, but the security police had harassed her and made her life almost unbearable in his absence. He, too, had found it difficult to stay composed, especially with the children. And her response on hearing he was leaving again in the morning still rang in his ears: "My father was right," she had said. "You are married to the struggle." They had left in tears.

By dusk that day the car was ready, parked just outside the kitchen, and their travelling arrangements were complete—he would pose as the chauffeur with Cecil as the back seat passenger. At the appointed time they made a few sandwiches in the main house's kitchen, filled a flask with coffee and said their goodbyes.

"Just give me a few minutes," said Nelson as he closed the kitchen door behind them. "There is something I must do."

He waited until Cecil was in the car before he began walking towards the spot where the pistol was buried beyond the chicken coop, counting each step as he walked. But he had measured the distance from the servants' kitchen, not from the house kitchen, and now was trying to recalibrate the angle and the distance as he walked. He should just have gone to the servants' kitchen and stepped it off from there. But he thought he would easily recognize the spot where the cache was hidden.

There was no obvious reason to be so secretive about the pistol among his closest comrades, but the fear of informers had plagued their resistance efforts for many years and the security forces were a constant threat. Besides, he had only just been trained in guerrilla tactics and thought it wise to practice his field craft. He hoped Cecil would assume he'd had a last-minute call of nature.

He found the spot where he thought he had buried the pistol, retrieved the hidden shovel and began to dig. After just a few minutes he knew something was wrong.

I must be digging in the wrong place. Maybe I walked off course or my estimate was wrong. And the trees and bushes all look the same in this light. Damn. I can't start digging holes all over the place, but I can't admit the commander-in-chief of the armed struggle has lost his personal weapon, the first gun of the revolution!

He cursed in frustration, covered the hole he had dug, hid the shovel under a shrub, and strolled back to the car. He got in behind the wheel but did not close the car door, then sat motionless as though deep in thought, his creased features illuminated by the interior car light.

"What's the problem?" asked Cecil from the back seat.

Trying his best to sound self-assured and decisive, he turned to Cecil. "Do you have a gun, Cecil, any type of weapon in the car?"

He could see Cecil's eyes widen.

"Um...uh...yes, Nelson, I do. It's in the cubbyhole. A revolver ...I think."

Nelson nodded and bent forward across the front seats to unlatch the lid of the cubbyhole on the passenger side of the wood-grained dashboard. He reached in, found the weapon, and sat back in his seat.

"Hmm...good," he said as he inspected the revolver. "But you really shouldn't leave it lying around like this. It's too easy to find."

"Yes, Nelson," said Cecil diffidently.

"Do you know whether it's loaded?" he asked as he checked the back of the cylinder. He had never handled a revolver but could see the dull brass gleam of at least two cartridges in their separate chambers.

"I think so," said Cecil. "A friend gave it to me. He said it was loaded."

"Well, your friend was right," he said, slipping the revolver into the split between the two tan-leather bench seats in the front of the car. Then he closed the car door, instantly extinguishing the interior car light, and started the engine. He left the headlights off as he sat for a few moments to allow his eyes to adjust to the dark. Then he engaged first gear, slowly released the clutch, and turned the steering wheel towards road.

"You never know, Cecil. We might need a gun on this trip," he said as he drove slowly up the incline out of the yard before taking the hard left turn and accelerating away from the house.

Just as the sun cast its last shadows of the day, the white man who had arrived with Mandela appeared and loaded a duffel bag and small suitcase into the trunk of the Austin. Then he started the car, backed it towards the house, shut off the engine, and reentered the house.

"Looks like he's planning to leave," whispered William. "Maybe we'll get another shot."

It was almost completely dark before the white man and Mandela emerged from the house. But for the light outside the kitchen, he might not have been able to identify Mandela, although the rising moon cast an eerie luminescence over the farmyard.

"Pa, over there," whispered Nicolas, pointing.

"Ja, I see him." He raised the rifle, made sure the safety was off, and adjusted his firing position. But instead of the white man getting into the driver's seat as before, he got into the back seat, like a rich man waiting for his chauffeur. That meant Mandela would get into the driver's side of the car, on the opposite side from William's firing position. He cursed the twist of fate. He could only just see Mandela's head above the car, still slightly illuminated by the kitchen light, but there was no chance of a shot.

"He's walking away, Pa... towards the bushes. I think he's going for his gun."

William lifted his head and watched as the dark figure receded into the shadows. "Ja, I think you're right. Let's hope he doesn't raise the alarm when he finds it's gone." He thought for a moment. "Pack our stuff, my boy, quickly. We might have to run like hell before you know it."

They packed, watched and waited.

"He's coming back, Pa," whispered Nicolas after a few breathless minutes.

The dark figure was barely visible as he emerged from the shadows on the far side of the car and opened the driver-side door. The interior car light came on, illuminating Mandela as he slid in behind the steering wheel. But he did not close the car door and the interior light stayed on.

William raised the rifle. It would have to be a head shot—not easy through the car's passenger side window, but at least he could see his rifle sights silhouetted by the car's interior light. Mandela was turned towards him as he talked to the man in the back seat, his large head and shoulders a good target. But just as William settled his breathing and touched the trigger, Mandela bent forward and almost out of sight.

"Ag, shit, what now?" he muttered. But then Mandela sat upright again, appearing to examine an object in his hand that looked like a revolver. Another damned gun, thought William as he raised the rifle again.

Relax... Breathe... Easy now, he reminded himself as he prepared to take the shot. His forefinger touched the trigger as his sights aligned with Mandela's head. He held his breath and began to squeeze the trigger.

In the next instant the image of Mandela was gone, lost in the inky darkness as the sound of the car door closing reached him a fraction after the interior car light extinguished.

"God Almighty!" cried William. "Jesus! Just another second—that's all I needed."

The car sat silent for a few moments. Then the engine started and the car turned, its headlights still off, and crept towards them as though seeking out the threat that lay hidden in the dark, before it swung away only yards from where they lay.

In a blur the black car swept past and disappeared like a wraith into the night.

The rolling waves of the Indian Ocean were mesmerizing. They were so close to the road he could hear the crash of surf and smell the salt and seaweed. It still thrilled him, even though his childhood village had been near the same ocean.

He was pleased to have spent time with Chief Luthuli, but it had saddened him to see the decline in health of a man so revered among the people, winner of the Nobel Peace Prize for leading their nonviolent struggle for human rights. And although the chief had always advocated a multiracial ANC, he had listened intently to Nelson's concerns—that they needed to change the image of the struggle to present it as the black man's struggle for freedom or risk losing the support of African leaders, including their blessing to operate from bases in their countries to conduct insurgent guerrilla operations into South Africa.

The chief had sighed, his misgivings evident in every crease of his venerable features, and said he would consider the plan. But his mental acuity seemed to be fading. It was especially troubling that he had failed to recall his endorsement of the armed struggle and the creation of Umkhonto.

The next stop was a meeting with the local command of Umkhonto and a Saturday night party in the Durban area, hosted by friends in the Indian community. He enjoyed the party, but as much as he liked being the center of attention, strutting about as commander-in-chief in his guerrilla khakis, he knew it was time to return to Liliesleaf and get down to the hard work of organizing and leading the armed struggle.

He was still basking in the afterglow of his celebrity status when they left Durban the next day to return to Johannesburg. And it seemed more appropriate that Cecil should be the driver and he the front seat passenger. There had been no encounters with the police and no indication the police knew his whereabouts. The party group the night before had even laughed about gathering under the nose of the security police.

He felt indomitable. The armed struggle was a reality and he, Nelson Rolihlahla Mandela, would lead the people to victory.

The rolling hills of the Natal Midlands drew them deeper into its folds as they drove through Pietermaritzburg and up the steep, densely forested escarpment, towards Howick and the waterfall he had heard about but never seen. He passed the time imagining offensive and defensive guerrilla tactics presented by the unfolding terrain, trying to adapt his field craft to the changing landscape.

It didn't require any field craft to notice the white Ford sedan that overtook them near Howick, filled with a group of white men, or to notice the two identical cars behind them. And when the Ford ahead slowed and outstretched hands signaled the Austin to pull over, he knew the regime had sprung its trap.

He glanced at the terrain on the left and right side of the road, trying to gauge whether an escape on foot was possible. He was in the front left passenger seat, closest to the roadside. The chance to make a run for it was tempting even though the banks on the left were steep and tree-lined. He knew the mountains of Lesotho were not far away, but he also knew it was a refuge he would never be able to reach.

"Who are they, Nelson?" asked Cecil with a tremor in his voice.

"Not friendly. Better stop," he replied tersely, anticipating the worst.

Cecil steered the Austin onto the shoulder of the road and braked sharply. Nelson glanced back and saw the two Fords pull over behind the Austin. When he looked ahead, four white men were getting out of the first Ford and moving towards the Austin.

His stomach tightened as he reached for the revolver between the front bench seats and calculated the odds. He was not sure how many men were in the cars behind him—likely as many as eight—but he knew there were four from the first car. Cecil's revolver had no more than five or six bullets, assuming it was fully loaded and assuming he would be deadly accurate with an unfamiliar weapon. The odds were not in his favor.

He took one more look around and shook his head. The risk of throwing away his life and getting Cecil killed in the crossfire was too high a price to pay for an uncertain outcome. He stuffed the revolver back between the seats, together with his notebook full of incriminating names and information.

"Nelson?" Cecil's plaintive supplication hung in the air.

"Don't worry, Cecil. Just sit still. No sudden movements. Tell them you don't know me—just giving me a lift."

He sat back and waited. The car seemed suddenly claustrophobic, the air thick with menace. His role as commander-in-chief was not supposed to end like this, so quickly and ignobly on the side of a road without even a shot fired.

The man closest to the Austin looked quizzically at Cecil in the driver's seat and then at him before approaching the passenger side of the car. Nelson rolled down his window and looked up at the lean, unshaven features of the white man.

"Name?" asked the man as he withdrew a small notebook from one shirt pocket and a pen from the other.

"David Motsamai," replied Nelson, using his favorite alias. "Who are you and why have you stopped the car?"

"I'm Sergeant Vorster," said the man. "And I will be asking the questions, not you," he added, the trace of a grin playing across his self-assured features.

"Where are you going?" asked the sergeant.

"Johannesburg."
"Where have you come from?"
"Durban."
"What was the purpose of your visit?"
"To see the sea."
The policeman dutifully made notes of his answers.
"Who did you meet?"
"Friends."
"What are their names?"
"You will have to ask them."

Exasperation flashed across the policeman's features. "Ag, man, enough of this bloody nonsense. You are Nelson Mandela and your driver is Cecil Williams. We know all about you, Mandela, and now we have you. I have a warrant for your arrest."

Nelson glared stone-faced at the policeman. Then he turned and looked around the Austin at the other policemen who now surrounded the car. He glanced again at the terrain closest to him. Even if he jumped and ran he would be either shot or captured before he could climb the wooded embankment.

There was no escape.

"Very well, I am Nelson Mandela. And you may have won this round, Sergeant," he said, trying to recover his composure, "but as any boxer will tell you, the fight is not over until the end of the last round."

"Humph," snorted the policeman. "Really, hey! Let me tell you something, Mandela. You are a flyweight in the ring against a heavyweight—and you have just been knocked out cold. Your little revolution is over before it even began."

"We shall see, Sergeant. We shall see," he said. "The wind of change is blowing, and you and your little tribe will soon be swept out of power. It's only a matter of time."

"Ag, man, the only wind blowing is the wind out of your arse. And the only change you'll see is when it turns to shit as the hangman's noose drops over your head."

They had left Liliesleaf in the dark and headed north to see the Monument outside Pretoria, then east to Majuba before working their way around the Drakensburg foothills towards the farm.

And although the prospect had sent a chill down his spine, he had taken Nicolas to Baboon Rock. The events associated with family members memorialized at that dreadful place had rekindled the coals that still burned through every fiber of his being. The memories had almost overwhelmed him as he stood with his son in silent remembrance of the brutal murders by Dingane and the terrible carnage on the infamous Kop. He had all but choked on his emotions as they remounted and turned away.

The only salve to the pain of the memories was the magnificence of the landscape as they made their way back to the farm. He experienced a powerful sense of the divine in the splendor of the mountain peaks and amphitheaters, the lush valleys and clear streams, the towering trees and fragrant meadows, as though a caring and creative God was embracing him, providing reassurance, every step of the way.

But whenever he reflected on the pilgrimage with his son, his thoughts turned inevitably to what they had found buried at Liliesleaf, an uncomfortable reminder of a disconcerting prospect.

The pistol felt like a malign presence in his saddlebag, symbolic of a cancer that might at any moment metastasize into bloody revolution and spread its evil across the country. He had thought of the Tommies as a godless invasive species, but these commie terrorists were another thing altogether—a homegrown cancer, alien to everything he held most dear. And he had missed his chance to cut out the heart of the tumor.

With every lurch of his horse, he felt the burden of failure twist like a knife in his soul. He had failed his family and his people.

It would be a long ride home.

"So what's Pa going to do?" asked Nicolas, seeming to read his thoughts as their horses ambled alongside a stream cut into a wooded hillside outside the town of Bethlehem.

"I'm not sure, my boy. What do you think we should do?"

"I dunno, but I think we should keep the gun."

"Ja, I agree. Who knows, perhaps it can be put to good use someday." He paused to swat at a few horseflies. "But it's a very big secret, my boy. Nobody can know about the gun or what we did at Liliesleaf."

"Ja, Pa. I know."

They rode on in silence for several minutes.

"Will Pa try again?"

"Try what, my boy?"

"To shoot Mandela?"

He grunted. "Ag, no, my boy. I'm too old for that sort of thing. Besides, you know what they say about Mandela—he's the Black Pimpernel. He'll just disappear, and who knows where or when he'll appear again."

"So is Pa just going to leave it then?"

"My boy, I had my chance. I can't go chasing a shadow. But I will go to my grave knowing I tried to avenge our family and to serve our people. I came close. Maybe the rest is up to you. Maybe you'll get a chance one day."

They rode on in silence broken only by the clomp of hooves in thick grass and occasionally by the raucous *har...har...ha-de-da* call of the Hadeda birds overhead. It sounded like demented laughter, almost as though the birds were mocking the folly of his attempt to kill Mandela.

"But if you do get the chance, make sure the safety is off before you pull the trigger," he added after a while, forcing a laugh.

"Ja, Pa," said Nicolas sheepishly. "So what's next, Pa?"

He thought a while before answering his son's open-ended question. "Well, my boy, the first thing to do is find a place to hide the gun. It's already wrapped in foil, so I think we'll wrap it all up in a bundle just like we found it and bury it again, under the tin plate."

"Where, Pa?"

William scratched his beard. "Under the willow by the river, underneath your grandfather's memorial stone."

Nicolas's eyebrows arched, but he nodded.

"And then, Pa?"

"And then, my boy, it's nearly time for you to go to Grey College for high school."

"But Bloemfontein is far from the farm, Pa."

"Ag no, my boy. It's not so far. And you'll be a boarder, not a day student. You'll go to Murray House with all the other new boys, just like I did. And the older boys will call you a 'new poop' to keep you in your place." He chuckled. "But you'll come home for the holidays, and we'll come watch your big rugby games, especially against Central High School."

He glanced at his son, who looked down in the mouth.

"Perhaps you'll play for Grey's first team when you get bigger," he added, trying to encourage the boy. "Maybe even play for the Springboks and wear the green and gold of South Africa. Some of our best rugby players have come from Grey. You could be one of them."

Nicolas brightened at the prospect. "And after Grey, Pa?"

"After that you go to the army, my boy."

"The army, Pa?" he said, frowning.

"Ja. All the boys have to do it. But after basic training you can maybe join the parachute battalion—it's stationed in Bloemfontein not far from Grey—or maybe go to the air force. But forget the navy—that's for sissies."

"And then, Pa?"

"Ag, my boy, who knows? Maybe you work the farm—it'll be yours someday. Or maybe go to university, hey?" He paused. "But God may have other plans for you, my boy. Who knows?"

36

THE POWER OF THE PEOPLE

1962

"*Amandla!*" called Nelson as he appeared at the top of the stairwell in the courtroom.

"*Ngawethu!*" roared his supporters in response. They were on their feet, their fists held high. The chant rolled back and forth, sweeping across the packed gallery like a wild fire fanned by the winds of change.

He thrilled at the cherished call and response—"Power! It shall be ours!" It seemed to invoke the soul of a people determined to shake off the shackles of bondage. He waved at the crowd and sat down.

The magistrate was speechless. The chanting was one thing, but nobody had expected Nelson to appear in full Xhosa tribal dress, including a leopard-skin cloak thrown over his bare shoulders, chosen to confront the white man's system of justice with the history and heritage of his own people—with the culture of Africa.

Even though he was representing himself, Nelson was surprised the magistrate had agreed to allow him to address the court before entering a plea. He stood, adjusted the leopard-skin cloak, rolled his shoulders and head as though preparing for the opening bell in his township boxing ring, and began to speak:

"First, as a preliminary matter, I must insist that Your Worship recuse himself from this trial," he said in a strong voice to make sure everyone in the gallery could hear his words.

The magistrate looked at him in disbelief. "I beg your pardon, Mr. Mandela. What did you say?"

"That you must recuse yourself, Your Worship. How can I get a fair trial in this court?" he demanded. "My case involves a clash between the aspirations of the black people and those of the white people. Yet the whites pass all the laws, appoint all the judges and make all the decisions." He glared at the magistrate. "How can anyone think the scales of justice are evenly balanced? I feel oppressed by the atmosphere of white domination that lurks all around in this courtroom—"

"Mr. Mandela," interrupted the magistrate, "I gave you permission as a courtesy to address the court before entering a plea. I do not expect you to take advantage of the courtesy and use the court as a political platform. You are charged with straightforward criminal acts that apply equally to blacks as well as to whites." The magistrate paused, stone-faced. "You are an officer of the court, Mr. Mandela. You and I know each other. You have always shown respect for the legal system and I expect you to do so now. I will not recuse myself. How do you plead?"

Momentarily stung by the reprimand, Nelson fingered his leopard-skin cloak as he gathered his thoughts. The magistrate was right and he felt a twinge of shame for taking advantage of a man he respected. But respect had run its course. Old norms no longer applied. This was a new chapter in the struggle, and he was writing the script on his feet.

"Your Worship, no matter how strong your own sense of fairness and justice might be, a system that makes a white judge sit in judgment over a case in which whites are an interested party cannot be impartial and fair. It is improper and against the elementary principles of justice to entrust whites with cases involving their denial of basic human rights to the black people of this country. The atmosphere inside the courtroom calls to mind the inhuman injustices inflicted on my people outside this courtroom by this same white domination."

The magistrate stared hard, tight-lipped, his jawbones flexing. There was not a sound in the courtroom—such a public exchange had never been heard before.

"Have you finished your statement, Mr. Mandela?" asked the magistrate, his expression dark, his tone terse.

"One more thing, Your Worship," he added. "This courtroom reminds me that I am voteless because there is a parliament in this country that is white controlled. I am without land because the white minority has taken a lion's share of my country and forced me to occupy poverty-stricken reserves, overpopulated and overstocked. And we are ravaged by starvation and disease."

The magistrate held up his hand as though demanding silence.

"Your Worship," continued Nelson, ignoring the implied command, "I hate discrimination most intensely and in all its manifestations. I have fought it during my life, I fight it now and I will fight it until the end of my days. Even though I happen to be tried by one whose opinion I hold in high esteem, I detest most violently the system that makes me feel that I am a black man in a white man's court. This should not be."

"Mr. Mandela! That is quite enough."

"No, Your Worship. With respect, it is not nearly enough." The two men glared at each other like gladiators, oblivious to their surroundings, intent only on the immediate existential confrontation. "The injustice in this court simply reflects the injustice in our society, Your Worship. The whites suppress our aspirations, bar our way to freedom and deny us opportunities to promote our moral and material progress, to secure ourselves from fear and want. All the good things of life are reserved for whites, and we blacks are expected to be content to nourish our bodies with such scraps as drop from the tables of people with white skins."

The magistrate was ashen, his eyes wide.

"This is the white man's standard of justice and fairness," continued Nelson. "Through bitter experience, we have learned to regard the white man as a harsh and merciless human being whose contempt for our rights—and whose utter indifference to the promotion of our welfare—makes his assertions to us absolutely meaningless and hypocritical." He paused, gathering himself. "This is an extremely dangerous situation for our country and for our people. If these wrongs are not remedied without delay, we might well find that even plain talk such as this is too timid, too little and too late." He paused again, meeting the exasperated magistrate's hard glare. "I make no threat, Your Worship, but it is almost past noon. If there is to be a peaceful transformation of our country, it must happen now."

The magistrate removed his glasses and pressed a thumb and forefinger into his eye sockets, as though massaging visions of violent revolution from his mind's eye.

"How do you plead, Mr. Mandela?" he asked again, clearly exasperated by the exchange.

"With respect, Your Worship, I do not consider myself legally or morally bound to obey laws made by a parliament in which I have no representation. I am not guilty of any crimes."

Nelson lost count of the number of witnesses the state called—sixty or seventy. All sorts of people from across the country gave testimony about his role inciting the strike. And the evidence about him being out of the country was indisputable, as was the fact he did not have a valid travel permit.

At the close of the prosecution case, the magistrate looked at him and, in a tired voice, said, "Mr. Mandela, you may call your first witness."

A hushed silence fell upon the courtroom, the stillness broken only by Nelson's chair scraping on the wooden floor as he pushed it back and stood to address the court.

"The defense will not call any witnesses, Your Worship," he stated in a matter-of-fact tone of voice. "The defense rests."

Sounds of consternation erupted from supporters as heads jerked in surprise at the announcement.

The magistrate looked down at him with an expression of disbelief. "Is that all, Mr. Mandela? You say you are not guilty of the crimes charged yet you offer no evidence to support your defense. Have you nothing more to say?"

"Your Worship, with respect, it is the government that is guilty, not me. The white government is guilty of the crime of discrimination and of enforcing policies through the courts that are in conflict with norms of justice accepted throughout the civilized world. I therefore submit that I am guilty of no crime."

The magistrate sighed audibly. "Court is adjourned until November 7, when I will hear argument on sentencing."

It was October 19, 1962. The trial had taken just four days but coincided with the first days of the Cuban Missile Crisis, fraught with potential nuclear catastrophe that reached a tipping point when the Soviets shot down an American reconnaissance plane, and Castro offered to sacrifice Cuba for the glory of socialism. The world seemed to hold its collective breath. Then Kennedy conjured a miracle, the Soviets withdrew and the crisis was over.

On the morning of sentencing, an orderly escorted Nelson

in from a side door to the dock. When he reached the dock, he turned to the black section of the gallery and raised his arm in a clenched-fist salute.

"*Amandla!*" he called out to his supporters.

"*Ngawethu!*" bellowed the crowd in response, rising to its feet like a multilegged, multicolored creature, angered to see its champion cornered and isolated.

The magistrate shuffled papers and appeared to ignore the commotion until the crowd was seated again and quiet. Then he cleared his throat to signal he was ready to deliver the judgment of the court.

"The defendant has been found guilty on both counts before this court. The court sentences the defendant, Nelson Mandela, to three years' imprisonment for inciting people to strike. The court also sentences Nelson Mandela to two years' imprisonment for leaving the country without a passport. The sentences are to run consecutively. There shall be no possibility of parole."

Nelson felt as if he had been punched in the solar plexus. As far as he knew, it was the longest sentence ever imposed for such offences in South Africa, a distinction that gave him cold comfort.

The magistrate banged his gavel. "Court is adjourned."

As the court rose, Nelson stood and turned to the black gallery, determined to show he was not cowed by the outcome of the trial. Standing tall, he raised his clenched fist and yelled, "*Amandla!*"

"*Ngawethu!*" howled the crowd in response.

Women wailed as he was led from the dock. But then, as if on cue, the crowd began to sing:

Nkosi, sikelel' iAfrika;	Lord, bless Africa;
Malupakam'upondo lwayo;	May her horn rise high up;
Yiva imitandazo yethu	Hear Thou our prayers
Usisikelele.	And bless us.

Yihla Moya, Yihla Moya,	Descend, O Spirit,
Yihla Moya Oyingcwele.	Descend, O Holy Spirit.

It was the last thing Nelson heard as he was led downstairs. The Lord may yet bless them but apparently was temporarily deaf to their prayers.

He had lost his liberty and his opportunity to lead the armed struggle, both unceremoniously stripped from him along with his leopard-skin cloak.

The shackles were painfully heavy around his ankles. And the stench in the back of the small, dark, windowless van was almost overwhelming—one bucket for the needs of four men chained together for a seventeen-hour, one-thousand-mile journey.

Every time one of his three comrades moved, the shackles that joined them all together clanked against the metal floor of the van, a noisy and coarse reminder of their predicament. The men sang, slept and endured.

After six months in a local prison he had been told in the middle of the night to pack his things—there wasn't much to pack—and taken to a small, dimly lit office, where the prison colonel waited with three other political prisoners.

"Where are we going?" one of the prisoners had asked.

"You lot are being transferred," the colonel has replied, clearly displeased at having had his sleep disturbed.

"Where?" a fellow prisoner had pressed.

"Someplace very beautiful," the colonel had said, his tone facetious. "To a seaside resort near Cape Town...to the Island."

No explanation had been needed. There was only one prison island—Esiquithini. Its notoriety was embedded in the psyche of his people and immortalized by the poet-warrior Makhanda, who had died trying to escape, leaving the people to wait in vain for him to liberate them. *Ukuza kuka Nxele*—a forlorn hope.

Nelson had more than enough time to think about the Island as the van traveled through the night. His five-year sentence now felt more like a life sentence, perhaps even a death sentence. Was the hope of his people for liberty, freedom and justice also a forlorn hope, as doomed as Makhanda's? Would they, too, wait in vain for a liberation that would never come?

He tried to get some sleep, but his mind swirled with questions about how he had come to be arrested and whether he had been betrayed. It pained him to think the police might have stumbled upon his trail through his own carelessness. He had scolded himself many times since his arrest for his sloppiness, for being beguiled by his persona as the Black Pimpernel, parading around as commander of Umkhonto and ignoring the basic principles of a covert operation. He was embarrassed to think his role as leader of the armed struggle had been so short lived.

But he was mystified by how the police had known he would be on the road to Johannesburg that Sunday. The only explanation was that he must have been betrayed. But that begged the question—by whom? Then it occurred to him. It was an open secret the Americans supported the South African regime's determination to crush revolutionaries like the ANC, and that the CIA exchanged intelligence information with the security police, the same police who had been so desperate to catch him.

He was still thinking of his betrayal when the van made a hard stop. Seconds later, the back door was flung open and shouted commands flooded the fetid atmosphere of their mobile prison cell. He was blinded by the sudden brightness as he shuffled towards the exit with his shackled companions, and gulped the crisp dockside air when he stepped out of the van. As his eyes adjusted, he glimpsed the monolithic mountain that watched over Cape Town, its flat top crisply highlighted by the setting sun, its ancient crags bearing silent witness to the events unfolding on the dock below.

Within minutes they were bundled down steep steps into the hold of an old wooden ferry rocking on the swell. The prisoners stood in silence, swaying, trying to keep upright as the ferry moved slowly away from the dock and pitched and rolled against the heavy sea. Their only reference point was a glimpse of the sky through the single open porthole above them, until a sudden spray of liquid cascaded onto their heads.

"What is that?" asked one of the men. "Ocean spray?"

Nelson licked at the droplets running down his face and recoiled. The laughter from above confirmed his suspicion. "It's urine! The bastards are pissing on us through the porthole."

His companions howled in disgust, which only raised the level of laughter from above. The men fell silent for the remainder of the journey, determined not to give their tormentors any further satisfaction.

About an hour later the ferry slowed, bumped against something and stopped. Even the swell under the ferry seemed to have abated. Then the hold opened and a torrent of threats, curses and orders cascaded over them as they lurched up the tiny stairwell, still chained together.

The sound of crashing waves, the smell of the sea, the screech of seagulls filled Nelson's senses as he emerged from the hold onto the deck of the ferry. For a fleeting moment he felt liberated. The feeling did not last long.

"This is Robben Island," shouted one of the white guards, a red-faced bull of a man. "Here, I am your boss. And here you will die!"

37

FREEDOM RISING LIKE THE SUN

1963

It started as a morning like any other—coffee in hand, sitting on the porch, unfolding the newspaper, the dog at his feet—until he read the headlines.

"My God! I don't believe it." The news was breathtaking. "Maria," he yelled, "look at this... It's unbelievable!"

Maria emerged moments later through the screen door with the air of one long accustomed to humoring her husband's outbursts. Nicolas followed, his eyes bright, his expression quizzical.

"Ja, William. Here I am. What is it this time?" she asked, wiping her hands on her apron.

"We caught the bastards," he said, waving the headlines at her. "In a raid on their hideout. Hah!"

"Ag, William," she replied apathetically as she sat down. "What raid? Who has been caught? But speak quickly—I have rusks in the oven."

"Mandela and his terrorist friends—the whole lot of them, all the leaders—caught like rats in a cage at their hideout in Rivonia."

"Ag, William, what are you talking about? We caught Mandela last year. You followed every report of his trial. I had to listen to you going on and on for weeks about Mandela and his chauffeur and their fancy car."

"Ja, ja, Maria, I know that. I'm not stupid," he replied, struggling to control his impatience. "Mandela's already in prison. But now the police have caught all his friends and found all sorts of plans for sabotage and violent revolution. And Mandela's name is all over the plans."

She slumped back in her chair. "All right. I suppose that is news. So what's the story and what's Rivonia?"

He swung his chair to face her. "Rivonia is a suburb, Maria, outside Jo'burg. The terrorists were hiding on a farm there called... uh... here it is... Liliesleaf." He did not want to sound too familiar with the hideout and hoped Nicolas would not say anything to betray their secret. "They used it for secret meetings to plan their revolution. And they had already put some plans into action—bombings and killings." He shook his head. 'Freedom after bloodshed.' That's what some of them are saying. Can you believe it?"

"Sounds terrible. But just read the story, William, before my rusks burn."

"Ja, okay, Maria." He turned to the front page and began to read. "At about three o'clock on Thursday afternoon, July 11, 1963, a dry-cleaning van drove slowly down the long dirt road towards the Liliesleaf farmhouse. In the driver's cab were two policemen wearing white coats. Thirteen more policemen were hidden behind a screen inside the van with a police dog called Cheetah." He looked up. "The police must have been tipped-off about what was going on at the farm."

"Ja, so it seems. Read on."

"As the van approached, the black farm manager stopped the van and told the driver there was nobody home. The van started to reverse but then shot forward into the main parking area. The doors flew open and the police and the dog jumped out. The men swarmed through the cottage and the main house. They ran down three terrorists who tried to escape out a back window of the cottage, and they caught another who tried to reverse away in a car but was stopped at gunpoint."

"How many did they catch, Pa?" cried Nicolas, gripping his father's arm.

"It says they arrested about eight immediately, including most of the leaders of the ANC and the high command of their terrorist army. Three white Jews—all communists and members of the ANC—were also arrested, together with some of the farmworkers."

"What else, Pa? Did they find guns and bombs and terrorist stuff?"

"Ja, my boy. It says they found a radio transmitter and hundreds of documents, including one they call the jackpot—Operation Mayibuye—a master plan for guerrilla warfare. Apparently the terrorists hoped it would inspire the masses to take up arms against our government. It was lying on a table in the cottage near the main house. But they didn't find any weapons—it says the guns and bombs were at a different hideout."

He stared at this wife. "Jesus, Maria. Guns and bombs! They really were planning to kill us all!"

"William! Do not blaspheme in front of Nicolas—or me for that matter. Don't think you're too old to have your mouth washed out with soap."

"Ja, ja, Maria, but this is incredible. The police say they found over a hundred maps targeting police stations, army bases, government offices, post offices and places like that. It's unbelievable!"

He stared at the paper, his hands trembling. "And listen to this. Mandela is the commander of their terrorist army, called Spear of the Nation. And a lot of documents are in his handwriting—a diary about guerrilla warfare, contacts with revolutionaries and notes on how to be a good communist—as well as letters and books and even a false passport."

He put the newspaper down. "Finally, Maria. We've got the bugger. He can't escape the noose this time."

She sighed. "Ag, William, we've been down this road before. The papers say this, the papers say that, and next week they'll say something else. But explain something to me—I understand the danger of armed terrorists, but why is a communist like a red rag to an Afrikaner bull?"

He was incredulous. "Maria, what don't you understand? This is all part of the Cold War, a global war between East and West. And now the war has come to us. The ANC terrorists get support from the Russians and Chinese and their pawns in Africa. Then they come back across our borders to attack us—to take our jobs, our homes, our homeland... everything." He was breathing hard. "Communism is evil, Maria. It's a cancer that has taken root in Africa in revolution after revolution, and now it's reaching into our people through the ANC. They're a godless menace. Even the Americans and British say so."

She shrugged. "Well, I'd rather think for myself, William. And all I'm saying is don't believe everything the government tells you. And don't jump to conclusions every time you read a report in the papers."

"Ja, well, Maria, you can think what you like. But I hope they all get the noose, especially Mandela."

"And that's another thing," she said, her face flushed. "For the last six or seven years I've heard nothing but Mandela this and Mandela that, how Mandela is on trial for one thing and then for something else." She got to her feet. "So how long will this trial last?

How many more years do I have to listen to you rant and rave about Mandela?" She shook her head in dismay. "I'm sick of it, William."

"Mandela's father is long dead, the son knows nothing of what happened to your family, and this terrorist thing is police business. All you do is fill your heart with hatred. It's not Christian and it's not good for our son to hear you go on like this, year after year. Vengeance is God's business, William, not yours."

He stared at Maria as though she were a stranger. "Mandela made it my business, Maria. The father made it personal. And now the son has made it a matter of life and death for our people."

She rose, shaking her head. "I must take my rusks out of the oven," she said as she disappeared into the house.

It had all happened so quickly, starting with the prison warder who woke him in the middle of the night and told him to pack his things. Within an hour he had found himself back on the road to Pretoria after serving only a few months of his sentence on Robben Island.

And now he was in yet another police van as it raced through the streets of Pretoria. He caught glimpses of the capital city through the narrow window bars but couldn't tell where they were until he saw the huge bronze statue of Paul Kruger—it stood high on a stone pedestal, complete with a stovetop hat, long coat and walking stick—in the center of Church Square.

The van slowed amid a mass of armed policemen watching over a growing crowd carrying signs that read, "We Stand With Our Leaders," while others read, "Let Them Die." Then he recognized the Palace of Justice, the handsome twin-turreted brownstone that dominated Church Square and housed the Pretoria Supreme Court.

As a venue for a show trial, the Palace of Justice was well chosen, he thought as he led his Liliesleaf comrades up the steep stairs into the center of the courtroom. The elements of the court—with its high ceiling and chandeliers, stained-glass windows and a huge cupola above a carved wooden dais for the judge—all seemed to coalesce into a formidable aura of regal, immutable authority, as though designed to declare to the world that if justice was to be found anywhere, this was the place.

He smiled broadly as guards escorted him to the front of the court. Then he turned and raised his fist in the ANC salute to the black section of the gallery. The courtroom was immediately filled with booming chants.

"*Amandla!...Ngawethu!*" and "*iAfrika!...Mayibuye!*" Power, it shall be ours; Africa, let her come home. He felt the emotion of the crowd surge through his being as though he had been injected with the most powerful antidote to colonial oppression.

He took his seat in the dock, surveyed the trappings of justice, and recalled the maxim that "justice must not only be done but must be seen to be done." At the end of the day, if the road to freedom was via the cross, then he had to make sure the world saw and understood what they were fighting for *and* what they were fighting against.

In a flash of inspiration, he remembered the words of Paul Kruger about the Boer War inscribed on the statue he had just seen in Church Square: *In confidence we lay our cause before the whole world. Whether we win or whether we die, freedom will rise in Africa like the sun from the morning clouds.*

Exactly, thought Nelson. We must lay our cause before the whole world, show everyone watching that the government is the guilty party, not us. And that whether we live or die, freedom will rise in Africa like the sun from the morning clouds.

William blinked hard before his eyelids finally unglued. His chest felt tight and he could hear the rasp of his breathing. He coughed and gasped in pain.

As his eyes adjusted to the light, he looked around, trying to remember. At least he knew where he was—the dimly lit bedroom had the familiar mustiness of the goose feather comforter he shared with his wife.

"Awake at last," said Maria as she entered the room and sat down on the bed beside him.

His mouth felt caked in sand, as though the grit of Spion Kop had been poured down his throat while he slept.

"Water...please." He wasn't sure his words were intelligible until he saw Maria reach for the glass on the bedside table and then hold his head while he sipped. "What happened?" he asked, licking his parched lips.

She smiled tenderly as she wiped the perspiration from his brow. "You collapsed, dear husband. Doctor says it's something to do with your heart. He says—"

"No, no, I mean what happened at the trial? With Mandela?"

She sighed. "Always Mandela," she said as Nicolas entered the room. "The world could be ending—facing Armageddon—and your only thought would be about Mandela."

"Please, Maria, the trial was about to start—just tell me."

She nodded with an air of resignation. "Let me think...the trial...Oh yes, I remember," she said. "The judge threw the case out of court. He set Mandela and his friends free."

William stared at his wife in disbelief as though she had spoken the most profane blasphemy. He knew she would smile if she was joking—that was their routine—but she remained stone-faced, her gaze unblinking.

"My God, Maria, what are you saying? That's not possible!" He looked at Nicolas and back at his wife.

"It's the truth, William. That's what happened."

"But how can that be? I don't understand. We caught them red-handed. We had all their plans. It was an open-and-shut case! Everyone said so—all the newspapers, all the politicians, everyone! How could they all be wrong?"

"Well, perhaps it was not idiot proof, William. Perhaps that was the problem."

He ignored the thinly veiled sarcasm. "Ag, please, Maria, don't talk in riddles. Just tell me what happened."

She took a sip of water and handed him the glass. "Where to start—that's the question," she pondered rhetorically. "So the prosecutor said Mandela and his ten co-accused planned a violent revolution through guerrilla warfare and armed invasion of the country, that they had already committed over two hundred acts of sabotage, and that they were part of a conspiracy with the ANC and the Communist Party to achieve the goals of communism in South Africa."

"Ja, ja, that's all true, Maria. So? What was the problem?"

"The problem, dear William, is everyone presumed they were guilty and thought the judge would just take the prosecutor's word for it." She paused. "He didn't."

William stared in open-mouthed disbelief. "But how could he be so stupid, Maria? Everyone knew they were guilty."

She shook her head. "It's what I've been telling you, William. Things are not true just because the government says they're true. Mandela was accused of over a hundred and fifty acts of sabotage, all committed while he was sitting in prison for that other business. How could that be? No wonder his lawyer asked for details of the offenses."

He scowled. "Who's their lawyer? Some clever Jew? Some damned communist?"

She smiled. "Actually, William, their lawyer is Bram Fischer, one of our own people. His father was judge-president of the Orange Free State and his grandfather was president of the old republic. He's the same lawyer who got them all off in the Treason Trial."

"Damned traitor!" said William scowling. "But why did we have to give them the details of our case?"

"Because the accused have to know what they are charged with doing. But instead of giving up the details, the prosecutor said they already knew the facts, so there was no need to tell them. Well, even I knew that was a stupid thing to say, and it didn't sit well with the judge either. He agreed with Fischer and quashed the indictment—set them all free."

"My God, Maria," he said in a bewildered, defeated voice, "I can't believe it."

"Believe it or not, William, it's true," she said with a thin smile. "But you're right about their lawyer," she added. "Fischer makes no secret of his beliefs—he is a member of the Communist Party."

William closed his eyes and shook his head. It was too much. He felt sick to his stomach. Nothing made sense. It felt as though his entire worldview had been turned upside down.

"So are they all free, Maria? Mandela too? Free to carry on and plot their bloody revolution?"

She shook her head with a bemused expression and told Nicolas to make two cups of tea from the fresh pot in the kitchen and to bring some rusks.

"Well, William, a funny thing happened after the judge left the courtroom." She paused to adjust his blankets. "While Mandela and his people were standing around and celebrating, the police rushed in and rearrested them all. It was complete chaos.

Policemen were falling over each other and jumping into the dock to grab Mandela and the others."

"What?" he cried, stunned by the unexpected twist in the plot.

"It's true," she said as Nicolas returned with the tea and rusks. "I don't really understand what happened. It was all a bit silly, but at the end of the day they were only free for a few minutes before they were all arrested again and taken back to jail."

"Thank you, God," said William, addressing the void above the bed as he fell back onto his pillow. "At least something went right." He lay for a few minutes, catching his breath, then sat up again to take his tea and a rusk from Nicolas.

"Any more surprises?"

"Lots actually, William, but it all seems like such a mess to me." She paused. "The raid was so dramatic. We were told our police had saved the country from armed invasion and bloody revolution. Their net was supposed to catch so many fish, and the Rivonia terrorists were the biggest fish of all. Then two of them, Goldreich and Wolpe, escaped the net—bribed one of our prison guards—and a third, who made a deal to be a star witness against his Rivonia comrades, just vanished."

"Well, that's not good, but what happens next?" he asked, dunking his rusk just long enough to avoid the sodden end breaking off into the tea. "Will there be another trial?"

She nodded as she stirred her tea. "Your old friend Vorster said a trial without Goldreich and Wolpe is like Hamlet without the Prince but that the show must go on. So yes, William, the show goes on—starts again tomorrow." Maria shook her head as she fingered a rusk. "And it's been quite a show! But the curtain came down so suddenly on the first act that I'm still not sure if it's a tragedy or a comedy."

He stared mutely at his wife.

"And I have no idea how it will end," she continued. "At least with Shakespeare the plot is clear. But this is more like a circus, an improvised act with clowns falling all over each other."

"I don't hear anybody laughing," he said, his temper rising. "It may not be a play by Shakespeare, Maria, but the plot is clear enough for anyone with eyes to see. The ANC was planning a revolution—an armed uprising and violent overthrow of the government. That's treason or sabotage or whatever they want to call it. And Mandela will hang for it. Vorster will make sure of that."

He fell back onto his pillow, exhausted. "Anything else I should know about?" he asked. "Any other surprises?"

She sighed as she shuffled through the newspapers from the past few weeks. There were not many local stories big enough to displace the Rivonia trial, but there was some international news.

"Not really," she said absently. "About a quarter of a million people—mostly Negroes—marched in Washington, the American capital. Someone named King made a speech about a dream."

"A dream! What was the dream?"

"Something about climbing a mountain."

"Humph," he snorted. "Anything more interesting?"

"And that boxer, Cassius Clay. He's the new world champion. I forget who he boxed against."

"Sonny Liston," added Nicolas. "It was a good fight, Pa. But Liston gave up at the start of the seventh."

"Liston quit? I don't believe it! Must have been a helluva fight," he mused. "I remember when Clay won gold at the Olympics, but nobody thought he could beat Sonny Liston."

"And there was something else." She paused, her brow creased. "Oh yes, my goodness, how could I forget? It was horrible. Just a month before Christmas the American president was killed—shot in the head as he sat in a car."

William gaped as he forced himself upright.

"Kennedy assassinated? My God, Maria. That is terrible news. I can't believe it." He took a sip of water then slumped back. "Kennedy was a good man. He said the fight against communism was a fight between tyranny and freedom, and that the battleground for freedom was in the southern hemisphere. That's us, Maria. That's what we're fighting for in Rhodesia and Angola, in Mozambique and South West Africa, and right here in our own back yard. For freedom against communism! That's why we banned the ANC and the Communist Party. They're our mortal enemies, the whole goddamned lot of them."

He stared wide-eyed at the ceiling. "My God, Kennedy dead. I can't believe they got him." Then he turned to face her. "We're next, I tell you. If we let our guard down for a minute, they'll be all over us."

He paused, his throat dry, his breath rasping.

"This is a fight to the finish, Maria. We have to keep our powder dry, our guns loaded, our wagons tight."

38

AN IDEAL TO DIE FOR

1964—1970

The prosecution finally rested in *The State v. Nelson Mandela and Others*.

Day after day, week after week, month after month the case against him and his comrades had been laid bare in mostly incontrovertible detail, until more than one hundred and seventy witnesses had testified and hundreds of documents, photographs, maps and books on guerrilla warfare, including all his personal papers found at Liliesleaf, had filled out the incriminating record.

Nelson agreed to lead the defense case by making a statement instead of testifying as a witness, to tell the story of the struggle without the risk of interruption by cross-examination. But it was a challenge to prepare the statement. He spent weeks sharing drafts with his co-accused at night and with his lawyers during the day.

One sticking point was the closing paragraph—he wanted it to be strong and uncompromising, but some thought it went too far. His lawyer, Bram Fischer, implored him not to read the last paragraph as written—that he was signing his death warrant unless he changed it.

"I understand, Bram," he said. "I know you are trying to save me from the gallows. So I will make one change and add *if needs be* to the last sentence, but nothing more. I must do this, Bram. I must say the things I truly believe."

Fischer just shook his head and buried his face in his hands.

"We are all guilty under the law, Bram," he insisted. "We know it, they know it, the judge knows it, and we will all probably hang for it. So I must take this opportunity to say what we all believe—to tell the world that in our struggle for the right to live, it was the government, not us, that plotted acts of violence against the majority of its own people, and that the government is the truly guilty party under the norms of civilized society.

"I'm not likely to get another chance, not in this lifetime. And at the end of the day, when all is said and done, I'm proud of the fight we fought. It was the right thing to do. And, the truth is, I *am* prepared to die for the right of our people to live."

Nelson could feel the tension grip his core as he sat waiting for the start of the defense case, but Fischer's opening address to the judge had a reassuring effect. And when Fischer announced in a firm voice, "I call on Nelson Mandela," he rose calmly to his feet, stood imperiously for a moment as he gazed out over the sea of expectant faces, then strode to the dock.

He stood for a moment, adjusted his notes and, freed from the burden of trying to prove their innocence, began to speak:

"I am the first accused. I hold a Bachelor's Degree in Arts and practiced as an attorney in Johannesburg for a number of years in partnership with Oliver Tambo. I am a convicted prisoner serving five years for leaving the country without a permit and for inciting people to go on strike at the end of May 1961." He took a deep breath. "I admit immediately that I was one of the persons who helped to form Umkhonto we Sizwe and that I played a prominent role in its affairs until I was arrested in August 1962."

He was soon into his stride, speaking in measured phrases of his youth, sharing his pride in his African ancestors, the origins of his political consciousness, the reasons for the ANC's resort to violence and his vision for the future.

"Above all, we want equal political rights." He paused—this went to the heart of the struggle. "I know this sounds revolutionary to the whites in this country, because the majority of voters will be Africans. This makes the white man fear democracy. But this fear cannot be allowed to stand in the way of the only solution which will guarantee racial harmony and freedom for all."

After describing at length the ANC's half-century fight against racism, he reached the last paragraph of his statement and Fischer's urgent warning rang in his ears. It was not too late to omit it—he could just sit down. He made his decision, laid his notes on the dock, looked directly at the judge, and delivered the lines he had worked so hard to perfect and had committed to memory:

"During my lifetime I have dedicated myself to the struggle of the African people. I have fought against white domination, and I have fought against black domination. I have cherished the ideal of a democratic and free society in which all persons live together in harmony and with equal opportunities. It is an ideal which I hope to live for and to achieve. But, *if needs be*, it is an ideal for which I am prepared to die."

He glanced at the courtroom clock as he sat down. Nearly four o'clock—he had started speaking at noon. His mouth was bone-dry, his spirit exhausted, but he had said what needed to be said.

The courtroom was so quiet it seemed as though the crowd must be holding its collective breath. There was not a sound for half a minute, until some women began to cry and a collective sigh swept through the crowd.

The judge seemed determined to proceed as though nothing unusual had just happened. After waiting a few moments for the gallery to settle down, he looked over to Fischer at the defense table.

"Mr. Fischer," he said matter-of-factly, "you may call your next witness."

Nelson squinted through the square window as dawn glistened on the wings of the vintage military airplane. The tranquil blue sky draped softly over the tip of the African continent appeared serenely disinterested in what had happened at the trial. There was no thunder or lightning to indicate the wrath of the gods. It was almost disconcerting, although the low throb of the twin aero engines pounding in his ears reminded him of the mind-numbing mountain of incriminating evidence that had hammered on his senses almost every day of the eight-month trial.

The judge's gavel had sounded like a gunshot after he pronounced their sentence, having already found them all guilty of high treason.

"What is it? What is it?" some had called from the gallery, while others had called, "How long? How long?"

"Life! Life! To live!" they had shouted in response. By some miracle they would all live despite having anticipated the opposite—that they would be taken away and hung by their necks until dead.

Perhaps Alan Paton's testimony had made a difference—it was impossible to say—but they *had* escaped the noose. Although a devout Christian opposed to violence, Paton had spoken of their courage, ability and sincerity—their devotion to the cause of their people and lack of any desire for racial vengeance—and how it could be understood that, after peaceful methods of protest had failed, they had come to believe that violence was their only alternative. Although he did not endorse their choice or believe violence could achieve the ends they sought, he had urged the judge—for the sake of the country—to exercise clemency in their case.

And Paton had spoken of the history of the Afrikaners being a striking example of a people who had refused to bow their heads and passively accept oppression, and had turned to armed revolt as their only alternative.

The judge, an Afrikaner himself, had seemed dismissive, his mind already made up—that even people with legitimate grievances were not entitled to break the law by force and normally were sentenced to death when convicted of high treason. And yet, despite such dreadful foreshadowing, the judge had decided to show them mercy.

The beloved country was still crying, as Paton had written years before, but at least some were now crying tears of joy that they had been spared, even if it meant a life behind bars.

The crowded gallery had erupted, with people pushing, jostling and rushing in every direction. In the streets outside the courthouse the people were in full throat, chanting *"Amandla!"* as the police vans carrying them away had raced back to the local prison after the sentencing. And, like an ancestral blanket of comfort, the anthem *"Nkosi Sikelel' iAfrika"* had rung out, sustaining their prayers, lamenting their pain. His spirit had drunk it all in as though storing nourishment for the journey ahead.

Power...it shall be ours...Perhaps not in my lifetime, but eventually...for surely God will bless Africa...raise her up...and give her back to her people.

His brooding meditation was interrupted when the drone of

the airplane's engines slowed sharply and the bulbous nose of the Dakota DC-3 dipped towards the flat top of Table Mountain overlooking Cape Town. The descent continued for several minutes before the aircraft banked lazily to the right towards a desolate island several miles offshore, isolated from the mainland by the frigid Atlantic Ocean. He was surprised the flight was nearly over. At least he had been spared another seventeen-hour ride in a cramped van shackled to his comrades.

It was some comfort that they had achieved their purpose. The London Times had declared, "The verdict of history will be that the ultimate guilty party is the government in power—and that already is the verdict of world opinion." And the New York Times had noted, "To most of the world, these men are heroes and freedom fighters, the George Washingtons and Ben Franklins of South Africa."

He drew a deep breath and slowly exhaled. He hoped it had all been worth it, that their lives had not been sacrificed in vain. And he wondered if he would ever see his wife and children again, whether his marriage to Winnie would survive. Then, as the wheels under each wing bounced on the wet airstrip and the aging airplane settled back on its tiny rear wheel, his thoughts turned to the harsh reality of his immediate future.

The Island—Esiquithini—place of forlorn hope.

The airplane taxied towards the waiting guards and shuddered to a stop. He shuffled to the doorway and gasped as the Cape winter sliced through his flimsy prison clothes.

It was June 13, 1964.

He was only forty-six years old.

He couldn't imagine spending the rest of his life on the Island.

Nicolas stood over his father's grave. It was the fourth anniversary of his passing, and the ritual with his mother at the family plot near the willow tree never varied—a prayer and a reading from the charred family Bible his grandfather had salvaged after the Great Murder.

In the silence that followed, he recalled their commando adventure to Liliesleaf. Even after so many years it still made his heart race to think of what they had so nearly accomplished that night. But at least they had kept a memento—Mandela's gun—buried beneath his grandfather's memorial stone under the willow tree. And he had kept his word to his father and never told a soul.

He closed the Bible and gently squeezed his mother's frail shoulder.

After a few more minutes of reflection, he walked her back up the hill to the farmhouse. The family dog trailed behind on arthritic legs, hanging its head as though sharing the pain of their loss.

"I'll move to town one of these days, so don't worry about me," said his mother as she settled into her porch chair while he adjusted the wrap around her shoulders. "I can't take care of the farm anymore, especially now that Solomon is gone too. And his son from the mines is no good—that apple fell a long way from the tree. But perhaps we can hire a manager until we decide what to do with the farm."

Nicolas looked at his mother—so self-sufficient, never wanting to be a burden, yet showing the unmistakable signs of a life drawing to a close. He poured two cups of tea from the freshly made pot brought to the porch by the maid. He wished he could do what he knew his mother wanted.

"I'm sorry, Ma, but I can't stay on the farm. I like the army. I have from the first day of basic training." He smiled at the recollection. "I still remember the sergeant who met us at the Ladysmith train station that day. "Snakes"—that was his nickname. Mean and tough, but I liked him. He helped get me into the parachute battalion after basics. But now I need a new challenge."

"Ja, I know, my boy. So what's it to be?" She squinted at him before taking the teacup he held out for her.

"Well, Ma, I've heard the army is starting a reconnaissance commando. I think I'll sign up. Pa would be proud if I was part of a real commando."

"Humph," she snorted over the brim of her teacup. "You not only look just like your father, except for the beard, but you think like him." She shook her head with an air of resignation. "So what does this commando do?"

"It's sort of a special unit, Ma, to stop the terrorists before they reach us. Our borders are too long with too many holes. So the idea is to go find them in their hideouts north of our borders. That's what I hear, anyway."

"Sounds dangerous, Nicolas."

"Ag, Ma, that's the world we live in. Pa once rode off and joined a commando to fight the Tommies. That was dangerous. Now it's my turn, my chance to ride off and join a commando to fight our new enemy, the ANC."

She sighed and stirred her tea. "Just because you're big and strong doesn't make you invulnerable to bullets, my boy. The Xhosas discovered that to their cost against the British. So did your grandfather." She shook her head. The sadness in her eyes made her look even older.

"And what about your rugby and the series against the All Blacks?"

It took him a moment to switch his train of thought from fighting terrorists to playing rugby. It seemed his thoughts of rugby always had the same prologue—regret that his father never saw him play for Grey College or be selected for the South African team. The old man had been happy enough to live to see Mandela sent to prison, but his heart had stopped one day as he sat on the porch smoking his pipe, before he ever saw his son reach his potential on the rugby field.

"I'm not sure, Ma, but unless Vorster allows the Maori players into the country, the All Blacks' tour might be cancelled." He shook his head. In the past the Kiwis had always agreed not to include Maoris in their touring teams to South Africa. But times had changed—now they insisted.

"I've heard Vorster might even make the Maoris honorary whites just so they can come and play. Sounds crazy, Ma, but maybe the prime minister can do such a thing. Anyway, I hope they find a way so we can play."

She looked off into the distance. "I hope you get to play the All Blacks. Your father would be proud. But political fires are being stoked, Nicolas, across the seas and here at home."

He shrugged and patted the dog at his feet. He thought he saw reproach in the dog's eyes for not wanting to stay on the farm.

"So what are you saying, Ma?"

She took a deep breath. "As your father might have said, Nicolas, there are cracks in our circle of wagons, the bindings are being forced loose and the masses are preparing to storm inside."

She paused to sip her tea, then set the cup down and reached for his hand. "So be careful what you wish for, Nicolas, that's all I'm saying. And be careful about this commando business."

PART THREE

1970—2010

The anti-apartheid movement gathered momentum after Mandela and his nine comrades were found guilty of sabotage and imprisoned for life on Robben Island in 1964. International boycotts of apartheid-based sports teams were among the first acts of the anti-apartheid movement, followed by cultural boycotts and economic sanctions.

Internally, black resistance efforts during the '60s and early '70s were contained by the regime until the chaos of the Soweto uprising in 1976 when thousands of black school students rioted, their rage fueled by a new law requiring half their subjects be taught in Afrikaans, considered the language of the oppressor. Although the army's focus at the time was the war along the country's northern borders, it was now also deployed in the townships to support police efforts to control the spiraling violence. It was a time of great turmoil that saw Winnie Mandela emerge as a powerful spokesperson for her husband and for the struggle, until she, too, became caught up in the violence.

As the violence escalated and political pressure mounted, clandestine meetings took place in the mid- to-late '80s between white leaders and black leaders, including separate secret meetings with the imprisoned Nelson Mandela. But the peace process was compromised by ongoing internal violence and the war in southern Angola against a Marxist regime, Cuban troops and Soviet armor, artillery and aircraft.

39

THE SWORD OF FREEDOM

1976–1988

Nelson shut his eyes as the pickax crashed against the quarry rock, sending splinters into his face and shards of pain knifing through his frozen hands. The rock seemed impervious, unyielding, refusing to be broken, protecting its seams of lime as though clinging to the glue of geological life.

His feet were numb with cold, his eyes ached from the glare, and grit had found pockets of refuge behind his weary eyelids. There was no respite from the razor-sharp winter winds that cut across the desolate penal outcrop, whipping up dust inside the craterlike limestone quarry carved into the hillside like a surreal and blindingly white amphitheater.

Before the quarry, his days had been spent sitting cross-legged in the prison courtyard together with about thirty others, crushing stones with a six-pound hammer—hour after hour, day after day, month after month—filling countless wheelbarrows with cracked stones.

That had lasted six months.

Then they were sent to the quarry. They were told the quarry stint would also last six months.

That was twelve years ago.

He was about to swing the pickax again when the guard called a work break. Without a word he dropped the tool and huddled with Sisulu inside a cave that had been hollowed out at the base of the quarry wall by a previous generation of prisoners. Today it would protect them from the worst of the frigid elements. Six months from now they would use it for shade as the midsummer heat transformed the quarry into a glaring, white-hot furnace, capped by meager green scrub clinging to life on its rim just as they clung to life below.

"The townships are in flames," said Nelson as he cupped his hands against his mouth, trying to warm them with his breath.

"The Americans had their revolution in 1776," mused Sisulu. "Perhaps we will have ours in 1976, led by our Soweto schoolchildren. Perhaps they are the ones who will ring the bell of liberty for our people."

The two men fell silent. It was hard to imagine the life-and-death struggle going on a thousand miles away in townships outside Johannesburg.

"Perhaps, Walter, perhaps." He blinked hard against the grit that irritated his eyes. "But I am worried about the level of violence. We must do something about it."

Sisulu stared at him. "The armed struggle was your creation, Nelson. You were the rebel, the hotheaded revolutionary, short fused and quick to quarrel, the warrior who pushed us into violent confrontation with the regime. You were our Garibaldi, our Che Guevara—the fearless sword of freedom in our fight against apartheid. Our young people are just following your lead, taking the fight to the oppressor, fighting violence with violence."

He knew Sisulu was right, but it gave him cold comfort as he reflected on the many ambiguities in the long history of the struggle and the role he had played.

"You know, Walter, since I came to this place, I've had a lot of time to think. To meet violence with violence only gives the advantage to the more powerful. If we ever hope to win the war against the regime, it will not be through the barrel of a gun. To win it, we have to understand what our enemy is thinking, not just what its leaders are saying. We have to understand their language, their culture, their hopes and their fears. And we have to speak to them in their own language, not in the language of their oppressors. So—"

"Surely you haven't forgotten Kennedy's warning," interrupted Sisulu, "that those who make peaceful revolution impossible make violent revolution inevitable."

He nodded. "I know the rhetoric of revolution, Walter. But I no longer believe violence is inevitable. The Boers aren't born hating us because of the color of our skin—they have to be taught to hate. And if they must be taught to hate then they can be taught to love—or at least to respect us as equals. For I have learned in my own life, especially on this island, that love comes more naturally to the human heart than its opposite. The Boers are no different. I no longer accept that violence is inevitable, that to have peace we must have violence. The contradiction is too great."

"But what alternative do we have?" countered Sisulu. "That's how we justified the armed struggle in the first place."

"You're right, Walter. I thought differently in '61 when we formed Umkhonto. But that was then and this is now. Their violence justified our violence, and now our violence justifies their violence. It's just a vicious circle."

He tossed a small rock across the quarry, then rubbed his hands together for warmth. He took a deep breath and slowly exhaled, knowing he owed Sisulu more of an explanation.

"I have gone from nonviolence to the armed struggle and back again to nonviolence," he began. "It's a question of tactics, Walter. Nonviolence, like violence, is just a tactic, not a principle. I will use any tactic as long as it works. If violence in the townships and in the streets forces the regime to the bargaining table, then I will sit down and talk. But I don't see that happening—we are outgunned. We must change our tactics."

He stood for a moment to stretch his legs, then huddled down again.

"And so I prepare for a future built on negotiation rather than confrontation. That's why I'm learning to speak Afrikaans even as our children protest against it and proclaim, 'To hell with Afrikaans.' It's a different kind of war, Walter. We must show the Boers our struggle is not just about liberating *our* people from the bondage of living *with* apartheid. It's also a struggle to liberate *their* people from the fear of living *without* apartheid."

He stood again and flexed his tired arm muscles. Then he glared at the inanimate quarry wall and hoisted the pick above his shoulder.

"It's guerrilla warfare without guns."

The blast was apocalyptic, as though the fist of an avenging God had smashed through the firmament and knocked the earth off-balance, or perhaps Armageddon had begun—except nobody had predicted 1983.

Nicolas coughed as he tried to regain his senses. Shards of pain stabbed at him from all sides as he sat up and peered out of the car into the maelstrom that moments before had been a placid street in Pretoria. Chaos swirled everywhere as plumes of gray-black smoke mixed with clouds of red-brown dust and billowed across the street. Through the veil of dust he saw people staggering, kneeling, lying still. And he heard pleas for help and screams of pain, adding visceral despair to violent destruction.

He kicked open the driver's door and stumbled out of the car, his feet crunching on the uneven debris of stone and glass. He stared dumbly around him, trying to make sense of what had happened.

In a flash it came back to him.

He had been in the driver's seat, leaning across to unlock the passenger-side doors for his wife and daughter waiting on the sidewalk beside the car.

Then the blast.

"Oh my God!" The hoarse cry erupted as the import of the explosion hit him as though for a second time and his military instincts belatedly engaged.

He dropped to a crouch behind the car door—there was always the chance of a secondary bomb or ambush of the rescuers. He looked up the street and easily identified the epicenter of the blast—the burning remains of a blue Alfa Romeo parked outside the offices of the South African Air Force.

Keeping low, he sprinted around the back of the car to the sidewalk and saw his loved ones immediately. They were lying on their backs about twenty feet away, still holding hands, surrounded by broken glass and blood. He reached them in seconds and dropped to his knees between their inert bodies.

Nicolas stared numbly at his wife—her eyes unseeing, the smile ripped from her face, the blood from a gaping wound at the base of her neck stark against her straw-colored hair. He had loved her smile—it always reminded him of their wedding that bright afternoon in 1980 during the annual rose festival in Bloemfontein. He lifted her head and cradled her to his chest. A low moan escaped his clenched teeth. Then he kissed her cheek and forehead, closed her eyelids and lowered her head to the ground.

He turned to their daughter, a miniature of her mother, born just ten months after they were married. She did not appear injured—perhaps Charlene had shielded her from the bomb. But she lay so still. He had seen death like that before—the blast alone was sufficient. Her green eyes and red hair normally sparkled with such vitality that the dull, dusty, lifeless form was almost unrecognizable. As he scooped up her limp body, a primordial scream erupted from the core of his being. He rocked her back and forth as he had done so many times to put her to sleep. Now he hoped to wake her.

No tears flowed, no words came to mind, no prayer filled his heart, just a forlorn hope to shut out the images of death, to remember them as they had been only minutes before—beautiful, loving and full of the promise of tomorrow.

He had taken them to visit the Palace of Justice where Mandela had been convicted. And together they had stood before the statue of Paul Kruger in Church Square and read his words about their Second War of Freedom: *Whether we win or whether we die, freedom will rise in Africa like the sun from the morning clouds.*

He never imagined the price of freedom would be so high.

Sirens and yelled instructions pierced his dulled senses before firm hands raised him to his feet. He watched in silence as Charlene was lifted onto a stretcher and someone took Saskia from his arms. He followed to a vehicle—it looked like an ambulance but could just as well have been a hearse—and climbed into the back. The doors slammed shut and the vehicle moved off, siren blaring.

He watched the paramedic go through the motions of checking for vital signs—Saskia first, then Charlene—her blue medic's coat contrasting vividly against the color of blood. Then she looked at him and shook her head.

"Both?" he asked hoarsely, hoping he was wrong.

"Your wife is gone... I'm sorry. But the little one... I'm not sure. The road is very bumpy." She paused. "I've never seen anything like it. Nineteen dead. Hundreds hurt. Ambulances from all over. It's too terrible."

"Car bomb," he muttered.

"Yes. Police say it was Umkhonto."

He buried his face in his hands. Umkhonto we Sizwe. Mandela had been its first commander. It seemed almost every heartbreak in his family's life bore the imprint of a Mandela, this latest atrocity the most cruel and personal of all.

The ambulance lurched around a corner, tires squealing, and bounced hard over the curb.

Saskia coughed.

Nicolas watched as the Soviet T-55 tanks advanced. He couldn't see his comrades from his reconnaissance position above the Lomba River, but he knew they were there, hidden from the marauding Sukhoi Su-20 and MiG-21 jets, ready to engage and push the Marxist enemy back to Cuito Cuanavale.

It was no secret that Pretoria and Washington were working together to resist Angola's FAPLA army, supported by Cubans, Russians, East Germans and Umkhonto fighters. But the geopolitics of the Cold War were not his concern. It was enough to know that commie bastards were threatening his homeland and committing acts of terror that had taken the love of his life.

The first contact took him by surprise—a barrage of mortar bombs followed by a salvo of Valkyrie rockets fired towards the enemy north of his position. But FAPLA countered with its own multiple-rocket launcher—the Stalin Organ—and its brigades advanced imperiously, as though daring anyone to try to halt their progress. At this pace, the FAPLA troops would soon cross the Lomba and penetrate deep into southeastern Angola, threatening the border with South Africa.

The reversal was as sudden as it was swift. The booming sound of South Africa's G5 field guns was unmistakable, as was the sight of low-level Buccaneer strike jets and Mirage F-1 attack jets. Everywhere he looked he saw the counteroffensive on the move, in Ratel combat vehicles and Olifant battle tanks, supported by Buffel troop carriers and truck-mounted Stinger anti-aircraft systems from America.

He realized he would miss the action if he stayed where he was and quickly made his way off the high ground to the plain below. He had no sooner clambered down the hill and into cover than a Ratel came into view, then stopped barely twenty yards from his position. He hesitated when he saw the black faces of the soldiers who emerged to secure some loose equipment on the Ratel. As tough as his Special Forces comrades were, the Buffalo Soldiers of 32 Battalion were a breed apart, their reputation well earned as "the terrible ones." But when he recognized their white commander from basic training, he broke cover.

"Got space for one more?" he called to the commander.

The commander looked up sharply, then waved. "Hello, De Beer. Ja, come on—climb aboard. We're part of the battle group spearheading the counteroffensive in the morning. So you're on your own when the shit hits the fan. Understood?"

"Understood," replied Nicolas, grinning. "That's the way I like it." He was confident his skills at survival, sabotage, and guerrilla warfare left the enemy with more to fear from him than he from them. The Ratel was soon on its way to the rendezvous on high ground about ten miles southeast of Cuito Cuanavale.

The night was cold and sleep in short supply. At 0300 the men were roused. He made sure his 5.56 mm R5 automatic assault rifle was loaded, one in the breech and the safety engaged. He had as many spare magazines as he had pouches to carry them, but he did not expect to run out of ammunition.

At 0400 the battle group moved out. Covering fire from mobile G5s started a while later, followed by Mirage jets that sounded like a rush of thunder overhead as they attacked FAPLA targets, their missiles like lightning strikes in the early dawn.

He was crowded inside a Ratel with eight Buffalo Soldiers. He could feel his stomach tighten, but he had long ago learned to control combat tension and to embrace the Recce motto—"Fear none but God."

His thoughts drifted as they crashed along the uneven terrain. Images of the bumpy ambulance ride after the Pretoria bombing were playing through his mind when he heard the turret gun above his head open fire. Seconds later the Ratel took a massive hit and shuddered to a stop.

"Out, out!" yelled the section leader as he forced the back doors open. The men scrambled out to the left and right to form a protective perimeter around the vehicle. Nicolas followed, sprinted a short distance to the three-o'clock position, then dove to the ground. His chest hit hard, his R5 at the ready.

The noise of the firefight was deafening—heavy-caliber booms, explosions all around and bullets flying in every direction, buzzing through the air like crazed bees.

Jesus, this is serious shit, he thought with grim satisfaction as he tried to identify the source of the threat.

"Tanks...T-55s...twelve o'clock!" someone yelled.

Nicolas rose in unison with the men close to him and ran for the cover of a ragged tree line twenty yards ahead. The trees provided scant protection against tanks, but some cover from enemy troops was better than none. He had no sooner reached the tree line than heavy-caliber gunfire erupted behind him and a squadron of Olifant battle tanks charged out of the dust and brush, their turret guns hammering away at the T55s.

Unbelievable, thought Nicolas. *A goddamn tank battle in the middle of the African bush!*

As the armored leviathans traded blows, it felt as though the whole world was lurching and grinding in spasmodic belches of fire and brimstone towards an apocalyptic end.

Then, without warning, the troops around him were also on the move. Nicolas was on his feet in an instant, crashing through the bush, trying to stay out of the way of the tanks and mobile artillery until, thankfully, the tank battle moved off in a different direction. And although he sometimes saw figures ahead of him, he couldn't risk firing at friendly troops in the disorientation and confusion of battle.

The dense bush suddenly opened up in front of him. Troops on his right and left were crouched low, staring at entrenched FAPLA positions about thirty yards ahead. He dropped to the ground, breathing hard. He took a quick drink from his canteen and spat out the sand and grit that caked his mouth.

It was oddly tranquil after the mad dash through the bush. He could still hear distant booms from the tank battle, but now it would be man against man. They would storm the enemy positions and fight it out at close quarters with the FAPLA troops.

As he waited for the signal, the terrain in front of him suddenly exploded in a blizzard of rock and dust. He scrambled back into the bush for cover as a couple of MiG fighter jets appeared from nowhere to strafe their position.

The threat passed as quickly as it had materialized. The troops around him reemerged from cover like an avenging horde and immediately rushed forward in a zigzag sprint across the open ground, firing short bursts at the enemy positions. Nicolas ran as hard and fast as he could, swerving left and right, his R5 alive in his hands, chattering spasmodically with each squeeze of the trigger.

He reached the enemy lines unscathed and leapt into the dugout, landing in a crouch, pivoting left and right to cover any threat from any quarter. But, like ghosts, the enemy had vanished under cover of the MiG attack.

After regrouping with the main battle group, the troops he was with settled in for another cold night and early start. But by the time the assault resumed in the morning, the FAPLA brigades had retreated to heavily fortified positions outside the town of Cuito Cuanavale.

It proved to be a frustrating stalemate, especially after elite Cuban troops and fresh Soviet hardware arrived to reinforce the FAPLA positions. And when the United Nations demanded that all foreign troops withdraw from Angola, the South Africa forces had no good options. They pulled back and headed home.

On the flight back to Pretoria, despite the rough ride in the four-engined Lockheed C-130 Hercules, Nicolas reached a life-altering decision as surprising as it was compelling. As a Recce he was merely a cog in a machine, an expendable pawn in a game of international politics, where victories won in blood could be lost in ink—just as his people had experienced in Natal after Blood River.

If the military couldn't protect the physical security of his people from the scourge of communism and ANC terror, perhaps he could reinforce their spiritual refuge in the church, embraced and protected by the everlasting arms of God.

Their borders might be porous and compromised, but their circle of wagons at home had to be impenetrable, their covenant faith unassailable.

40

IN THE NAME OF FREEDOM—AND OF THE FATHER

1990-2010

Nelson gazed down from the balcony of city hall onto the sea of multicolored faces squashed together on Grand Parade, the oldest public square in Cape Town, cheering and singing so much more joyfully today than all those years ago at his trial. The crowd was so tightly packed the people seemed joined at their hips, their unity and elation a vindication of the long and lonely years of struggle.

Alternating chants of *"Amandla...Ngawethu!"* and *"iAfrika... Mayibuye!"* swept across the public square and reached up to the balcony where he stood, lifting his spirit as he waited to speak.

Nelson smiled as he recalled the Grand Parade was the site of Jan van Riebeeck's fort when the Dutch settlers first came to South Africa in the 1650s—a fort to protect them from the natives. But like the Berlin wall of shame that had fallen just three months ago, the Boer fortress of shame—apartheid—that had also seemed impregnable for so long, had finally been breached.

The euphoria of freedom rising, of oppression crumbling, of a future for all within grasp, was almost palpable. Just like the event that had symbolized the end of the Cold War, today's natives would use this day, at this site, to celebrate a victory that no fort or laager had been able to prevent.

It had all seemed so dark after the schoolchildren of Soweto transformed the political landscape in 1976. The spiral of violence through the rest of the '70s and '80s had been gut wrenching as a fever of insurrection swept through the townships. And, on the national stage, Umkhonto had attacked fuel storage facilities, launched rockets at a military base, bombed a nuclear power station, and, in the worst act of terror in the country's history, detonated a car bomb in Pretoria that killed nineteen and wounded two hundred and seventeen. The ANC had declared 1986 "The Year of Umkhonto we Sizwe, the People's Army" and vowed to turn every corner of the country into a battlefield.

The Afrikaner leader, P. W. Botha, had been convinced that South Africa faced a "total onslaught," and the regime's resolve—to hold on to power until the bitter end—had seemed unshakable. The country had degenerated into a police state in all but name, and the military had gone on the offensive, deploying troops along more than a thousand miles of borders from Namibia to Mozambique, taking the fight deep into Angola and conducting preemptive strikes against ANC targets in neighboring countries.

Nelson drew a deep breath, glanced over the crowd and thought about what he was about to say to all these people and those watching on television. As he reached into his coat pocket for the speech, Lincoln's Gettysburg Address came to mind. Only two hundred and seventy words in ten sentences, yet those few sentences, delivered in just a few minutes, had captured the essence of liberty, equality and democracy for an entire nation torn by a bloody civil war, a fate many had predicted for South Africa.

He knew his speech lacked the eloquence and grandeur that

Lincoln had mustered so concisely, but it could not be helped. He had been released so hurriedly that the speech had been a group effort, rushed and difficult to compose, and he worried it would give truth to the old saying that "too many cooks spoil the broth." It had turned out stodgy, a thick stew of partisan red meat that offered little sustenance to a nation hungry for transformation, for a vision of the future.

He fingered the button of his gray suit. He was hot and uncomfortable and the plain white collar and gray-purple tie felt too tight around his neck. It had been a hectic day and a chaotic drive from his winelands prison into the center of Cape Town, not the dignified release he had wanted. He was almost three hours behind schedule and the sun was already setting over the city.

His thoughts drifted further afield as he waited, to the efforts during the 1980s that had culminated in his release from prison. He had been moved to Pollsmoor Prison in a suburb of Cape Town in 1982, after eighteen years on Robben Island. In '85, amid the escalating violence, Botha had offered to release him if he renounced violence as a political weapon. He had publicly refused—his daughter Zindzi had read his statement to thousands of supporters at a stadium in Soweto.

Then, in late '88, he had been moved again, this time to a comfortable three-bedroom cottage with his own swimming pool and personal chef. The cottage was set in a secluded area among trees on the grounds of the Victor Verster Prison in the Cape winelands, about thirty-five miles from Cape Town. He smiled as he recalled the irony of the minister of justice—his jailer—presenting him with a case of wine as a housewarming gift.

The illusion of freedom had been almost beguiling—there were no bars on the windows or locks on the doors. He could sleep, eat, swim and walk outside whenever he pleased, and receive guests from the outside for private meetings. But he was still inside a prison, its walls laced with razor wire.

And he still had work to do—the struggle was not yet won, the long walk not yet finished.

He would never forget the secret meeting with President Botha in July '89 in the president's formal office in Tuynhuys, a Cape Dutch house in the Company's Garden in the heart of Cape Town. He remembered how tense he had been at the prospect of meeting the finger-wagging tyrant—an archconservative with the temper of a cantankerous old crocodile—who had once dismissed him as an arch-Marxist destined to spend his life in jail.

It was supposed to be just a courtesy visit, an icebreaker, but the anticipation of an explosive encounter had been almost palpable. To his surprise, Botha had greeted him with an outstretched hand and a disarming smile and even served him tea. And when he addressed Botha in Afrikaans and spoke with empathy about the Afrikaner struggle against the British—the Boer War, the Rebellion of 1914, and how Afrikaners were the "first freedom fighters"—the ice had been broken.

Although they had not directly addressed the current political conflict, he had been sure the mere fact of the meeting and the personal relationship established with Botha had represented a major step towards peace and reconciliation. Yet no follow-up meeting was scheduled—it seemed the president was content to fiddle while the country burned. Then even the fiddling stopped when Botha, who had previously suffered a stroke, unexpectedly resigned in August of '89.

After years of trying to deal with Botha's regime, he had despaired at the prospect of starting all over to negotiate with a new president. But only a few months later, in early December, he had been taken without warning to Tuynhuys for a second secret meeting, this time with the new president, the lawyerly F. W. de Klerk.

The meeting with De Klerk was no tea party. Serious political issues were deliberated in a respectful manner, the thorniest being how to accommodate the principle of majority rule while protecting minority rights. He still recalled De Klerk's words: "It's a dilemma that goes to the heart of the situation," the president had said. "We're not sellouts. We cannot accept a simple majority-rule formula. We whites are about ten percent of the population. Yours and the other nonwhite groups make up about ninety percent. We have to avoid domination by the majority. We will not sacrifice the safety and security of our descendants on the altar of simple majority rule."

Despite the seemingly intractable issue, De Klerk had asked what could be done in the interim. His unequivocal answer had been prepared in advance by leaders of the struggle—release all political prisoners, legalize all political organizations, end restrictions on political activity, stop all political executions and lift the state of emergency.

He had left the meeting encouraged that he might yet see an end to apartheid in his lifetime. But just two months later, at the opening of parliament in February 1990, De Klerk had responded publicly. In one breathtaking pronouncement after another, the new president had unraveled almost the entire grand tapestry of apartheid and, saved for last, announced that he would be released from prison unconditionally and almost immediately.

Now here he stood, only a few days later, on a balcony draped with the ANC's flag of black, green, and gold next to the solid red of the Soviet flag with its yellow hammer and sickle, about to give a speech as a free man after twenty-seven years of captivity. He hoped he would be able to read it—he had forgotten his reading glasses at the prison and had to use Winnie's.

He felt a nudge and realized the moment had come. All eyes were on him as the crowd's calls and responses subsided. He unfolded the speech, adjusted his wife's reading glasses as best he could, and began to speak into a microphone held for him by Cyril Ramaphosa.

"Friends, comrades, and fellow South Africans. I greet you all in the name of peace, democracy and freedom for all." The crowd erupted. "I stand here before you not as a prophet but as a humble servant of you, the people. Your tireless and heroic sacrifices have made it possible for me to be here today. I therefore place the remaining years of my life in your hands." He paused until the cheering subsided. "On this day of my release," he continued, "I extend my sincere and warmest gratitude to the millions of my compatriots and those in every corner of the globe who have campaigned tirelessly for my release... I salute the African National Congress... our president, Comrade Oliver Tambo... the rank and file members of the ANC... combatants of Umkhonto we Sizwe... the South African Communist Party... and my beloved wife and family."

He kept reading, page after page, until eventually, his duty to the ANC done, he reached the last page.

"In conclusion," he said, his voice strong as he returned to a familiar theme, "I wish to quote my own words from my trial in 1964. They are as true today as they were then." He paused, recalling with a shudder the drama of that time, his last appearance in public before being shut away for so many years. He took a deep breath. The words were not only still true, but he still recalled them as clearly as he had twenty-seven years before when he addressed the judge:

"I have fought against white domination and I have fought against black domination. I have cherished the ideal of a democratic and free society in which all persons live together in harmony and with equal opportunities. It is an ideal which I hope to live for and to achieve. But, *if needs be*, it is an ideal for which I am prepared to die."

"In the name of the Father, the Son and the Holy Spirit," intoned Nicolas in formulaic fashion, "go in peace."

After greeting members of the Stellenbosch congregation at the door as they left the historic Mother Church in the heart of the Cape winelands, he walked around the back of the church into the graveyard. He liked to spend a few moments under the oak tree after Sunday morning services. And as he fingered the charred family Bible he still cherished, his consciousness flooded with the circumstances that had brought him to this sacred place—the heart of Afrikanerdom.

There had really been only one option after his return from the war in Angola, only one portal into the faith of his forefathers—the Stellenbosch University Seminary and the Dutch Reformed Mother Church. His studies were demanding and exhausting, but he had finally graduated and been ordained. And now he served at the altar of his people's covenant faith. The congregation knew him as a former Springbok rugby player and now a man of the cloth. They also knew he had served in the military, but they did not know his robes cloaked a former Special Forces Recce who had dispatched at least as many terrorists to hell as he had brought sinners to God.

Dappled light streamed through the oak leaves to form irregular patterns on the gravestones, the flickering mosaic conjuring images from the passage of his life. There was something about the tree—its constancy and resiliency, its towering embrace—that reminded him of his mother and gave him comfort as he thought of his loved ones, especially those memorialized beneath the fierce indifference of a baboon's skull.

His mother had died in her sleep only two weeks after she saw him play against the All Blacks in the '76 series. But at least he still had Saskia. She had grown strong, a marathon runner about to graduate as a pediatric oncologist, a thoroughly modern woman. She made him proud, but he was not sure what she thought of him or how she would remember him. He had run a few marathons with her, and she had completed a few triathlons with him, but aside from that, his only private recreation was golf, which she did not play.

His passion for golf was a guilty pleasure, an extravagance in a country dominated by oppressive poverty, but he treasured the opportunity it provided to decompress. He liked to play alone at sunrise and never allowed the golf to spoil a good walk. There were times on the course, especially with the sun rising through the trees and lacing wispy clouds with its glory, that he felt at peace with the universe, at one with the divine.

His thoughts turned to the sermon he had preached a few minutes earlier, the familiar themes still resonating in his mind in the quiet of the graveyard. Just as the Jews had created and defended their homeland, surrounded by hostile nations intent on their destruction, driven by an unshakable conviction they were chosen to fulfill the will of God, so too had the Afrikaner people created and fought for their homeland, surrounded by hostile nations intent on their destruction, driven by a bedrock belief they were a people chosen to fulfill a sacred covenant.

And yet he knew the cherished historical themes so familiar to him were also at the heart of a more contemporary and controversial manifestation of human motivation—Israel's treatment of the Palestinians equated with apartheid, and apartheid reviled as a crime against humanity. The cruel irony was stark. For those fighting for their survival and a land to call their own—the Jews after a two-thousand-year diaspora and the Afrikaners after three centuries of struggle—the drive to protect themselves and their identities had been an all-consuming imperative textured by faith, sacrifice, and the instinct for self-preservation. But it could not be denied that, having suffered so much for their own freedom, they had turned that imperative against their neighbors and countrymen—oppressed others to protect themselves—and denied to so many the very freedoms they had struggled so hard to attain for their own people.

He still struggled with the paradox, and with the fact his own church had been integral to it, part of the foundational warp that had shaped the fabric of their apartheid society and held it together for so long. But now that fabric, and the social pattern so carefully woven over so many years, had been stripped from the loom and replaced by new fabric being woven by new weavers creating an entirely different pattern, unrecognizable from the old. It was their right to be the weavers, to control the levers of the country's loom and to create a new tapestry from organic threads colored by natural dyes—an African form for an African people.

But he did not like what he was seeing. The corroding stain of corruption—of poverty, cronyism and inequality—was discoloring the fabric and distorting the pattern, producing a grotesque caricature of the cherished values enshrined in their new constitution.

He had never spoken publicly of his despair for his country.

And he had never spoken of his own grief or the history of his family. But it still hammered at his consciousness like a constant reverberation across the membrane of his soul that, after all the treachery and murder, wars and concentration camps, hardships and suffering, his people had given it all away—to Mandela of all people!

It had all become fresh and raw that hot summer day in 1990 when Mandela walked out of prison instead of serving a life sentence—hailed as a savior as though risen from the dead—and became president when the ANC won the election in '94. He had imagined his father rising from his grave to rage in protest at the injustice of it all. And then, adding gross insult to extreme injury, the ANC leaders after Mandela had plundered the country as though its wealth was a vast and bottomless trough set aside just for their pleasure, while the people they were meant to serve suffered every day and in every conceivable way.

It seared his conscience to think of it—the mockery of democracy, the crisis of freedom—and it exposed his impotence in the face of it. Perhaps Neptune or Poseidon could have diverted the Titanic from striking the iceberg on her maiden voyage and sinking to the bottom of the frigid North Atlantic Ocean. But there was no god, mythological or otherwise, that could save his country from disaster in her maiden journey under ANC leadership as she lurched inexorably towards self-destruction. And there was surely nothing that could be done by a single white clergyman well past his prime.

But in a flash of insight it struck him—like a "sheet of lightening at midnight" as Emerson had said—a moment of illumination as he stood fingering the charred symbol of his family's sacrifice and his people's struggle.

He had spent the last twenty years in the pulpit while his people and his country staggered on the edge of the precipice under the ANC's leadership. He had tried to be a faithful shepherd to the congregation and pass on the principles that animated his faith—to act justly, love mercy, and walk humbly before God—the simple credo by which his mother had lived her life and impressed upon his. But all at once he knew with awful certainty that what he was doing was not enough.

It was time to step into the arena, to make a stand against tyranny and corruption, regardless of personal cost.

After all, David had killed Goliath with just one stone, a Philistine giant who boasted of capturing the Israelites' Ark of the Covenant during their exodus from Egypt as they searched for their promised land. Maybe with just one bullet he could avenge his family and shock the nation into a cleansing fire of moral and political reform. Perhaps, like a phoenix—the scarlet and gold eagle-like symbol of resurrection and immortality from ancient mythology—there would be life after death and a renewed nation would rise from the ashes, take wing and soar.

The new resolve raced through his senses, through every fiber of his being and wrapped itself around the core of his soul. He knew the chances of success were remote—that "tyranny, like hell, is not easily conquered" as Thomas Paine had said of the American revolution against British oppression—but he would rather die trying than submit to a life of defeat. After all, the people of South Africa had beaten the odds before—apartheid had been conquered—and now the tyranny of the ANC had become an evil that could no longer be endured.

He refused to be a "sunshine patriot" and shirk his duty. He would answer the call. For if ever there was a time in his beloved country to "try men's souls," now was that time.

He knew his mother would have been proud that he had turned to the church. But the existential battlefield had been transformed over the past twenty years. Now it was time to follow his father's example, and turn to the gun.

Perhaps even Mandela's gun.

41

THE CALABASH

2010

The Calabash appeared ablaze in the afternoon sun, like an enormous gourd atop a flickering fire, as though the stadium on the edge of Soweto was being pre-heated for the stew of ninety thousand football spectators who would soon pour into the pot for the opening game of the World Cup—Mexico against South Africa—at four o'clock the next day, June 11, 2010.

Nicolas stepped onto the platform and set the suitcase down. The five-mile train ride from Johannesburg had been uneventful. He straightened his black suit, smoothed his hair and adjusted the black fedora until its brim almost touched the frame of his dark glasses. The clerical collar was a little tight around his neck, but he had long reconciled himself to the chaffing it represented. He fingered the return ticket in his pant pocket—he didn't expect to need it.

He climbed the steps to the promenade and began the long walk towards the stadium. He marveled as he took in the spectacle—it looked otherworldly, as though a giant patchwork quilt of earth-tone panels had been thrown over the stadium's original frame, transforming it into a vibrant, curvaceous melting pot, a crucible for the hopes of a nation dreaming of football glory. He was perspiring by the time he reached the turnstile entrances.

"Good day," he called brightly to an attendant, hoping to take advantage of the instinctive deference accorded ministers of religion. "How are you, my good man?" he asked with an engaging smile as he made to walk through the turnstile.

The black attendant nodded an acknowledgement but said, "I'm sorry, Reverend, you can't come in without a security pass."

Nicolas stopped in his tracks, looking pained. "A pass? Really? They didn't say anything about a security pass at the office in Pretoria."

The attendant frowned. "What office?"

"The Department of Sports and Recreation."

"There are many offices in that department," said the attendant skeptically. "Who did you speak to and what is the nature of your business?"

"You're a smart fellow," Nicolas said with a smile. "I spoke to Deputy Minister Gert Oosthuizen—he and I are members of the Inter-Ministerial Organizing and Planning Committee for the World Cup. He never mentioned a pass but said I could use his name if there were any questions."

"Really," said the attendant as one accustomed to tall stories.

"Yes, we're old friends, ever since we played rugby against each other. He played for Rustenburg High School and I played for Grey College." Nicolas had never met the man and was relying on the government's website. He hoped the attendant would not bother to verify the story. "In fact," he continued quickly, shifting the narrative, "I played for Grey College when Morné du Plessis was there. Remember him?"

"The one who managed the Springboks when they won the Rugby World Cup in '95?"

"The very same," said Nicolas. "Even Madiba was there, wore the Springbok jersey when he came onto the field—number six—same as our captain."

"I was there," said the attendant beaming. "I saw it all. Did you see the film they made?"

"*Invictus?*"

"Ja, that's the one. It was good. Made me proud."

"I saw it," said Nicolas. "And I was at the final in '95...invited as a former Springbok."

"You played rugby for the Boks?"

"Yes, in the '70s. I was on the team that beat the All Blacks in '76. Morné was our captain. Man, those were great games."

The attendant extended his hand. "Proud to meet you, Reverend," he said, his handshake firm. "And Madiba will be here tomorrow," he added.

"Really," replied Nicolas, feigning surprise. "At the game?"

"Ja, at the opening ceremony. It will be great to see the father of our nation again."

Nicolas nodded and smiled.

"So, Reverend, what's your business here?"

"Ah," he responded, pointing to the sky. "The Lord's business."

The attendant smiled indulgently. "And the suitcase?"

"Bibles for the skyboxes," he said, balancing on one leg as he opened the suitcase on the knee of his other leg. "To remind our visitors that God is on the side of Bafana Bafana, the twelfth man on our team when we play Mexico."

"Good one, Reverend," said the attendant with a grin. "Our witchdoctors have thrown the bones and made magic muti too." He laughed. "Go ahead, Reverend. Whatever it takes, hey."

"I agree, my good man," said Nicolas, doffing his fedora as he passed through the turnstile. "Whatever it takes."

He headed into the stadium towards one of the eight large ramps that provided access to the upper tiers. Nobody paid any attention to him as he made his way to the top tier. He could see the setting sun through the stadium's mottled patchwork of exterior panels as they curved gracefully over his head.

From above, he imagined the stadium must have looked like an open pot with a wide brim. From below, the underside of the pot's brim was cantilevered in a sweeping curve from the upper concourse towards the center of the playing field before stopping in midair, leaving a graceful oval opening over the field. A translucent, sand-colored membrane covered the underneath of the cantilevered roof, revealing blurred impressions of the matrix of braces and struts that supported the overhanging structure.

He had made sure to reconnoiter the stadium at a recent game between the AmaZulu team from Natal and the "The Clever Boys," the nickname of a local team affiliated with Wits University. It had been a full rehearsal for tomorrow's opening of the World Cup, complete with cheering fans waving flags and banners and blowing cacophonous vuvuzela trumpets. And during a halftime reconnaissance walk, he had identified the best place to access the roof—from one of the twelve huge concrete supports that ringed the stadium, the one directly opposite the players' entrance to the field.

Satisfied with his plan, he moved down the ramp to a kitchen on the hospitality suite level and slipped inside. He closed the door and flipped on the light switch. There were several appliances against the walls, and a tall stack of potato chip boxes in one corner. A stainless-steel island counter stood in the center of the room. He opened the suitcase on the counter and unpacked the Bibles that took up the visible space. Then he lifted out the false bottom of the suitcase, revealing a hidden compartment about five inches deep. Not original, he knew, but adequate.

In the compartment, in a bed of hard foam with shaped cutouts for its various pieces, lay an Arctic Warfare Covert model .308 bolt-action rifle handmade by Accuracy International. The AWC's detached twelve-inch barrel with its integrated silencer was lying at an angle across the main body of the rifle with its folding stock and Schmidt & Bender telescopic sight. There were smaller cutouts for the bolt, a bipod, a ten-shot magazine and a spare box of cartridges. Not the lightest at just over thirteen pounds, but definitely the best, most compact sniper rifle he'd been able to find through his Recce contacts.

He assembled the rifle, inserted the preloaded magazine, worked the bolt action with quiet precision to chamber a round, then engaged the safety.

Next to the foam rifle bed—which took up about two-thirds of the available space in the hidden compartment of the suitcase—and tightly packed in the remaining space, were the other items he needed: a fixed-blade Ka-Bar knife in a leather sheath, a laser range finder, his well-worn tawny-colored beret, low-profile running shoes that packed almost flat, a telescoping aluminum tube, a roll of duct tape, a pair of rubberized gloves and a length of black synthetic rope knotted at two-foot intervals attached to the eye of a lightweight and collapsible grappling hook. There was just enough space left across the top of the hidden compartment for a few toiletries, a change of underwear, a pair of socks, a fresh shirt and a pair of blue jeans.

And Mandela's gun.

He racked the pistol's slide to chamber a round and made sure the safety was set.

Nicolas emerged from the kitchen just after one o'clock in the morning wearing his black cleric shirt and pants, his black running shoes and the rubber gloves, with the rifle in one hand and the pole, rope and hook in the other. The Ka-Bar's sheath was looped through his belt at his back and the Makarov lay snug in a holster inside his waistband. The duct tape and range finder were in his pant pockets.

He kept low as he made his way up the ramp, moving quickly through the multipatterned shadows of the Calabash to the upper tier. There was nobody in sight. He took a moment to catch his breath and wipe his face with his beret—an old habit—before he crossed to the concrete support structure he had selected to access the roof. It stood about twelve feet high, two feet thick, and fifteen feet deep—a solid support for the overhead trusses that rested on its crown.

After slipping the rifle strap over his head and across his chest, the rifle snug against his back, he prepared to climb. First he extended the top section of the telescoping aluminum tube, unfolded the three claws of the grappling hook, locked them in place, then inserted the neck of the hook into the top of the aluminum tube. He had precut a narrow slot in the top section of the tube for the neck of the hook to slip inside the tube but allow the rope attached to the hook to hang free. The idea was to lift the hook into place with the tube while holding the free end of the rope. He had dismissed the idea of trying to throw the hook over the trusses—too noisy and too unpredictable.

Next he extended the telescoping tube to its full length and raised the hook towards the trusses above the concrete support, aiming for the main truss that encircled the stadium. When he judged one of the claws to be above the main truss, he lowered the tube until he felt the hook snag the truss and then tugged on the rope to make sure the hook was secure. Satisfied, he telescoped the tube to its shortest length, slipped the tube into his pant belt and started to climb. He used his arms and hands to pull himself up, his gloves providing a dependable grip on the knotted rope, while the running shoes provided silent, tactile contact with the concrete support.

It took less than a minute to reach the top of the support and the main truss. Leaving the hook in place, he reeled in the dangling rope and stuffed it with his gloves and the tube into a crevice created by the intersection of two roof trusses.

So far so good, he thought as he contemplated the cavernous wedge-shaped gloom of the cantilevered roof. From where he stood at the wide end of the wedge, the top and bottom of the wedge extended at a slight incline into the murky darkness until they came together over the perimeter of the playing field. He could just make out a maze of braces that connected the top and bottom struts of the roof like a futuristic, three-dimensional spider web. And beneath the struts the roof was covered with the translucent membrane he had seen from below.

He inched his way along one of the inclined struts until he reached a section of the roof he judged optimal for his purpose. Then he unslung the rifle and lowered himself onto his stomach. The strut was not comfortable but just wide enough. He jammed his feet against the vertical brace behind him and laid the rifle across the strut ahead of him and in front of another vertical brace to hold it in place.

He took a moment to orientate himself before unsnapping the clasp around the stacked leather handle of his Ka-Bar. Then he unsheathed the knife, reached forward and cut two long parallel slits about twelve inches apart and three feet long into the membrane below him. Next he made a horizontal cut across the top of the two slits. The rectangular flap fell out of sight, replaced by a sudden rush of winter air through the opening that caused his eyes to water. Fortunately, it would be warm when the time came to be clear-sighted.

Although it was too dark to make out any detail of the football pitch through the narrow flap, he could see a single light directly opposite him in the players' tunnel leading onto the field. His range finder indicated just over 140 yards from his position across the width of the playing field to the touchline on the far side. He assumed the players would form a traditional line to sing their national anthems and be greeted by dignitaries. The custom would give him direct line of sight to his target across the field. The bullet drop would be minimal over such a short range, and the air inside the stadium would be still, eliminating any wind factor.

He retrieved the rifle, unfolded the stock and checked the sight adjustment. He had zeroed in the telescopic sight on the farm of his father's friend outside Krugersdorp where he had stayed the past week. His three-shot groupings over 150 yards had been within a hair's breadth of perfection through an empty coffee can. He made a minor adjustment to the sight for the actual distance measured with the laser—his estimate had been pretty close. Then he stretched out with his left arm across the strut, nestled the butt of the rifle against his right shoulder with the forestock across the back of his left hand, and adjusted his position until he was aiming through the opening in the membrane at the single light in the players' tunnel.

It was awkward, but he would not miss at this range, even with the short barrel of the AWC. He checked to make sure the safety was still engaged before returning the rifle to the braced support strut in front of him.

The last task before he settled in for the long wait was to deal with the hanging flap he had cut. Reaching down into the void, he pulled the loose end up through the opening and taped it back in its original position. It would take sharp eyes to notice the slits from below. When the time came to reopen the flap, he would use the tape to secure the flap on his side of the opening and make sure it did not hang below him and attract attention.

Nicolas settled in for a solitary vigil he knew so well from a different time and place—the uncomfortable hours lying in ambush in Angola, sometimes on sand but often on rock, his R5 ready, his every nerve alive to the night sounds that might betray his quarry or reveal his position.

He was pleased he had used the restroom earlier.

It would be a long night.

In the bush war, the ANC terrorists had been indistinguishable from locals—none wore uniforms—which made identifying them impossible until an AK-47 materialized in their hands. The Recces all wore camouflage outfits but avoided visual cues of rank or leadership—no insignia or saluting—to deny enemy marksman a prized target.

But there would be no effort at subterfuge when the founding commander of the ANC's armed struggle entered the stadium—his aura was his rank—and everyone around him would show him the utmost deference, as though welcoming a messiah.

He thought about his exit strategy. He knew his instincts and training would engage when the time came, but the truth was he didn't expect to get away with it. His only chance would come during the confusion after the shooting. If he could get out of the roof and down to the kitchen unseen while everyone's attention was focused on the field, he might find a way to get out alive.

Despite the odds, he did not regret his choice of the Soccer City stadium. Even before it was transformed into the Calabash for the World Cup, it had achieved iconic status in the black community, a place of mourning and of celebration. It was where the funerals of prominent leaders of the struggle like Chris Hani had been held, and where Mandela had addressed over eighty thousand supporters two days after his release in 1990. And in just a few hours it would host the opening of the 2010 World Cup, blessed by Mandela himself.

He had hoped to use Mandela's pistol as his primary weapon, but the stadium opportunity required a rifle shot. Still, it was useful to have a backup—he might just need the pistol before all was said and done. Besides, in a curious irony, the feel of the gun at his side was like having Mandela with him above the stadium as he waited for the dawn. He found himself drifting into dialogue with Mandela, expressing all the anger and bitterness that weighed so heavily on his spirit, saying all the things that needed to be said if he ever got the chance.

Aside from his thoughts, his only companion for the night was whatever he could hear through the earbuds of his mobile phone. He made sure the ringer was off and checked his Internet connection. Then he selected a playlist of Albrecht Mayer's oboe concertos and closed his eyes. Moments later his silent world was transformed by a virtuoso who somehow compressed soaring lyricism and unadorned darkness into exquisite double-reed harmony through the tiny bore of a woodwind instrument handcrafted from African blackwood.

As he lay suspended high above the stadium listening to the music and thinking about the day to come, his thoughts flew to the top of the mountain fortress of Masada, overlooking the Dead Sea. The ramps of the Calabash became the ramp built by the Romans to storm the fortress—the last holdout of the Jews in their rebellion after the Romans destroyed much of Jerusalem in AD 70. He saw himself among the thousand covenant people on the mountaintop, knowing their end was near, trying to decide whether to fight to the last or to take their own lives—men, women and children—rather than give the Romans the glory of victory and the satisfaction of the rape and slaughter to follow.

And he heard himself pleading with the rebel leaders to fight—that God surely would give them a great victory as His chosen people in their promised land even against the overwhelming numbers of soldiers massed in the valley below. But the rebels chose mass suicide, and Masada fell into Roman hands. Yet the Jewish people had learned from their defeat—and the subsequent diaspora that split them apart for nearly two thousand years—when they reclaimed their promised land in 1948. Masada became an icon of resistance, an enduring symbol of their determination to live free, to never give up despite being surrounded by enemies on all sides.

It was the Jewish story; it was the Afrikaner story. Overwhelming numbers had also surrounded them. They had fought but ultimately surrendered. Thankfully, there had been no slaughter. Yet now, twenty years later, the reconciliation forged by Mandela and De Klerk faced an existential threat from the tyranny and corruption of ANC leadership. The ties that bound them all together in "a single garment of destiny," as Martin Luther King had said of the American people, were being ripped apart.

Nicolas drew a deep breath as he thought of his beloved country...and of his beloved family. He had chosen a lonely path that would likely lead to a lonely death.

The commando trip with his father started playing through his mind's eye like a grainy old film...the horse ride from the farm...the terrorist hideout...the buried gun...his father taking aim...

His head jerked. He rubbed the sleep from his eyes and checked his watch—nearly five o'clock in the morning. Although he had plenty of time before the game, he was immediately filled with a premonition that something was wrong. He reached out in the dark to make sure the rifle was still resting on the strut, the knife secure in its sheath, the Makarov safely holstered.

All was as it should be—yet nothing was.

He had learned to rely on his instincts, and they seldom let him down. It had to be something else, something out there, beyond his dark world above the stadium. He took out his mobile phone. No texts and no calls—just a few spam emails.

He pulled up the *Mail & Guardian* news website.

"Goddammit!" he erupted under his breath. "Jesus, I don't bloody believe it."

He reread the breaking news: a concert in Soweto featuring Shakira and the Black Eyed Peas...thirteen-year-old Zenani Mandela killed when her driver lost control on the way home after the concert...her heartbroken great-grandfather, Nelson Mandela, staying home...not attending the opening ceremony of the World Cup at the Calabash.

42

FOR THE LOVE OF LIFE

2010

Nicolas was filled with a rush of desire to live. Too much was at stake to waste his life on a nonevent. But he needed to get out of the roof and into his clerical garb before the workers and the crowd started arriving for the game.

He slung the rifle across his back, retraced his route along the strut, retrieved the tube and rope, slipped on his gloves, dropped the rope over the main truss and climbed down. He decided to leave the rope—it would take precious minutes trying to recover the grappling hook with the telescoping tube. Instead, he flung the loose end up and over the concrete support—not a perfect solution, but at least the rope was more or less out of sight and not dangling at eye level. Then he ran down the ramp and slipped into the kitchen.

He snapped on the light, set the suitcase on the table and lifted out the false bottom. His hands flew as he disassembled the rifle, folded the stock, laid the pieces into their foam cutouts and repacked his gear before replacing the false bottom of the case.

He was reaching for his jacket when he heard it—somebody whistling nearby.

The tune was instantly recognizable, an old Boer song, "My Sarie Marais," about a homesick soldier longing for the love of his life and the land of his birth. Whoever the whistler was, he was very close to the kitchen door.

He quickly slipped on his jacket, stepped into his black shoes, adjusted his clerical collar and put on his fedora.

The door opened behind him.

"Hey, what's going on here? What are you doing?" The gruff male voice betrayed an Afrikaner origin.

Nicolas forced his best Sunday smile and turned to face the man.

"Ag, sorry, Reverend," the man stammered. "I didn't mean to give you a fright. Just checking the facilities."

"No, that's all right, Sergeant," responded Nicolas, noting the three-striped chevron on the stocky man's uniform. "I was just having a quiet moment before setting up a stall for this afternoon's game. A good opportunity to reach those who believe God comes in the shape of a football."

"Good luck converting this lot, Reverend," said the sergeant, advancing towards the table. "So what's in the case?" he asked. "I have to check, you understand, with all the dignitaries scheduled to attend."

"Certainly," agreed Nicolas, moving aside as the sergeant stepped up to the table. "As you can see, Sergeant, a case full of Bibles to hand out today to anyone who will spare me a minute."

He turned to face the suitcase and positioned himself shoulder to shoulder with the sergeant as the man reached in and picked up one of the Bibles. Just as he began flipping the pages, the sergeant glanced at the space the book had occupied. Then he held the spine of the book horizontally against the outside of the suitcase, as though comparing the thickness of the book with the depth of the case.

Nicolas tensed.

The sergeant laid the Bible aside, reached into the case, and pushed on the space where the book had been. The false bottom of the case depressed under the sergeant's hand.

"Reverend," he began in a puzzled tone, "what's under—"

Nicolas hit the man as hard as he could with a short, vicious elbow punch to his solar plexus. The sergeant let out a startled grunt and doubled over. Before he could recover, Nicolas grabbed the back of the man's head and smashed his forehead into the table. The sergeant went limp and crumpled to the floor.

Nicolas quickly closed the kitchen door and unsheathed his knife. But as he looked down at the helpless sergeant, he heard again the strains of "My Sarie Marais" in his mind's ear and knew he couldn't kill him, despite the fact the man had seen his face.

After a moment's indecision, he retrieved the duct tape from his suitcase and taped the man's mouth closed, his ankles together and his hands behind his back. A quick search of the man's pockets produced a two-way radio and a mobile phone. He switched them both off, then dragged the man behind the stack of potato chip boxes. Satisfied, he shut his suitcase, straightened his suit, lifted the fedora to finger-comb his hair and walked to the door. He turned off the light, stood for a few moments in the dark, breathing deeply, then opened the door and put on his dark glasses.

There was nobody in sight. He quietly closed the door behind him, walked briskly down the ramps and headed for an exit gate. Early arrivals were already crowding the turnstiles. No one paid any attention to him as he exited and headed for the transit station.

The train ride back to Johannesburg gave him time to consider his options. Airplanes were fast but airport security tight. Car rentals were efficient but required too much paperwork. Trains were slow but security was lax. By default, trains seemed least risky, and he was already using the rail system.

He considered heading northwest to Victoria Falls or northeast to the Kruger National Park, or perhaps west towards Botswana and the Okavango Delta. But he still had unfinished business with Mandela. And although he had no idea of Mandela's plans, his instinct told him to head for Cape Town. It was home to the Houses of Parliament, the office and official residence of the president, and site of the brand-new World Cup stadium on the waterfront. It was also nearly a thousand miles from the Calabash, far enough to put some distance between him and what had happened at the stadium. Besides, it was less than an hour's drive from his own home in the Cape winelands.

He breathed easier, knowing he had a destination and the rough contours of a plan. But his plan was based on a fast train leaving as soon as possible, not some milk train that stopped at every little station along the way. He did a quick Internet search on his phone. His best option was the Blue Train if he could get a seat at the last minute on one of the most luxurious travel options on the continent of Africa.

The website showed only one berth still available for today's departure—a deluxe suite with twin beds and a shower—providing a luxurious mobile sanctuary for the twenty-seven-hour journey to Cape Town. But timing was tight—the train left Pretoria at eight thirty, in less than three hours, and the commuter connection via Johannesburg would eat up much of that time. And he had to take the risk that an online credit card purchase could destroy his alibi. But he didn't have enough cash for the ticket or enough time to find a bank.

He bought the ticket.

The next problem was his appearance—too distinctive as a pastor. He considered changing clothes in the train's restroom, but onboard security cameras would record the change. He decided to wait and take advantage of the anonymity of a busy Johannesburg station restroom.

His train arrived in the city behind schedule, and it took several minutes to locate a restroom. As he walked in he noticed a janitor's trolley with a box of large black garbage bags. He stripped a bag from the box and stepped into a private stall. He quickly removed the Bibles from the suitcase and dropped them into the garbage bag, changed into his spare shirt and jeans, pulled on his running shoes and stuffed his black clothes and religious trappings into the suitcase. Satisfied, he exited the stall, jammed his fedora into a waste receptacle, and moved to a handbasin where he shaved with hand soap, combed his hair and put on his dark glasses. Then he left the restroom and, after dropping the garbage bag next to a garbage can—he couldn't bring himself to dump bibles into the trash—boarded the commuter train to Pretoria.

He found himself willing the commuter to reach Pretoria in time to make the Blue Train connection. Under normal circumstances he would have taken the time to pay his respects at the Voortrekker Monument outside the city. It always reminded him of the Jewish memorial to the holocaust in Jerusalem—Yad Vashem—in remembrance of the most grotesque crime against humanity in recorded history. Like the Jews, the Afrikaners were determined to honor and never forget the suffering of those who had gone before. His parents had spoken with such pride about the monument, and how they had gone with the wagons to Blood River where they were married, while others had gone to Pretoria to lay the foundation stones for the new monument.

The train shuddered. The jolt forced him to focus on the task ahead. He was still dissatisfied with his appearance—he felt acutely underdressed for the Blue Train wearing just a shirt and jeans and running shoes. He needed something more, perhaps a jacket, not only to look more respectable on the luxury train but also to conceal the knife and pistol when he was in public places.

Fortunately, when the commuter train did finally pull into the Pretoria station, he had more time than expected to make the Blue Train connection and just enough time to look for a jacket. But it was just a train station—there were no shopping options for men's clothing. Frustrated, he decided to take a minute to use the restroom—it had been a long night—and afterwards found himself standing at the handbasins next to a well-dressed man about the same size as himself. The man had rolled up his sleeves and was about to wash his face. Just behind the man stood a wheeled briefcase and, draped over its retractable handle, a denim sport coat.

The opportunity was irresistible. Nicolas snatched the jacket the moment the man dipped his head to wash his face and quickly left the restroom. Then he nonchalantly slung the jacket over his shoulder and, with less than five minutes to spare, climbed into the gleaming blue cocoon of the luxury train and slipped inside his cabin. He took a moment to search the pockets of the jacket, finding nothing more than a used train ticket.

He smiled as he looked around at the understated elegance of the luxury suite. The design elements were appealing, even to him—the African-motif scatter cushions, soft pewter-colored upholstery, brass light fixtures set into wood paneling, fuchsia-colored flowers in a delicate vase, the exquisitely detailed wooden table beneath a panoramic picture window, and a double bed and private half bathroom with marble surfaces and gold fittings.

After showering, he plugged in his mobile phone to charge, then sat back on the settee, the monogrammed dressing gown sensual against his skin, and closed his eyes. It felt so good it was almost decadent.

He could feel his heart rate slow as the tension drained. His thoughts drifted to the roof of the Calabash...The long night and the news report...The mad scramble out of the roof...The headlong rush to escape.

He opened his eyes and was amazed to discover the train had left the station without him sensing the motion. He glanced through the window at the silent blur of the Highveld and then at the neatly printed itinerary propped up against the vase on the table—brunch at noon and afternoon tea at three thirty.

And a stop at Kimberley, including a visit to the Big Hole.

43

THE BIG HOLE

2010

Kimberley. The prospect immediately conjured up images of his grandfather digging for diamonds. He still remembered the stories passed down through his father, vivid images of brutal mining camps—hard living, hard drinking, hard times and a sprinkling of good fortune.

And the story of a black miner—a strange story about a diamond and a flogging and his grandfather helping the man, even taking him home to the family farm at Sannah's Post.

The farm. His tired brain began threading together the tapestry of his early years, bringing to life the bucolic strands of early morning roosters and mourning doves, the pungent odor of the cattle barn, the snort and stamp of his favorite horse and the aroma of lamb stew on the coal stove. And, as his eyes grew heavy, he heard again the reassurance of his mother singing the Lord's Prayer at Sunday services, his father saying grace over evening meals, the earnest dignity of Solomon's reports about crops and cattle, and the family stories recounted by his father from the comfort of his favorite chair in front of the fireplace...

He woke with a start. It was midafternoon and he was

hungry—he had slept through both sittings of brunch. The only option before dinner was high tea in the lounge car. It would have to do.

He pulled on his jeans, spare shirt and running shoes, adjusted the pistol holster and knife sheath around his waist, and put on the jacket. It was stylish, good quality, fit him quite well and looked almost fashionable over his untucked blue-green checked shirt and slightly creased jeans. It also draped comfortably over the two weapons around his waist.

He locked the suitcase and hid it under blankets on the overhead luggage rack. He did not have much confidence in the security of his suite, but it would look ridiculous if he took his suitcase to tea. Besides, it was a luxury train full of wealthy travelers and tourists—the risk seemed low.

He passed through several cars on his way to tea and was surprised to discover each car had a butler cabin at one end. He had never had a butler wait on him and noticed several on his way to tea. As he reached the dining car, he glanced back into the adjoining kitchen car and marveled at the tight but efficient culinary incubator of the meals he would soon enjoy, already a hive of activity. He passed through the dining car into a lavishly appointed nonsmoking lounge car with attentive waitstaff and a curved bar counter midway along its length.

The lounge appeared almost full—it took a moment to spot a vacant armchair. As he sat down, a woman seated adjacent to him caught his attention. In a car full of older guests, her youthful elegance was as conspicuous as it was stunning, crowned by an auburn wave that swept down and across her alabaster complexion like an exotic shroud. It took all his willpower not to stare.

The tea service was immaculate and the waitstaff deferential. He selected rooibos and a scone with blackberry jam and clotted cream. As he set his plated scone down on a travel magazine lying on a side table, he heard the woman choose Earl Grey with lemon. And when the waiter moved away, he noticed the title of the book she had laid aside to take her tea. *Pride and Prejudice*. He had not read it, but Charlene had adored Jane Austen and loved to share all the complex social plots, so much so that he still recalled most of the leading characters.

He glanced at the woman's face and was astonished to see her looking directly at him, her amber-colored eyes piercing the reddish-brown veil of hair, her demure smile only fractionally wider than the Mona Lisa's—a fraction that made all the difference. Then she looked away, opened her book and resumed reading.

He sat for a while looking out of the opposite picture window as the train meandered through the winter landscape at a leisurely fifty miles per hour. It was all so genteel. He had a second scone and another cup of tea, flipped through the travel magazine and occasionally stole a glance at the woman. Just as he was about to get up and return to his suite, the woman leaned towards him holding out a folded napkin with a pen. He instinctively took the items and glanced at her as their fingers touched. The demure smile again. Then she looked away.

He unfolded the napkin and read the neatly printed message. "Dinner? Second sitting?"

He looked up. She was reading. He hesitated, thinking about what lay behind him and what might lie ahead, then smoothed the napkin on the magazine, took a deep breath and wrote, Yes & Yes. Then he refolded the napkin, stood up and nonchalantly laid it and the pen on the padded armrest of her chair as he walked past.

She did not look up.

He smiled and returned to his suite.

The train drew to a stop in Kimberley. Within minutes the passengers were snaking disjointedly along the platform towards the railway museum and the waiting coach. A five-mile drive took them to the Big Hole and the complex of buildings that included a visitors' center with shops, a theater and an underground mining experience.

He detached from the group before it reached the visitors' center and headed directly into Old Town. Set among the collection of buildings was a replica of an old family farmstead. He took pleasure imagining his grandparents in the kitchen, in the bedroom, on the porch, living and working among men and women driven by the quest for life-changing fortunes. From the farmstead he wandered past the old Digger's pub, the Boxing and Skittle Alley, the Rothschild Auction Market, and into the visitors' center. He saw his tour group returning from the viewing platform and headed in their direction and towards the platform, sipping from a bottle of water he had brought from the train.

He emerged from the visitors' center onto a huge red ramp, supported by a web of overhead cables, extending to a cantilevered observation deck that overlooked the Big Hole. The observation deck turned out to be a square walkway, offering views over the outside and inside of the deck.

The view was astounding. The fact that he was alone added to the grandeur of the moment. He knew from an information board he had seen that he was looking at the largest man-made hole on the planet, with a rim about a mile in circumference and nearly eight hundred feet deep, although the lower vertical walled crater of the original open-cast mine was now filled with aqua-blue water. Above the water-filled crater and reaching up to the rim beneath the observation deck, the vertical hole became a steeply sloped funnel shaped like a martini glass, with a scattering of shrubs and trees clinging to the precipitous grade. A patch of trees almost directly below the deck was unusually dense, creating a canopy over the rocky terrain.

It was almost impossible to believe that hands wielding only picks and shovels had dug a hole so big. It had taken about forty years, the miners working claims the size of the deck he was standing on—thirty square Cape feet. He shook his head as he thought of his grandfather digging somewhere in the vast hole beneath him, playing his part in the obsession that yielded more than fourteen million carats of diamonds before the mine was closed at the start of the Great War.

Movement caught his eye. He glanced back towards the visitors' center. Two men were walking down the ramp towards him—one white, one black, both burly—and showing no interest in the view, their attention focused on him. When the men reached the junction where the ramp split at right angles in opposite directions, they exchanged glances before separating, each taking an opposite leg of the walkway.

Nicolas immediately recognized the threat. He was trapped between two tough guys—the white guy hunched like a front row forward in a rugby scrum intent on battering the opposition, the black guy moving like a light heavyweight looking to deliver a knockout punch.

He quickly assessed his options: the Makarov, but he would need two shots—too noisy; the knife, but that meant fighting both men at close quarters—too risky; the Big Hole, but he might not survive the jump—a dead end in more ways than one. Then fate intervened with a fourth option when the white man drew a pistol from a concealed holster, a silencer protruding unmistakably from its short barrel.

A tight smile creased Nicolas's features as the outline of a plan came together.

"What can I do for you gentlemen?" he called amiably as he visualized the next few minutes.

The men had rounded the corners of the deck on opposite sides of him and were now closing in on him. He kept his back towards the Big Hole, unscrewed the cap of his water bottle and transferred the bottle to his left hand.

The white man on his right with the pistol spoke. "You are Nicolas de Beer?" It sounded more like an accusation than an inquiry.

"Yes," he said agreeably. "It's a family name. Who are you?"

"We're with internal security," the man said. "We're investigating an incident at Soccer City in Soweto this morning—some funny business in the roof of the stadium and a police officer was attacked in one of the kitchens. A single white male was seen leaving the stadium by train and a single white male bought a ticket on the Blue Train at the last minute. You're the man who bought the ticket. You can understand why we need to ask you a few questions."

Nicolas nodded, as though impressed by the logic. "So why the gun? And why the silencer?"

"We can't afford to take any chances," the man said, pointing the pistol directly at his chest. "And you never know when a silencer might come in handy."

Nicolas smiled—his thoughts exactly—as the two men advanced to about ten feet from him, one on each side.

"Well, you're right," he said. "I am a single white male. My wife died many years ago in a terrorist bombing. And I did buy a ticket at the last minute today—the wife and I always wanted to take a trip on the Blue Train, but we never got the chance. And if I'd thought about it too long, I would never have bought the ticket—too damned expensive. But you only live once, hey."

He chuckled, inviting the men to share his indulgent pleasure. "But as for the Soccer City business," he continued, "well, I wasn't there, so I can't be the man you're looking for. I'm sure the police officer has given you a description of his attacker."

He knew he was taking a chance, but he had to know.

The man stared hard at him. "The officer has a head injury—he does not recall the attack." He paused. "You'll have to come with us, De Beer. We need to talk to you at the local police station."

The pistol in the man's right hand waved towards the visitors' center.

"Ag, no... please, man," protested Nicolas. "If we do that, I'll miss the train." He turned to face the black man. "I've waited too long and paid too much for the ticket," he implored, backing towards the man with the pistol. "Give me a break. You guys know I'm on the train. Can't our little talk wait till I get to Cape Town?" He backed closer. "And if you can't get to Cape Town, I'm sure you have people there who can meet me and do the interrogation."

"Hey, you heard me," demanded the man behind him, jabbing him aggressively in the back with his pistol. "Let's go!"

Nicolas raised his hands as though to comply, then flipped the open water bottle end over end at the black man and yelled "Catch!" As the spray of water whipped into the man's face, Nicolas spun clockwise around the ball of his right foot and, leading with his right arm bent at the elbow, knocked aside the man's pistol hand with his forearm.

He heard the muffled explosion of the shot fired harmlessly over the Big Hole. In the next instant, as though recoiling from his first effort, he drove the heel of his right hand straight up at the tip of the man's nose. He heard the crunch of nasal bones shattering, caught the man's pistol hand as he stumbled backwards, forced his right forefinger into the pistol's trigger guard on top of the man's trigger finger and immediately swung the pistol toward the sound of the black man charging at him from behind. The arc of the swinging pistol and the man's lunging hands came together in a blur of movement that lurched to a sudden stop when Nicolas pulled the trigger. The man staggered—eyes wide with shock—then crumpled face-first to the deck at Nicolas's feet.

He glanced at the visitors' center. The shots were surprisingly loud despite the silencer, but the noise hadn't attracted any obvious attention.

Without a second thought, he lifted the white man under his armpits until his limp body was draped backwards across the rounded barrier railing, then tipped him over the edge of the deck. The man was still holding the pistol as he tumbled silently into the gaping chasm below. Then he squatted over the black man, grabbed his trouser belt in one hand and the back of his heavy coat collar in his other hand and, as though performing a weightlifting clean and jerk, lifted him to chest height, paused for a moment, then straightened his legs and thrust the man's body up and over the edge of the deck.

He looked to where the men had fallen into the canopy of trees—their bodies could not be seen from above. Then he checked the deck surface—the smear of blood where the black man had fallen would be hard to miss. He looked for a solution and saw his water bottle lying where it had fallen, still with some water in it. He took off his shoes and socks, poured a little water over the blood smear, wiped the blood with one sock and dried it with the other. Satisfied, he rolled the socks into a single damp ball and threw it as far as he could towards the Big Hole. He watched it land on the slope and roll over the edge of the crater into the water below. Then he put on his shoes and walked quickly back to the visitors' center.

He was breathing hard, unsettled by the violent encounter.

But his options had been limited, his combat skills and instinct for self-preservation reflexive. He headed into the restroom to wash his hands and face and finger-comb his hair. He stared at his reflection, thinking of the two men. Poor buggers—just doing their duty against an internal threat as he had done in the border wars against an external threat. He dropped his head and said a silent prayer—that by some miracle the men would survive their injuries despite the peril that would present for him. He shuddered, exited the restroom and slipped into the rear of the movie theater for the last minutes of the documentary about the Big Hole.

He closed his eyes and took several long, deep breaths, willing his heart rate to slow. The soundtrack signaled the closing credits. As the lights came up, he opened his eyes and saw the Englishwoman sitting on the far side of the theater looking at him. She smiled. He nodded.

The tour group exited the theater and reconvened in the lobby where the guide announced the train's departure was delayed for technical reasons. They boarded a coach and were driven a few miles to the Diamond Pavilion for some additional shopping to pass the time. Although he was not a shopper, there were a few items he needed. It didn't take long. The Trappers store had it all—a khaki shirt and long pants, a pair of his favorite *veldskoen* ankle boots, as soft as they were durable, plus hiking socks and a button-down pale-blue Oxford shirt with a matching tie.

He knew men were supposed to wear a jacket and tie to dinner on the Blue Train and was sure the Englishwoman would be in eveningwear. Despite the violence at the Big Hole, he did not want to cancel their dinner arrangement—he thought it might help him build an alibi to avoid being implicated in what had happened on the observation deck. And the truth was, he was looking forward to their dinner.

He paid in cash.

The Blue Train left Kimberley just after eight o'clock, an hour behind schedule. But his escape was still on track, at least for the next several hours...as far as he knew.

44

THE BOY FLOWER

2010

It felt as though unseen hands were reaching for him through the night as the Blue Train snaked southwards through the semi-desert Karoo towards the majestic mountains of the Cape. As much as he enjoyed the train's creature comforts, he now knew the whisper-quiet refinement had induced a false sense of security. He had narrowly avoided disaster, but his trail was fresh and there to be found.

He showered and dressed as carefully as his limited options allowed.

The delayed second sitting was called at ten o'clock. He entered the opulent dining car a little after ten. The ambiance was enchanting, even seductive—the clink of silverware against monogrammed white plate ware, the scent of flowers creatively arranged in silver vases, the bouquet of red wines glowing in cut-glass stemware, the tang of charbroiled meat and pan-seared fish, and the elegantly dressed waiters pampering the select few in hushed tones.

The Englishwoman was seated halfway down the aisle, attentively scanning a menu. Her ecru-colored evening dress—satin or silk, he couldn't tell which—hung like an afterthought from tiny spaghetti straps over bare shoulders, a perfect canvas for her striking features.

"May I join you?" he asked when he reached her table.

She looked up, eyebrows arched. "That depends, sir."

"On what?" he asked, smiling but feeling a little awkward being challenged as he stood in the aisle.

"On whether you agree that a single man in possession of a good fortune must be in want of a wife."

"What?"

"You heard me—do you agree?"

"No."

"Are you?"

"Am I what?"

"In possession of a good fortune?"

"No."

"In want of a wife?"

"No."

"A single man?"

"Yes."

She smiled. "That'll do very nicely," she said, gesturing to the chair opposite her.

He extended his hand as he sat down, uncomfortably aware of the pistol and knife beneath his jacket. "I'm Nicolas. Nice to meet you."

The woman took his hand—light and soft and warm. "Nice to meet you, too," she said warmly. "I'm—"

"No, let me guess," he interrupted. "Your name is... Emma."

Her auburn hair flew as she threw back her head and laughed, the sound as warm and pleasing as her touch had been.

"Not quite," she said with a playful smile. "Care to try again?"

He nodded, tilted his head, stroked his chin, and did his best to appear in deep thought as he considered her from every angle. She appeared to enjoy the scrutiny. Then, as though experiencing a divine revelation, he laid both hands on the table and said, "I have it!"

"Oh yes? Pray, do tell."

He leaned forward and, in a stage whisper, as though revealing a great secret, said, "Your name is Elizabeth, but your friends call you Lizzy."

Her smile froze as she stared wide-eyed before recovering her composure. "However did you know that?" she asked, astonished. "You must be clairvoyant... or a spy."

He shrugged. It had been a wild guess. The story of his wife's love for Jane Austen, especially the character of Elizabeth Bennet in *Pride and Prejudice*—known to her friends and family as Lizzy—was not one he wanted to tell. Not now, not to this woman, even though she was reading the novel.

"So, Elizabeth, what's a beautiful Englishwoman doing traveling alone on the Blue Train?"

"You may call me Lizzy," she offered, "for I have a feeling we shall soon become great friends." She smiled again—a ready and easy smile. "Well," she began, "I'm more likely to be a tourist than you, an Afrikaner, judging from your accent, traveling alone at great expense on a train renowned for attracting well-heeled foreign tourists. So I might ask you the same question. What's a handsome Afrikaner doing traveling alone on the Blue Train?" she asked, appearing to scrutinize him in much the same way he had just done to her.

The question hung between them for several moments while an elderly couple walked slowly past their table.

"I'm hoping to catch a single woman in possession of a large fortune and in want of a husband, or at least in want of a man. Are you one?"

Sheer delight erupted into laughter, transforming her iridescent features into a glowing landscape that he found utterly captivating.

"You wish," she said, laughing. "No, alas, I'm a humble freelance journalist on a mission to uncover the truth about the new South Africa."

"And doing it in style," he observed. "What story are you following?"

"The World Cup...and Mandela, of course. With a bit of luck there will be another moment of magic like the 1995 Rugby World Cup. I saw it on TV—and in the Invictus movie—but this time I want to be there in person. Too bad about the accident—there won't be any Madiba magic at the World Cup today."

"You mean the girl who died in a car crash last night?"

"Yes. I was supposed to be at today's opening ceremony. But not much point in being there if he's not there—there are more than enough sports writers to cover the game. So I'm going to Cape Town. Bought the train ticket in the wee hours as soon as the news broke—there were only a couple of berths left."

He knew the problem only too well.

"Why Cape Town?"

"Let's just say my reporter's radar tells me that's where he'll appear next," she said with an enigmatic smile.

"Like the Black Pimpernel, popping up unexpectedly here and there."

"Perhaps, although he has no reason to hide anymore."

"Maybe, maybe not. Anyway, where are you staying?"

"The Mount Nelson."

Nicolas raised his eyebrows.

"Yes indeed—*that* Mount Nelson," she said and smiled. "Named after the British Lord Nelson, not the African Lord Nelson," she added, enjoying her own joke. "I love it. Such a wonderful 19th century hotel right in the heart of Cape Town, and Churchill once stayed there. Besides, it's pink, for goodness' sakes. How could I possibly stay anywhere else?"

He chuckled as a black waiter appeared at their table, immaculately dressed in shades of Africa, including a black jacket with zebra-striped lapels and cuffs, and politely inquired if they were ready to order.

"Will you share a plate of Knysna oysters as an appetizer?" she asked.

"Sure, why not?" said Nicolas amiably. "Although I can't say oysters are a regular part of my diet, dear lady. But then again, I'm experiencing a time of firsts in my life, so why—"

"And for your entrée, madam?" asked the waiter, interrupting his soliloquy.

"The ostrich fillet... with seasonal vegetables."

"Very well. And for you, sir?"

"Karoo lamb... medium rare... roast potatoes with vegetables," he said curtly, annoyed at having been interrupted.

"Any wine this evening?" asked the waiter.

"Red?" inquired Nicolas, looking at her.

She nodded.

"Do you have the Allesverloren Shiraz?" he asked without looking at the wine list.

"Yes, sir, we do."

"Then that's what we'll have."

"Very good, sir," said the waiter as he gathered the menus and wine list before disappearing into the kitchen car.

"Allesverloren?" she asked with a coy smile. "All is lost... just because I'm not an heiress looking for a husband?"

"These are desperate times," he said. "Besides, I have to figure out how to pay for the train ticket once I get the bill. This little jaunt is ridiculously expensive."

"Ah, but it's a jaunt with benefits," she said with a smile. "We'll just have to try to ease the pain of your lost fortune and impending ruin, won't we?"

He felt fire dance across his face before it raced down his chest and past his waist. He reached for the glass of iced water, drank half and busied himself arranging the napkin across his lap. Then he looked up. Her Mona Lisa smile widened as their eyes met.

"These orchids are sometimes called moccasins," she said, lightly touching the flower in the silver vase on their table, "although I call them lady's slippers."

Not to be outdone, he pointed at the flowers on the opposite table, their individual red oval-pointed leaves cradling a single, long bulbous stem carrying tiny, virtually invisible flowers. "And those red anthuriums are also known as flamingo flowers."

"Hmm," she mused thoughtfully as a smile played across her features. "I've heard them described as boy flowers."

He glanced at the erect and swollen stem of the flower and instantly felt the fire return to his face. He took another drink of water and wished for the wine. The evening was heading down a path he had not fully anticipated. He was not sure he had the physical or emotional stamina—it had already been a draining day interrupted by moments of extreme violence, perhaps even death. But, when he looked across the table at the alluring woman smiling at him through strands of auburn hair, he was powerless to prevent his mind's eye from slipping beneath the satin.

Or was it silk?

"So, Mr. Oyster-less Nic, what takes you to Cape Town?"

"Adventure," he said, improvising. "I want to dive with great white sharks, hear the spouting of southern right whales, taste wines from every estate in the Cape, bungee jump off the Bloukrans Bridge, paraglide off Signal Hill, hike to the top of Table Mountain and spend the night in the Mountain Club hut on the back table."

"My, my," she said with a bemused expression, "quite the bucket list."

"It grows by the minute," he added. "I also want to look down from Table Mountain onto the Mount Nelson and keep an eye on you."

She smiled. "Any other firsts you have in mind?"

He paused to drink more cold water. "Well, you never know," he said. "I may have a eureka moment, discover a new truth about life or change the course of a nation—make my mark in history."

"My goodness, such lofty goals. Anything more practical, more achievable, more immediate?"

"Perhaps," he said, taking the bait. "It's been a day full of surprises already. Who knows what might happen before the day's carriage turns into a pumpkin?"

The waiter reappeared and offered the wine for approval—Nicolas declined the taste test—before pouring half a glass for them both and setting the bottle down on the table.

"And what do you do for a living to support this adventurous lifestyle?" she asked.

"Ah, well... this is more like a midlife crisis than an adventurous lifestyle," he said, raising his glass.

"To adventurous midlife firsts," she toasted.

"To making history," he countered, swirling the wine before he sipped and swallowed. He drew a deep, satisfied breath, then set the glass down.

"But to answer your question," he continued, "I'm what you might call a freelance motivational speaker. You know, two cups of self-help, a tablespoon of spiritual truth and a pinch of political reality."

"Hmm, sounds...interesting," she said dubiously. "So is this an organized adventure tour of the Cape?"

"More or less. A friend arranged it. I'll just hook up with him and see what he's got planned."

The oysters were served on crushed ice in a silver platter and positioned like the spokes of a wheel around a half lemon. He watched Lizzy drizzle one with lemon juice, deftly loosen it from its half shell with her cocktail fork, then delicately slurp the meat from the wide end of the shell together with a little of the filtered seawater. It did not look appetizing.

He turned and looked out of the window at a landscape shrouded in darkness and obscured by reflected images from inside the car.

"Out there is the Great Karoo," he mused. "My father was with Smuts on commando during the war. They came down into the Cape—maybe even followed this railway line—and fought their way across the bottom of the continent from east to west until they reached the Atlantic."

"Yes, I know," she said. "About the commando, I mean. Deneys Reitz was on commando with Smuts. I read his book."

"Really?" he said, surprised but pleased. "Reitz and my father were friends—they were both at Spion Kop and then with Smuts in the Cape. So you're interested in our history?"

"Oh, absolutely! Such an enthralling saga with so many colorful personalities—from Gandhi, who served the British as a stretcher-bearer at Spion Kop, to Churchill, a war correspondent, captured when a Boer commando ambushed a British armoured train, who escaped by scaling a 10-foot prison wall in the dead of night, and then was in the thick of it at Spion Kop. And the battle for Spion Kop—what terrible carnage—memorialized in football stands all over England. In fact, my father used to take me to see Liverpool play, and we always watched from the Kop amongst the most passionate fans in football—real do-or-die stuff—as though reliving the cut and thrust of battle with every touch of the ball."

Before he could get a word in about his father fighting at Spion Kop and his grandfather dying trying to protect him, she was already talking about Paul Kruger, "a sort of caricature of Abe Lincoln with his stovetop hat and long coat and—"

"And Smuts," he interjected, "a caricature of an Englishman who used guns and bombs against his own people and then betrayed them by siding with the British in both world wars."

"That's a bit harsh, Nic," she replied. "Whatever you may think of Smuts, the world thinks of him very differently—as an international statesman. After all, he was invited to join the British Imperial War Cabinet, helped draft the charter for the League of Nations after the Great War, and is the only world leader to have signed the treaties ending both world wars. If that were not enough, Smuts played a role in founding the Royal Air Force, was appointed a field marshal in the British army during the Second World War, and has been described as one of the three most outstanding members in the five-hundred-year history of Christ's College, Cambridge, the other two being John Milton and Charles Darwin."

She took a sip of wine and smiled disarmingly. "There's even a statue of Smuts outside the Houses of Parliament in London, alongside Churchill, Lincoln and Mandela, among others. That's pretty select company, by anyone's standards. So all in all, dear Nic, although he was not without fault—no politician ever is—Smuts was a unique individual and hardly a caricature of anyone."

"Humph," snorted Nicolas, appalled by the tribute and thinking Lizzie had just made his point better than he could—that Smuts had turned his back on his own people to serve others. He stabbed at an oyster with his fork as though to exact revenge on the hapless mollusk for Smuts's betrayal. Then he stabbed it a second time for good measure, for the death of his father's first wife when Smuts's air force dropped a bomb on her.

"And then there's Lord Roberts," she continued, "scrambling to defeat a ragtag army of Afrikaner farmers who managed to run rings around the mighty British Empire and its quarter of a million trained troops. That is, until my countrymen resorted to scorched-earth tactics and concentration camps."

"I know all about their tactics," said Nicolas quietly, "and about their camps."

The two fell silent for several moments.

"Did you lose family members during the Anglo-Boer War?" she asked tentatively.

He washed an oyster down with wine before answering.

"If you mean our Second War of Freedom, then the answer is yes. My grandfather was shot dead at Spion Kop, my grandmother was burned off our family farm and my aunt raped. She died with her mother in a concentration camp outside Bloemfontein."

Lizzy looked ashen. "I'm so very sorry, Nic," she said gently. "I know the history of the war, but I've never met anyone on the Boer side who was so affected by it." She paused, reached across the table, and lightly draped her left hand over his as it rested on the stem of his wineglass. "I've seen the monument to your women in Bloemfontein. It's a special place, the simple obelisk a shrine to the suffering of the innocent. Even Emily Hobhouse is buried there. Boer women called her the 'Angel of Love'."

She sighed. "Do you have any other family?"

He nodded. "Wife and daughter," he said and felt her hand lift from his. "My wife was killed by an ANC bomb in '83. My daughter survived." Her hand lowered. He felt the gentle pressure of her comfort.

"Dear God, Nic. I'm so sorry," she said. "I can't begin to imagine what your family has been through."

They sat quietly for several minutes. He looked out the window into the blur of night, imagining the carpet of vibrant wildflowers that would bloom in the spring, and recalling the old proverb that all the flowers of tomorrow are in the seeds of today. The corollary was inescapable—that the same applied to weeds, except that weeds choked life rather than enhanced life when they bloomed. The people of his homeland were choking on the weeds their ANC leaders were sowing.

He was distracted by Lizzie's reflection as she swirled the wine and held the glass to her nose, as though trying to divine the vagaries of life from its crimson depths and complex bouquet.

He thought to change the subject but heard himself saying, "And then the ANC's terrorist-in-chief, Nelson Mandela, hails Cuba's revolution as an inspiration to all freedom-loving people, fawns over Castro for sending troops to support the Marxist regime in Angola, and celebrates the battle of Cuito Cuanavale in '88 as a defeat of the South African army and a victory for all of Africa."

She sat back for a moment before responding. "Well, the battle was a pretty big deal," she said. "Some call it a turning point in the struggle to free South Africa."

"Well, they're wrong! I was there," he said, struggling to control his anger. "We stopped the bastards in their tracks. Chased them all the way back to Cuito, a hundred and twenty miles away. Even the Americans called it a 'stunning humiliation' for the Soviets," he added, gesturing with air quotes. "But somehow Mandela saw it as a victory for Africa." He paused for a mouthful of wine. "Christ, Lizzy, he even rushed off to celebrate the anniversary of the Cuban revolution with Castro in '91."

She sipped her wine slowly before responding. "Well, it's a complicated story," she began. "Think about it. The Cuban missile crisis happened in the middle of Mandela's trial for leaving the country to raise support for the ANC struggle. The Cold War was at its most fierce and, as it turned out, the only friends Mandela could find were among communist countries, a fact that handed your government a prized propaganda weapon in its fight against the so-called terrorists."

"There is nothing 'so-called' about—"

"Your ostrich, madam," said the waiter, interrupting, "and your lamb, sir, medium rare." He refilled their glasses of wine and moved off.

"Labels like 'terrorist' are so easy to throw around," she continued, "usually by our governments at their enemies, and we are told to believe what they tell us. But the truth is always more complicated. By today's definition, even George Washington would be called a terrorist for his revolutionary war against the British government—the Mandela of his time."

Nicolas shook his head. "All I know is Mandela and his Umkhonto killed my wife and almost killed my daughter. It was pure terror. It *cannot* be defended in the name of freedom."

"Yes, it was terrible—so many innocent people killed. I'm not defending it, Nic, just trying to show how labels can be used to obscure a more complicated truth and justify a more draconian tyranny."

They sat quietly for several moments before she excused herself to visit the restroom. He sat and stared out of the window, his food and wine forgotten, as the dark landscape behind the reflections morphed into images of Boer freedom fighters and ANC terrorists before dissolving again into darkness, into the pain and aching loneliness of the last two decades.

"I'm sorry, Nic," she said as she sat down again. "Truly sorry for your loss." She sniffed and squeezed his hand across the table. "I detest stereotypes and generalizations and the way we label others. I'm always telling friends and family not to generalize about people—about 'Muslims' and 'Americans' and other groups—as though they all think and behave alike. It's just not true. Even your people suffered the same thing—no news coverage complete without reference to the 'racist apartheid regime,' the history of your country and people compressed into slogans and ten-second sound bites on the nightly news. Labels are just too easy—too often a refuge for ignorance and bigotry and self-righteous hypocrisy. The truth is almost always more nuanced, more complicated."

She sighed then turned her attention to her ostrich fillet. "Hmm. It's actually quite good," she said, chewing delicately. "Tastes like a cross between chicken and steak." She smiled and took a sip of wine.

"So anyway, my dear Nic, what do you think of the situation now?"

Nicolas took a deep breath. "You really don't want to know what I think. Trust me. But as for my people," he continued, "we're stumbling through the debris of our dreams, lost and alienated in the land we love, hiding behind barbed wire and security fences, hoping somehow to find a way back into a place of pride in who we are as a people."

He could feel himself slipping, caught in a riptide of despair. Even the perfectly prepared lamb tasted like rubber, the wine flat and insipid.

"This just won't do—the Allesverloren must have gone to your head," said Lizzy with a beguiling smile. "But if you've truly lost you way, dear Nic, then you've found just the right person to help you find your way back."

"What?" he said, nonplussed. "What are you talking about?"

Instead of answering, she began to hum a tune and play an invisible piano that hovered just above the table. He was startled and just a little embarrassed when she began to sing in a playful half whisper across the table:

"You've been living with a shadow overhead... You've been sleeping with a cloud above your bed... You've been lonely for so long... trapped in the past, you just can't seem to move on... All you need to do is find a way back into love... You can't make it through without a way back into love. Oh, oh, oh—"

"What is that?" he said, interrupting, forgetting his embarrassment. "What the hell are you going on about?"

She laughed. "You, of course, silly! It's my version of the theme song from one of my favorite Hugh Grant movies—*Music and Lyrics*—sung just for you."

He shook his head—her vivaciousness was irresistible. "So what's it got to do with me, or me with it?" he asked as a smile crept across his haggard features. He took a sip of the wine, its bouquet and flavors of black cherries and pepper coming alive again as his spirits began to rise.

She smiled. "It's about a guy living in the past who believes he's all washed up. He meets a girl who shows up to water his plants. She kills his plants—even the plastic ones—but gives him a reason to take another chance on life. It's sweet and silly and absolutely charming."

"And does he...? Do they—"

"Yes," she interjected. "Under a grand piano!"

He laughed out loud and held up his glass of wine. She did the same.

"To high notes," she offered.
"To low notes," he countered.
She smiled. "To two-part harmony."
Their glasses clinked over the empty oyster shells.

Breakfast in Lizzy's double bed was delicious. The aroma of sausages, bacon and eggs, toast and marmalade, tea and coffee saturated the air as her suite gently rocked with the motion of the train. The stimulation of his senses enhanced the memory of the night before, not least because her bare leg against his still radiated warmth, while her roving hand aroused appetites he did not associate with breakfast.

Undressing after dinner had been awkward. The pistol and knife strapped to his belt had felt radioactive, likely to ruin the mood in an instant, but he had managed to discard his clothes in an untidy heap that covered the weapons. Her silky dress had barely floated to the floor before he joined her under the sheets.

As exhausted as he had been, drained by the day's events, he had found her passion irresistible, entirely beyond his experience or control. And it had been so long since the last time.

The bathtub was far too small for both of them after breakfast, but it was fun and the tight squeeze led directly, dripping wet, back to bed. This time he took the lead and discovered a willing and playful partner in degrees of intimacy he had only ever imagined. Her damp skin, moist hair and succulent femininity produced an experience so luscious, so satisfying and joyful that he felt reborn, fully alive for the first time in decades.

After just a few hours together she seemed as essential to his life as breath itself. And yet he knew a long-term relationship was as unlikely as the goat in Chagall's painting of the bride being transformed into a groom. But perhaps goats, like blind pigs, sometimes got lucky.

Despite the odds, he made plans to meet her at the Mount Nelson after his "adventure" was over.

45

CHARIOTS OF FIRE

2010

It was already eleven o'clock when he stepped back into his suite. And he had a problem. He had to assume the police were following the lead that had so nearly proved disastrous at Kimberley. If they now had a description of him, then he would almost certainly be walking into a trap when he arrived in Cape Town.

He needed a plausible subterfuge or disguise before the train reached the station. It came to him in a flash of inspiration—the butler. Not the one assigned to his car—too short and heavy—but the one about his size and weight in the adjoining car.

He moved quickly. Fortunately, there was a lot of activity in the cars. Nobody paid any attention to him carrying his suitcase and shopping bag from one car to the next as passengers mingled in the corridors preparing for their arrival, enjoying the scenery on the outskirts of Cape Town.

He did not have long to wait before the butler appeared, distracted by a document in his hand. Nicolas followed him along the corridor and into his cabin. He set the suitcase and package down quietly, slipped the Makarov from its holster and stepped behind the butler. The man started to turn just as the pistol crashed against the side of his head.

He caught the butler as he fell, laid him on the floor, and quickly locked the cabin door. It was awkward undressing a limp, heavy-set man, but he needed the butler's bow tie, waistcoat and shirt. Luckily, his clerical pants and shoes were the same color as the butler's—black. He hoped the disguise would serve its purpose as he buttoned the six brass buttons down the front of the waistcoat, clipped on the black bow tie and slipped into his shoes.

He considered using duct tape to restrain the man but decided against it. Two officials knocked unconscious and bound exactly the same way with the same tape within twenty-four hours of each other would be too easily connected. He used the cabin's towels instead and stuffed a facecloth into the man's mouth. Then he laid the butler on the bench seat facing the wall and draped a blanket over the inert form.

Satisfied, he slicked his hair with water and set the peaked uniform cap on his head. He looked in the mirror and noticed the brass nametag pinned to the waistcoat—he would have to pass as "Jannie Botha" long enough to get away from the station. He sat down next to the unconscious butler and waited.

At a minute before noon, the Blue Train rolled past the dockyards on one side, the Castle of Good Hope on the other, and then into the station. It eased to a stop just as the hands of the station clock aligned at the top of the hour.

Nicolas scanned the platform. There were no obvious signs of a reception committee, but he knew the threat was more likely out there than not. He waited until some passengers disembarked, then stepped onto the platform carrying his suitcase like a tray between his hands, with the Trappers package on top of the suitcase shielding his face. He hoped his laden appearance would dissuade anyone from asking for assistance carrying their luggage.

He made his way past the Blue Train lounge, found a restroom and slipped inside an enclosed stall. He stripped off the disguise, stuffed it into the suitcase and dressed again in his jeans, shirt and jacket, and running shoes. Then he inverted the plastic Trappers bag so the logo was not showing, put on his sunglasses, and left the restroom carrying his suitcase and bag normally, one item in each hand.

He exited onto Adderley Street, walked past the terminus he had used to get to the airport for the flight to Johannesburg, crossed Adderley at the intersection with Strand and entered the parking ramp. He took the stairs to the second level and cautiously approached his midnight-blue Volkswagen R32 Hatchback, checking for signs of surveillance near his parking spot. Seeing none, he unlocked the driver's door, tossed the suitcase onto the passenger seat and settled in behind the wheel. The black leather interior of the hatchback still had that new-car smell, even after two years, and the spirited V6 fired at the first turn of the key.

Traffic was moderate although the streets were crowded with pedestrians and hawkers. He headed towards the Convention Center and then onto Nelson Mandela Boulevard near the foreshore of Table Bay before taking the N1 exit onto the freeway.

In forty minutes he would be in the middle of the winelands—in Stellenbosch—and safely home.

A sense of wellbeing coursed through him as he drove into Stellenbosch—the City of Oaks—and up Dorp Street, as though the luminous aura of the Mother Church was enough to dispel the dark cloud hanging over him.

He passed the historic Old Town and turned left onto Drostdy, the road that led to the church. It was a short street, the top of a T-junction with Church Street, a longer street that led back into Old Town. He often thought of the two streets as forming the Cross of Calvary, with the church at the top of the cross representing the head of Christ.

He saw the unoccupied white sedans almost immediately. Two were parked awkwardly against the flow of traffic in front of the twin-gabled Church House. Another was parked further ahead in front of the neo-Gothic Mother Church with its stained-glass windows and dark, rapier-like spire capping the white bell tower above the front entrance.

So much for a safe haven, he thought—the net cast for him had already reached into the heart of his sanctuary. He did not slow or look towards the church buildings before turning left onto Church Street and heading back into Old Town. He felt sick at heart as he made the turn—as though taking the first steps down his own via dolorosa.

He turned right at the Mill Street junction at the bottom of Church Street and headed past the original village green on his left towards the university, then right again onto Merriman and through the heart of campus until he reached the intersection with the provocatively named "Hell's Heights" road.

He idled at the stop sign for several moments trying to think what to do, where to go. Decision made, he turned right and accelerated, redlining the all-wheel-drive manual transmission through each gear change as he drove as fast as possible towards Franschoek and the remote mountains and valleys that cradled the winelands to the east of Stellenbosch. Ancestors on his mother's side had been among the handful of Huguenots who sailed from La Rochelle in France during the 17th century to escape religious persecution. It made emotional if not rational sense to head towards their original settlement of Franschoek.

Within minutes he passed Tokara at the crest of Hell's Heights Pass. It was one of his favorite wineries. He loved the sculptures and art gallery, the glass-walled restaurant and late harvest dessert wine, and the vineyard draped vistas over Stellenbosch and False Bay. He drove on, past the Boschendal winery with its magnificent Cape Dutch farmstead, towards Franschhoek, driving too hard to enjoy the glorious countryside cradled by spectacular mountain ranges that he loved so well.

He slowed through the pretty town as he approached the Huguenot Monument with its three tall arches—each symbolizing one part of the Christian trinity—surrounded by imposing mountains on three sides. He turned left at the T-junction and, as he passed the monument, recalled the Reformation motto highlighted at the site: *post tenebras lux*—after darkness comes light.

Exactly, he thought as he accelerated into the mountains. He had to find a way to light a fire of reformation across the land, to replace corruption with covenant, darkness with light.

The road wound past the Mont Rochelle Nature Reserve and into the serpentine Franschoek Pass—its heights pockmarked by gray boulders seemingly pushing through a stubble of green-brown growth—before a twisting descent to a dam crossing and then a steep climb over Sir Lowry's Pass and down towards the spectacular eighteen-mile-wide False Bay.

He had driven just over a hundred miles in nearly a complete circle since leaving Cape Town. But he couldn't keep driving in circles—he needed a contingency plan. He braked hard, pulled to a stop on the side of the road, selected a number from his contacts list and made a call. A few miles farther he turned off the highway to Cape Town and onto Baden Powell Drive.

His new route followed the shoreline of False Bay. He had always thought the bay misnamed—there was nothing false about it, except that early Portuguese explorers had confused it with Table Bay on the other side of the narrow Cape Peninsula.

The nearly twelve-mile beachfront road separated two shantytowns from the ocean before it reached the bay's western edge and the Cape Peninsula. Although he had seen glimpses of the shantytowns of the Cape Flats many times, he had never appreciated the scale of the black township of Khayelitsha and the adjoining colored township of Mitchells Plain, the one mostly Xhosa speaking, the other mostly Afrikaans speaking. The shanties were packed together in a drab patchwork of multicolored fabrics and metal sheets strewn among the sand dunes, an irregular single-level landscape connected by a labyrinth of asymmetrical dirt roads that looked like the ragged veins of a mutant organism struggling for survival. And dispersed among the shanties were incongruous signs of technology—electrical poles with lines draping in all directions, like intravenous drips delivering life-saving energy directly to patients on life-support; and satellite dishes, like vacant eyes staring heavenward, beseeching the entertainment gods for relief from the crushing oppression below.

He drove on through Muizenberg and past the cottage where Cecil Rhodes had died—the narrow beachfront road snaking between the ocean on his left and the mountains on his right—then through the towns of St James and Fish Hoek, before turning away from the ocean towards Chapman's Peak Drive on the other side of the Cape Peninsula.

He opened the car's windows, took a deep breath and smiled as memories of the sights, sounds and smell of the Two Oceans Marathon flooded his consciousness. It had been his favorite marathon, and this was its signature section—the torturous run up Chapman's Peak, its sheer cliffs falling away into the ocean on the left as the narrow road twisted toward the summit, then the descent into the stunning natural harbor and fishing village of Hout Bay. And on the other side of the village, beyond the twenty-six-mile marker, the punishing run up the short but steep Contantia Nek, before the relief of the final miles past the gardens of Kirstenbosch to the finish at the University of Cape Town.

As he drove the well-trodden course, he heard again the music from *Chariots of Fire* that had boomed across the course from huge speakers. There were times he thought of it as the soundtrack to his life. Perhaps when his life had run its course, when the bleeding of his homeland had been stanched, he too, like the prophet Elijah, would be taken up to heaven by a whirlwind in a chariot of fire.

He coasted into Hout Bay past the crescent-shaped beach awash in sunshine—its leopard statue on a seaside rock always reminded him of the mermaid statue in Copenhagen. He headed directly for the quaint harbor watched over by a massive rock formation known as the Sentinel. He could almost taste the crayfish, prawns and calamari as he passed the multicolored fishing boats lashed together as though seeking refuge from the South Atlantic sea, their gunwales barely as high as the quayside itself, their rugged-looking crewmen cleaning and repairing nets as voracious seagulls squabbled for every morsel.

He turned left just beyond Mariner's Wharf—its iconic seafood restaurant, filled with seafaring memorabilia, a perennial favorite—onto the short road that led to the open parking lot alongside the dock. He turned right as he entered the lot and parked near the Lookout restaurant, its landmark waterfront facade marked by a sixty-foot tall watchtower painted in huge bands of red and white.

A broad-shouldered sailor wearing a captain's hat emerged from the restaurant and headed towards his car.

Nicolas took a few minutes to remove the rifle pieces from their protective foam cutouts and carefully wrap them in a sweater, then transferred all the gear he needed to a backpack. He stepped out of the car and handed a set of his car keys to the sailor just as a nondescript sedan pulled up alongside.

The sailor exchanged a few words with the driver then grasped Nicolas by the hand. "Fear none but God," said his former comrade-in-arms before walking away towards Mariner's Wharf.

Nicolas settled into the passenger seat, the backpack at his feet, as the car headed up Victoria Road and over the hill towards the seaside village of Llandudno. Ahead lay the sweeping oceanfront road that meandered along the Atlantic coast under the imperious gaze of the Twelve Apostles, a majestic ridge of mountains abutting the southwestern edge of Table Mountain.

The sun was low in the western sky and brilliantly illuminated the surf crashing onto the rocks below the road on his left before its dying rays swept over the road and up the mountainside.

At the beachfront town of Camps Bay, the driver turned away from the ocean and headed up Kloof Nek road towards the gap between Lion's Head and Table Mountain. As the car crested the neck, Nicolas could see Cape Town and Table Bay below him and, to his right, the cable car ascending to the westernmost tip of Table Mountain as though trying to escape the darkness that would soon envelop the city.

A few minutes later the driver stopped on Queen Victoria Street, a narrow lane just outside the Company's Garden in the heart of Cape Town.

Without a word, Nicolas got out of the car, slung the backpack over his shoulder, and entered the iconic haven through an elegant white gabled entrance about halfway up the length of the rectangular garden refuge.

The Garden, developed by the Dutch East India Company in the 17th century, was home to the national museum, art gallery, planetarium and Houses of Parliament. And among all the grand buildings set against the backdrop of Table Mountain stood a stately old Cape Dutch house—Tuynhuys—used as the state president's office, although his official residence was on the magnificent Groote Schuur estate on the other side of Table Mountain in the shadow of Devil's Peak.

Nicolas looked to his left towards St. George's Cathedral just beyond the edge of the Garden closest to the harbor. The "People's Cathedral" had been such a bastion of resistance against apartheid, especially when Desmond Tutu had been the archbishop. Whereas Tuynhuys had symbolized apartheid, St. George's with its bell tower had stood like a physical and audible rebuke, and Tutu—the charismatic "rabble rouser for peace"—had spoken truth to power at the height of apartheid while Mandela sat silenced behind the bars of Robben Island. Nicolas admired Tutu, not least because he had remained committed to nonviolent change and never supported the ANC's armed struggle, but also because he had never compromised his faith despite his contextualized black African theology. The diminutive clergyman had been a giant among men, truly "a man for all seasons."

Nicolas turned away. He knew he was compromising his own faith by turning to the gun. He was reconciled to the contradiction.

He paused at the Delville Wood Memorial to more than two thousand South Africans who had died in the five-day battle in France during the First World War. The memorial featured a sculpture depicting two men clasping hands over the back of a horse. It was titled "Brotherhood" and designed to represent the unity of Boer and British soldiers. Nicolas shook his head. They might have been allies, but brothers they were not.

He headed up the terraces away from the harbor, past the art gallery and planetarium, towards Table Mountain and exited the Garden at it's highest point where it butted up against a city street. Across the street stood the colonnaded Prince of Wales Gate, the entrance to the tree-lined driveway leading to the Mount Nelson Hotel.

The Pink Lady and the lovely Lizzie were just a short walk away.

46

MADIBA'S MAGIC

2010

Nicolas felt shabby and out of place as he approached the porticoed entrance, avoided the immaculately dressed concierge, and pushed through the graceful wooden revolving door into the refined lobby of the five-star icon.

To add to his discomfort, Lizzy had told him where she was staying but not her last name. His options were limited—he could either skulk about like a dung beetle on an oriental carpet in the hope of bumping into her elegant pumps, or he could take a chance on a name that forced itself upon his imagination with an insistence that was either inspired or absurd.

He decided to take the chance.

He turned to the reception desk on his left. "Ms. Elizabeth Bennet, please," he said to the attractive young woman behind the desk.

"Yes, sir," she replied, appearing to wrinkle her nose but not reacting to the literary allusion as she tapped on a keyboard. She stared at the monitor for a few moments.

"Who shall I say is calling, sir?"

"Mr. Darcy," he said.

He watched the clerk make the call, a courteous exchange that caused the clerk to smile.

"Ms. Bennet says she will be down shortly, Mr. Darcy. She invites you to take afternoon tea with her in the garden around the fountain."

"Thank you," he said with exaggerated courtesy. "Which way to the garden?"

The clerk's directions were easy enough to follow—straight ahead, past the Planet Bar on the left, through the patio doors directly opposite the main entrance.

The garden setting around the fountain was a tableau of stylishly dressed guests relaxing on white wrought-iron furniture offset by colorful cushions and waited upon by uniformed staff serving a variety of exotic teas, finger sandwiches and sweet desserts. It was a lifestyle he had never experienced and one to which he did not expect to become accustomed.

He selected a two-seater that offered a little separation from the other guests and sat down.

He did not have long to wait. Lizzy soon appeared at the top of the terrace stairs wearing a form-fitting pair of cream-colored slacks and a salmon-colored long-sleeve blouse. The pink hotel rose behind her like a generously proportioned grande dame with her arms—the two wings of the hotel—outstretched as though presenting Lizzie to the gathered assembly. He half expected her appearance to be announced by an English-accented herald. She looked as comfortable in the plush surroundings as he felt awkward.

"Mr. Darcy, I presume," she said, approaching with her hand outstretched. "So glad you overcame your pride, as I did my prejudice."

"Hello, Lizzy," he said, rising to take her hand. "Nice to see you again. It's been a while."

"Yes." She laughed as she sat down. "All of five hours. Did it take that long, Mr. Darcy, to convince yourself—against your will, your reason, and even your character—how ardently you admired and adored me?"

He felt the blush and laughed to cover his embarrassment. "I've never thought of myself as a character in a Jane Austen novel, but believe me, dear lady, I didn't need any convincing to find my way back to you." He smiled. "By the way, is your last name really Bennet?"

She laughed. "Yes, it really is. Spelled exactly as Austen spelled it. But I've had more Wickhams in my life than Darcys, despite my best efforts to avoid cads and catch lords." She smiled. "Still not sure which category you fall into, but maybe you're in a category of one, a latter-day Saint Nicholas."

He smiled and shook his head. "I am many things, Lizzy, but I assure you I'm no saint. And I've never been mistaken for Santa Claus."

"Oh well, worth a try," she said. "But Nicolas is a good name—derived from Greek—means 'victory of the people.' " She smiled. "One of the few benefits of my classics degree from Cambridge."

"Yes," he said with a thin smile, "I know what it means. Question is, which people?"

She looked at him for a moment as the rhetorical question hung unanswered between them. "Anyway, enough airy persiflage," she said as the moment passed. "So what happened to your great adventure?"

"My friend got rear-ended by a drunk driver just outside Gordon's Bay. He's laid up for a few days with whiplash."

"Oh dear, that's too bad," she commiserated and signaled a waiter.

She ordered the signature tea blend, he ordered rooibos, but they both passed on the sandwiches.

"So what are you going to do now?" she asked.

"Not sure, actually," he said. "Seems I have some time on my hands."

She raised her eyebrows. "Well...the Pink Lady is very accommodating," she offered, her decorous assurance belied by her mischievous smile as the waiter set their tea down on the wrought-iron table.

He returned the smile. "Sounds promising. But why is she so pink?"

"She was painted pink in 1918 to signify peace after the Great War. She's been pink ever since," she added over the brim of her porcelain teacup.

Nicolas gave her a wry smile and glanced up at the imperious monolith of Table Mountain, so constant yet witness to so much change. "Peace and disarmament...like truth and reconciliation...but then we had the Second World War in Europe and now we have violence and corruption at home. High minded aspirations—treaties, democracies and constitutions—are all very well, but they can't save us from the craven instincts of man."

"Perhaps a subject for another time," she prompted with a demure tilt of her head.

He shrugged and smiled. "Yes, you're right. So anyway, how's room service?"

She laughed. "Well, it depends what you like...but I have it on very good authority that the service is exceptional."

The seductive experience was enhanced by the Mediterranean ambiance of Lizzy's room—the pastel décor, open double doors leading to the balcony, and the warm ocean breeze lightly caressing the sheer fabric of the curtains and luxurious linens of the king-sized bed.

A room service dinner was followed by a reprise of exquisite intimacy. The transition from ecstasy to sleep was seamless, a perfect glidepath from pleasure to rest.

They were both up early the next morning, she to swim in the heated water of the secluded Cottage Pool, he to admire her languid stroke from a poolside deckchair. The setting could not have been more Lizzy-esque—a private pool bordered by flowering trees, next to a lane of charming Victorian-era cottages, each complimented by colorful English gardens behind delicate white picket fences. He regretted not having a swimsuit but was content to watch the water ripple sensually in her wake, and to contemplate the whispy tablecloth of cloud draped over the leading edge of Table Mountain.

He did not need a swimsuit in the shower after her swim.

Neither did she.

"You said you had lost your way," she began as they sat down at the Oasis Bistro overlooking the main pool for a late breakfast, "when I asked you on the train about the situation in South Africa."

"I did," he said, "meaning our people have lost their way."

"How so?" she said.

"Where to start…" he mused.

"Start at the very beginning," she said with a lilt. "A very good place to start."

"Not if you're going to start singing again, Lizzy, especially not from *The Sound of Music*. Besides, to start at the very beginning would take too long, and it doesn't mix well with breakfast."

"Okay, just pick up the story wherever it makes sense. But I don't promise not to sing if the spirit moves me—it's divine inspiration, like Mozart at a piano, Da Vinci at an easel, Michelangelo at a block of marble. I could go on." She laughed. "Sorry, Nic. You were about to say?"

He smiled fleetingly, drew a deep breath and slowly exhaled.

"Mandela said in his inauguration speech in '94 that we had entered a covenant where black and white could walk tall, where no one would suffer the oppression of one by another, a rainbow nation at peace with itself. It sounded so noble, so enlightened, despite the fact his guests of honor included Fidel Castro, Yasser Arafat and Muammar Gaddafi—hardly paragons of the virtues he espoused."

He paused to sip his grapefruit juice. "But the high has worn off. Madiba's magic has been replaced by a witches' brew that would make Macbeth blush. Fair has become foul and foul is truly fair. And so my poor beloved country sinks beneath the yoke—it weeps, it bleeds and each day a new gash is added to her wounds."

"My goodness, Nic, a Shakespearian tragedy in sub-Saharan Africa with words and commentary by the Bard himself. Who would have thought?"

"There's nothing new under the sun, Lizzy," he said. "History is but a stage—the players change, the plots remain the same. In fact, I often wonder what Lincoln would say in this time and place if he looked out over the Gettysburg of our struggle."

"Lincoln! Whatever next?"

"I can almost hear him," he went on, ignoring her incredulity. "I think he would speak of how our fathers, black and white, brought about a new nation in 1994 dedicated to the proposition that all are created equal, but that now we find ourselves in crisis, engaged in a great human rights struggle to test whether our nation, so conceived, can survive." He sipped more juice, then added, "And I think he would say it's the great unfinished work of our times—that it's up to the next generation to complete the task, to give the last full measure of their devotion, so that those who died to consecrate our birthright will not have died in vain, and our nation, under God, might have a new birth of freedom."

"I don't know whether to weep or applaud," she said, shaking her head.

"I weep. The country weeps. And so should every right-minded person weep for the tragedy that has befallen our beloved country. The high hopes of a rainbow nation and democratic society have been cast into the dirt like pearls before swine, trampled by comrades with their *viva* this and *viva* that, invoking the legacy of Mandela so fervently, yet betraying it so completely."

"That's rather bleak, Nic. I mean, imperialism, colonialism and then apartheid produced quite a legacy. For the ANC to turn it around can't be easy. Perhaps expectations were too high," she offered, nibbling at a square of melon skewered to her fork. "After all, democracy is a risky enterprise. I think it was Lord Acton who said, 'The pervading evil of democracy is the tyranny of the majority'."

"That's exactly the evil we feared and resisted all those years. Their chants said it all. *Amandla, ngawethu*—power, it shall be ours. They cloaked it in the rhetoric of freedom and democracy, but now that their power is absolute, so is their corruption. Besides, trying to conform this crowd to the principles of a democracy is like trying to squeeze a donkey into a wetsuit. It's never going to happen."

She threw back her head and laughed. "Good one, Nic. As political metaphors go, that one takes the cake."

His smile was fleeting. "We were fooled into thinking Mandela's successors would be like him. The great irony is that imprisoning Mandela for all those years was the best thing that ever happened to the ANC."

Her eyes went wide. "Whatever do you mean?"

"Prison froze him in time as a freedom fighter, preserved his image as the symbol of resistance and injustice, and captivated the imagination of the world. He was never seen or heard from for nearly twenty-seven years, yet achieved more for the ANC in prison than they could ever have achieved if he had been a free man. And when he was released, he was a complete contradiction that disarmed our people. Gone was the angry agitator, the Black Pimpernel, the guerrilla fighter and militant leader wearing Xhosa beads and leopard skins. Out came a gray-haired senior citizen in a three-piece suit, a soft-spoken negotiator, a diplomat and conciliator."

He shook his head. "The illusion Mandela created was that ANC leaders would be like him and could be trusted to govern the country. Zuma is the last straw, an emperor without clothes, whose first impulse is to fuck anything wearing a skirt and everything that is sacred, a village idiot whose corrupt and ignorant vulgarity is beyond belief, a grotesque distortion of the ideals of freedom and democracy."

He paused and looked around, conscious that the sumptuous setting seemed to belie the austere picture he was painting. "The illusion is all that's left, Lizzy, and that's the sad truth of the situation." Then, recalling a motif from one of Springsteen's songs, he added, "The ANC turned dust into gold with Mandela, but when they were done, they broke the mold."

"A depressing view, Nic, I must say. I prefer to think that hope may yet prevail. I mean, if a notorious minister of law and order, responsible for hit squads and assassinations, can kneel before a black man he tried to kill and wash his feet, asking to be forgiven for what the regime did and tried to do, then anything is possible."

He shrugged. He knew the story—Adriaan Vlok's contrition had made international news—but it would take more than soap and water to cleanse the corruption that infected the body of the ANC. Besides, this was not the time for Christlike humility. It was a time to be bold, to step into the arena, to dare to do the unthinkable for the only cause worthy of such a sacrifice.

He knew his mother would never have agreed that the end justified the means. But then again, Christ was crucified to reconcile mankind to God—a redeeming end that had apparently justified such an agonizing, humiliating and brutal means that Jesus thought God had forsaken him as he hung dying on the cross. A local artist had even painted Mandela as Christ in his vision of Da Vinci's *The Last Supper*, with Mandela seated between Gandhi and Martin Luther King, together with other iconic civil rights figures. Mandela had endorsed the image, and if he saw himself as a Christ figure then he understood the sacrifice he might have to make. After all, he had declared in his most famous speech that "if needs be, it is an ideal for which I am prepared to die."

There is power in sacrifice, thought Nicolas. *The cross is proof of that, and the re-birth of our nation demands nothing less.*

His thoughts turned to Lizzy's notion of high expectations and that hope could still prevail.

"Hope is such a fleeting thing, Lizzy. It filled our sails after the end of apartheid, raised our expectations high on the main mast—we had chartered a new course. But the ANC has shredded our sails and shattered our mast, leaving us adrift in rough seas and unpredictable currents." He rubbed his temples. "Sad to say, but our ship of hope has floundered and is about to go under."

"But may be returning to port for repairs," she said, brightening. "My sources tell me there's a secret meeting in Cape Town this weekend between African leaders who are here for the World Cup. Apparently Mandela is committed to the meeting as the figurehead of African democracy. All very hush-hush."

He leaned back in his chair. "That may be news, but it's hardly a recipe for national renewal."

"Perhaps Madiba still has some pixie dust left," she said with an impish smile.

"Humph," he snorted. "Pixie dust is for fairy tales. We need something a lot stronger, more like a miracle. We need someone to turn our water into wine—like Jesus did at the wedding at Cana—someone to turn the foul water the ANC forces down our throats into a full-bodied cabernet, accessible by all. Perhaps, in this marriage of our people that Mandela presided over in '94, he saved the best wine for last and will serve it soon." He cracked a thin smile. "We can only hope," he added drily. "Anyway, do you know where they're staying? Hopefully not all here."

Her eyes glowed. "I'm not sure about the rest of the group, but my source says Mandela is staying at Groote Schuur—the Rhodes mansion—tonight and maybe Sunday night. Then he flies back to Jo'burg for his great-granddaughter's funeral on Thursday."

Nicolas shrugged, as though indifferent to the news, but the pieces of a plan fell together in an instant.

47

MENSA'S MAJESTY

2010

"How about taking the cable car to the top of Table Mountain?" he suggested when they got back to the hotel room. "There's no better place to see the sights. And we really should try to do some sightseeing before it gets crazy around here with VIPs strutting about and roads being blocked."

"Sounds delightful, Nic. Do you know Table Mountain has been nominated to be one of the new seven wonders of nature?" she asked rhetorically. "I read somewhere that there are only six floral kingdoms in the world, and one of those kingdoms is right here in the Cape, most of it in the Table Mountain National Park. That's why the Kirstenbosch Botanical Garden on the other side of the mountain is so special."

She looked at him with arched eyebrows. "Well, my good man," she demanded imperiously. "Did you know that? Some of that? Any of that?"

"Flowers not quite my bag, dear lady, I'm sorry to say."

"Flowers not your bag?" she responded, feigning surprise. "You mean aside from boy flowers, which I happen to know are very much part of your bag."

He felt the color race to his face. "But did *you* know," he countered, trying to recover, "that Table Mountain is the only natural feature on earth to have a constellation of stars named after it?"

"Oh? And what constellation is that, pray tell?"

"*Mensa*. Latin for 'table,' visible only in the southern hemisphere, just below Orion, around midnight in mid-July." He paused and smiled. "And I didn't have to study classics at Cambridge to know that."

"Humph," she snorted. "Don't try to change the subject, which is your lamentable ignorance about what's visible all around you twelve months of the year. And in solemn penance for your grievous moral and floral failure as a citizen of the fairest Cape of them all, you will escort me to the Kirstenbosch gardens on the thirteenth day of the sixth month in the year of our Lord 2010." She paused and smiled. "That means tomorrow, Sir Nic."

He bowed in mock deference. "Your wish is my command, dear lady."

She beamed. "Of course it is, dear boy, that goes without saying. And as for today's little outing, can we take your car? I assume you drove here."

"Uh... actually, no. I took a taxi. But it's such a nice day for a walk, don't you think?"

"Sounds lovely, Nic," she said, looking around the room. "I'll be back in a minute. I think I left my sunglasses at the pool."

He was relieved to have a few private minutes. He quickly emptied his backpack and carefully wrapped the rifle pieces in hand towels from the bathroom before packing them carefully into the backpack. Then he checked and repacked the other contents of the backpack—a first-aid kit, water bottle, fire starters, matches, flashlight, flare gun, wire cutters, rubber gloves, camouflage crayons and binoculars. To that he added the extras from his car, including his charred Bible, a couple of smoke and tear gas grenades, a few short ropes and wads of cloth, the grappling hook and a foreign passport under an alias. The khaki outfit went in last with his running shoes and black sweater. The knife and pistol were stuffed into a front zipper pocket for easy access.

The minibar yielded several bottles of water, two mini bottles of wine and several packets of snacks, which he slipped into pockets on the sides of the backpack. Then he scribbled a quick note to Lizzy on the hotel's writing pad and slipped it into *Pride and Prejudice* at the same page as her bookmark.

He sat down, laced up his suede *veldskoens* and clicked on the TV just in time to see the morning show interrupted by a bulletin describing the search for a single white man in the Cape Town area, complete with a grainy photograph of himself wearing sunglasses, the clerical collar and his fedora. He heard Lizzy open the door and switched off the TV just as she entered and announced that all she needed was her hat and her walking shoes.

"Ready?" she asked a minute later, standing in the bedroom door, looking like Katharine Hepburn in *The African Queen* about to take on the German gunboat.

"Yes, ma'am. Ready, able and willing," he said, grinning. "And I packed some stuff for a lunch on the most spectacular picnic table in the world."

"Wonderful," she said as they stepped into the elevator. "And I have arranged a carriage, horses and all, to take us to our picnic."

He stared at her, hoping it was a joke.

"You didn't order a taxi, did you, Lizzy?" he said good-naturedly. "I thought we agreed to walk."

"The concierge told me it was too far. But walk we shall, my dear Nic, on top of the mountain, not beneath it." She laughed. "Our carriage will be waiting outside. Not quite horse-drawn, but with more than enough horsepower to carry us to the cable station."

"And you told the concierge where we were going?"

"Of course I did, silly. They always ask when you order a taxi."

Nicolas forced a smile. "Well done, Ms. Bennet. How very resourceful."

"Thank you," she said, flicking her hair from her face as she exited the elevator before striding imperiously through the lobby to the waiting taxi.

They were halfway down the palm tree-lined driveway when he heard the sirens. Seconds later two white cars, sirens blaring, raced through the Prince of Wales Gate and past their taxi towards the hotel.

Like a script from a James Bond movie, thought Nicolas, as he sank a little lower in his seat. Somebody must have connected him with Lizzy on the train, and then traced her to the Mount Nelson.

"Probably just making arrangements for you know whom," she observed as she adjusted her seat belt. "I always wear my seat belt," she added, "ever since Princess Diana died in that awful car crash."

The cable car station towered over them as the taxi pulled to a stop less than ten minutes later. Its angular gray profile seemed to mimic the buttresses and crags of the mountain it served. The taxi had made the drive in good time, but when Lizzy strolled towards the edge of the parking lot to view the natural bowl cradling the city and harbor a thousand feet below, he intervened, swept her off her feet and made a joke of carrying her over the threshold into an airborne carriage.

Timing is everything, he thought as they boarded the cable car last in line just before its doors closed.

"It looks like a giant hamburger dangling from a chain," she joked as the car lurched away from the cable station. It was half-full—about thirty people—and the floor rotated to give everyone breathtaking views from every angle during the five-minute, two-thousand-foot ascent to the top of Table Mountain. He smiled in response to her delight but kept an eye on the winding road leading to the cable station below.

During the last and steepest section, as the cabin floor rotated away from the mountain—it seemed close enough to touch—towards a panoramic view over the city and Robben Island, he saw two white cars speeding up the road to the lower cable car station. He knew the cable cars could be put into reverse and silently urged the cable car to go faster, to reach the upper station before the police reached the lower station.

Moments later the gaping mouth of the upper station swallowed the cable car and it lurched to a stop. For a moment he imagined being sucked into the cavernous eye of a huge baboon skull, caught up among family members in a scene of violent and bloody death. The terrifying image had stuck with him ever since his father had described what his grandfather had imagined at the makeshift burial site beneath Baboon Rock after the Great Murder.

He shuddered and realized he had been holding his breath. He stepped out of the cable car and gasped as fresh winter air filled his oxygen-starved lungs.

Lizzy turned left and headed for the closest viewing point. She seemed mesmerized by the cobalt-blue horizon beyond the harbor city that seemed to stretch endlessly over the hazy inland mountains before swinging out over the glistening Atlantic Ocean. A tendril of white cloud on the horizon added an ethereal dimension to the spectacle.

"It's beautiful, Nic. Absolutely glorious. Like standing on the edge of eternity."

She was right, although his attention was focused on the surrounding terrain and the threat he faced, on avoiding a premature encounter with eternity.

"Lizzy, I need to find a restroom. I'll meet you in the café for coffee before we head out. Okay?" She nodded absently, her faraway gaze fixed on the majestic tapestry of the Cape. He stared at her profile, trying to memorize every nuance of tone and curve, every detail of texture and color, before he kissed her lightly on her cheek and walked away.

He forced himself to concentrate on the mission ahead. He needed to create a diversion, use his resources sparingly, anticipate the moves of his pursuers and figure out the optimal route to his target—the Groote Schuur estate, just below Devil's Peak.

The ancient mountain could not be taken lightly. Older than the Rockies, Alps or Himalayas, it bore the scars of a past contorted by massive shifts and upheavals of red, purple and gray sandstone, immense rock formations that now were textured by a rugged carpet of boulders and *fynbos*, the unique shrubs of the floral kingdom Lizzy had described.

He would have to use the designated trails if he wanted to stay ahead of his pursuers.

He checked his watch as he headed for the Table Mountain Café and the gift shop—a quaint stone building with a peaked roof and tall chimney—and threaded his way between the café and the shop. He paused at the top of the curved stone stairway that lead down to a large stone terrace overlooking the beach at Camps Bay and the Twelve Apostles mountain range that formed the southwestern back of Table Mountain.

It was just after one o'clock. He had about ten minutes before the next cable car arrived with at least eight military or police. The terrace below and to his right was packed with sightseers—young and old of every shape, size and color. The café patio on his left was filled with the same make-up of lunchtime guests, some intent on their food or their phones, others gazing at the stunning view or fending off the hungry birds.

He stepped down to the terrace level and found the restroom on the left beneath the café patio. He slipped into a stall, quickly changed into his khaki shirt and pants, stuffed his beret into his waistband, two red smoke grenades into his pant pockets, and wrapped a fire starter in one of the hotel towels. Then he stepped out of the stall, stuffed the towel into the plastic waste bin and lit the fire starter, just as a heavy-set man entered the restroom and shuffled behind him towards a stall. He waited until the man disappeared into the stall, then latched the restroom door against the wall to keep it open and stepped down onto the sunlit terrace path.

He checked his watch again—six minutes until the next cable car arrived. Despite the urgency, the view over the cloud-draped Twelve Apostles to the spectacular coastline below caught his attention. It was breathtaking, as intoxicating as Lizzy's unexpected presence in his life. His resolve wavered for a moment, but there was no going back—the die was cast, the fuse lit.

He activated the two smoke grenades, tossed the first underhand towards the middle of the large terrace, then casually lobbed the second onto the patio above him just as the heavy-set man crashed out of the restroom yelling "Fire! Fire!"

Sounds of chaos erupted within seconds—screams, falling tables and chairs, breaking glasses and plates, frantic shouts. He knew his diversions were modest at best—tear gas would have been more effective but also more dangerous to the sightseers.

Still, the smoke grenades would buy him a little more time, and that was all he needed.

He pulled on his beret and began to jog away from the café along the stone path that led across the level plateau towards the eastern table of the mountain and Devil's Peak.

He did not look back.

48

THE DEVIL'S SHROUD

2010

The challenge was to get off the mountain and then to Groote Schuur.

The most direct route was about one and a half miles across the front of Table Mountain to its eastern edge. But that route provided no good option for getting off the mountain. Besides, it would expose him to easy detection, especially from above if they deployed the air force against him.

The quickest route that also provided some cover was down the narrow Platteklip Gorge that separated the western table from the central and eastern tables of the mountain. The gorge was on the same north side of the mountain as the cable car and less than half a mile from the café. It was an option he thought his pursuers were least likely to anticipate—that he would try to get off the mountain under their noses so soon after reaching the top. And he could reach the gorge in less than five minutes.

As he jogged, a layer of cloud slipped over him from the south. He grinned as he recalled the legend of the mountain's cloudy tablecloth—a smoking contest between the devil and a pirate—and gave silent thanks for the cover it provided. But he had no sooner embraced the legend than a second metaphysical presence crept up on him, the unnerving sense of being chased by the hound of heaven—the grace of God—even as the devil offered him protection.

Within minutes he reached the War Memorial overlooking the gaping chasm between sheer rock faces that created the precipitous gorge. He crouched for a few moments, looking and listening, but there were no indications of pursuit. He checked his bootlaces, re-cinched the straps of his backpack, then launched himself down the gully into the narrow crevice with its flat stones that gave the gorge its name. He had jogged up the two-mile trail several times training for marathons but had never imagined being chased in the opposite direction. He hoped the cold, cloudy conditions would keep day hikers out of the gorge.

The trail down the gorge was fairly straight at first. But, as the cliff faces on either side closed in towards each other, the trail became a treacherous series of slippery switchbacks under his flying feet. In most sections the best he could do was a sort of jog-hop down the steep sections, forced to focus on each step to avoid crashing over the edge or into the ragged barbed wire fencing along sections of the lower side of the trail. Tight switchbacks in the upper gorge gave way to long twists in the lower gorge. His urgency was heightened by the irrational sense of pursuers surfing the icy cascade of water around him, catching up with him, carrying him away.

A little more than halfway down the mountain, he reached the intersection he was looking for—a contour path that traversed the slopes of Table Mountain. Below him the gorge path continued beside a stream down to a road. To his left, the contour path led back to the lower cable station and, to his right, towards Devil's Peak.

The cone-shaped Devil's Peak rose almost as high as Table Mountain and overlooked the Groote Schuur estate. Bridging the gap between the peak and Table Mountain was a depression known as the Saddle, marked by a huge boulder called Saddle Rock. His route off the mountain to Groote Schuur lay across the Saddle and down the other side of the mountain through the Newlands Forrest.

He turned right towards Devil's Peak and lengthened his stride.

The contour path was much easier going after the steep gorge, but it was exposed and ran parallel to the road just a few hundred feet below. He might have a chance if the cloud cover held until he reached the Saddle, less than a mile away.

Running blindly through the fog, he missed the fork on his right to the upper contour path. He realized his mistake—he was on a lower traverse—just as the cloud began to lift. He swore at himself but there was no going back. He plunged ahead until he reached the intersection with a trail that led from the road below straight up to the Saddle. He veered right and scrambled up the zigzagging path, climbing as fast as he could to keep up with the rising cloud cover.

The path finally leveled off below the crest of the Saddle after intersecting with the upper contour path he had missed. He followed the path as it curved left towards Saddle Rock and was about half way there when he heard it—the unmistakable gearshift and drone of a Buffel—the six-cylinder troop carrier and fighting vehicle he knew so well from the border war. And the sound was getting louder, heading in his direction on the road below.

About thirty feet ahead of him was a group of flat rocks just off the lower side of the path. If he stayed where he was, he would be hopelessly exposed. He sprinted for the rocks, focused on one that was big and flat enough for a firing position. He reached the rock in seconds, pulled off the backpack, threw himself down and unzipped the main compartment. He was unwrapping the rifle pieces when two Buffels came into view at the bottom of a gulley and stopped about three hundred feet below him.

He dropped flat on his stomach, watching for any sign of threat.

The two open troop carriers were occupied—he estimated about ten personnel in each. He couldn't tell if they had seen him or were even looking for him. It could be a training exercise heading towards the King's Blockhouse around the far side of Devil's Peak. Then the Buffels moved off just as quickly as they had appeared.

He turned on his back and heaved a sigh of relief.

"Jesus, that was close," he said to the blue sky above him, now devoid of cloud cover, and smiled as the luscious melody from *Rhapsody in Blue* flooded his senses. Just like Gershwin, he thought, he was improvising under a tight schedule.

He lay on the ledge for several minutes enjoying the respite. But the threat of pursuit compelled him to get moving. That and the fact he couldn't hear the Buffels. He turned and looked down. The troops who minutes before were being carried away were now fanning out along the road and up the mountainside.

"Shit!" he muttered as he repacked his backpack, threw it over his shoulders and began to run. It was not far to Saddle Rock and the path over the Saddle, but he worried about being completely exposed as he ran. Then, out of the clear blue, a heavy tongue of cloud appeared and reached down towards him from the Saddle ridge on his right. It seemed the devil was still smoking and beckoning him to cross the Saddle beneath his ghostly shield.

He didn't second-guess his good fortune and ran as hard as he could towards Saddle Rock. After a few minutes of heart-pounding effort he reached the unmistakable rock on the left of the path, then swerved right and plunged through the *fynbos* towards Pulpit

Rock and the Dark Gorge on the far side of the Saddle. He could feel the presence of Devil's Peak on his left as he ran, as though the devil was urging him on, pleased with the screen he had created for his minion's escape. As he ran, he reminded himself not to overrun the far side—the drop-off into Newlands Forrest was like the edge of a knife in places.

The path off the mountain down Newlands Ravine to Groote Schuur was the obvious route—well marked, frequently used and relatively easy. The path down the Dark Gorge was less obvious—unmarked, seldom used and treacherous. Both led to deep cover under the dense, indigenous canopy of the Newlands Forest. He decided on the Dark Gorge for exactly the reasons that made it unsafe—his pursuers were unlikely to think he would take that route.

The fog of cloud was heavy and the path narrow and overgrown through the dense *fynbos*. He passed the turn to Newlands Ravine and within minutes was at Pulpit Rock, the jagged pile of boulders on the edge of the Saddle that looked more like a castle turret than a pulpit. To his surprise, he couldn't see the Newlands Forrest below or the southern suburbs beyond—the mantle of cloud before him obscured everything beneath it and seemed to stretch all the way across the peninsula to False Bay.

Despite his urgency, he was overcome by a surreal sense of peace as he gazed out over the blanket of clouds that looked for all the world like an enormous goose down comforter of the purest white.

The moment was shattered in an instant.

With a thunderous roar a black reptilian creature burst through the cloud below him, as though the devil had spat up his most vile creation from the bowels of hell. The creature stopped just above eye level, hovering, pointing its narrow and venomous snout straight at him, blowing a maelstrom of turbulence in his face, sending his beret flying off his head and throwing him onto his back. It took several heart-stopping moments before he recognized the prototype attack helicopter—the Rooivalk—with its stepped cockpit, nose-mounted 20 mm cannon and short, stubby wings carrying rocket pods on both sides of the fuselage.

He scrambled to his feet and waved, trying to signal that he was a friendly. He hoped the pilots would conclude from his clothes and behavior that he was part of the search party.

The black creature hovered as though trying to make up its malevolent mind. He braced himself, imagining its cannon erupting, shredding his muscle, splintering his bone and splattering his life's blood across the dense *fynbos*. But the beast suddenly leapt upward and veered off towards Devil's Peak, the pilot waving an acknowledgement as the Rooivalk swept away.

Watching the attack helicopter soar towards the peak reminded him of the time when three air force jets had crashed into the peak in low cloud while practicing for the tenth anniversary of Republic Day. Eleven airmen had died. He didn't wish that fate on anyone, not even his pursuers, but the fact of the chopper suggested the search was closing in on his position.

He had to find refuge as quickly as possible. He retrieved his beret and headed for the entrance to Dark Gorge about thirty yards to his right. The entrance was impossible to miss—it was signposted by a tall green sign that warned "extremely dangerous—do not attempt descent."

He saw the "V" shape of the top of the gorge as he approached. It was cut into the mountain, barely visible above the layer of cloud, and pointed down towards the gorge. He couldn't see the cleft of the gorge below the dense clouds but he knew it was almost impossibly narrow, as though the mountain had been split by a giant ax.

He swore at the ethereal void below him. The cloud engulfing the gorge was too thick—a descent would be suicidal. The devil's smoke screen that had been his salvation now threatened his survival. He would have to go down Newlands Ravine instead. He turned away and crashed through the *fynbos* and over a knoll towards the ravine, another hundred yards to his right.

The top section of the "U" shaped ravine was relatively easy-going. It felt wide and generous even under the heavy cloud, although the switchbacks between rugged mountainsides slowed him down, forcing him to jog-hop down the steep sections. He was about to enter the tree line when he heard a dog bark. He stopped and crouched behind a boulder. Another bark. Human voices too. It was impossible to be sure but the sounds seemed to be coming from below, advancing towards him. Right or wrong, he couldn't take the chance.

"Fuck!" he swore as he turned and pounded back up the steep ravine. The Dark Gorge was now his only option, a gorge that had claimed several lives over the years.

He reached the top of the ravine and plunged through the *fynbos* back over the knoll and down to the sign that marked the entrance to the gorge. It seemed to seethe with portents of disaster, as though the devil was expecting him and now demanded recompense for his favors up to that point.

He took a deep breath. *Fear none but God*, he thought as he took his first tentative steps. There was no clear route down—it seemed to lie wherever the rubble of rocks from the giant ax blow had fallen. The cliffs pressed in on him on both sides and trees clung as perilously to the uneven surfaces as he did to them. He tried to keep three-point contact at all times, testing each step and handhold—rocks, roots, limbs and vines—a precaution that saved him several times when a foot or hand slipped on the treacherous surfaces.

He was sweating profusely as he passed the cairn of stacked

rocks marking the trail and through the steep top section. He knew it was a minor miracle to have made it without a fall, but aside from a few scrapes he had emerged unscathed. The fog was less dense in the lower section—at least he could see his hand in front of his face—but the route was no less difficult, winding through a matted undergrowth of roots, vines and fallen trees.

He could hear distant barking and voices but nothing close enough to pose a threat. He pressed on until he emerged onto the contour path above Newlands Forest. He wiped his forehead with his beret and crossed the path. He needed to find a hideout further down in the forest while there was still daylight.

He slid down the steep slope below the contour path using his hands, heels and backside to control his descent. Within minutes he came across a mossy overhang that formed a cave-like shelter on the lower side of a towering forest tree. The overhang protected him from the path above and gave him a vantage point over the forest and any movement below.

He could still hear dogs in the distance, but they were not getting any closer. He drank some water, relieved himself under cover of a nearby tree, and settled back beneath the overhang. Dusk was creeping inexorably over the peninsula as the sun set behind him on the other side of Table Mountain—the sunset view from Lion's Head a favorite spectacle for locals and tourists alike.

He glanced at his watch—four thirty—sixteen thirty hours as he instinctively defaulted to mission-critical military time.

He finished a packet of trail mix in two gulps and got to work. He retrieved the knife and Makarov from the backpack and strapped them around his waist. Then he used camouflage crayons to apply streaks of green and black to his face, neck, and hands.

As an afterthought, as though granting himself a last request as a condemned man, he drank a mouthful of the cabernet he had taken from the Mount Nelson. Then he pushed the two mini wine bottles neck first into a soft section of the overhang behind him and covered the holes with handfuls of damp earth and leaves. He hated littering, but the extra weight would slow him down. He made a mental note to retrieve the bottles if he ever got the chance.

He would make his move in less than an hour, using the last light of day to get off the mountain. He was no more than a mile and a half from the Groote Schuur estate in the ever-darkening shadow cast by Devil's Peak.

He settled back to wait and to relive the past twenty-four hours with the extraordinary Ms. Elizabeth Bennet. It felt as though he had crammed a lifetime into those few brief hours.

49

DESTINY'S YOKE

2010

Dusk fell—it was time.

After clearing his shelter of any sign of human presence, Nicolas moved cautiously through the forest to the Woodcutters Path that led down the mountain past the Newlands Reservoir.

As he descended, the cool mountain air thickened with floral accents drifting over the forest from the nearby gardens of Kirstenbosch. Beyond the reservoir was the highway, and just beyond that lay the Groote Schuur estate.

He skirted a dirt road used by the forest station and angled past the reservoir towards the National Park offices and the road that wound up behind the university to the Rhodes Memorial. Staying just off the tree-lined road's right shoulder, he followed it down towards the intersection with the highway and the stream of red and white car lights crossing in front of him.

He felt a shoelace loosen and stopped to retie it, then retied the other as well for good measure. When he looked up, three sets of headlights were reaching up the hill towards him. He dove to his right over a rock and rolled onto his stomach behind a tree trunk.

"Damn it, Nicolas—stay focused," he muttered angrily, lying motionless as the trucks rumbled past him and up the road towards the Rhodes Memorial. Chastened, he decided the streets were still too busy to risk going any further for the time being. He angled back towards a dense stand of trees, set his watch alarm for two thirty, pulled on his black sweater and settled down to wait.

As he rested, using his backpack as a pillow, he took a mental tour of the Rhodes mansion, trying to recall the details of what he had learned from the guided tour he had taken years before.

Rhodes had bought the property in the 1800s, commissioned an English architect to restore the original Cape Dutch character of the mansion and replaced the Victorian ornamentation with art objects from all over the world. He had also added a new west wing, including a master bedroom above a billiard room, both with enormous bay windows overlooking the terraced gardens and facing the eastern buttress of Table Mountain and Devil's Peak. And just beyond the terraced grounds—landscaped with a mass of hydrangeas, roses, bougainvillea and fuchsias—the estate had included a private reserve of antelope, zebra and wildebeest on the gentle slopes beneath Table Mountain. Then, at the turn of the 20th century, Rhodes had bequeathed the entire Groote Schuur estate to the nation.

Nicolas took pleasure in the fact that Rhodes's architect had also designed the dining hall of his old boarding school at Grey College. The continuity was strangely gratifying, as was the knowledge that almost every Afrikaner leader of the country, starting with General Louis Botha in 1910, had used the mansion as his official residence. When Mandela became president in 1994, he chose instead the mansion next door—once home to the British governor-general—as his official residence.

His thoughts drifted to bygone times...Playing rugby...His wife...His daughter...The car bomb...

He came awake just after two o'clock. Within minutes he was heading down the dark street. Traffic had all but disappeared from the highway as he approached the intersection with Princess Anne Avenue. Moving at a crouch just off the road, he followed the curve of the avenue as it swept under the highway. On the other side of the highway he crossed the avenue to the heavily wooded neighborhood of ministerial mansions abutting the Groote Schuur estate.

Staying in the deep shadows beneath the highway, he noted the high chain-link fence that surrounded the mansions and a second interior green palisade security fence with spiked pales about three inches apart and eighteen feet high. The formidable looking security fence was set about fifteen feet inside and parallel to the chain-link fence. He was surprised to see security cameras set on the palisade posts about fifty feet apart—he had not taken that possibility into account. The cameras all pointed to his left along the line of the security fence and did not appear to cover the exterior chain-link fence.

He kept to the shadows on a path that ran parallel to the chain-link fence until he reached the road that served as a boundary between the ministerial mansions and Groote Schuur. The road was served by an off-ramp from the highway that was blocked by an ornate Cape Dutch style wooden double-gate. He could just make out another gate about a hundred yards down the tree-lined road but, unlike the first gate, there was nothing ornamental about the second gate. It appeared to be a palisade style security gate, the same as the security fence.

Nicolas looked left and right, then pushed through the wooden gate, closed it behind him, and crossed to the chain-link fence on the side of the road closest to the Groote Schuur mansion. He crept along the fence until he found a section where branches from the trees overhung the fence. Using his wire cutters, he cut an opening in the fence and squirmed through, pulling the backpack through behind him. Then he tied the cut section of fencing back in place with two short strands of rope. The rope would also serve as a marker for him to find the spot on his way out.

His next challenge was the security fence. He decided to climb the fence on the immediate right of one of the posts supporting a camera. The camera would be pointing away from him and he would be furthest from the next camera fifty feet away. He knew the cameras posed a risk but he decided to take it. After all, the mansion was now a museum and had not been used by the country's presidents since 1994. There was no reason to monitor the cameras or even to switch them on.

He would know soon enough if he was wrong and guards were watching his every move.

He sprinted across the fifteen-foot gap to a fence post and froze in place for several minutes, listening and watching for any sign of discovery. Then he crouched low, extracted the black climbing rope from his backpack and tied a noose in the end opposite the grappling hook. It took three tries before he landed the noose over the spike of one of the pales and watched it drop onto a horizontal rail that ran the length of the fence about eighteen inches below the top of the spiked pales. Next he used his knife to cut the rope to the length he needed for the climb and stuffed the remaining rope with the grappling hook into his backpack. Then he slung the backpack over his shoulders and began to climb.

The spikes at the top of the pales were awkward but the horizontal rail helped him avoid impaling himself. Once at the top he pulled the rope up, dropped its loose end over the inside of the fence, and used it to climb down. He decided to leave the rope hanging from the fence—there was no good alternative if he needed to get out again in a hurry—and even a conscientious security guard would not easily see the black rope in the dark.

He dropped to the ground and sprinted at a crouch along the fence line through the trees to the tennis court. From there he followed the angle of the court to the tree line at the top of the terraced gardens.

He reached the trunk of a stately tree and there it was—Rhodes's masterpiece—the Groote Schuur mansion. He was just thirty yards from the back of the mansion—the pale-white outline of its scrolled gables strangely bright and crisp despite the darkness.

He knelt, retrieved the Swarovski binoculars from his backpack, then sank to his stomach in the deep shadow of the tree. From his position, the back of the two-level mansion was shaped like an "L" with its long leg to his left and its short leg pointed straight at him. A balcony extended the full length of the long leg and wrapped around the short leg. The bedrooms were all on the second level—the main bedrooms in the long leg and the Rhodes bedroom in the short leg.

He had no idea where to start looking for Mandela and couldn't risk groping around in the dark checking the beds of visiting African dignitaries. But the longer he stared at the mansion the more convinced he became that if Mandela were there with other visitors, he would be given pride of place, even if it meant resting his head where Africa's preeminent colonialist and arch-imperialist had slept a century before.

From his elevated position on the upper terrace, Nicolas had a view of the Rhodes bedroom through its bay windows that faced him. He recalled a hall and staircase at the far end of the bedroom, beyond the bedroom doorway, and that a curtained side door led from the hall onto the balcony. But to get to the bedroom he had to get past whatever security guarded the mansion's occupants.

Using his high-performance binoculars to see what would otherwise remain unseen in the low light, he spent thirty minutes watching for any sign of movement around the mansion.

The first surprise was the lack of guards. The only one he could see was seated against the wall outside the back entrance to the mansion about halfway along the colonnaded veranda below the balcony. The man's head was slumped on his chest. There didn't seem to be any roving patrols on the property.

Odd, he thought. Perhaps they were around the front of the mansion, or perhaps Lizzy had been mistaken about the whole thing. Or perhaps there was only one guest at the mansion, a guest renowned for preferring privacy to publicity.

The more he thought about it as he brought each area of the mansion and gardens into sharp focus through the binoculars, the more he thought it likely the other African leaders would have gone to one of the many luxury hotels around Cape Town, like the Twelve Apostles or Mount Nelson.

He decided not to dwell on imponderables—he would stay focused on the Rhodes bedroom and deal with the situation as he found it. And if it was a mistake and his efforts in vain, he would extract himself as best he could and try to avoid being associated with what had happened at the Calabash and the Big Hole.

It was time to move—time to step into the arena.

He fingered the Makarov at his hip to make sure the safety was on, repacked the binoculars and cinched the straps to his backpack. Then, skirting the flowerbeds on the terraces that rose up towards him, he sprinted at a crouch on a direct line down the terraces to the end of the veranda next to the billiard room. After reaching the veranda, he paused to catch his breath and to make sure he had not aroused any unseen guards. Then he darted from one column to the next, quickly advancing along the short leg of the veranda, the darkened billiard room on his right.

At the juncture with the long leg of the veranda that extended to his left, he peered around the corner to make sure the guard was still asleep. Satisfied, he crossed the veranda to the ornate teak doors that led into the hall beneath the Rhodes bedroom. He tried the doors, careful not to force them or risk making a noise. They were locked. He would have to go the long way—past the guard, through the double doors of the rear entrance, and then backtrack via the interior rooms to the hall and stairs that led up to the Rhodes bedroom.

He unholstered the Makarov and moved silently across the veranda's black-and-white marble floor towards the sleeping guard, relieved not to be treading on creaky floorboards made of the same antique wood featured in the veranda's ceiling.

The guard never knew what hit him. He went from sleep to unconsciousness in an instant. Holstering the Makarov, Nicolas bound the guard with two short lengths of rope and gagged him with a wad of cloth before unclipping the ring of keys from the man's waist belt. Fortunately, the keys were tagged. He selected the key to the inner hall, quietly unlocked the double doors, dragged the guard inside and relocked the doors.

He stood for a moment until his eyes adjusted to the gloom. Despite the lack of light, details of the décor came alive—the whitewashed walls and dark wood furniture, the smell of old tapestries, oriental carpets and heavy drapes—the musty colonial opulence of it all. Then he dragged the guard across the marble checkerboard floor and lowered him into an antique storage chest beneath the teak staircase that led up to the main bedrooms.

He felt a sudden chill and stood frozen, certain he was being watched from behind. His hand gripped the Makarov as he slowly turned towards the staircase. He was right. Sinister-looking Zimbabwe birds perched on the newel posts were watching over the hall with imperious expressions carved into their sharp soapstone features. He slowly exhaled, then turned back and crossed the hall, past the dark stinkwood table where Rhodes's body had lain in state after his death. Hanging on the wall to the left of the table was a large tapestry depicting an exotic America, with a Dutch sailing ship at anchor near an island now known as Manhattan.

He slipped through an unlocked arched door into the dark dining room, the gloom intensified by a heavy carpet and wooden floors, wall panels and ceiling. He glanced to his left down the length of the formal dining room. The mother-of-pearl details in the chair backs around the table were luminescent in the dark, as was the tapestry hanging across the full width of the room at the far end portraying European royalty beneath a Greco-Roman cupola.

He began to feel the cold sweat of tension. It was too quiet. There should be more guards. Then, just as he was about to pass through another arched door into the small hall beneath the Rhodes bedroom, the tall grandfather clock inches from his head erupted in a series of hammered chimes.

"Jesus!" he hissed into the gloom, his heart pounding. He stood for several moments until his heart rate slowed, while a melodious syncopation of chimes crashed through the darkness from the six or seven similar case clocks scattered throughout the mansion.

He checked his watch. At least the clocks were correct—six o'clock. Sunrise would be at around seven forty-five. He felt his stomach tighten. He had to keep moving. The sands of time were suddenly an inexorable agent in his immediate future.

He crouched as he entered the small hall. The complete silence after the chimes was unnerving. He was now in the newer west wing of the house beneath the Rhodes bedroom and in the wing where he expected guards to spend the night. A vibrant Afshari oriental rug lay on the checkerboard marble floor. To his left stood a camphorwood chest with intricate brass fittings and, against the far wall, a large Baroque cupboard sat stark against the whitewashed walls. To his right, a small staircase to the Rhodes bedroom hugged three sides of the hall.

He stepped carefully up the wooden stairs, keeping as close to the walls as possible to avoid putting his weight in the middle of the century-old treads that were likely to creak despite the plush carpet runner. He moved silently, step by step, across the first landing, past a small Kazak prayer rug hanging on the wall above the second landing, then past a tapestry near the top of the stairs showing the Queen of Sheba surrounded by African animals.

He crouched low as his head reached the top level of the stairs. He expected a guard to be posted outside the bedroom door. There was a chair but no guard. Straight ahead he could see through an alcove to the door of the Rhodes bedroom. It was slightly ajar. His sense of disappointment grew as he stepped onto the second-floor landing. It should not be so quiet, so deserted. This was beginning to feel like a mistake, a foolish misadventure that could cost him his life.

He glanced over the balustrade to the ground floor below to make sure no guards had entered the hall behind him. There were none. But he sensed something...some disquieting presence below him. As he gazed into the gloom his vision suddenly filled with a spectral image of the hound of heaven padding unhurriedly up the stairs behind him to the first landing where it paused...beneath the prayer rug...and stared up at him through soft, radiant eyes, as though willing him to make the next move while patiently drawing ever closer.

He shook his head to dispel the unsettling image, then turned to face the bedroom door. He moved forward but stopped next to the curtained door on his right that led to the balcony. He pushed the curtain aside and tested the glass-paned door—it was unlocked. He considered checking the bedroom first, but decided he needed an exit strategy regardless.

He slipped through the glass-paned door onto the balcony. Crouching, he scanned the long length of the balcony past the main bedrooms, then the short length alongside the Rhodes bedroom on his left. The balcony was starkly vacant, aside from a guardrail system around its perimeter supported by slender posts. Still crouching, he moved along the whitewashed outside wall of the bedroom and quickly covered the thirty feet to the guardrail post at the edge of the balcony next to the bedroom's bay window.

He knelt and stayed still, focused on any sight or sound of danger. Reassured by the languorous silence, he unzipped the backpack and set to work. First, he opened the grappling hook, hooked it around the base of the guardrail post, then peered over the balcony to make sure there was no obstruction below. He laid what was left of the attached length of rope next to the post—it would not reach all the way to the ground but would get him close enough to drop the rest of the way. Next, he assembled the rifle, rested it on his backpack against the wall, and laid the flare gun and tear gas grenades next to the rope. Last, he retrieved the charred family Bible, held it briefly to his lips in silent prayer, then slipped it back into his backpack.

He stood slowly and looked at the gardens and terrace below. If he could make it back to the trees, he might have a chance. Then he turned and looked at the roof of the mansion, trying to judge the best angles to the front lawn and driveway to direct his limited diversionary arsenal. Satisfied, he crept back to the balcony door, opened it and peered past the curtain to make sure there were still no guards outside the bedroom. Seeing none, he quietly reentered the hallway and silently closed the door behind him.

He waited a moment until his senses readjusted to the interior gloom. Then he moved along the wall towards the alcove outside the bedroom door, rolling each step from heel to toe to avoid sudden concentrated weight on the wooden floor, staying as close to the wall as he could until he reached the alcove.

It was the moment of truth.

He pushed gently on the bedroom door. The antique hinges creaked so loudly it felt as though a nerve in his spinal column had been stripped from its roots. He stopped, heart pounding, and pushed again. Another creak, then another, the effect like shards of glass slicing into the same spinal nerve that had just been laid bare. But at last he was able to slip past the door. He wanted to push it back into its former position, slightly ajar, but he couldn't risk any more noise. It was enough that he was inside the Rhodes bedroom, the gloom only slightly diluted by early morning light through the half-moon alcove of bay windows at the far end of the bedroom.

Ahead of him in the middle of the room was a writing table and chair standing on the center medallion of a large oriental carpet. On his immediate left a tall Cape armoire towered over a small bedside table and lamp. And, next to that, squatting against the wall in the corner of the room, a four-poster bed, its short wooden posts thick and square, supporting elegantly carved head and footboards.

The bed's sturdy bulk dwarfed the solitary figure lying beneath the covers.

Nicolas resisted the urge to immediately identify the bed's occupant. His instincts and training compelled him to take in every detail of his environment, to avoid surprises before committing to a course of action.

Above the bed were several small images framed in assorted sizes. Beyond the foot of the bed was a large fireplace with an octagonal mirror on the mantelpiece. And beyond that were the bay windows set into an alcove. A single brass chandelier hung from the vaulted ceiling over the writing table in the center of the room. Against the wall opposite the bed was a writing bureau on top of which stood a statue of young Napoleon. And on the wall above the bureau hung an etching of an older Napoleon. It showed him snatching the crown of the Holy Roman Empire from the pope in a grasp of power that seemed symptomatic of a compulsion deeply imprinted into the genetic character of mankind.

Satisfied the room concealed no hidden threat, Nicolas moved towards his target.

The prone figure was breathing audibly in deep sleep. A halo of short white hair offset an ebony face, the deep lines of fatigue and age visible even in the low light, the features unmistakable. He stood for several moments looking down at the man the world had come to revere and whom he had come to kill.

Nicolas inhaled deeply and slowly exhaled. Then he turned to the desk in the middle of the room, picked up the armless chair and set it down near the foot of the bed facing its head. He stood for a moment, then unclipped the Makarov from its holster, made sure the safety was still set, and tapped the sleeping figure firmly on the shoulder with the barrel of the pistol. Then he stepped back and sat down. The chair's antique rawhide seat creaked in protest.

Nicolas watched impassively as the icon known as Madiba grunted, blinked his eyes, then slowly lifted his head as though reluctantly surfacing from the comfort of well-earned rest after a lifetime of struggle.

EPILOGUE

2010

"There *must* be another way," insisted Nelson. "Killing me—plunging our people into another cycle of violence—will not bring peace and freedom to our land."

The assassin nodded, as though acknowledging the paradox. "Perhaps," he mused. "But no-one can predict how this will end...which way the wind will blow after the fire is lit."

Nelson shook his head in dismay. The image of a national conflagration filled him with an unspeakable dread. "It will never—"

"But that's not all," continued the man. "There is something else...something you should know before you die."

The man closed his eyes, drew a deep breath and slowly exhaled. When he opened his eyes they seemed vacant, unfocused, as though their focal point had extended to a faraway place and time, or perhaps turned inward towards some point deep in the man's soul.

Then, in a halting voice thick with emotion, the man spoke: "My family suffered unspeakable horrors at the hands of your family, horrors that led me by one hand to this moment just as surely as our nation's suffering led me here by the other hand."

Nelson stared, completely bewildered. "I don't understand. What are you talking about?"

"The treachery of your father led to the humiliation and death of my father's mother and sister in a concentration camp, and to the destruction of our family farm."

Nelson shook his head. "I know nothing of these things."

"Maybe so," said the man. "But God says the sins of the father shall be visited upon his children."

"My father was a *good* man," replied Nelson with conviction. "He died in my mother's hut when I was young from a lung disease after working in the gold mines. But everyone who knew him said he was a good and honorable man."

The assassin shrugged, as though dismissing the self-serving testimonial. "It is not only the father who sinned. Your Umkhonto detonated a car bomb in Pretoria that killed my wife and nearly killed my daughter."

Nelson sighed. "I am very sorry for your loss," he said in a respectful tone. "I was in Pollsmoor Prison in Cape Town at the time of that bomb."

"Umkhonto was your creation," retorted the man, "the violence and bombings part of your plan. You bear ultimate responsibility. Nobody else."

The man's jaw set hard. Then he raised the pistol.

"Jesus said, 'Not my will, but thy will be done.'"

Nelson saw the skin whiten around the assassin's trigger finger.

"Your Jesus also said to turn the other cheek," he said in a rush of inspiration, "to love your neighbor as you love yourself, as a brother. I am your brother. My burden is yours to carry as yours is mine to bear. We are both crippled by the past but need each other's strength to walk the road to freedom together, for all our people."

"Enough! It's time, *Madiba*. It's time."

The finality of the man's pronouncement was chilling, yet somehow clarifying. He took a deep breath, savoring every last molecule of oxygen, then slowly exhaled as he recalled a passage from Shakespeare's *Julius Caesar* that had fortified him in his struggle to survive the long years on Robben Island. In a tone of somber reflection, as though drafting his epitaph, he said, "'Cowards die many times before their deaths, but the valiant never taste of death but once.'"

In the deadly silence that followed, he took fleeting comfort in the solace of the moral universe—that, as Martin Luther King had said, its arc was long but it eventually bent towards justice. And yet, even as he embraced the comfort, he knew it was far from certain the universe was moral, and there was nothing preordained about the shape of its arc. Only men and women of courage and integrity could bend it towards justice.

Then, unbidden, the first lines of the anthem enveloped his soul and he began to sing, his resolute baritone filling the silence:

Nkosi sikelel' iAfrika	Lord bless Africa
Maluphakanyisw' uphondo lwayo,	May her spirit rise high up,
Yizwa imithandazo yethu,	Hear Thou our prayers,
Nkosi sikelela, Nkosi sikelela	Lord bless us, Lord bless us.

He held the man's gaze, determined not to flinch. But still, the shot did not come.

Seizing the moment, he sang part of the old Afrikaner anthem, knowing it would be as provocative to the man with the gun as his "if needs be" statement had been to the judge when he had all but challenged the court to sentence him to death:

Ons sal antwoord op jou roepstem,	We shall answer to your calling,
One sal offer wat jy vra	We shall give whatever you ask
Ons sal lewe, ons sal sterwe	We shall live, we shall die
Ons vir jou, Suid Afrika.	We for you, South Africa.

His voice trailed off. The pistol never wavered. All he could hear was labored breathing.

And yet, as the cathedral-like stillness deepened, it seemed not only to herald the impending sacrifice but simultaneously to petition for grace.

"I have answered the call of our country," he began in an unyielding voice, gazing directly at the man. "I have done my duty on this earth, given what was asked in our people's struggle. Your people were afraid of democracy and turned to apartheid for a solution. And so we fought back, just as your people did against British oppression." He paused, breathing hard. "I have always been prepared to die for justice and freedom, so that all our people—yours and mine—can live in peace and dignity. We are not there yet, and killing me won't bring us any closer."

The man's jaws clenched as the pistol barrel wavered, then dipped for a moment, revealing the man's face.

Nelson held the assassin's gaze, willing his spirit to pierce the darkness of the man's soul. He saw the man's eyes constrict, as though to shield his resolve from the intrusion.

Then the pistol rose and held steady, aimed at his chest.

Nelson felt his stomach contract, his breath become tight and shallow. He wondered if he would notice the man's trigger finger move before the bullet exploded from the barrel.

Then he saw it.

The man's finger moved.

But it was his thumb, not his trigger finger—a short upward movement on the left side of the Makarov.

The soft click was unmistakable.

The safety was engaged.

Filtered light from the sunrise began to fill the bedroom as the man lowered the pistol, the early morning stillness disturbed by a rising clamor that signaled discovery of an intruder.

"It is time," said Nelson, "time for you to go…time for you to *let* go."

As their eyes locked he sensed the genesis of understanding behind the man's gaze, a dawning recognition of the ties that bound them, for good or ill, in life and in death.

Without a word the big man rose, drew a deep rasping breath as he reached his full height, and slowly exhaled as though expelling the breath of life itself. He stood still for a moment, the pistol at his side. Then he stepped closer to the head of the bed and, with an almost imperceptible nod of acknowledgment, laid the pistol on the bedside table, turned and left the room.

AUTHOR'S NOTE

Amandla was conceived as a legacy for my two daughters, a desire to tell them an entertaining but informative story about the controversial country that is part of their DNA through their father. That desire found a purchase point in history when I read a 2006 BBC interview of Nelson Mandela describing a gun he had buried at his hideout at Liliesleaf in 1962, a gun that has never been found. That fact inspired me to write a work of historical fiction about the DNA of the country itself. In the telling of it, I did not want to retell the story of Mandela's life (a life already well documented by historians, biographers and by Mandela himself), nor did I want to fictionalize his life. That said, the scene in the Rhodes bedroom of the Groote Schuur mansion is complete fiction. But even in that scene, and wherever Mandela appears in the novel, I tried to remain faithful to the historical record of his words, ideals and character as revealed in his speeches, writings and actions. For his thoughts and unrecorded reflections, I allowed myself the liberty to imagine what they might have been.

The lives of Mandela's grandfather and father, however, are fictionalized. Their life stories are undocumented as far as I know except for brief accounts of the later years of his father, Henry Gadla Mandela, as counselor of two Thembu kings. Not knowing any better, I gave his grandfather the name Gadla and created a fictional life story out of whole cloth for him and for the undocumented earlier portion of the life of Henry.

By contrast, the story of the De Beer family is complete fiction. And although it does intersect with the story of two De Beer brothers who discovered diamonds on their farm in the Kimberly area before selling it for £6,600 in 1871, the fictional De Beer family of the novel is not intended to represent the family history or story of those two De Beer brothers in any respect. It is true, however, that the brothers' farm did become part of the De Beers Mining Company created by Cecil Rhodes in 1888, and the brothers' last name did become forever associated with a company that monopolized the international diamond industry for more than a century.

It has been said that the story of America, described as the oldest constitutional democracy in the world, is an experiment in democracy that continues to evolve. At the other end of the spectrum, the story of post-apartheid South Africa, one of the youngest constitutional democracies in the world, can be described as an experiment in democracy that has only just begun to evolve. It is my hope that its tree of liberty will constantly be refreshed by men and women of courage and integrity—faithful to the ideals for which Nelson Mandela was prepared to die—as the rainbow nation continues to evolve towards a more perfect union of all its peoples.

ACKNOWLEDGEMENT

Writing this novel was a lonely process. It consumed evenings, weekends and vacations over the course of more than a decade while I steadfastly heeded conventional wisdom not to quit my day job. During every phase of the process, the love, support and companionship of my wife never faltered—and for that I am truly grateful.

Lightning Source UK Ltd.
Milton Keynes UK
UKHW010718171121
394120UK00001B/281